RHYN ETERNAL
VOLUME TWO

Darkyn's Mate, The Underworld

LIZZY FORD

Cover design by Lizzy Ford

www.LizzyFord.com

Darkyn's Mate, The Underworld copyright ©2018 by Lizzy Ford, *www.LizzyFord.com*

Cover design copyright © 2018 by Lizzy Ford

www.LizzyFord.com

Darkyn's Mate

Book Three

Prologue

F rom *"Gabriel's Hope"*

SUDDENLY, Past-Death's words about how Deidre became Gabriel's mate clicked. Would the reverse also work? If Past-Death was dead again, was Deidre next in line to be Gabriel's mate?

Deidre faced the door, mind working quickly.

"Wait!" she called. "Your soul. If you can't do what I did in a week, I get your soul."

"Fuck off, human."

"Who's the coward now?" Deidre demanded. "You're incapable of loving him the way he deserves, and you know it."

Past-Death froze at the door. Her face was red, her eyes glittering. "You will wager your soul as well?"

"Yep," Deidre said. "Deal?" She held out her hand and drew near. "One week. Your soul and mine on the table."

Past-Death shook her hand. Cold energy shot through Deidre,

and she flinched. The door opened, and they both looked towards it.

"Which one of you is mine?" Darkyn's growl made her blood run cold.

"As I promised. My payment for your services." Past-Death snatched Deidre's arm and yanked her to the side for him to see the tattoo.

The demon lord smiled. Past-Death pushed Deidre towards him.

Deidre dug in her heels before she reached him. The heat of her anger vanished, replaced by fear.

"Deal settled," Darkyn said, stepping aside. "With regards to our arrangement about reviving you…"

"We'll talk later," Past-Death said and brushed by him.

Darkyn watched her go. Deidre saw the look on his face, the same one Past-Death gave her when admiring the product she created. His attention returned to Deidre. His fangs were lengthening. She backed away, unable to fathom the idea of being trapped with him in Hell for eternity.

"Rules," he reminded her and entered the chamber. He closed the door behind him.

"No running. No fighting."

You must obey him, no matter how much you do not wish to. Your life is not the only one dependent upon this.

She stopped in place as Fate's words returned her. Unable to quell the panic flying through her, she wasn't willing to test the waters to discover if demons were restricted from harming their mates like Immortals. In a week, when Past-Death lost her end of the bet, Deidre would be free.

She just had to survive.

Deidre closed her eyes as Darkyn's arm snaked out to grab her neck. He dragged her against him. Breathing ragged, she tilted her head in submission.

One week.

"Welcome to your new home, love," the Dark One said a moment before his teeth sank into her neck.

For Gabriel.

Day One

Chapter One

In Hell, human-Deidre sat next to the hearth hours after she made the deal with the goddess who stranded her. She hadn't seen her new mate, Darkyn – the Dark One – since he drank his fill of her hours before and left. Her lightheadedness was gone and she was grateful his bloodsucking was pain free. Not by his choice, which was clear. If she hadn't bartered for a painless existence, she'd be trying to kill herself to get away from him.

If, for some reason, she was stuck here forever, at least he wasn't going to hurt her, as long as she followed his rules.

No running. No fighting.

Either of them was too much of a turn on to a demon that reveled in causing pain. The idea made her panic. How long would it take Gabriel to find her and rescue her?

Would he be able to, if he thought the goddess Past-Death was his mate?

Her stomach growled. A look around her bedchamber with its black, stone walls, ceiling and floor revealed nothing remotely edible. The large bed was set in a similar stone bed frame and covered with dark coverings. The room was allegedly the most comfortable Hell had to offer. She wasn't able to tell what time it was in Hell. There were no clocks and she had no cell phone. Her room was made of black stone and quiet with no sounds except the crackle of fire.

It wasn't bad. She had no intention of spending eternity there, though.

She stood, hungry. Made of material softer than silk, the black dress she wore pooled at the top of her feet. Her back was bare to display the name of *Darkyn* amid the Immortals' geometric writing that marked her as an Immortal mate.

She put her hair down to hide the mark, horrified by the idea of belonging to the devil.

Deidre's hand went to her neck, where Darkyn had placed a slender collar. If his name scrawled across her shoulders didn't mark her as his, the collar did. She didn't think any demon in Hell was going to mess with the Dark One's mate. At least, she hoped not.

She stood in front of the door nervously for a long moment, not certain it would open.

It did.

There were no longer demon guards outside her door, maybe because Darkyn knew she couldn't leave. If her bond to him was like hers to Gabriel, he'd be able to find her no matter what.

She couldn't think about such things without wanting to break down and weep. First things first: she needed food to survive. Bracing herself, she stepped into the hallway. No one attacked her or told her to stop. She also had no idea where to go.

Deidre closed the door behind her and walked down the hall-way. The dress moved with her like a second skin, draping her curves and swishing silently around her legs. She rubbed her mouth. It was dry and her gums irritated. She could use some water, too.

She walked for ten minutes, carefully remembering where she went, so she was able to find her way back. The first demons that crossed her path made her freeze in place. They didn't notice her, and she released her breath.

Deidre continued through the halls lined with torches bearing black flames. She reached a stairwell and descended to a floor with wider, taller corridors, as if she'd gone from the wing with private chambers to a more public area. There were more demons on this level, a couple of which eyed her before moving on, leaving her a bit more confident she wasn't going to be eaten. The stone doors lining each side were all closed.

One of them yawned opened as her eyes fell to it.

With an anxious look around to make sure no one was watching, Deidre peeked into the open door, hoping it led to a McDonalds or some other place with food. What she saw puzzled her.

Hell had a library?

At the far end of the library was a creature that made her think twice about entering. White-gray fur covered a body with moth-eaten wings, a hideous face and yellowed fangs. It was hunched over a book large enough to cover half the black stone desk at which it sat. As she watched, the creature rose and hobbled from the desk to a nearby shelf. It wheezed, its body bent by time. The small book it hefted made its stooped posture almost double over. He staggered.

She had the sudden urge to assist him. Whatever creature it was, it had to be ancient. She hesitated then crossed the library.

"Do you want help?" she ventured timidly.

The ugly face turned towards her, and she slowed.

"What are you?" it asked in a voice as old as its leathery face.

Uncertain how to explain things, she turned and swept her pink-dyed hair from her back to show him the mating mark.

"Ah." It said then concentrated on holding onto the book.

Deidre reached him just as he dropped it. The tome was far heavier than she expected, made of something much different than cardboard and paper. The two of them toppled to the floor with the book.

"It only *looks* small," the creature said, peering at her. "The Dark One's never had a mate."

"Ever?" she asked. She stood and bent. The book was the size of a paperback she'd buy at an airport but had to weigh fifty pounds. With a grunt, Deidre lifted it and carried it to the table. She returned to the creature, which was climbing to its feet with difficulty. She took its arm and helped him up.

"Ever," it answered with a wheeze. "But … there has only been one other Dark One before Darkyn." Its breathing was labored, and it sighed when they reached its chair. "Was the oldest ... deity remaining. Very powerful. Don't know ...how Darkyn did it."

"Maybe he made a better deal," she suggested. "That is what he does, isn't it? Makes people horrible deals that screw them over for eternity?"

"This is true. Darkyn is smart. He doesn't make ...mistakes."

She shivered, not wanting to imagine what Darkyn was capable of or how hard it might be to outmaneuver him to leave Hell. As ugly as the aged creature before her was, there was something about him that left her feeling safe for the first time since arriving to Hell.

"Do you have a name?" she asked.

"Do you?" It looked irritated at her question. "Of course demons have names."

"Sorry," she murmured. "I'm Deidre."

"A human mate and so soon after he's taken command." The ancient demon shook his head in disapproval. "You can call me Zamon. My real name is too hard for you to say."

"Nice to meet you, Zamon."

"There was a time ... young girls ran when they saw me," he sounded annoyed then sighed. "That time is gone."

"If it helps, I'm scared." Deidre rubbed her upper lip again. Her gums were irritated, reminding her she hadn't eaten or drunk water in a while. "Do you want me to run away so you feel better?"

"No." Zamon growled. He pushed the small book around then opened it.

"What kind of library is this?" she asked with a glance around.

"I keep our histories, record bloodlines, manage the deals that come in. I will record you now," Zamon said.

She watched him turn a page and touch it. Strange writing appeared.

"You are recorded," he stated, reading the words. "The Oracle says you made your first deal as his mate. You learn fast." He nodded in approval. "Your deal holds the power of the Dark One to enforce the debt, since you are his."

"That doesn't sound good," she said. Her first deal was made more out of emotion than anything else. She'd challenged Gabriel's new mate to win him over in one week, or one of them lost their souls.

During the quiet time she'd had since then, Deidre began to think she'd made a bad bet. Gabriel and Past-Death had a relationship that spanned thousands of years. He'd chosen to stay with her that long, and she'd broken Immortal laws to take her place as his mate. Gabriel's intense hatred was born of intense love and pain, and he'd clearly never made up his mind about her in the time they were together.

In a week, Deidre would be dead or back with Gabriel. At least, this was what she hoped when she made the deal.

"It is dangerous. You should not make deals, until you learn how," Zamon said sternly. "A bad deal by a deity or its mate will ruin the universe."

"Okay," she said, startled by his calm statement. "I'll be careful. How do I learn?"

"Darkyn."

She frowned. Since he was the one she wanted to learn to outsmart, in case things broke bad, she doubted he'd teach her anything. Another thought crossed her mind as she stood in Hell's library.

"Can you … teach me things about the Immortals?" she asked. "I don't know anything about this place. I was a normal human two weeks ago."

"Maybe."

Her gaze returned to him. He was concentrating on turning pages and recording things she was unable to read.

"If Darkyn agrees," Zamon added. "The Dark One likes to control those close to him."

"You mean there's more than me?" she asked.

"His daughter."

"Seriously?" she exclaimed in disbelief. "That … he's a father?"

"Yes. She was hurt by an Immortal and is in a coma of sorts."

Deidre stopped herself from pursuing. There was no way she was going to learn more. She had no intention of staying here.

Worse, she wasn't about to give the creature that tricked her into Hell and turned her Immortal an ounce of compassion.

Her stomach growled again.

"I was looking for somewhere I could get food," she said, reminded of her initial reason for wandering out of her room.

"Human food?"

"Um, yes."

"You will not want to go where the other human blood monkeys are. Darkyn would not approve. You will have to ask him."

Deidre sighed. In a place that operated on rigged deals where demons didn't seem to lose, she was certain anything she asked Darkyn for was going to cost her. That he'd beat out the original Dark One in a deal did not bode well for her.

She was trying hard to keep her fear away so she could figure out this new world. First the unfriendly Immortal society, now this nightmare. She'd promised herself she wasn't going to cry today. Half an hour after leaving her room, she was ready to break down.

"I'm going to lay down," she said.

"If you ask him, and he agrees, you can come back," Zamon said. "I will make time for you."

"Thank you."

Zamon nodded once, attention on the book. Deidre retreated into the hallway and started back towards the stairs. There was no way a creature like Darkyn, who valued control over everything, was going to let her talk to Zamon. Or eat. Or anything else.

Her eyes grew misty, and she rubbed them to keep tears from coming.

A door along the hallway ahead of her opened, startling her. Several demons exited, and the stone door closed silently. She ceased walking to wait for them to move down the hallway.

One caught sight of her and stopped. Unlike the others whose paths she'd crossed earlier, he didn't ignore her. This one nudged the demon beside him. Within seconds, all four of them were watching her like lions a wounded gazelle.

Darkyn warned her about running. Demons loved a challenge

and a fight. She held her breath and stayed still, praying their interest was passing, and they'd move on.

They didn't. One smiled coldly, revealing its sharpened teeth, while another was the first to take a step towards her. Deidre clenched her fists as the four surrounded her in the middle of the hallway.

"Darkyn's blood monkey," one demon said, eyes on the band around her neck.

She hadn't thought to put her hair up; it blocked the name of her mate on her back. Or maybe they didn't care. Maybe *he* didn't care what happened to his mate.

"You know she'll taste good," another agreed. "He takes the best ones."

"He shouldn't let you off the blood monkey floor."

"Human?"

She nodded, heart racing. All four growled, hunger in their eyes.

"We'll give you a head start," the one in front of her said. He stepped out of her path. "I'll count to three."

Deidre shook her head.

"I'll count to five?"

"No," she replied. "He won't want you touching me." *I hope.*

Two of them laughed.

"You must be new."

"As long as we leave some for him. Blood monkeys are afforded no protections here, and he always shares with us. Whatever deal you lost, you'll suffer demon mercy for as long as we keep you alive."

Demon mercy. She had a feeling it was a horrible inside joke.

"I'll count to ten."

"I'm not running," she managed.

"Very well. This is less fun, but we still get to eat." The demon on one side snatched her arm and dragged her to him. His canines lengthened. She shoved at him unsuccessfully. He grinned at the attempt and grabbed her hair, yanking her head back to expose her neck.

Suddenly, he looked up, an uneasy expression crossing his

features. Unable to see what he saw, Deidre prayed it was Darkyn, and the demon lord wasn't going to join them in passing her around for dinner. The sound of bodies hitting the stone floor behind her preceded Darkyn grabbing her by a few seconds. Deidre was yanked away from the demon holding her then released. Something jarred her, a flash of magic, one that made her more nauseous than what she saw happen next.

Darkyn snatched the demon that intended to make her its dinner. Deidre covered her face as the demon lord tore out the demon's throat with the same fangs that drank from her. Warm blood sprayed her. He gripped her arm, spun her until her back was to the remaining demon and pushed aside her hair.

"Spread the word," he snarled.

"Yes, my lord," the demon said in a hushed voice.

Deidre opened her eyes, distracted by the flow of cool magic from Darkyn into her. The remaining demon stumbled away. Her eyes dropped to what was left of the other three then flew up to the wall.

"Go," Darkyn ordered and released her.

Deidre didn't face him, afraid of what she'd see. She stepped over the dead demon between her and the stairwell without looking directly at the bloody mess. He'd told her not to run, but she found herself sprinting as soon as she was free of the dead demons. She fled up the stairs and down the hallways she'd memorized on her trip to the library.

She pushed her door open and slammed it shut. The demon blood on her face and arms disgusted her, just like the sight of the ease with which Darkyn shredded three demons with bodies like humans. But it was the thrum of magic lingering within her that disturbed her most.

It was the same thrum she felt with Gabriel, after she'd been claimed as his mate. Instead of Gabriel's warm energy, this one was Darkyn's cool energy, the soul-deep connection to a demon horrifying her. Would it be as strong as hers had been to Gabriel, where she'd ached for him to touch her, no matter how little sense it made?

No. It couldn't be. It was probably just Darkyn's magic, which he used to kill the demons. The alternative – that her own body was about to betray her to the devil – wasn't something she could handle. She felt overheated already, like she did when she was starting to get a cold.

Her gaze went to the bed. She'd never thought about how long Darkyn might wait to claim his mate by Immortal law in *that* way. Gabriel gave her space. Something told her Darkyn wasn't so considerate.

She wiped blood from her face and crossed to the small bathroom off the bedroom. She was no closer to food, but she could at least drink water out of the sink. Her mouth was dry.

Deidre grimaced at the sight of blood on her arms. She cleaned them off with hands that trembled from the confrontation. One question was answered: Darkyn was obligated to protect her in some way. He didn't do so out of the kindness of his heart. She cleaned up and left the bathroom, freezing.

Darkyn stood beside the hearth. Deidre swallowed hard. The sense she was falling ill grew stronger. Her skin was clammy, her forehead hot.

Her eyes were riveted to his frame in a way that warned her the bond she'd felt with Gabriel was now with this creature. Just under six feet tall, wide-shouldered and lean, Darkyn's youthful appearance was framed by short, dark hair. His eyes were blacker than Gabriel's, and his plain features deceptive. He didn't look like the threat she knew him to be.

"As my mate, you have the ability to draw off my power. Anything you ask of Hell, it will do," he said.

She wasn't expecting the information.

"Try to summon human food," he directed.

Not at all certain what he meant, she was hungry enough to test his claim. She willed a cheeseburger to appear. One did on the mantle above the fire. Deidre stared at it.

An odd sense entered her mind, dulling her senses. The cheeseburger was quickly forgotten. She shook her head. She almost felt as if she was … drugged? Her thoughts weren't entirely hers.

Darkyn extended his hand, drawing her from the thoughts

before it was able to form fully. A small hourglass with black sand was in his palm. Sand had already begun to trickle into the bottom.

Deidre approached him with trepidation, stopping only close enough to reach out and take the hourglass.

"What is it?" she asked.

"When the sand runs out, your deal with Past-Death is finished."

Her eyes flew up in shock that he knew about her plan to get Gabriel back. She clenched the hourglass, waiting for him to explode.

"It was a clever deal," Darkyn said, approving.

She searched his face, uncertain how to take his response.

"I'm counting on you winning," he added. "The deal of my mate is sealed with my magic. It would not be seeming for the first deal of my mate to be a loss."

Fear fluttered through her. If Darkyn wanted her to win, what had she forgotten to add to the terms, so *she* won? Not Past-Death, not Darkyn. *She* wanted to win, so she could return to Gabriel. She was missing something.

Or he was already a step ahead. Zamon's conversation with her about Darkyn tricking his predecessor left her feeling like she walked into a trap when she made the deal with Past-Death.

"Come here."

The parting words of Fate's short visit the day before were all that kept her from flipping out. He'd said she had a chance not only to leave, but also to help save Gabriel's life, if she did exactly as Darkyn said.

Comforted by Fate's words, Deidre obeyed Darkyn's order with trepidation but no hesitation, assuming he meant to drink from her again. His nearness rattled her senses in a way that reminded her of how she felt around Gabriel. She swallowed hard, willing herself to remember that she was meant for Gabriel, even if it was Darkyn's name on her back.

The heaviness of her mind grew, until she wasn't certain why she should resist Darkyn in the first place. She was fighting a fever, one that made it hard for her to focus.

"No demon should ever harm you again. But, if an Immortal or human or deity corners you, and you aren't able to summon me, you need to know how to defend yourself," Darkyn started. His voice was the only thing that penetrated the haze coating her thoughts. "I'll show you how to kill the simplest way possible."

As he spoke, he peeled off his shirt to reveal a whip-like, muscular upper body coated by a thin layer of tan skin. Gabriel's body was built for power; Darkyn's was crafted for agility. He tossed his shirt on the chair behind her. He reclaimed the hourglass from her and set it on the mantle of the fireplace. When he took her hand, she almost cried.

She didn't want to be attracted to him, to feel the fire in her blood and the calm at her core when he touched her. She was too aware of the expanse of his chest, the heat of his closeness, the strange fog that grew thicker in her mind.

"I prefer to kill painfully," he said. "You probably do not. Have you ever killed anyone?"

"No. I've never even hit anyone."

He assessed her for a moment before continuing. "To kill a man, Immortal or demon fast, touch him here." He placed her hand at his neck.

Worse than seeing him was feeling him. His skin was smooth and warm, stretched taut over an athletic body. The Dark One felt like a *man*.

"Or here," he said and moved her hand to his chest. "Also, instant death."

She flattened her palm against the spot over his heart. His hand fell away, but hers remained. He had a heartbeat, one that reverberated through her as if it was her own. She wasn't able to reconcile the creature that turned her Immortal with the man before her.

"How?" she managed, needing to focus on something other than him. She ran her tongue over her gums then licked her lips. Despite the water, her mouth was dry and aching almost to the point of pain.

"You will them to die-dead. As my mate, you are able to use a limited amount of my power," he explained. "Try it. Will me dead."

Her attention shifted to the hand over his heart. He felt too *real*. She hadn't been able to break up with a boyfriend she was sick of for fear of hurting his feelings. She couldn't kill anyone.

She shook her head.

"You turn down a chance to kill the Dark One?"

She almost screamed at herself. He wasn't a man. He was the creature who trapped her in Hell. The thought of hurting him made the hand she pressed to his heart tremble. It wasn't anger she felt towards him but … hunger.

He smelled like a heady mix of male musk and something so faint and sweet, it made her want to press her face to the skin of his chest for a better smell. It was this compulsion that was like a drug weighing down her thoughts and making her hungry, like walking past a bakery first thing in the morning and trying not to look at what was in the window. His solid frame and heat were creeping into her senses, tugging at her resolve to resist.

He stood at ease before her, unconcerned with teaching her to kill then exposing himself to death at her hands. She couldn't bring herself to try, just like she couldn't remove her hand. His body was covered with faded scars that fascinated her, made her want to trace the lengths of them with her fingers then her tongue.

She'd experienced one night with an Immortal mate, and it was the most incredible night of her life. What would it be like to run her hands over Darkyn's lean frame the way she had Gabriel's, to feel his sharp teeth nip the delicate skin of her inner thighs and breasts? What pleasure would it bring if he drank from her while making love to her?

The erotic visions in her head made heat bloom in her lower belly and the fire of desire spread in her blood.

Deidre struggled against the sensations. She needed control of her own mind back, but the feverish fog was too thick.

Was what she felt for Gabriel nothing more than destiny and Immortal laws she knew nothing about? Was she destined to feel that for Darkyn, despite knowing what he was? Was there no choice in who she loved?

"No," she said out loud. "It can't be true."

"The laws from the time-before-time are absolute. They are the only ones," Darkyn's growl was unusually soft, almost a purr. "Past-Death fucked you over by letting you experience another mate first, when you were meant for me alone."

"No," she said. "This is...this is temporary." She dropped her hand and prayed the sensations within her left.

"How certain are you that what you feel is not real?"

Deidre met his gaze. He always knew how to read her. He had since they first crossed paths in the shadow world, when he offered her a choice: to cure the inoperable brain tumor killing her or to outright kill her before she declined, whichever outcome she preferred.

His gaze was penetrating and direct, stirring desire and fear within her. His features were masculine and strong. His nose bore the appearance of having been broken and set incorrectly more than once. Where Gabriel was always clean-shaven, Darkyn's strong jaw was shaded by a day or two of growth, lending danger to his appearance. His fangs were long, his eyes burning with more than hunger.

"Certain enough to make me a deal?" He touched her, his hand settling on her arm. Her breath caught. Cool energy worked its way into her. The simple, purposeful touch reinforced what she already knew. This was too similar to what she physically felt towards Gabriel to be anything other than the Immortal bond that branded Darkyn's name across her shoulders.

If she could only think straight for a few seconds! But her thoughts were falling under the control of something else.

"It's not fair," she whispered in a choked voice.

"It is the nature of the mating rite. You were never meant to belong to Gabriel. It took me too long to find Past-Death's soul. You almost waited too long to seek me out for a deal," he said. "A few more days, and even I wouldn't have been able to undo what Wynn did."

Had the deity Fate betrayed her like everyone else did? His advice had been to give in to Darkyn. Why try to help her, if he knew her destiny already?

"You're trying to trick me again," she said with resolution.

Darkyn cupped her cheek with one hand, the cool energy spreading as his thumb rubbed her cheek lightly. She shuddered at the contact. With his other hand, he removed the slender collar he had placed around her neck when she arrived. It dissipated.

The odd scent was closer, and she found herself breathing in deeply to try to capture it.

"Think about it. When you win your deal with Past-Death, there's no requirement for her to be rendered dead-dead at the end of the week. She may live an eternity, even if her soul comes to you eventually," Darkyn explained. "Gabriel cannot kill his own mate. It's against the Immortal laws. Which begs the question: What happens to *you* in one week?"

It was the same question she'd been asking herself. She didn't know the answer. She was terrified to find out. As he spoke, he continued the light stroke of one thumb and trailed a finger down the side of her face and traced her jaw. A line of cool fire remained. His touch went down the side of her neck, lingered on her collar-bone then continued down her arm. Mesmerized by the sensations, her confusion and his direct gaze, she had to concentrate hard to register what he said.

"I, um, don't know," she murmured then shook her head. "I mean, this is temporary. It won't happen that way."

Darkyn's hand rested on her hip. He drew her against him. Deidre found herself leaning into his solid frame without resistance, entranced by the combination of his hot, hard body and cool fire on her swimming senses. The faint, sweet scent was close. Calling to her. Tugging at her ability to reason.

She nuzzled the hand cupping her cheek, and his thumb traced her lips. He lifted her hand to his heart. Instinctively, she flattened her palm against his chest once more to feel his heartbeat. It was the opposite of hers: calm, steady, strong.

"You don't sound certain enough to make a deal with me."

"I ... I'm not sure why I should."

Touching him felt too natural. He was saturating her senses, seducing her somehow. She'd walked away from Gabriel, because he all-but-pushed her away. Darkyn's intentions were the opposite. He was using the truth to hammer down her resistance and his power to seduce her. She didn't expect it; she expected him to lie rather than point out the flaws in her desperate logic.

The fog around her thoughts grew heavier.

Waiting for him to snap or yell as he had when she arrived to Hell, she touched him timidly with her other hand to begin exploring the ridges of the scars on his chest.

"Touch me, taste me, scratch me, bite me," he whispered. "You can't be too rough for me."

"You can be for me," she said uneasily.

"I made you a deal. I know how to give pleasure without pain." By the distaste in his voice, he wasn't happy about it. "I won't hurt you, unless you ask me to."

Her hands ceased quivering as she ran them across his chest, over his firm shoulders and shapely arms before returning to his chest.

"Yes or no, love?" he purred. "Will you take your place in my bed as my mate?"

"You won't wait a week?" she asked.

"Only if you make me a deal."

She groaned. The same instincts that warned her against the last deal with him told her she'd never win any bet with the devil

"I'll give you the terms first this time. You can gauge the risk." He chuckled, a sinister sound. "You can fuck me here, now, the way mates should. Or, when you lose our deal, you can fuck the Dark One." He nuzzled her neck, and she tilted her head. His teeth grazed the sensitive skin without biting.

"Oh, god," she breathed. No part of her was willing to risk an encounter with Darkyn's other form. The world around her was dark around its edges. The fever had taken her out of her mind and into the alternate reality of a dream.

Except, when he touched her, it felt real again.

Unable to exit the dream fully, Deidre had no concept of how long they stood before the black flames of the fire.

"Choose."

"Yes," she whispered.

Rather than drink from her, he kissed her. Unlike Gabriel, who was gentle, teasing, Darkyn was demanding. Deidre felt herself breathless and consumed before the end of their first kiss, yielding to the intensity of his kiss and the firmness of his touch. He slid her dress free, his hands moving over her body possessively before he lifted her and carried her to the bed.

His body was solid and strong, the sensations of his skin against hers and his scents intoxicating her. She fell headfirst into his spell. True to his word, he was aggressive without hurting her. The nip of his fangs at her neck, inner thighs and breasts almost drove her over the edge while his hot tongue and hands explored every part of her.

She found herself nipping back at his chest and neck, something she'd never done before. The faint scent was there, pulling her. She was almost able to catch it before it fled her again. She tasted his skin, but it, too, wasn't enough. She wanted something as elusive as the scent. He eased into her body at first then made love to her hungrily, relentlessly pushing her deeper into the haze of pleasure and desire, until she arched beneath him, her body on the verge of shattering.

His fangs sank into her neck.

This time, there was a combination of distant pain and pleasure as he bit her that almost pierced the hazy dream. Deidre gripped him, craving something she didn't know how to ask him for. He drank deeply. The pain faded once more, and the experience became too dreamlike to be real.

He lifted his head, whispering,

"Bite me."

Lost in the heady sensations, Deidre wriggled and strained beneath him. He pinned her hands above her head to keep her still then whispered the command again. Desperately trapped by need unlike anything she'd ever known, she obeyed.

She bit his neck gently, not wanting to hurt him despite the strange dream and hunger in her body screaming to be filled.

"Harder." Darkyn moved in and out of her slowly, taking her closer to her climax.

Overwhelmed by the pleasure, Deidre bit him hard enough that she tasted him. Distant alarm was overwhelmed by need. *This* was what she smelled, what she ached to taste. The warm liquid in her mouth didn't taste like blood; it was virtually flavorless, tainted by a sweetness hard to quantify. The consuming need to drink from him swept through her mind, dulling the rest of the world.

"Drink." His voice was hoarse, his body straining. He growled from low in his chest.

Barely aware of anything outside of his commands, she obeyed. She pulled more of him into her, trying to identify the elusive flavor that left her intoxicated. He pulled away, and Deidre's eyes fluttered open. He whispered words she wasn't able to make out then bit her again, this time hard enough for the pain to piece her dreamlike stage.

Deidre's world shattered. She cried out, body convulsing under waves of pleasure intense enough to push her towards unconsciousness. He rested on top of her, breathing hard, as he pressed her into the bed. She panted. Their bodies were slick with sweat, and she lingered in the afterglow, lost in the heat and silk of his skin. The effect of his blood in her body was twofold: she felt it moving through her, changing her, while her mind once more was lulled into dreamy confusion. One thought emerged, fed by urgency that was quickly swallowed by cool magic.

She slept with the Dark One – drank his blood like a demon might. No part of it felt unnatural.

Or was it a nightmare only?

Bite me.

There was no way it was real. She'd never drink anyone's blood!

Deidre lay still for a moment before her eyes opened. She was alone in bed. Fevered and shivering, she felt too weak and hungry to focus well, but the shape of the black hourglass was unmistakable. It sat on the nightstand beside the bed. She reached for it. Her clumsy hand missed it, and she stared at the black sand as it fell towards the bottom of the glass.

It's too late. Like her other thoughts, this one escaped before she was able to understand its meaning. Whatever was working through her system was making her sick. The dream of Darkyn was no doubt a fever dream, one that caused distant alarm despite her illness.

Exhausted, her eyes fluttered closed. Deidre stopped fighting her body's cry for sleep and fell into a deep, dark slumber.

Day Two

Chapter Two

Deidre awoke alone and naked in bed. Her head hurt, and she felt grimy from the night sweats. The night was a blur in her mind, a combination of strange, fuzzy dreams about blood and tossing and turning from the horrible fever. She remembered touching Darkyn's chest and feeling aroused by the idea of his hands on her. From there, the night was a blurry fever dream. She'd dreamt of sleeping with Darkyn. Just the thought made her head hurt worse. The dread and guilt at the pit of her stomach were countered by the confusion of knowing that she'd fallen into the grip of the Immortal laws first with Gabriel then with Darkyn.

Was any of what she felt real?

Was Darkyn or Fate right about what was supposed to happen?

She was so hungry! Distraught, she rolled over to find the first surprise of the day on the block of stone that acted as a nightstand: an obsidian tray of fruit and fresh pastries. The scents made her stomach roar to life.

Hell had a magic library. Did it have a magic bakery, too?

Unable to dwell on how Hell knew what she liked for breakfast, she wolfed down the pastries and a banana before crossing to the bathroom for a shower. She scrubbed herself down, angry at the Immortals as a whole for tolerating a system that screwed over their mates and eliminated free will. Darkyn's assertions about her destiny being with him left her in a foul mood.

The Dark One was not capable of a healthy relationship. Gabriel had been, and she was furious at herself for not taking him more seriously and for choosing to accept Darkyn's deal instead of taking a chance with Gabriel. If Gabriel had killed her while trying to save her, he'd kill the soul in her head, too, the one that damned Deidre to Hell. All of this would've been avoided.

She hadn't been ready to die, though. Did it make her a bad person for wanting the best chance at life? She hadn't thought so, but then again, she never expected to end up in Hell.

Unwritten terms, Darkyn called them. The ones only he knew that let him win.

Maybe Zamon had answers. He might at least explain what these laws were that condemned her to Darkyn. She didn't believe that her bet with Past-Death wouldn't make a difference. If Past-Death being dead had rendered Deidre the mate of Gabriel, why wouldn't it work again, once Deidre won their deal?

"I feel like crap," she muttered and rested her forehead against the black stone wall of the shower. The water was hot and the water pressure brutal. It helped wake her up without completely lifting the fog of a fever that had been present since yesterday.

Darkyn's amusement at the deal made her shudder. She had to figure out what she was missing fast and how permanent it was to be an Immortal mate.

Deidre turned off the shower, some semblance of a plan comforting her. She dressed then went through the motions of brushing her teeth and dressing without the aid of a mirror, irritated that the only mirror in the bedroom was in the inside door of the wardrobe. She wiped the last of the toothpaste from her mouth and glanced down. Blood bubbled from the cut on her index finger. She stuck it in her mouth and cut it again. The wounds healed almost instantly.

Puzzled, she studied her finger, not understanding what was cutting it. She had no old wounds she was reopening. She ran her tongue across her gums again and froze.

Deidre whipped the door open, ignoring the sting of her wet hair against her shoulders. The dress shifted around her as she hurried to the wardrobe. She pushed open the door with the mirror and stared. Petite, white, pointed fangs extended from her upper gums to rest on her plump lower lip.

"No, no, no," she whispered and pushed at the teeth with a finger. They were real. She bared her teeth. Her two canines were larger than before and gave her the appearance of a vampire.

Or demon. The Dark One was going to turn her Immortal. Had he made her a demon?

She controlled her breathing to keep her frantic emotions from consuming her.

Her eyes went to the mantle where the hourglass remained. Deidre strode to the hearth and picked up the time marker that was no larger than her pinkie. She tilted it. The sand only moved one way, even when upside down.

She found herself poking the new teeth with her tongue to confirm they really were there.

Maybe they were temporary. When the sand ran out, she'd have no Darkyn tattoo, no demon fangs, no Past-Death standing between her and Gabriel.

How certain are you? Darkyn had baited her.

She wasn't. At all. What if she won but stayed a demon? What if she lost and stayed a demon? Whose bright idea was it to turn her into a demon anyway? What if she lost the bet entirely?

She swallowed hard to keep tears from forming.

There had to be a way out of this. Fate said to do what Darkyn said. Fate wanted Past-Death dead. Thus far, he'd been the most helpful of the Immortals. He wasn't going to abandon her, too, was he?

Deidre went back to the mirror and gazed at herself. She wore the Grecian style gown of Hell: secured around her neck by a loose band, it draped over her curves and pooled at her feet, leaving her arms, shoulders and back bare to the hips. She wore the metal collar that marked her as Darkyn's food source. The scars the Dark One created when he turned her Immortal were more faded today than yesterday.

Her pink hair was up in a bun that revealed the delicate cut of her elfin features. Her large blue-green eyes were clear and calm, the curves of her slender frame complemented by the cut and drape of the dress. Her lips were red and her features flushed from the fever. She sensed more than saw the largest difference within her. The sunny glow she was known for was gone, replaced by a sultriness rendered dangerous by the fangs resting on her lower lip.

She looked seductive, no longer sweet. The distinction left her feeling torn. She'd lost something when the Dark One turned her. At the same time, the petite woman in the mirror was beyond gorgeous, the combination of shimmering seductiveness and cool beauty stunning.

She had fangs.

Deidre closed the door, near tears once more. She raised the hourglass. She had to make it only a few more days.

"You still don't believe me."

She tensed at his low voice. She hadn't heard him enter but doubted the Dark One used doors.

"I don't know what to believe," she replied. "None of this is real."

"It is."

"What did you do to me?"

"I turned you."

"Into what?"

"What do you think?"

Deidre faced him. Across the room, Darkyn held the tension of a taut rubber band. His predatory gaze was on her. No part of his stance or piercing look was welcoming and yet, she felt the urge to cross to him. A flash of a dream went through her mind. It was of his lean body pressing her into the bed while they made love. She shook her head, not about to believe anything of the sort happened outside her nightmare.

Darkyn's hands were clasped behind his back. He approached her, eyes on her lips. Deidre didn't move, afraid of provoking him.

He reached out to take the hourglass, grazing her skin in the act. Her breath caught at the cool electricity that ran through her. She flushed. His gaze flickered to hers. He was coldly amused. He held up the hourglass in the space between them.

"Let's talk, shall we?" he asked.

"I don't think I want to," she replied. She felt too fragile to deal with him.

"Assume you win your bet. Do you really think you'll become Gabriel's mate?" he started, ignoring her. "The chances are slim it will work. Both of you bear the mating marks now. She had none before her death. She'd have to be dead-dead which could happen next week or in a millennium."

Deidre swallowed hard. She recalled the other thing she hated about interacting with him: he always knew how to read her deepest fears. He was good at throwing them back at her, too, like he was doing now.

"So? What if I can … um, expedite that?" she asked.

"Love, you couldn't kill me. You can't kill her."

Deidre met his gaze. To emphasize his words, he lifted her hand and placed it over his heart. Her chin trembled at the steady pulse of his heartbeat beneath her fingertips. She'd felt it last night, too, before … before the fever dream about them having sex.

It had to be a dream, except that she remembered the heat of the skin beneath his shirt and tracing the scars she knew covered his body.

"What do you want from me, Darkyn?" she asked, afraid to admit how right he was.

"For you to accept that this is where you belong." He tossed the hourglass onto a chair. Her eyes followed it. It was her one hope out of this place.

She shook her head. Deidre's heart was flying at his nearness. His magic crept up her arm and into her body. She dropped her hand from his chest, needing to think.

"Very well. The chances are slim that what you want will

happen. I prefer the alternative of them being non-existent," he said. "There are three bonds that are older than time. The mating bond is one, used by Immortals and deities. A blood bond is another, practiced between demons in place of the mating bond. There's only one entity in the universe that can transform a human into a new form that can be blood bound to a demon."

She didn't have to ask which entity that was. She touched her mouth and felt the canines at the mention of transforming her. She suspected he was one step ahead, but she wasn't expecting him to reveal his plan.

"We will be blood bound. Think of it as …insurance. That slim chance you leave here becomes no chance."

"I won't do it."

"You are mine already," he said in a quiet voice. "If the blood bond takes, there is nothing that can break a double-bond. No deal, no manipulation by Fate, no breaking of the laws from the time-before-time."

Deidre's quick breathing was loud in her ears.

"I don't lose," he added. "Ever." He touched her face. "The bond is voluntary. You've already got the teeth."

She shuddered and quickly lifted her chin.

"I won't," she said, unable to stomach the idea that he turned her demon or that there was no chance she ever left Hell. "Nothing you do will convince me."

"No?" He touched her arm.

Deidre backed away. If his touch was hard to resist last night, it was crippling today. Anger and panic bubbled within her. She fell into his trance last night; she needed to keep her head clear to deal with him this time. Except she was suddenly hungry again, the faint, sweet scent winding through her senses.

Darkyn pursued calmly, eyes glowing. He touched her again. She moved away. He was amused at whatever game he played as he closed the distance between them once more. It fed her fury. He took her arm, and she yanked away from him.

"Don't touch me!" she hissed.

He reached for her once more, and she slapped his hand away.

"If there *is* a way out, I will find it!" she snapped. "Fate said …" she stopped, recalling the blond deity's warning about not revealing he had visited.

"You trust Fate over me?" Darkyn mused. "Interesting. What did he tell you? Obey me, and you'd leave?" He continued to move closer.

"Yes." Her senses addled, Deidre was forced to retreat.

"What *exactly* did he say? That you'd leave?"

"That I'd be …" *relatively okay.* Fate hadn't said anything about leaving. She shook her head to clear the memory. "I mean, he didn't say leave … he …" A sick sense of betrayal sank into her stomach. "Survive. He said I'd survive."

"Maybe he wanted to ensure I didn't kill you before we were bound." Darkyn pretended to consider.

"You made a deal for me. Why would you kill me?"

"If I don't like what I find, I'm not obligated to keep you alive before the bonds form," he said pointedly. "You interpreted what he told you in a way that gave you hope."

She knocked away his next attempt to reach her, fully aware he was distracting her physically while whittling down her resistance mentally.

"Of all the Immortals and deities fucking with you, I have no need to lie. Yet you trust him over me."

"I don't trust any of you! From the first minute I was dragged into this fucked up world, I've been lied to and used. Past-Death claims to – stop! Don't touch me!" she said with a shudder at the fire his fingers sent through her arm. "Past-Death almost killed me and you trick me into coming here. Now you want to make sure I never leave!"

"I saved your life. By law, you are mine twice over even without the blood bond."

Her back hit the wall. He stopped close enough for their bodies to touch if she breathed in too deeply.

"I'm the only one who hasn't lied to you. Even Gabriel has," Darkyn said.

"No," she said flatly. "You won't turn me against him."

"Why? Because you felt the mating bond with him first? The same one you feel with me? He did nothing but hide the truth from you. Your illness, Wynn, Past-Death. He was in love with a ghost and unwilling to take a chance on *you*. Did he tell you who he was before he fucked you?"

"Stop!" she grated. His words struck her as true; they were the same doubts she'd had about Gabriel since she met him. Feeling claustrophobic, she broke the plane between them and shoved him. Darkyn caught her hands and pushed them down to her side. His magic shot through her. His nearness was driving her crazy. She smelled something faint, familiar. Entrancing. It was calling to her. She felt as if she hadn't just eaten a large breakfast. She was starving.

"You know the Immortal mating bond is what made you connect with him," Darkyn continued.

"No," she insisted. "You can never understand." She stared hard at his chest as she struggled with her anger and need. They were spinning out of control, fed by the direct contact with him and the elusive scent that was making her mouth water. Her whole body was burning up with something she never, ever expected to feel for a demon: need.

"So you feel nothing now," he stated. "Say it. Lie to me and tell me you aren't about to throw yourself at my feet and beg me to fuck you."

His mocking tone infuriated her. She wrenched free of his hold and pushed him hard enough to slide out from between him and the wall.

"I wonder what your Gabriel will think when he finds out. Fucking the Dark One. Blood bound to the Dark One. And only the Dark One."

"It won't happen."

Breathing raggedly, she tried hard to rein in the emotions that were close to landing her in trouble. She hated his rules, but she wasn't fighting him. She was trying hard not to run. She wasn't going to give him an excuse to attack her. It struck her that he was baiting her, perhaps for that reason.

"I am sick of this shit," she said. "I'm sick of deities and Immortals tricking and lying to me. What do you want? Or are you just tormenting me for the fun of it?"

"Does it matter?"

She faced him again. "You wouldn't be here if it didn't. You won't convince me what I felt towards Gabriel wasn't real, and there is nothing you can do to make me do this blood bond."

"You already know the Immortal mating is what made you feel that way towards Gabriel. If you thought otherwise, you wouldn't have fucked me last night," he said, meeting her gaze.

"What? I ..." she gaped at him. "It was a dream!"

"It was the final stage of your transition into a demon. It might have felt like a dream, but I can assure you it was not," he said, smiling.

"I refuse to believe you," she cried. "Tell me what you want or just leave me alone!"

"I did. I want you to accept that you belong here, and I want to hear the words."

"What words?"

"The ones where you tell me you're mine."

She shook her head.

"You've started to admit the truth to yourself," he added. "I want to hear it out loud."

"If I say the words you want, are you manipulating me into this bond, the same way you did to get me into Hell?" she demanded.

"You're mine either way."

"No, I'm not. I'm Gabriel's," she retorted.

Darkyn gave a slow smile. "How certain are you?"

"I'll never say those fucking words, and I'll never be blood bound!"

"My bet is that you will do both before the hourglass runs out."

"I'm not about to be tricked into another bond or whatever it is you're trying to trick me into," she replied.

"No tricks," he said. "How about this. A private deal, just between us. If we become blood bound, you say the words."

"If we don't?"

LIZZY FORD

"You don't," he said with a shrug.

"What about the unwritten terms?"

"None. Simple deal."

She studied him. She'd never let him blood bind her, but he wasn't someone who took no for an answer, even if it was allegedly voluntary. Double-bound, though, meant she was fucked as far as Gabriel.

"I'm not playing your game," she said and turned away again. Her body was trembling. She didn't know why, couldn't get control of either her emotions or the hunger in her blood. They left her beyond confused, terrified and certain she didn't want anything to do with Darkyn right now.

"You know I'm right. You know Past-Death will stop at nothing to get what she wants," Darkyn said. "I foresee you winning your deal. I also foresee Gabriel refusing to kill her. He cannot. She's his mate by Immortal laws, and we both know how seriously he takes his duty. He will protect her, as is his obligation. No one will challenge Death to kill her. Which leaves you here. With me. For eternity. My informal deal is one week. At the end of it, if you've not bound yourself to me, then the deal expires. We can spend eternity together and you never say the words."

Darkyn was right. She knew Gabriel. He'd sworn to protect her, even while pushing her away. He followed the laws. She found no flaws in Darkyn's logic, which only made her despair soar.

"Are the words part of the blood binding rite?" she asked. She was almost ready to say whatever he wanted to get rid of him. Her world was crushing her; she needed to be alone.

"No."

"It must be voluntary?"

"On both our parts."

"Why are the words so important? Me being your mate isn't enough?" she guessed. "You want complete surrender."

"You did that last night, no matter what you choose to remember." The husky laugh made her stomach flutter. "Mentally, you are holding out. I spent my life at battle. There is no such thing as half a

36

victory. I won't let you think there's a chance this isn't real or permanent."

"So, that's it?" she asked.

"That's it. Private deal. One week."

The idea that it bothered him enough to provoke a deal made her brow furrow. All she had to do was make it a week without agreeing to the blood binding. There had to be a catch with Darkyn's deal. She didn't see it, though, unless he intended to force her to do it, in which case, she was fucked anyway. The words would mean nothing to her at that point.

"Fine," she said, at the end of her rope with him. "Will you leave me alone now? Please."

"Not quite. I came to feed as well."

Deidre heard him approach from behind. She tensed, waiting for the flip to switch and him to grab her. He touched her, trailing his hands down her arms. Her body responded to him in a way that made her angrier. He nudged her head to the side to reach her neck, and she pushed back, refusing.

His hands on her arms made her body betray her again. It was harder to resist him than it was Gabriel, which made her want to weep. She didn't understand it. It wasn't possible she was meant for Darkyn. He nudged her head once more. She refused him.

"Rules," he reminded her.

"Fuck your rules," she said. "And fuck you if you think I'll ever volunteer to be bound to you."

"That's why I have insurance."

He pulled her into his body, and the intensity of the strange hunger within her expanded. She focused on what he said to keep herself distracted from the yearning growing in her body. She felt his arousal against her backside, while his other hand rested on the bare skin of her hip. Hot nips started down the side of her neck. Overwhelmed, she instinctively tilted her head in submission, exposing her neck to him.

"I don't lose deals, Deidre," he repeated. "You were bound last night."

The images he placed in her mind were of her arching beneath him, crying out his name, while he drank from her. She recalled biting him and the taste of his blood. It was thick in her mouth, slightly sweet, and made her ravenous. It was her fever dream without the heaviness of illness to blur it.

"No," she said. "You're messing with me."

Darkyn responded by removing his hand from her body. He ran one finger along her lips. She felt a drop of warmth and instinctively licked it. Warm, sweet.

Him.

Her hunger became crippling. She wrenched away from him, desire and thirst making her head reel.

"Look in the mirror," he said, nodding his head towards the wardrobe. "You've got the demon marking already."

Deidre fled to it, needing something to bolster the defenses that were dropping too fast. She yanked the wardrobe open and turned to peer over her shoulder.

She had two markings on her back: One burgundy, the familiar Immortal mating tattoo, and the new one black, positioned directly beneath the original. Both displayed Darkyn's name. Shocked, she wasn't able to move.

"You will never have a chance with Gabriel, even when you win your deal." Darkyn touched her arm again, his cool energy making her snap.

"You son of a bitch!" she whispered. "I will never say those words!" Deidre slapped him hard. Darkyn's tongue flickered out to catch the drop of blood from the corner of his mouth.

She raised a hand to slap him again, but he grabbed her. Any control she had slid away. She struggled against him, not caring what he did to her now that he'd taken away her only real hope of leaving.

He kissed her. The taste of the blood in his mouth ensnared her instantly. She stilled, arrested by the flavor and texture. All conscience effort to think fled and was replaced by a new instinct, the primal need to feed. He released her. Deidre took his face in her hands, hungrily trying to taste more of him as she explored his mouth with fervor.

Only when every last lingering fleck of blood was gone did her ability to think return. She dropped back on her heels, staring up at him in surprise. Darkyn's dark eyes glowed. His fangs were out, his attention riveted to her.

"Blood bond," he said quietly. "The original bond from the time-before-time. Demons are the only who still practice it. Immortals and deities have mating marks. Demons have blood marks. I am both a deity and a demon, which means you have both. Insurance." He stepped away, towards the bed, peeling off his shirt as he went.

Deidre couldn't register what he said and how permanent he claimed it was.

"I know you are hungry. Come feed with me."

She *drank* blood! Horrified, Deidre started toward the door. She needed to run away, far away, until this nightmare was over.

Darkyn stopped where he was and lifted a hand. He slid a fingernail across the pad of his thumb.

The scent of blood was crippling.

She tried to turn away, but the smell filled her senses with inhuman hunger and desperation. Deidre sank to the floor, not trusting herself. She wanted – *needed* – to taste him again. It was painful. Instead, she wrapped her arms around her knees and tucked her face in the crook of one elbow.

Wake up, Deidre! She ordered herself.

Too aware of him, she tensed as he crouched beside her, the scent too potent to be a dream.

"I can't … do this." She shook as much from need as fear.

"You already have."

"It's wrong."

"You feed me. I feed you. We give each other life. What is so wrong in that?" he countered. His cool touch calmed her this time, parted the reeling emotions and chaotic thoughts.

On some level – in the newfound instincts that wanted to taste him – his words made sense. Even with him taking the edge off, reality still wasn't real. This place, him, her situation – they *couldn't* be, or she was going to go insane.

"Let me go. Please," she whispered, raising her head to see him.

"It's too late for that."

"Is there no part of you capable of …" she stopped. His eyes were so cold and ancient. Hard. Unforgiving. Merciless.

"No, there's not," he replied just as softly.

"Am I so bad that I end up married to the devil?"

"You are the only innocent soul in Hell." His chilling smile did nothing to make his statement more tolerable.

Darkyn tipped her chin up, until she met his gaze again.

"This is where you belong. You must accept that. You must accept me. I didn't just turn you Immortal; I turned you into one of my kind. A demon. One who must feed on blood to live."

He offered his bloodied thumb. With effort, she turned her head away.

"I can't be like you. I can't hurt people or drink their blood," she said.

"You don't have to. You will only drink from me. You will only hunger for me."

"And you?" she asked, bitterness in her voice.

"The same."

Uncertain if she understood him or not, Deidre studied him. He had yet to lie to her, and she didn't think he was now. He had no need to; this was his domain. In his mind, she was already his.

"I will only drink from you," he said slowly, clearly. "It is what being blood bound means. Think of it this way, love. You are saving five lives a day, simply by being my mate." He smiled.

Deidre's mouth almost fell open. "You were killing so many people?"

"Bled them dry. This will help you rationalize and accept your place here, I believe."

She swallowed. "You turned me into a demon."

"I did." He shifted forward as he spoke and nudged her head aside with his. The low purr in his chest was audible. He nuzzled her neck.

Deidre closed her eyes, hating that she was turned on by the thought of him feeding from her. Of her needing his blood.

He turned her into a demon. A creature that required blood to live. More tears squeezed from her eyes. She already sensed she was fighting a losing battle. She wanted him so bad, it hurt.

"Drink," he whispered.

The impulse to do as he bid was too strong. She touched his neck with trembling hands and felt his pulse. He, too, was a demon, but he had a human body, a heart, blood.

He waited.

"There's no going back," she said hoarsely.

"No, there's not." Sensing she was yielding, Darkyn drew her into his body.

Deidre's breathing was ragged as she tried to process what she was about to do. She found herself nuzzling his neck, compelled by the elusive scent and taste. Why didn't the idea disgust her like she thought it should?

"This is really happening," she said in disbelief.

"It is. You can't hurt me. Drink."

"If you knew I was blood-bound, why provoke me into a deal you already won?" she asked.

"You need to confront what is before you. Gabriel's biggest mistake was not forcing you to accept your new world from the start. I will not make the same one," he replied. "And I like to know you've got some fight in you. I'll teach you how to fuck like a demon before the week is out."

She hesitated. Need was thick in her body, an inhuman craving she knew now how to satisfy. She bit him timidly, failed to draw blood, then closed her eyes and bit him hard.

He growled, a sound that made his chest vibrate against hers in a way not remotely human. He didn't tell her to stop. The growl faded to a purr. She drew his blood into her mouth, immediately appeased by the elusive flavor that made her blood burn. She was tasting *him*.

The unnaturally deep intimacy of the moment wasn't lost on her. Deidre eased against him, the tension fleeing her body. Her senses became saturated quickly by his scent and heat. She withdrew her teeth from his neck, not at all certain what to think of what she'd done.

"You are the first and only to draw my blood." His purr was husky.

She rested her cheek against his, and they breathed the same air, his steady and hers erratic. Deidre felt the wetness of her tears. She was confused again, unable to shake the memory of Gabriel or fully accept this new fate.

"That means something important, doesn't it?" she asked.

"It means I accept you as my mate," he said. "It means you can fight me now."

"How about running?"

"Try it and see."

"I'm not ready for that," she replied. "I'm not ready for this. For you."

"The bonds are complete." His shifted, and his tongue flickered out to capture her tears. "There's nothing else between you and me, except you accepting it."

Deidre wasn't expecting his version of kindness. He was too hard and cold to offer much in that way, but he spoke the truth softly and then kissed her hungrily. She responded, her sorrow and confusion feeding her need. He lifted his head.

"No more tears," he said. A cunning smile crossed his face.

She stared, not understanding. She smelled it suddenly and jerked, scouring his body to find the blood whose scent stirred her senses. She spotted the maroon drops on the pad of one thumb and drew his hand up to her lips. Before she could capture the drops, he lifted his hand above his head, out of her reach. He stood.

"What are you doing?" she asked, confused. She rose with him.

"Provoking you."

Hunger roared within her. Deidre stretched but couldn't reach. He pushed her away and moved towards the bed. The sensations within her churned and burned in a way that demanded she do something. She treaded to him and pulled his head down to kiss her then nudged it aside instead to reach his neck.

Darkyn pushed her away again. Madness was settling into her at the scent and sight of his blood. She could neither control her body's reaction to it nor satiate it.

"Come on. I'll teach you to play with your food." The light of challenge was in Darkyn's eyes. He waited.

Deidre caved, unable to take the newfound hunger. She went to him. She ran her hands over his chest and leaned forward, nipping him hard enough to draw blood.

"Nice try," Darkyn chuckled. He grabbed her hips, kissing her hard and leaving her breathless. He drove her back onto the bed, pressed her down and rested on top of her.

Deidre reached for him, straining to ease the need to taste him. Darkyn played keep away, until she was drowning in heat, desire and the hot hunger that felt like it was going to consume her. His solid body was on top of hers yet unattainable. He withheld kisses and blood, refusing to sate either of her cravings.

"Come on. Play," he whispered into her ear. His direct look managed to stir what part of her wasn't already desperate.

Near frenzied, Deidre fought to pull some part of him close enough for her to taste. He growled in response and nipped her neck, pushing her away roughly. He was different than the last deity she'd slept with. Whereas Gabriel was willing to give-and-take, Darkyn toyed with her and demanded submission in exchange for controlled pleasure.

He alternately let her feed just enough to drive her mad then drank from her, while he commanded her body relentlessly. Only when he finished with her did he relent.

Panting and exhausted, Deidre couldn't have moved, had he not shifted to hold her against him.

"Drink," he whispered.

Deidre let her newfound instincts guide her. She fed. The hunger abated, and she dropped her head back to the pillow, satisfied. Her body entwined with his, she breathed in his scent as deeply as she could. Her mind returned now that her need was gone, and she opened her eyes.

She drank blood. She slept with the devil. Why wasn't she freaking out?

"I am very satisfied with you, my little human," Darkyn said, his lips moving against her temple.

"I get to live another day," she murmured.

"Maybe two, if you please me again."

"You're not funny."

"You have nothing to fear from me now."

"Is that true?" she asked. "Like, really true?"

"I have no need to lie to you."

Deidre was quiet. Physically at ease with him, she nonetheless had no idea how to talk to a lover who was neither one she chose nor human. She couldn't help thinking the creature whose job it was to trick people into Hell wasn't above lying to the human mate he took.

"You're not afraid I'll try to run away?" she asked.

"You need my blood and don't yet understand how to curb the hunger. If you leave, you won't stay away long or go far."

Her face warmed at how desperate she'd been for a single drop of him, to feel him inside her while his fangs sank into her neck.

"Insurance," she whispered, distraught. "You're serious about keeping me."

"I don't lose. I love a fight and an absolute victory even more," he replied.

Her eyes blurred with tears. She wiped them away. Darkyn was quiet and still, his body relaxed for the first time since she'd known him. He slid a pointed fingernail down her arm. Blood bubbled up. The scratch healed itself as fast as it formed.

"You will be able to use some of my magic," he said, following her gaze. "You will heal like I do. You will have the instincts of a demon and a human. I've assessed that you are vulnerable to the deception and depravity of others. In time, the ability I've shared with you will enable you to determine deception, weakness and threat from others."

"Like a human lie detector?"

"Of sorts. You will sense without reading minds."

"If I had that originally, Wynn couldn't have almost killed me and I wouldn't be here now," she murmured.

"It's useless to dwell on what might've been. What is and will be are all that matters."

She ran her hand down his arm and side, unable to shake the desire to saturate her senses with every part of him. The thought of an eternity with someone incapable of caring for her was a nightmare beyond those she had already lived. She tried to distract the building panic.

"Do demons have emotions?" she asked.

"They are not of your understanding," he replied. "The blood bond is the greatest obligation a demon can take to another. It is not based on emotion."

"You did it to make sure you win a deal. That doesn't seem ..." *smart.*

"Smart," he repeated, even though she hadn't spoken it. Darkyn lifted his head to study her. "How would a human who lived a fraction of one life judge *my* actions as foolish?" He tensed.

"You're angry. That's an emotion I do understand," she said. "It scares me."

He said nothing for a moment then lowered his head to nuzzle her neck. His body relaxed. Deidre took it as a sign he was passing on the subject. She did the same, unwilling to provoke him.

"Why me, Darkyn?" she asked, distraught. "I'm nothing like you."

"You see the stars and the moon instead of how dark the night is." He quoted, trailing hot kisses along her collarbone.

Her whole body deflated at his mocking tone. They were the same she'd said to Gabriel on the beach, the night they met. She'd been on the verge of dying, discussing how her impending death forced her to decide whether she wanted to live or mourn.

"That's so cruel," she whispered.

"I made a deal for *you.* No one else."

She considered his words anew as she heard her own. He wanted a mate. He wanted *her.* Darkyn was like a housecat that dragged in beheaded birds and left them in the middle of the floor for its owner. Was the offering a compliment or a complaint?

She was too unsettled by the past two days to give him the benefit of the doubt.

"Can demons love?" she asked.

"No," he replied. "We have no need for such a human emotion."

"Not even for affection?"

"I know pleasure."

"That's physical. Is there no demon equivalent for … mental pleasure? Fondness?"

"There's no difference for demons."

Deidre had the sense of speaking a different language, even though she understood his words. How did they not have emotions when she saw signs of them?

"Humans are emotional," she said.

"It's a weakness I exploit."

She frowned.

"Do you really kill five people a day to feed?" she asked, a streak of raw fear going through her. She couldn't fathom the amount of pain he had caused over his lifetime.

"Sometimes more." He nuzzled her neck again. "Now I'll only need you."

She was comfortable in bed with him – yet silently panicking as well. Deidre didn't understand how to balance the two sensations, the physical need that made her want to drink more of him and beg him to make love to her again, and the inability to believe her fate was at the side of the Dark One. She was saving lives, yes, but she wished there was a different way to do it.

She sought a safer topic, one that wouldn't leave her ready to scream.

"I found Zamon yesterday, before uh, the incident with the other demons," she said.

"You do not *find* Zamon. He lures you to him."

"Hmm," she said, troubled. "He's not out to eat me, is he?"

"No. He asked me if he should be talking to you."

"And you said …"

"You're the mate of the Dark One. You can do whatever the fuck you want."

His irritated honesty startled her enough that she started to laugh. The sound surprised her after the intensity of their interactions. She choked it back quickly, appalled she was able to find humor at such a time.

"The only thing he can't do is teach you to deal. I alone will do that," he added.

"You're not afraid I'll learn something to break the bonds?" she asked.

Darkyn pushed her far enough to meet her gaze.

"You're mine. There's no going back."

At the reminder, she looked away, uncertain how to handle her newest foray into the weirdness that was the Immortal world.

"The taste of a human and the stamina of a demon. I want to fuck you like this every night," Darkyn said and nipped her neck.

"You only have a week," she retorted.

"That reminds me. Someone lost a bet," he said.

She shook her head, emotions stirring one more.

"You lost the deal." He gripped her chin and forced her to meet his gaze. Cold and merciless, this creature was her mate for all time. The brutal reality was that he'd double-bound her to ensure he didn't lose – and not because any part of him was capable of affection. She was stuck with the creature behind the evil in the world.

There was no going back.

"Look at me." His tongue flicked out to taste her tears. "Say the words."

She drew a shaky breath. Darkyn's face hovered next to hers. The ancient intelligence in his gaze terrified her, and she couldn't escape the scent of blood and sex that left her feeling intoxicated and wanting more of him.

"I'm yours, Darkyn," she whispered.

The predatory smile crossed his face. She tried to twist away from him. He held her in place.

"You got what you wanted," she objected. "You win!"

"Say it again."

She stopped struggling, overcome by feelings.

"I'm yours, Darkyn," she said.

"You don't yet accept it," he observed. "You will soon, love. You will know before the week is out where you belong."

She rolled away from him, not wanting to cry in front of him but unable to prevent the tears that were starting to form.

Darkyn left her silently. Only when he was gone did she let herself cry.

Day Three

Chapter Three

Deidre looked over her shoulder at the reflection in the mirror displaying the two markings on her back. She gripped the hourglass, a symbol of her hope at leaving, even after learning that there was no real hope.

"That was one chain of events." Fate's reflection moved into her line of sight. The blond deity with multi-hued eyes and a quick smile was dressed for a dressage event, complete with helmet and crop.

She sighed. "I want nothing to do with you." She tucked the hourglass into the small pocket inside her dress at waist level.

"Love the fangs. Super sexy."

"I'm one of those TV vampires."

"More like a little fruit bat. Harmless."

Deidre faced him, face warm. The way he said it made it clear he was making fun of her. He was studying her. He offered a small smile, not nearly as large as the one he'd given her the day he gave her the advice that ended up condemning her.

"Didn't go the way you planned?" she asked.

"Yes and no," he admitted. "I manage the destinies of billions of the living. It always pains me to see some preferred outcomes involving the innocent."

"You knew."

"I always *know*."

"Then why did you tell me what you did?"

"To ensure this preferred outcome came to fruition. Darkyn has been spinning out of control for many years. Now that he's the boss down here, it's a dangerous combination. He needed something to take that edge off."

"So you kept me quiet long enough for the marking to appear." She wanted to slap him, more because he was making it obvious how right Darkyn was.

"I kept you quiet long enough for the bond to *stick*. For you, it was instant. For a creature from the time-before-time, it's not always the case," Fate said. "The mating bond has to take. The blood bond has to take. Otherwise, he can kill you."

"That sounds like a preferred outcome to me!" she snapped.

"Silver lining, fruit bat," he said, grinning. "You always find one. You will find one here in Hell. It will become all that stands between your mate and the human world. Trust me."

"No way. If I've learned anything, it's never to trust a deity or an Immortal or a demon."

"Darkyn did what Gabriel should have," Fate mused. "Made you face the truth before the first day was out."

"Funny how the devil is the one who's deceived me the least. He taught me how to kill someone, by the way," she added.

"The danger with Darkyn is dealing and you, my dear, are harmless," he replied. "A creature that powerful has no need to lie, until he wants to lure you to Hell. You're already here."

"Was that how he became the Dark One? He out-dealt the other Dark One?"

"Yes. It didn't hurt he's old enough that he's had time to build his power as well. When the timing was right, he had the advantages of strength and negotiating without the hindrance of mercy or a conscience."

She shivered. Darkyn didn't have compassion. He hadn't killed her, because of the bonds and a deal she made without knowing how important it was. An eternity with someone who was unable to care for her?

"If it helps, you are the only pure soul in Hell," Fate said, reading her expression. "If anyone can make him less ... him, it's you."

"Great. I have no purpose but to make others' lives easier. Why is any of this happening?" she asked, throat tight. "Did I screw up somewhere along the line?"

Fate gazed at her for a moment. "Have you ever seen the web of a black widow?"

She shook her head.

"It's a disaster. Other spiders weave these beautiful, symmetrical, ethereal webs whose designs have been the inspiration for art and mythology for as long as there were spiders," he explained. "That is what people think of when I tell them about the chain of events. In truth, destiny is like the web of a black widow. Take all the webbing of a normal spider, wad it up and tangle everything together then attach it to random points. It's more of a cluttered box than a web. That's the real chain of events. I can follow the threads, but no one else can, and there's always the chance that something unexpected gets caught up in them. Sometimes it's even a surprise to me."

"Was I unexpected?" she asked.

"No. It's just an example. You were one of the first threads in this web."

"Then you admit to lying to me to make sure I was stuck in your web."

"I did what I had to in order to ensure the web never crashes down around the spider," he said. "This is what I do. Imagine trying to monitor zillions of these webs."

"Who is the spider in my web?" she demanded.

"Who says there's a spider? Those fangs are so sexy." His gaze was on her mouth. "You'll want to be careful when you go to the human world."

"Is that general advice or forecasting?" she asked, frowning.

He winked.

"You are so frustrating. Like every other deity I meet."

She wanted to ask him more, like what happened when her bet with Past-Death was up. It didn't matter, since she was bound to Darkyn, but she found herself wondering anyway. She didn't think she could trust anything he told her.

"I'm glad you're okay," Fate sounded sincere. "Now I know you'll remain that way."

"You said something similar two days ago, before I became the mate of the Dark One."

"I mean it this time." He chuckled. "I'm okay with you hating me, now that I know you'll be okay. One last tip. Three doors down on your left."

Deidre almost cringed at the thought of leaving the chamber after her first venture out that landed her not only in trouble but also in Darkyn's bed. She twisted her hair into a bun and felt the warm energy of Fate fade with him.

When she was done, she studied her reflection. The sultriness was present, along with the calm steadiness of her blue gaze. She felt centered and refreshed this morning, the newfound hunger for the blood of her mate sated for now. She was surprised to find the idea of tasting him didn't repulse her, as if the intimate bond with him was natural.

She should be disgusted. Deidre shook her head in frustration and left her room. She lingered outside her door, waiting for someone to attack her. When no one did, she paced three doors down and paused.

Fate had a way of setting her up. She wasn't so sure she wanted to know what was behind that door.

She was also tired of being afraid.

Deidre knocked. A moment later, the door opened, and she gasped. The Immortal who posed as her only friend and surgeon for years – who also nearly killed her – stood before her. His dark skin was offset by brilliant turquoise eyes, his noble carriage and cold features giving him the appearance of an ancient prince.

"Wynn!"

He raised an eyebrow in the only sign of surprise. His eyes

settled on the fangs resting on her lower lips. Self-conscious, she felt her face grow warm and crossed her arms. She pressed her lip together to hide her fangs.

"He lost no time in turning you," Wynn said. "Come in." He opened the door wider to display a chamber the same size as hers but outfitted as if for a hospital.

Deidre entered uncertainly. A girl in her mid-teens lay still on the hospital bed central to the room. Half her face was disfigured.

"Double-bound? I didn't even know it was possible." Wynn was unable to hide his surprise this time.

Unwilling to admit to the bonds let alone talk about them, Deidre focused on the girl.

"Is this …"

"His daughter."

Deidre wasn't certain what to think at the sight of the girl on the bed. She drew nearer, eyes sweeping over the medical equipment in the room. The girl appeared to be sleeping, her breathing deep and steady.

"What's wrong with her?" she asked.

Wynn took up position in a seat near the bed. There were dark circles under his eyes, and his face was drawn.

"Sasha, one of my sons hurt her. He was on the Council until shortly after I died-dead, after which he betrayed the Immortals to work for the Dark One, Darkyn's predecessor. Darkyn cracked down on him, and Sasha hurt his daughter."

"If he fixed me, why can't he fix her?" Deidre frowned, disturbed by the idea of some psycho hurting the girl. Darkyn's daughter appeared frail and gaunt, her skin a shade or two darker than the white pillow beneath her head. The damage done to half her face caused horrible scarring that left her features lopsided and her skin knotted. The other side of her face displayed facial features that were heavy rather than feminine, resembling her father's.

"I'm assuming it was because a deal went bad. I guess the time this all happened was when Darkyn took on the Dark One. He wouldn't say much else, other than she cannot be fixed with the magic of Hell," Wynn explained. "She's in a stasis right now, caught between life and death. I've been charged with curing her. Or I'll never leave Hell."

Deidre felt no pity for him, despite the circumstances. After what he'd done to her, she wasn't able to. Wynn's eyes fell to her fangs again then drifted down her body.

"He changed you," he murmured. "You won't be leaving here after your deal is up with Past-Death."

"How do you know about that?"

"I was waiting in the portal room with her when Darkyn came to tell me I wasn't leaving," Wynn said with mild amusement. "He stripped her deity powers, said she had to earn Gabriel the same way you did."

Darkyn did two things that she almost agreed with. Deidre didn't think it was a good sign that she cheered on the Dark One. Did it make her bad, too?

"Lesson learned. Don't screw over his mate," Wynn finished.

"It wasn't for my sake," she assured him.

"He knew exactly what he was doing."

"Darkyn doesn't lose. As I learned, my deals hold the same power of enforcement as his. He was making certain I win," she said. "I'm assuming he kept you because you're the best surgeon there is. Even if you did use your skills to try to kill me."

"I'm not the mate of the Dark One. Those skills give me a small chance of leaving," he reminded her.

"I was destined for this," she returned. "Past-Death told me how she made me in her image to trick the laws into making me Gabriel's mate." Deidre hugged herself, disturbed. "She said she made me, used me and was done with me. She traded me to him, Wynn, like I'm nothing. Maybe I shouldn't be, but I'm glad Darkyn stripped her power. Maybe she'll learn a thing or two about being human."

Wynn studied her, warmth in his eyes. "I don't know how this all unfolded," he said. "You truly are an innocent caught in the politics of the Immortals and the scheming of deities. You are the last person who deserves to be here."

"You always say the right thing," she murmured. "Even while

you were killing me."

She paused, knowing she shouldn't ask what she'd wanted to since finding out what he did. At this point, there was no reason not to.

"How could you, Wynn?" she asked, with more emotion than she intended.

"It's done, Deidre," he said.

"It's that simple to you? I mean nothing to you, like I meant nothing to her? I'm disposable?"

"Deidre," he stopped then continued with some effort. "I loved you in this life and the last. I lost you in both, too, once by the choice of Past-Death and once by my own. There is no part of me that wishes I couldn't go back and save you from this. He won't let me out of here alive, I don't think."

Deidre returned her attention to the girl. Wynn regretted what he did; he regretted the impact to him more. Immortals and deities didn't have the capacity to care for others. Would she be alone for eternity?

"Can you help her?" she asked.

"I am doing my best. My deal with your mate is dependent upon me succeeding. He gave me five days."

"If the magic of Hell can't cure her, can yours?"

"Not so far. I've tried traditional medicine" he motioned to the machines lining the perimeter of the room "and my magic."

"Poor girl," she murmured, recalling all her years of pain and misery with the brain tumor Wynn caused to expand. Her deal with Darkyn damned her, but also saved her life. "Is she demon?"

"Half-breed like Rhyn. Demon and Immortal. Mother is long dead, most likely one of the blood slaves. Darkyn was known for going through them like tissue paper."

The reminder of what her mate was made Deidre nauseous.

"At least I can save other women from that destiny," she said. "The mating bond is absolute, isn't it?"

"It is. Neither mate can have someone else on the side. Yours is more so. He's dependent upon you for blood, a condition that transcends the normal mating relationship."

She deliberated on this information. Darkyn was determined to keep her, determined enough that his *insurance* limited him more than her. He was serious about not losing.

Wynn was looking at her again, an odd light in his eyes. It made her uncomfortable.

"He was wise to turn you quickly," he said after a long silence. "He can't harm you now with the double-bond. Did the transition hurt?"

"He's never hurt me. Terrify me? Definitely."

Wynn's smile was fleeting. "I don't suppose you'll put in a good - or bad - word for me."

"No," she replied firmly. "Your deal is with him. You made your choices, Wynn."

"More than fair."

Deidre. The summons was quiet. It was accompanied by a vision of her chamber. She felt compelled to go there.

"I'll come back," she said. "Will you tell me if you need something to help her?"

"Without a doubt."

Deidre left, troubled, as she returned to her room. It didn't make sense that nothing could save the girl, or that Darkyn was capable of trying to. It meant he cared. Or he was obligated. She'd learned a lot lately about how obligation held more sway in the Immortal society than truth or emotion.

Her heart quickened as she entered her room. The sight of Darkyn's lean frame was enough for her blood to heat before his piercing gaze caught hers from across the room.

I am yours.

She hated him. She *needed* him. She couldn't navigate through the emotions.

Deidre approached unbidden and stood before him, wishing she understood him and their bond better. His black eyes saw through her; his cold features were expressionless. He scared her, and she touched him instinctively, wanting his cool energy to help calm her emotions.

"I'm sending you somewhere," he told her.

"What? Where?"

"On an emissary mission."

Surprised, she sought some sign he was testing her or baiting her again.

"You trust me to go somewhere without making a deal you can't live with?" she asked.

"Clever," he murmured. "You want something."

"I won't make any deals this trip if you teach me how when I return."

He considered. "Two conditions. One, what I teach you can never be shared. Two, there will be no official deals between you and me. Private deals only."

"Ones that can't be enforced, in case you lose?" she challenged. "You think I'll beat you eventually?"

"Insurance," he replied mockingly.

She rolled her eyes at him and dropped her hand.

"You've gotten brave, love."

"You like a fight, don't you?"

The light in his eyes was response enough. It made her heart race.

"Deal or no?" he asked.

"Deal."

"You'll be taking a message from me to them."

"Really?" She frowned. "What's the message?"

"You are."

Gabriel. Her first thought was that he was sending her to Death as a means of torturing her or at least, nailing home the point that he had won this round with Gabriel.

The slow smile she distrusted spread across Darkyn's face. Did he know what she thought? Was it so obvious?

She dropped her gaze.

"You will soon learn that those who lose deals with me are a desperate lot. They will see you as a target. Do you remember what I taught you about killing?"

She placed her hand on his heart. He remained relaxed despite giving her a loaded weapon then telling her to take the kill shot.

"To summon me, simply say my name," he added. Darkyn tipped her chin up to meet her gaze. "You think I'm sending you to *him*."

"It would be awkward," she said in a hushed voice.

"Then you'll have to trust me, won't you."

"You enjoy baiting me too much for me to trust you."

"So honest, so pure," he said.

"Don't mock me," she said, thinking about how Fate did the same. "I get it. This is your game. You don't lose. You'd send me to Gabriel on a silver platter to get your point across. I assume that's where I'm going."

"You'll find out."

Deidre wanted to deck him again. And cry. And run. She hated that he'd always known exactly what to say to get to her. From the moment he first offered her the deal that landed her in Hell, he read her.

Darkyn flicked a nail against the pad of his thumb. The blood ensnared her senses at once, compelling her attention to the maroon droplets. Her hunger demanded action. The wound healed, leaving the drops on his thumb. He pressed the pad to her lips. They parted instinctively, and she tasted him.

She closed her eyes and shuddered in pleasure. He'd worked her into a frenzy the night before by dribbling a similar amount of blood, enough to tease her without satisfying her. This time, the few drops quelled the hunger and her distress. It left her calm.

"When you're finished, call a portal," he instructed.

Her eyes opened. His attention was on a point behind her, and she turned to see a portal waiting.

Deidre's hand dropped from his chest. This had to be a test. He was sending her out and expecting her to return. Did he trust her or assume she knew better than to run?

She ran her tongue over her teeth to capture the last of his blood. She'd seen how hungry he was last night. He wasn't going to let her go for long, since she was his singular food source.

One of the yellow portals beckoned her. Deidre entered the shadow world and shivered, her exposed skin chilled. She glanced back over her shoulder to see Darkyn standing where she left him, hands clasped behind his back, watching her with the cold smile that told her there was more going on than she suspected.

The calm of his blood offering kept her uneasiness at bay as the portal behind her closed. She hurried to the one waiting for her and paused. He could be sending her anywhere.

To Gabriel.

At least, if she saw him, she could determine which parts of what she felt were real and which stemmed from the bond. Deidre drew a shaky breath and stepped through the portal.

She recognized the surroundings. The Immortals' stone fortress. She was in the middle of an unfamiliar, tall hallway. She heard the sound of a weapon scraping a scabbard behind her and turned.

Red tattoos flashed on the arms of the two Immortals in the hallway. She didn't recognize them from her short stay there. One had his sword raised, the other's was down. They scrutinized her.

"Rhyn," she said, uncertain who else to ask for.

"Wait here," one said. "No quick movements."

She nodded.

The second put his weapon away and darted off down another hallway. Deidre waited nervously, uncertain what to think about the Immortal staring at her. His sword lowered as the time grew on. The light in his eyes was like that in Wynn's, one she couldn't place. It was almost the fire of desire, yet too raw.

It made her uncomfortable.

"Fuck."

Deidre recognized the growl of the half-demon and faced him. Flanked by the Immortal she knew as Kiki and two more, Rhyn stood several meters away. The silver-eyed half-demon was tall and muscular, the air around him rippling with power. It was the opposite of Darkyn's, whose was subtle and calming. Rhyn's energy made her edgy.

"You've been gone, what? Three days? And you come back with a double-bond to someone new?" He shook his head. He motioned for the Immortal behind her to leave. "Does Gabe …"

Her sharp intake of breath stopped him.

"Double-bond," one of those behind Rhyn said. "What is a double-bond?"

"It's what the Dark One does when he doesn't want his mate disappearing on him," Rhyn said. "I sensed you arrive."

He approached and circled her, pausing behind her. Self-conscious in front of Gabriel's closest friend, Deidre faced him, tilting her head back to meet his liquid silver eyes.

"Did you say Darkyn is the Dark One?" Kiki asked.

"Looks that way," Rhyn replied. "No one else can turn a human into a demon, and only demons blood bind."

"He is," Deidre confirmed.

"I thought you were in Atlanta."

"It's a long story," she replied. "One Gabriel doesn't know and probably shouldn't for another few days."

"We match." Rhyn bared his teeth to display canines similar to Darkyn's that would lengthen when he was hungry.

"Mine don't retract," she said with a grimace.

"The teeth of a demoness don't. You left Gabe's human mate and came back a demon bound to Darkyn. He wasted no time in turning you and blood-binding you." Rhyn studied her for a moment. "What the fuck happened?"

Uncertain how to respond, Deidre laughed uncomfortably at the amount of bewilderment his question contained.

"Rhyn, care to share?" Kiki asked.

The half-demon looked over her head at the group behind her. He frowned. Deidre tried to figure out what it was she was supposed to say. She wanted to ask after Gabriel but didn't. She also wanted to step outside and see the forest. She missed nature in the time she'd been in Hell.

"We need to talk in private," Rhyn said for her ears only. "There's another issue you haven't figured out yet."

She frowned. Rhyn took her arm and started away.

"I'll let you know, Kiki," he called to his half-brother. "We're going to talk about demon shit."

"What? Rhyn, you can't –" Kiki objected.

"Later, Kiki."

Deidre didn't resist, uncertain why he looked grim suddenly. They didn't go far. He led her into a large study with a huge, brown leather couch near a dead hearth. She brightened at the sight of the comfortable seating. Rhyn released her and locked the door behind him then paced, rubbing his jaw.

"What's wrong?" she asked, concerned by his actions.

"You shitting me?" he returned. "You come back a demon and want to know what's wrong?"

She flushed.

"A demon of human origin. It's like Gabe being turned Immortal. You reek of Darkyn's power."

Deidre tucked her knees to her chest and wrapped her arms around them, watching him pace.

"First. What are you doing here?" he demanded.

"I don't know. Darkyn sent me. He said he had a message, and that I'm the message," she said. "If you don't know, then I'm not sure."

"Oh, I get the fucking messages."

"What are they?" she asked, puzzled.

"One, he's letting me know he's the Dark One. I'm assuming the transition happened recently. We didn't know. Two, this is a personal fuck-you, addressed to me from the Dark One. Three," he paused, studying her. "You. His mate. His *human*, blood bound mate."

"Why is that important to you?"

"No demon can waltz into the middle of my stronghold without being chopped to pieces. If you were a demon and his mate, you'd be missing your head. You're a *human* mate, or were originally, which means I can't hurt you. I'm the only Immortal who can walk into Hell. The last time I did it, I robbed him of a few prisoners he didn't want to lose. He's showing me he can do the same," Rhyn said. "There's no fucking chance of bringing you back, even if somehow you were to escape the mating bond."

"I know that," she replied. "He didn't hesitate to claim me once the marking appeared."

"Are you okay?" Rhyn's voice carried genuine concern.

"Sort of," she said. "He didn't hurt me, if that's what you're asking."

Rhyn didn't look convinced.

"I'm, uh ..." she swallowed, tears blurring her vision. "Scared. Horrified. A demon."

"Yeah, there's no reversing that."

"Really?"

He raised his eyebrows.

"I guess I know that," she whispered. "He's determined to keep me."

"I see that. The good thing is that he can't hurt you now. The blood bond between demons is to ensure one of them doesn't get too hungry and bleed the other dry."

"Good to know," she mumbled. "He hasn't hurt me yet. But he doesn't lose, does he?"

Rhyn shook his head. "For someone like him ... he never even bowed down to the Dark One. The bond creates more than dependency; it gives you a helluva lot of influence over him."

"I don't see it," she said with a snort.

"Trust me. The mating bond alone makes it easy for a woman to control her mate. Add a blood bond to it? You become the only person in the universe that can influence him. The other deities can't even do that."

She frowned. She didn't see that happening. Darkyn was always too far ahead of her, twisting her into knots to keep her in place.

"Talk," Rhyn ordered. He threw himself down in the seat across from her.

"Well..." Deidre sighed, sorting through her thoughts. She met his gaze, uncertain what to tell him.

"Gabriel doesn't know," he guessed and sat back.

"Not yet. At least, I don't think he does. There's a deal on the table," she explained, mind on Past-Death. "I'll start from the beginning. I, uh, made a deal with Darkyn a few days ago for him to remove my brain tumor. It seemed simple enough. He saves my life. In exchange, he keeps the tumor."

"But that didn't make you his mate."

"Indirectly it did. The tumor in my head had a soul in it. Past-

Death's soul," Deidre continued. Her throat tightened as she spoke. "I guess she made a deal with Darkyn. He brought her back, and she gave him me."

Rhyn growled low in his chest.

"I made her a deal that expires in four days, thinking I could reverse the bond. I gave her a week to make Gabriel fall in love with her, or I get her soul. I thought if she was gone, the bond would reverse, return me to Gabriel," she said. "Darkyn calls the blood bond his insurance for when I win. I can't go back to Gabriel, even if I do win."

Rhyn was quiet, his gaze intense.

"There's more, but …" She shook her head, hands trembling. "Darkyn never loses."

"I wouldn't say he won. He had to sacrifice his freedom to keep you," Rhyn said. "It'll give you an advantage in deals with him."

She almost groaned. She'd signed away that advantage already. Another thought occurred to her as she thought about Katie, the half-demon's mate she met when last at the fortress.

"Rhyn, is any of what you feel when you become a mate real?" she asked. "The bond I shared with Gabriel. I mean, as soon as Darkyn's name was on my back, it shifted, like none of the emotions I felt for Gabriel were real … and now with the blood bond…"

"Gods. I'm the last person to ask this touchy-feely stuff," Rhyn said and rubbed his jaw again. "The bond brings you together. You still have to … make a relationship. One is physical, the other mental. They're both real."

"Gabriel and I didn't get that far. He kept pushing me away," she said. "Darkyn's been relentless in pursuing me."

"There's another reason for that," Rhyn said slowly. "Deidre, you can't be around normal mortals or Immortals for long or even really demons outside of Hell."

"Why?" she asked, fear spiraling through her. "Does something happen to me?"

"How do I say this…" he sighed. "My mother was a sex-demon. It's a sub-class of demons. You are, too."

"Meaning …"

"Meaning you might be one of them. Every man you cross will do what it takes to try to fuck you."

She gasped. "What? Why?"

"Why?" he echoed. "Because you're a sex-demon."

She stared at him. Rhyn rose and motioned her up. He crossed to a mirror and pulled her in front of him. She saw the same woman here as she did in Hell: sultry and sweet, beautiful of face with a body enhanced by the dark dress.

"You don't see it?" he asked.

"No."

"I'm dealing with enough shit," he muttered. "Trust me. You've got that vibe. Darkyn is relentless because of the fucked up double bond and whatever subclass of demon he decided to turn you into, which I'm guessing was a sex-demon. It's good for you. Might give you an advantage with him if you're willing to play the seduction game."

Deidre shook her head, not seeing this either. There were no advantages with Darkyn and she was the last person on the planet who would try to seduce anyone, especially a demon. Darkyn had to know this. Was this some sort of twisted sense of humor on his part?

They returned to the seating area. Rhyn grabbed an iPad off the desk. He considered her.

"I have to show you something," he started. "It's bad. But since he sent you, I want you to see it." He paused to pull up photographs on the screen. "Before a few months ago, the Immortals and demons had an understanding that the normal humans are off limits. Things have gone to shit fast, partly because I can't get the fucking Council to agree on anything." Rhyn snorted. "Darkyn recently decided to send his demons after human kids. They've been attacking schools all over the world. We're getting better at tracking them, but haven't been able to stop them." He handed the device to her.

Deidre almost dropped it at the pictures displayed. Horrified, she wasn't able to look away. The children were all elementary age, their dismembered bodies nothing but carnage. There were dozens of them.

This was what she was bound to for eternity, the monster behind all the evil in the world. Rhyn snatched the iPad as it slid from her fingers. She stared at the floor. Fate said she was a balance for the out-of-control demon, but how could she live with something like him?

"If you have any influence over him ..." Rhyn prodded. "I'll make you a deal to stop this. Just let me know your terms."

"I can't make deals," she whispered. "Rhyn, I ..." The images in her head were brutal. "I was terrified of Gabriel, knowing he was Death. This is something so far beyond what he was." She stood and paced anxiously, hugging herself.

"You're his mate, his representative. As much as I hate to do this, I need for you to help me fix this," Rhyn said. "It's been going on for two weeks, and it's getting worse. Redirect the violence at the Immortals. Human children are off-limits."

Deidre was silent, grappling with the issue and her emotions. Her chest was too tight for her to breathe deeply. What power did she have to do what Rhyn wanted?

She caught sight of her gaze in the mirror again and stared. Distraught, she was also clearly the mate of the Dark One. The only person who might influence him, based on what Fate and Rhyn believed.

She was beyond terrified of the power Darkyn held. What he was in their insulated world in the bedchamber was far removed from what he was outside. She'd accepted her place in his bed. How did she accept her destiny as his mate?

What part of her was able to live with not trying to help spare innocent children?

Claustrophobic, she started to panic.

"I, uh, I need to go," she said.

"Alright. If you need anything ... I have no fucking clue if I can help, but ask." There was concern on Rhyn's face.

Deidre nodded, focused on calling a portal. It yawned open for her. She left, stopping in the shadow world to try to calm herself. She wasn't able to make an official deal with Darkyn to save the kids, and she had nothing to offer him. What the fuck did she do?

The portal to Hell glowed darkly. Deidre moved towards it, recalling the last time she'd crossed through it. Her eyes filled with tears, but she forced herself to do it.

It left her on the covered landing where Darkyn first brought her. It was where he told her she'd never leave Hell, where he'd first drawn her blood. The landing overlooked the parched desert surrounding the black fortress. The dual sub orbs were dim, casting a sickly light over Hell. She leaned against the waist-high wall.

This was her eternity. The only innocent soul in Hell. There had to be a greater purpose to all of this, a reason why she was trapped. A reason why she was the only light in a very dark place. Was it to help the innocent? To blunt the bloodlust of the Dark One? Was this her silver lining? If she didn't find one, she'd spend eternity weeping.

Her heart slammed into her chest at the thought of confronting the devil. With a deep breath, Deidre summoned him.

"Darkyn."

As before, he appeared instantly. She turned away from the desert and crossed her arms. He stood a few meters away, hands clasped behind his back. His black eyes scoured her features and lingered on her lips.

"Rhyn ... showed me what the demons are doing to human kids," she started uncertainly.

"And?"

"They're just children!"

"The Dark One is not known for mercy or kindness," he said, amused. "The source of my magic is from the forbidden, the depraved. The death of innocents, the weakness of a man's honor, heart or soul."

"You've shown me mercy," she said, approaching him until they stood toe-to-toe. "What will it take to stop this now?"

"How strongly do you feel?"

"I'll play your game," she said firmly.

"The first lesson in making deals: make the terms yourself. Don't let anyone else determine them," he said. "For example. I'll do as you ask, if you can make it to our bedchamber by the count of five."

"I don't even know where it is from here!" she exclaimed.

"Then you lose before you begin."

Deidre stared at him. He stepped aside, out of the way to the corridor leading into the fortress.

"This is it? This is all you'll give me?" she asked, torn between fury and sorrow at the impossible challenge.

"Second lesson: you will do whatever it takes to win the deal."

"Like blood binding yourself for insurance," she said in frustration. "Or stripping Past-Death's power."

"Exactly."

She had to focus. There had to be a way. He'd told her she wasn't able to travel via portal when she was human. Yet she drew off his magic now. She was able to kill and call a portal from the human world.

"One."

Her gaze flew to him.

"Two."

Deidre bolted, silently willing a portal to appear as she sprinted into the fortress.

"Three."

A black cave yawned open before her. It was different than the other portals; there were no doors visible through this one, just a hole in the world. She flung herself through it, not caring what waited for her on the other side.

Deidre emerged in her room, a full second before Darkyn did. It took a moment for her to register the truth.

"Omigod! I did it!" she breathed. She hurried to him. "You lose. You have to stop hurting them." Praying she hadn't missed some term of the deal, she waited for his reaction. For a long moment, Darkyn was quiet. Deidre's despair began to form anew, along with tears. She started to shake, unable to bear the idea of more children dying or living with the creature behind it.

His cold smile scared her, until he spoke. "Done."

"Is this your insurance plan where you don't follow through because it's not binding?"

"I always execute my terms," he replied. "There will be no more attacks on human schools."

She waited another few seconds for a catch before letting herself believe him. Relief made the tears she'd been holding begin to fall. Deidre reached up to him and fluttered kisses across his face and neck. She nuzzled him there, smelling the blood so close to the surface. It made her hungry to taste him.

"Lesson three. If you win or lose, let it be on purpose," he said.

"You let me win?"

He chuckled as she nibbled timidly at his neck. "You don't need an invitation to drink, love."

At the amusement in his voice, she flushed. She nudged his chin aside but wasn't certain about biting him. His fangs were lengthening, and he lowered his head, nudging her back. Darkyn rested his hands on her hips and drew her into his body.

"I beat you," she whispered into the shared space between them. "Even if you let me. I'll take it." She pushed his chin aside with more force and kissed his neck before closing her eyes and letting her fangs sink into him.

He growled in response. Deidre drank until she grew sleepy. She released him at his nudge.

"Does it hurt?" she asked.

"Yes," he said. "Since you are demon now, there is pleasure in it for you. If you are pleased enough about your victory, you will grant me leave to show you."

She hesitated. "Just once?" she ventured.

He locked one arm around her in response, the other holding her head. His canines were four times the length of hers. Before she could tell him she'd changed her mind, sharp pain penetrated her neck. Deidre clutched at the material of his shirt. After the initial shock, she felt the pleasure, warm and hot, burning and mixing with the pain. It raced through her body, lulling her into a strange trance of heightened senses while he drank.

When he withdrew, she rested against him. She still didn't quite trust he'd keep his word, but she prayed with every ounce of her soul that he did.

"Why did you let me win?" she asked.

"Because it pleased me to do so."

"Seriously?"

"The humans mean more to you than they do to me. It was an extremely easy victory for me." He bit her hard. "You are happy enough I no longer need to dull the pain."

She shuddered at the pleasure-pain.

"I said once, didn't I?" she murmured.

"You only have to agree once."

Damn unwritten terms. She didn't think she'd ever win with him, but she was thrilled knowing she'd done something right. For once.

In Hell. In a deal with her mate, who just happened to be the devil.

With the hum of their bonds and the satiation of the blood exchange, she ventured a look at him. His head was bowed near hers, eyes closed, as if he was…pleased to share the moment with her. Deidre touched her cheek to his and reached up with one hand to his other cheek. She was perplexed by this creature. He was yielding now, as he'd been last night. As if sensing she'd noticed, he straightened and moved away, breaking contact to stand a few feet away. The intimate moment was gone, replaced by the tension that always filled the space between them.

"Did the half-breed receive my message?" he asked.

"All of them," she replied. "He also said I need to be careful in the human world. Is there something wrong with me?"

The cunning look on Darkyn's face did nothing to reassure her.

"Lesson four. Deals made while the negotiator is distracted or emotional are easier to win," he said. "I only enhanced what appeal you already had. It'll make it easier for you to deal with others, and it's no sacrifice for me to want to fuck you every time we meet."

"Why did you have to do that?" She flushed, humiliated. "I take it the *distraction* won't work on you in our private deals."

He flicked a fingernail against his thumb in response, commanding her complete attention. Deidre groaned as the hunger returned.

"Does it work on you?" Agitated, she bit her thumb.

"I can control the hunger." He smiled and waited.

Deidre paced for a moment before caving. She needed contact with him as much as the blood. Leaning into him, she sighed when he placed his thumb at her lips. The calm spread through her again. He licked her finger free of blood.

"You are already a distraction for me," he said gruffly.

Triumph fluttered through her at the admission. Maybe Rhyn was right; maybe she had more power than she knew.

"You should've thought of that before you blood bound me and turned me into a sex-demon," she retorted softly. "I guess that's *my* insurance, isn't it?"

"I find it entertaining that you were willing to do whatever it took for humans you never knew, but those who knew you weren't willing to do the same," he said.

"What do you mean?" she asked.

"I offered Wynn and Past-Death deals for your safety. Neither was willing to bargain with me for your life." He sounded pleased once more.

Disturbed, Deidre withdrew from his embrace. She scoured his features.

"Why are you telling me this?" she asked, her upbeat mood fading.

"Why do you think?"

"I don't know. I don't expect them or anyone else to make deals with you for me," she said, hurt as much by his words as the thought that there was no one outside of Hell who wished her well. She stared into the hearth.

"You are true to your nature. I can assess that you would make deals for them."

"Why did you have to ruin this, Darkyn? I did something good. Why couldn't you let me have my victory?" she whispered.

"I'm closing the doors around you, until there's only one that's open."

Deidre looked up at him.

"When you accept that, you can celebrate what victories you have. Your victory today hasn't gone anywhere," he added. "I always keep my terms."

He took her arm. She pushed him away, upset. The demon lord gripped her more tightly and wrapped her in his arms. Deidre strained then sighed, letting her head drop back against his shoulder. His cool magic calmed her thoughts. He nudged her head aside, and she yielded, albeit unhappily.

"Fight me, love. You want to. I feel it," he said.

"You people have the lowest standards when it comes to quality of life."

"The spirit of a human and the bloodlust of a demon."

"Bloodlust? No. I mean, I only want your blood. I think," she said, puzzled. "Don't I? Oh, god. I'm not going to want to drink the blood of others am I?"

"Only mine. Such is the nature of a blood bond."

"You hurt my feelings, Darkyn."

"Good. You are too trusting. What I do will help you survive."

It wasn't the first time she'd heard such a thing, but it sounded far worse coming from the devil than it had Wynn.

"I'm being summoned. You can fight me later," he said and released her. He strode towards a waiting portal.

Deidre watched him. It really did hurt to think that Darkyn outright tested others and they failed when it came to her. Of course, he chose two of the most selfish people she knew. She wanted to think that Gabriel wouldn't turn his back on her so quickly.

In hindsight, she really didn't know any of them. She wasn't an Immortal or deity. She held no sway in what happened or played no larger part in their twisted doings.

In spite of that, hope flickered through her. She'd helped Rhyn stop Darkyn's demons. Darkyn himself had shown some signs of being affected by her, perhaps not as much as she liked, but more than she ever expected.

Maybe she could make a silver lining here, protecting the innocent.

Breakfast was on the magic obsidian tray next to the bed. She wolfed it down, satisfied she was still able to eat real food in addition to drinking from Darkyn.

Day Four

Chapter Four

T he next morning, Deidre found herself at the wall overlooking the red deserts of Hell. The air was hot and dry, the two suns too dim to shed much light into the black fortress. Any thought she had of trying to make it here faded whenever she saw the desert or thought about how Darkyn manipulated her.

She was scared again. The pictures Rhyn showed her wouldn't leave her thoughts, even if Darkyn had agreed to stop the slaughter. He would do it again. It's what he was.

She started to panic.

Deidre drew a deep breath. She missed nature. Real nature, not the barren landscape of Hell. She glanced around her, wondering what would happen if she just … left. Even for a short time to try to relax. Darkyn would find her no matter what, but she had the urge to see trees. Water. Grass. Anything familiar. . She absently reached for the hourglass and realized she'd left it on her nightstand.

She tried not to get her hopes up that a portal out of Hell would appear. Stilling her mind, she calmed herself. The portals didn't answer her at all when she was upset.

It opened at her request. Deidre was startled. She expected

Darkyn to have severed her ability to leave. Glancing down at herself, she decided there was only one logical place for her to start.

Deidre stepped into the shadow world and paused. No one stopped her. Darkyn didn't appear to force her to return. She crossed the shadow world to the glowing portal that would take her where she wanted to go.

The mate of the Dark One does whatever the fuck she pleases, Darkyn had claimed. She was almost surprised to see he was serious.

She stepped into her own apartment and stopped. It smelled horrible, probably because of the blood-soaked second bedroom. Otherwise, it looked the way she left it, except that the air conditioning was off.

Deidre looked around, struck by how different the place she lived for two years felt. The pile of mail she left on her desk was still there, the living room neat and quiet. With the rest of her life in disarray, she didn't expect her apartment to look … normal. Like it was just waiting for her and her boyfriend to come home.

One choice. She'd made one choice, and she'd never come home to this place again. She crossed to her desk, where a red journal sat. In it was her bucket list, a list of things she hoped to do before she died from the terminal brain tumor she no longer possessed.

Now, she had an eternity to fulfill the list. An eternity in Hell at the side of the Dark One.

Deidre set down the journal, needing to distract her thoughts before she started to panic again. She sat down on her couch, recalling the nights she spent watching television after work. This world had been all she knew three weeks ago. Now, she felt out of place, like she was sitting in a display at a furniture store. Nothing in the living room was hers.

She went to her bedroom and pushed the door open. It was as she left it. She'd packed her favorite clothes to take with her to Wynn's a few days before she ended up in Hell. She had a ton left and began sifting through her drawers for jeans. She couldn't walk down the streets of Atlanta in her Hell gown. She was going to draw enough attention as it was being a sex-demon.

Demon.

Deidre still couldn't fathom that she'd been turned into some sort of supernatural creature. She paused to look in the mirror. Yes, she looked different. But she didn't have horns or a tail or anything. Just her little fangs and the odd presence she found subtle but which apparently had a staggering affect on men.

Shaking her head, she pulled out a t-shirt and jeans, tossing them on the bed. She reached for the band around her neck securing the dress.

The sound of someone in the hallway made her freeze. The footsteps were soft, but it sounded like more than one person. Her thoughts went to Darkyn but her instincts warned her it wasn't him. She didn't fully understand the demon senses that Darkyn indicated were part of her now. But if they told her she was in danger, she was going to listen.

She tiptoed to the closet and slid inside, peeking through the slats of the door. Two large men entered. Red tattoos flashed on their bodies, indicating they were Immortals. They were dressed more like Gabriel than the Immortals she met at Rhyn's.

Death dealers.

The demon side of her recognized what they were, even if the human side didn't. The idea that Gabriel's people were there brought confusion. If he knew she was there, wouldn't he come himself? Her instincts were at full alarm, but she didn't understand what she had to fear from Gabriel's death dealers.

Unless more than Harmony had betrayed Gabriel. She recalled how his former right hand dealer had turned traitor. Deidre sank back into the closet. She began to steady her breathing and focus, so she could draw a portal when they were gone.

One of them entered the bedroom, cold eyes taking in the surroundings. He walked farther in, appearing to be listening.

Deidre held her breath and hoped her heartbeat wasn't as loud to him as it was to her. He neared the closet, and she pushed herself back into the clothing. He moved faster than she was able to follow. The crack of the wooden door registered a short second before his hand gripped her throat. She was hauled out of the closet and tossed on the bed.

"Found her!" the death dealer called.

"Anyone else?"

The death dealer looked at her. "You alone?"

She swallowed hard and nodded. His gaze lingered then went over her body. The familiar light appeared.

"Kin, Anyone else?" the other dealer asked again.

"No," Kin answered.

"I'll let Harmony know."

Deidre's hope sank. So they weren't there on Gabriel's behalf but on Harmony's. Deidre had no bad interactions with the death dealer, but she suspected anyone who betrayed Gabriel wouldn't be interested in helping her.

"Up. Come on," Kin said, motioning to the hallway.

Deidre rose and crossed her arms, walking ahead of him into the living area. A portal was open, and the second death dealer was waiting. Deidre's heart beat hard. She could summon Darkyn, though she feared his reaction to her leaving more than what these people would do to her.

Kin stood right behind her, way too close for her comfort. One of his hands brushed her hip then returned.

"Sexy little thing, isn't she?" he murmured. He walked around her, trailing his hand around her midsection.

Deidre tried to ignore him, afraid reacting would only draw more attention to herself. He touched her hair and the sensitive skin around her neck. She flinched away as his fingers rested on the clasp of her dress.

"Fangs?" the other dealer asked, frowning. He was older, in his mid-thirties, and the light took longer to appear in his eyes than it had the younger man.

Kin's hand rested against the bare skin at the small of her back then continued south. Deidre stepped away.

"Hey," Harmony said, stepping through the portal. "You got her."

"You didn't tell me she's fucking hot," Kin said. He took

Deidre's arm and pulled her against him, rubbing his hips against her backside.

Panic was beginning to set in. Darkyn gave her the power to seduce without the knowledge on how to turn off its effects, if it was even possible. The second dealer was moving closer, and she couldn't free herself from the thick arm wrapped around her.

She strained against him. He snatched her neck and squeezed until her ability to breathe was hindered. Deidre went still.

"Stop it," Harmony said. "Something's not right here." She looked Deidre up and down with assessing green eyes. "Turn her around."

Without releasing her neck, Kin spun her and locked the arm around her body again. Deidre felt Harmony's light touch as the death dealer brushed her hair aside.

"Shit," the dealer murmured. "This isn't the right girl. You were supposed to grab Gabe's mate, not Darkyn's."

"Darkyn's?" Kin asked, uneasiness replacing the glow in his eyes.

"Get rid of her," Harmony ordered. "Take her soul and brain. Darkyn can read either to find out who grabbed her. We'll make it look like the Immortals did it."

"Can I have a little fun first?"

"I don't give a shit but make it fast. Darkyn can track her. If she's here, it's because she's allowed to be here."

"I'm due back in two minutes," Deidre voiced.

"Even has a sexy little purr," Kin said, lust crossing his features. "I only need one."

He dragged her by the neck down the hallway. Deidre choked. He threw her on the bed again. Her eyes watered, and she coughed. The death dealer stripped off his shirt and weapons to display a muscular body.

Deidre rolled off the bed, darting for the hallway. He snatched her around the waist and laughed, dragging her onto the bed with him. She struggled. The dealer slapped her hard enough to daze her. He placed a knife at her neck. It bit into her skin, and she gasped, afraid to move. Kin shoved her knees a part and yanked up her dress. His face glowed with frenzied need while he worked quickly to unzip his pants.

She whispered the first name that came to mind.

"Darkyn."

Deidre sucked in a deep breath, praying the demon lord answered the summons.

"One of Harmony's men."

Kin froze at the inhuman growl. Deidre squeezed her eyes closed, not wanting to see Darkyn response and afraid his anger might be directed at her.

"Did he see your markings, love?" Darkyn asked.

"No," the dealer said, scrambling off her. "My apologies, my lord."

Deidre released her breath as the knife left. She opened her eyes. Darkyn's dark gaze was on her, not the dealer. She didn't feel him rifling through her thoughts, but she sensed it was what he did. Her blood stirred at the sight of his lean frame. Smaller than the dealer, he nonetheless radiated quiet power. And the sweet scent of his blood made her gums itch.

The demon lord glanced at the dealer and tilted his head to the side. The death dealer snatched his shirt and left quickly.

Darkyn held out a hand to her. Deidre took it, shaken by the experience. She met his gaze then looked away quickly. His scent and warmth only made her panic increase. Deidre braced herself for his violent reaction or words. The demon lord released her hand, silent, with her standing before him. He lowered his head and nudged hers aside, nipping at her neck. His growl turned to a purr.

Surprised by the intimate motion that seemed meant to comfort her, Deidre glanced up at him before nuzzling his neck. The scent of his blood made her mouth water, and she breathed him in.

"You're not angry at me?" she whispered.

"If I didn't want you leaving, I'd close the portals," he replied. "You summoning me shows you've begun to accept your place, love. If anything, I am satisfied, or will be, after I deal with the death dealers."

"What will you do to them?" she asked.

"Do you want to know?"

"They didn't hurt me," she said, not wanting to think about what he planned to do.

Darkyn touched her neck. She flinched. His fingers came away with blood.

"Stay here." He stepped away from her and strode through the doorway. He closed the doorway behind him.

Deidre's insides shook. She sat on the bed, panicking silently. At any minute, she'd hear him tear them apart and then, she'd freak out.

No sounds came from the living area. He had almost been kind, or at least, as kind as he was capable of being. She waited, wishing she'd never come. Wishing she'd gone somewhere other than here.

She waited for Darkyn to return but was too scared of what he was capable of doing to open the door and see the damage.

Chapter Five

Deidre. The summons came.

She stood, terrified of what she'd find when she went to the living room. Granted, she hadn't heard anything, but she knew Darkyn well enough to know he didn't plan on leaving anyone alive.

Deidre hugged herself and padded down the hallway, her heart flipping in her chest. She was expecting to see some gruesome scene like that in the second bedroom caused by Darkyn's demons a week ago or what he'd done to his own demons who tried to drink her blood in Hell.

What she saw was worse.

"Gabriel," she breathed.

Death was a dark, towering, muscular figure in the living area of her apartment, clothed in black and wearing an expression that mirrored what she felt. He was armed but hadn't yet replaced the trench coat she cost him soon after they met. His dark eyes swept over her, lingering at her neck, where her wound had healed with Darkyn's power.

"Deidre?" he faced her fully. "You're alive."

She nodded, unable to speak. Her heart was breaking again or maybe, her hope crumbling. She wasn't certain what to feel: angry at Darkyn for setting her up or sorrow at facing the mate she'd never have.

Gabriel was speechless for a long moment.

"What the fuck is going on?" he demanded.

She jumped at the harsh words. She glanced at Darkyn, who was still. Silent. Watching. She fought the urge to cross to him. This felt like another of his tests or maybe, his way of closing another door.

Gabriel's eyes were on her.

"I, um, made a deal with Darkyn. I went to Hell and …" she drifted off. She crossed her arms, close to panicking. First the death dealers attacking her, now Gabriel.

"…had the tumor removed which happened to be Past-Death's soul. Darkyn brought Past-Death back, fulfilling their mystery-deal, and you were at the mercy of Darkyn," Gabriel finished for her.

She nodded. "As his mate."

"His *mate.*" His disbelief was clear.

He started towards her. Deidre skirted away, placing the recliner between them. Darkyn had tensed at Gabriel's' movement. Though the demon lord didn't move from his spot, she was afraid of causing any sort of confrontation between them.

"I just want to see the mating marks. That's it," Gabriel said.

She hesitated and glanced at Darkyn. He didn't move.

She nodded at Gabriel.

"You okay?" Gabriel asked in a hushed voice.

Another nod.

Gabriel stretched towards her slowly. Deidre braced herself, hoping not to feel the warm energy of his magic. She didn't feel ready for it yet. It was hard enough for her to stand before him, knowing they could've been together.

He took her arm with one of the hands that had explored every part of her body not two weeks before. He tugged her out from behind the chair then turned her gently. He pushed her hair over one shoulder, and his hands dropped. No warm magic drifted through her. Was she glad or upset?

"Gods, Darkyn," he muttered, astonished.

Deidre looked at the demon lord. Darkyn's eyes were on Gabriel.

"I win this round," Darkyn said, a faint smile on his face.

She recalled how much he loved to conquer. Right now, he was savoring a victory.

"Double bond. You weren't about to take a chance that you lose her," Gabriel said, sounding baffled.

Gabriel turned her to face him again. Deidre looked up at him, trembling. She couldn't decipher what he had to be feeling. He seemed mainly angry.

His attention fell again to the blood on her neck, caused when one of his death dealers attacked her.

"Tell me Darkyn did that to you, and I'll fucking destroy him," he said.

Deidre shook her head, a smile slipping free. He cared. As much as he tried not to show her, he really did. She wished she'd realized that a few days earlier, before it was too late to matter.

She'd tried to hide her fangs from him, but smiling brought his attention to them. She pressed her lips together for a moment.

"One of your death dealers attacked me," she told him.

"What?"

"I came here to … visit," she said with a quick glance at Darkyn. "They found me."

"Followed her," Darkyn corrected. "Your doing, Gabriel?"

"Of course not," Gabriel snapped.

"Harmony was with them," Deidre added.

"The bitch betrayed me to *you*, Darkyn. Which means this could be your doing," Gabriel pointed out.

"The funny thing about traitors," Darkyn replied. "You can't ever really trust them. Harmony was granted access to use Hell to go to your underworld. I can assure you if she's found going through my portals again, she'll be sent straight to me."

Deidre's eyes drifted to Darkyn in a sense of longing. As much as she hated herself for feeling it, she needed his touch to calm her.

"How many were here?" Gabriel asked her.

"Two," she replied. "And Harmony."

"They hurt you," he said, lifting her chin to see the blood.

"Yes," she said. "Darkyn rescued me from them. He has the two I think."

Gabriel faced the demon lord. Darkyn stepped out of the corner where he stood and Deidre grew edgy, fear fluttering through her. The two were tense enough to worry her that they meant to fight.

"There were two who attacked my mate," the demon lord said. "I'm taking the dealer who hurt her." He paused. "My … spies report that you can't keep dealers and have no idea what's going on in the underworld. The other dealer you can have."

"This sounds like a favor," Gabriel said, frowning.

"It is."

"What do you want in return?"

"Harmony. When you find her."

Deidre glanced at Darkyn in puzzlement. Why would he want the dealer behind those who hurt her? A strange sense went through her, one she might think was jealousy. How insane was she to be worried about Darkyn drinking the blood of another woman?

"By letting them attack you, Harmony made a personal affront to the Dark One," Gabriel explained. "I can't imagine that will go well for her."

"What does that mean?" Deidre asked uncertainly.

"I imagine an eternity of punishment as only the Dark One can devise. Same for the dealer who hurt you today."

"But I'm okay. He didn't hurt me," she said, looking at Darkyn with renewed fear. "An eternity? For one mistake?" She couldn't fathom the idea. The reminder of what her mate was left her trembling harder.

"Even I won't go to bat for him," Gabriel said. "Either of them. Mates are sacred."

"But it's my fault," she said. "Darkyn, I never should've come here. I don't want him paying for something I did."

"He will pay for drawing your blood," the demon lord growled in a tone that made her jump. "Anyone who raises a hand to my mate also raises a hand to me and will be dealt with accordingly."

"For once, I agree with Darkyn," Gabriel said.

Deidre was quiet, troubled. The two deities were bristling. She sensed it was because of her. Were they talking in their heads to one another? She couldn't tell, except that the tension in the room was increasing.

"Has he hurt you?" Gabriel asked, looking at her once more.

"No," she replied. Her distress was rising with their tension. Darkyn motioned to her.

Deidre crossed to him quickly, almost relieved. She leaned into his body. Sensing her anxiety, Darkyn rested a hand on her hip. His cool energy worked through her, calming her. She sighed and breathed in the scent of his warm skin and the lingering, faint smell of blood.

"Agreed," Gabriel said. "Harmony for the dealer you have."

"I'll have him brought to the shadow world and summon you," Darkyn said. His low growl vibrated against her.

Deidre twisted her head to see Gabriel. Tense and rigid, he was watching her with no small amount of emotion in his features.

"You don't deserve to spend your life in Hell," he said, pacing. "Gods, if I could send *her* home with that demon in your place, I -"

"Gabriel!" she exclaimed, startled by his bitter emotion.

"Would you consider a trade, Darkyn?" Gabriel asked.

"She did what she did because she loves you, Gabriel," Deidre said. She moved away from Darkyn to stand in front of Gabriel, searching his gaze. She wasn't certain how he could say such a thing about the woman who gave up everything for him. Deidre had a reason to despise Past-Death but Gabriel ... he was too good for such an emotion.

"After all she did to you, how can you say this?" he demanded, glaring down at her. "She'll be lucky if I let her survive the day."

"I was angry at her," Deidre admitted. "Maybe I still am. But you can't kill her! She deserves a chance."

"To *what?* Turn on me again? To make my life hell?" Gabriel shook his head.

"To have a second chance with you," Deidre answered softly.

"I knew something was wrong. Her story just didn't make sense." He looked away, towards the window, hands on his hips.

"When you thought I was dying, you weren't willing to take a chance," Deidre added sadly.

"Deidre, I –"

"No, wait. You weren't, Gabriel. You did exactly what she did. You hurt me to protect yourself," Deidre pushed forward with what she needed to say. "I had to make a choice without knowing what would happen or even if you would be there for me in the morning."

He was quiet.

"I don't want you to apologize, Gabriel," she said with a sigh. "I want you to see what I do. You both made selfish choices. You both have a chance to make it right."

"And leave you in Hell with *him?*"

"I made a choice, too. I chose to live, no matter what the consequences. That path lies in a direction I never would've expected. But I accept that, Gabriel. There's a greater purpose than myself. You and she never understood that, when it came to caring for someone else. You have that chance now."

He studied her.

"I guess what I'm trying to say is…" she drifted off.

"You're breaking up with me," he said, smiling faintly.

"Oh, god," she mumbled with a look at Darkyn. She sensed he demon's imperceptible tension rise. "Deidre gave up everything to be with you. You weren't willing to do that for me. Maybe you can set aside your pride for her."

"You're too nice to be involved with any of us."

"The only innocent soul in Hell, I've heard," she said and rolled her eyes.

"If Darkyn ever, *ever* hurts you, you have a place to go."

"Thank you, Gabriel." She wasn't entirely convinced yet she wouldn't need the open invitation. Gabriel was disturbed. She wanted to cry again. Gabriel made her heart flutter; Darkyn made it fly.

The demon lord was gazing at her intently. Deidre held his gaze, wishing she knew the right answer to anything. A double-bond couldn't be broken, but did she want it to be? Yesterday, she saw the power she could have to help people from Hell.

Today, she had left, because the idea of eternity in the red desert with a creature incapable of caring for her was too much for her to bear. Standing between the men who could claim her as a mate at some point in the past week, she was caught in the need to taste Darkyn and the desire to have the love of an Immortal whose heart was never hers to start out with.

"We're done here," the Dark One said to Gabriel. "Send my regards to your mate."

Gabriel was still for a moment. A portal appeared behind him, and he left without another word.

Deidre watched the portal close.

"Come," Darkyn said.

He scared her. He probably always would, but she went to him. Deidre stopped only when they were toe-to-toe and leaned into him, needing the heat and solidness of his body to quiet her distress. She was ten seconds from fleeing. She nuzzled his neck, the scent of his blood intoxicating enough that her body relaxed in response. Darkyn nudged her in return, assuring her he wasn't angry. She was shaking from the experiences in her apartment.

"Why did you choose to come here?" he asked in a measured tone.

Deidre moved away from him. "I don't know."

"You do."

"I ... I guess I keep hoping when I walk out of my apartment next time, things will be normal."

Darkyn trailed her. She leaned back against a counter. He planted a hand on either side of her, dark eyes piercing. She swallowed hard. His rugged features were unreadable.

"You know that's not the case." His tone was neither harsh nor teasing. Factual. The same way he wore down her resistance before.

"I know," she whispered. "Are you angry?"

"What reason do you think I have to be angry?" He tilted his head in a sign of genuine curiosity.

"That I left. That I came here. That I want to … to reset things. That I still have …" she stopped.

"… feelings for Gabriel."

She nodded.

"You want him. You *need* me. It's not a competition," he said simply. "As for the rest, you are working through the human stages of grief. But you've started to accept your fate." Darkyn nudged her head aside. "I'm hungry, not angry."

Deidre's body grew warm from the inside out as he nuzzled her neck, preparing to bite her. This time, she felt his fangs pierce her neck and jerked. He wasn't trying to numb the pain. The brief pain turned quickly into pleasure intense enough that she began panting, her hands roaming his body. He caught her wrists and pinned them behind her, more interested in feeding. When he lifted his head, her body was roaring with need. She strained against him.

"You see why demons love pain?" he whispered. Chuckling, he pushed her head away as she tried to reach his neck. "Now, show me you need me."

Darkyn kissed her, hot, hard and demanding. She struggled to reach him, even if only to touch his skin or for her little fangs to graze his neck. He overpowered her easily and maneuvered her down the hallway to her bedroom, stripping her and tossing her onto the bed in one move. He followed, and Deidre reached for him. The feel of the hot skin of his chest against hers made her groan.

"Play, love," Darkyn growled, nipping her hard.

Uncertain what possessed her – beyond pure emotion – she complied. Deidre fought him for a taste, a kiss, soon breathing hard from effort as he grappled with her, teased her with nips and kisses, and dribbled single drops of blood over her lips. He didn't numb the pain this time, and it drove her mad with need.

A short time later, when she was too exhausted to move, she lay still and silent on her side. Darkyn drank more from her than before, leaving her lightheaded. With her belly full of his blood and her body worn out by the rough sex, she couldn't remember being more content.

He leaned away from her neck but nipped her collarbone down to her shoulder. She shivered.

"There is nothing I will do to you that you cannot handle now that you're a demon." He wrapped an arm around her, securing her body against his. "You will not come back here, Deidre."

Deidre opened her eyes and shifted her head back to see his face.

"What do you mean?" she whispered. "To the apartment or my world?"

"Apartment."

"I understand," she murmured. It wasn't her home anymore. Still, she felt a sense of loss. The man in whose arms she lay was not only her husband by Immortal and demon laws but the Dark One who turned her into a demon.

"You're still fighting it." This time, he was amused. She knew why; it was a futile fight.

"You terrify me," she replied. "I didn't ask for any of this. What should I feel?" Her eyes brimmed with tears, and she ducked her head to hide them from Darkyn. "Why did you make me face Gabriel today?"

"Curiosity."

"You were tormenting me."

"Your fate lies with me. I wanted to see what you would do when confronted with the man you thought you were going to return to," he replied.

"Cruel."

"Closure."

"Closure," she repeated. "Another door closed." Deidre pushed herself up to see his face.

"A battle is only truly won when the opponent believes he's been beaten," he said. "You were forced to admit it. You were forced to let go."

Deidre sat up and wrapped her arms around her knees, pink hair falling down around her. She didn't move from Darkyn's body.

"There are so many moments where I don't think I can do this," she said. "You can't understand that or how I feel. You never will."

"I am a survivor," he corrected her in a growl. "I do not feel like a human, but I know what it is to survive."

"How do you survive a life and a world that's so … foreign?" she rested her temple against her knee.

"Simple," he said. He sat, his warmth surrounding her once more. With his hair mussed and his youthful features, he didn't look like the devil she knew him to be. "It's the same key that got you into Hell."

"My tumor?"

"To bring people to Hell, I uncover their weakness and I exploit it. What did I exploit to get you to Hell?"

She was quiet for a moment.

"Hope," she murmured.

"Hope," he agreed. "I gave you what you were looking for. A silver lining."

Her eyes flew up to him at the words Fate had spoken to her.

"You read my mind a lot," she said.

"I rarely stop."

"That's really not …" she sighed, sensing he'd provoke her, if she let him. "Did you have a silver lining to survive?"

"My ambition is far different than yours."

"You wanted to rule Hell."

"And the mortal world."

She shivered again. Fate's words returned to her. With their faces inches a part, they assessed each other.

"I won't let you hurt my world," she said.

"You can't stop me."

"But I'm the only one who has a chance to try."

A slow smile spread across Darkyn's face. It scared her, and she saw his fangs grow.

"You can beg me," he said and kissed her hard enough to rob her of breath. "And fight me." Another kiss, this one harder. "And bleed for me. If you satisfy me, I might consider whatever you ask of me, but I will never willingly spare your world."

Deidre stopped his next kiss by placing her hand on his heart. Darkyn didn't back down, and the light of lust flared in his gaze.

"You are the only one I'd ever try to kill," she whispered.

"I'm the only one you never could kill, even if you used all my power against me," he replied. "You are my mate. It's not possible."

"You're bluffing," she said, searching his face.

"Am I?"

She couldn't tell, but she doubted it. Anger stirred within her at the satisfaction on his face. He was serious about destroying the mortal world. If he was half as creative at torturing people and planning his battles as he was in bed, he was more than capable of doing it.

"We are nothing alike," she said.

"I am what I am. You are what you are. Your purity and my depravity. It will make eternity intriguing." He leaned forward to kiss her once more, his fangs fully extended.

Deidre pushed him away. The demon side of her was always turned on by him, the human side of her determined not to let him do anything to her world. Before he could start another round of rough sex on his terms, she leaned into him, using her body to press him to the bed. Darkyn didn't resist. His hands roamed her body, his long nails leaving trails of blood down her skin. They healed fast and brought exquisite little pricks of pleasure.

She bit his neck harder than she had before, and he chuckled.

"Now you're ready to play," he assessed. "Drink deep, love. What I plan on doing to you would kill a demon ten times over."

Anger burned in her blood. Deidre did as he said and fed long, prepared to put up an honest fight this time. Her fear was tamed by fury. No part of her would let Darkyn hurt her world. Ever. No matter what the cost to her. She'd show him she wasn't afraid to back down in bed or anywhere else.

Day Five

Chapter Six

D eidre. She frowned, not recognizing the voice. Darkyn said nothing about leaving Hell after they returned from her apartment. She hesitated, though, not wanting to walk into another trap of Harmony's death dealers. Darkyn wore her out, and when she'd woken, she was alone.

On her way to see Zamon, she stepped into an empty hallway before trying to call a portal. She saw someone waiting for her in the center of the in-between world and recognized Rhyn. At ease with the half-demon friend of Gabriel, she entered the shadowy land. He waited for the portal behind her to close.

"Thought I'd check up on you," he started. "Figured you had to make a deal that broke bad for you."

"Um, no. Why?" she asked curiously.

"Five minutes after you left, he called off the attacks." Rhyn eyed her. "I don't want you to hurt yourself to make a deal that benefits me. I'll make a deal with him first."

Deidre grinned. With a whoop, she twirled in the middle of the shadow world.

"So you did do something," he said, waiting.

"I think so," she replied. "I basically asked him to stop."

"Just like that."

She blushed, smile on her face.

"This is the creature that nearly wiped out the planet and the human race, who's building an Army of Souls to make a second go at it, who has eaten more people than you'll ever know, even if you live forever, and who's got the largest source of power of any deity," Rhyn said. "You *asked* him not to kill a few kids, at the request of the half-breed he fucking hates, and he just agreed."

"It's purely on his terms," she added. "Why he chose to agree, I don't know. I think …" She was pensive for a moment. "No, I have no idea. I've been trying to figure him out for the past few days and have no clue. I didn't know what to do after you showed me those pictures, Rhyn. I knew I had to try. I can't out-deal him. I can't lie to him. I can't manipulate him. All I could do was ask. Maybe he's got something worse planned. I don't know why he agreed."

Rhyn studied her. "I think I do."

"I'm all ears."

"You'll figure it out," he said. He held out something to her. "I brought this, in case you needed a negotiation tool to use to protect yourself from him."

She accepted the small vial. It was the size of her thumb and filled with blood.

"A little birdie in my spy network fills me in on shit going on down there from time-to-time," he started. "Past-Death said Darkyn kept Wynn, and the birdie told me awhile ago the reason I think he did. Darkyn's daughter?"

Deidre nodded.

"That is the solution." He raised his eyes at the vial. "Not enough for him to duplicate, but enough for you to make a deal."

"What is it?" she asked.

"My mate's blood."

She met his gaze, surprised.

"She has an anomaly that makes her immune to young and old Immortal magic, all the way back to the Ancients. Whatever my half-brother did to her, that should fix it," he explained. "Consider it a thank you. Use it how you will. If you need the negotiation tool, use it. If you want to use it elsewhere, do so. No one will know but you and me."

"Wow," she breathed. "Thank you, Rhyn. But really, he humored me for his own reasons. What if it starts up again tomorrow?"

"It won't."

"You know this how?"

"His game isn't the one you think he's playing. I'll leave it at that. Just promise me one thing," he added. "Don't give that vial to Wynn. He'll bargain a way home and swallow it on his way out. If you use it for his daughter, dump it in her mouth yourself. If you keep it, hide it somewhere safe until you need to make a deal. Darkyn will know what it is the minute he sees it."

"I promise. I know better than to trust Wynn," she said with a sigh.

"You did what no one else has ever done and convinced the Dark One to stop slaughtering innocents. Be proud of that," he said. "Now, get your ass back to hell before your mate hunts me down."

She gave him another smile and turned away, retreating through the black portal. She emerged on the landing and stopped to study the vial. He was right. It'd make a good bargaining tool for a deal. Her thoughts returned to the sight of the girl in the bed.

How many days, months, years had she prayed for a miracle like the one in her hand? Diagnosed with a brain tumor as a child, she was pronounced terminal over three years before. The pain, the surgeries, the rollercoaster of hope and despair. Was the girl in pain?

Should it matter that she was Darkyn's daughter? Deidre wasn't certain what to feel in that regard. The daughter of her mate for eternity, who terrified her and ordered the slaughter of innocents.

Who'd stopped because she asked him and showed some sign of yielding to their bond, if not to her.

In either case, Deidre never put a stupid *deal* over the life of another suffering as she had. She'd be helping Wynn out of Hell as well. The idea he got out causing all her suffering made her frown. Deidre wasn't vindictive, but she still didn't fathom the amount of evil in one's heart it took to kill them slowly while smiling and saying they'd get better.

Yet the alternative was that Darkyn probably killed Wynn tomorrow, when he failed. It was too easy of a death for the first Ancient.

She'd make him a deal. One he couldn't turn down.

She wrapped her hand around the vial and focused on calling a portal back to her room. The hole appeared, and she cringed as she went through it. She'd never liked the portal system outside of Hell; this one was scarier. There were no doorways, just a hole.

She ended up in her room as expected and left for the girl's room three doors down. She knocked, and Wynn answered.

"I hope you have good news," he said and pushed the door open, stepping aside. "I don't."

"Just checking in," she murmured. Her eyes fell to the girl. "What's her name?"

"Selyn."

Deidre crossed to her and touched the girl's forehead. Wynn paced to the desk in one corner, pushing the papers around with frustration.

"Your time is almost. up, Wynn. What will you do?" Deidre asked carefully.

"I don't know, Deidre. Chances are he kills me or sells me back to Rhyn at some great cost."

"Or leaves you here somewhere," she mused.

"That would be the worst of the options. Have my magic stripped and turned into a blood monkey for demon scum."

"Can you make him a deal?"

"Maybe. I'm well aware of his reputation, though."

"I wouldn't make him a deal, and I'm his mate," she said with a snort. "I get Hell for eternity and you get …death. Or to leave."

"Fate is a cruel master," Wynn said.

His nonchalance made her angry. She sat down and pulled her knees into the chair.

"Do you have any regrets, Wynn? I mean, this time around, I guess."

"You want me to say I regret what I did to you."

"It'd be nice to hear you wish you hadn't almost killed me." Deidre smiled sadly as he glanced at her. She rested her head against the back of the chair. Nervous about proposing a deal, she also feared doing it wrong. Darkyn's first few lessons returned to her. She went over the wording of the deal in her mind.

"I do," Wynn said in a considering tone. "In some respects."

"I think you do a little. I mean, why else did you want to ask me out to dinner at the end?"

"I did what little I could to assuage my guilt."

"But not for my sake," she murmured. "For yours."

"The greatest lesson I've learned this life is survival. In my previous life, I was nearly invincible. My magic was stunted this time around. It's made me cautious and appreciative of the importance of self-reliance. Caring for someone is a vulnerability."

She heard what was behind his message, the cunning edge Darkyn didn't try to hide behind pretty words like Wynn did. No, she didn't trust the Dark One, but she doubted he'd cover up what he was.

"I miss my friend Wynn," she admitted softly. "I trusted you with everything I had."

"See where that got you," he teased.

"Well, what if our roles were reversed?" she started with thoughtfulness. "What if I could help you meet your deadline? Would you trust me?"

"I imagine if you had that ability, Darkyn would've discovered it."

"What if he didn't?" she asked. "What if the silly, innocent, clueless little girl you spent years lying to actually had something that you need to leave here?"

"What are you saying?" Wynn faced her, alerted by the note in her voice. His sharp gaze took her in.

"Just that," she said with a shrug. "What if there was something I could do to help you?"

"The Deidre I know wouldn't put politics over helping someone in need, like Selyn," he replied.

"True," she agreed. "Though I could always wait until tomorrow, after Darkyn deals with you."

"You're not vindictive. I know how good you are. You'll forgive Past-Death for hurting you. You've probably already forgiven me. You'll be the one person in the universe who finds an ounce of good in that creature, Darkyn."

His words struck home. They always did. Only now, she understood he was manipulating her. Darkyn's shared sense warned her. She heard it in Wynn's, saw it in the ruthless gleam in his eyes. The knowledge made her want to scream, knowing she'd spent years blindly letting him talk to her like this and encourage her with pretty words, while he ensured the tumor in her head killed her.

This was the kind of man whose depravity Darkyn preyed on.

"I have forgiven you," she said. "Not because you deserve it, but because I understand you had a weakness that consumed you."

"Darkyn's bond has given you insight."

"Either that or being screwed over by everyone you trust," she replied. "It doesn't matter. I have forgiven you, Wynn. I am sorry you did what you did. I'm even sorrier to know that it didn't change you." Her throat tightened at the words. "You're right. I'm not vindictive. I don't want to see you hurt here or killed."

He appeared wary for the first time since she'd known him.

"I have a solution that might work. It's not guaranteed, but it's a shot," she said.

"Why should I trust this?"

"Because if it fails, it costs you nothing. We both walk away, and it never happened."

"You are offering me a deal."

"Didn't think this silly little girl that believed your lies for years had it in her?" she asked in a bitter tone.

"I didn't think you'd hesitate to help someone if you could."

"I'm not. Offering you a deal is helping you both."

He considered.

"No obligation to hear the terms. You can always walk away," she told him, repeating the words Darkyn used to lure her into the deal they made originally.

"Very well. What are the terms?"

"If this solution works, you owe me a favor of my choosing. If it doesn't, you owe me nothing."

"Carte blanche?" He shook his head firmly. "No, Deidre."

"What's it worth for you to be able to leave here? Darkyn always keeps his terms. You don't have a solution. You're running out of time," she reminded him. "Whether or not you take my deal, I'll help her. It's just the when that I'm looking at."

"You won't help her today, if I don't agree," he said.

"No."

"You'd let Darkyn torture or kill me, knowing my death is on your head."

"It's not on my head. You have a chance to save yourself. If you choose not to take it, it's your decision, not mine."

"And if I tell Darkyn you've got a solution?" Wynn challenged. "He checks in daily."

"You think he'll choose to spare you?"

Wynn studied her for a quiet minute. Deidre held his gaze, heart quick but calm in her decision.

"It's right here," she said and held up the vial. "Your ticket out of Hell. I know it's a high price."

"Carte blanche is beyond high," he said. His gaze, however, was riveted to the vial.

"If it doesn't work, no harm, no foul," she said. "If it does, wouldn't you rather take a chance to owe me than be in debt to Darkyn?"

He was thinking hard about it. She sensed weakness and dwelled on the instinct for a moment. He was going to fold. One more push. She'd never before been able to tell when someone lied to her or when they were manipulating her.

Was this how Darkyn knew how to make deals? Was this a benefit of her bond to him?

Oh, to have had this instinct years ago, when she met Wynn!

"You'll have to trust me, Wynn, the way I trusted you for all those years," she continued in a hushed voice. "You'll have to trust

I'm nothing like you, that what I eventually ask of you doesn't do to you what you did to me."

"Agree or I'm fucked," he summarized.

"Yes. You can take credit for curing her, if it works."

Another long pause. Wynn wiped his face.

"Very well," he said reluctantly. "I agree to your terms."

Deidre rose and held out her hand. He hesitated once more but took it. Cold energy sealed the deal as official.

"Don't toy with what time I have left," he said. His features remained stoic, but she felt his concern. She'd judged right; he'd do whatever it took to survive.

Deidre twisted the top of the vial open and neared the girl.

"Wait," Wynn said. He repositioned Selyn's head then gripped her chin and squeezed her cheeks until her mouth opened. "Okay, now."

Deidre held her breath as she poured the mystery blood down the pale girl's throat. Blood speckled her lips. Deidre tipped the vial to tap the last of the liquid out and glanced up at Wynn.

"I wonder how long-"

Selyn's eyes fluttered open. She started coughing.

"Prop her up," Wynn snapped.

Deidre helped him lift the hacking girl into a sitting position. Wynn propped her upper body with pillows.

"Bring me that tray," he ordered Deidre, indicting the table to his right.

She scampered around the bed to obey, beyond thrilled that the blood worked. She took him the tray. Selyn appeared confused at the sight of them, her dark eyes unfocused. Her skin began to flush until it was pink enough to look human rather than the sleep of the dead.

"Omigod, Wynn," Deidre exclaimed. "We did it!"

"Hush."

She clamped her mouth closed, watching him check Selyn's vitals with the urgency and diligence of a man whose life depended upon the results.

"Can you hear me?" Wynn asked. He lifted Selyn's eyelids and shone a light to watch her pupils.

The girl's opened her mouth to answer. What came out was a pitiful squawk.

"Your vocal cords did not heal correctly," Wynn told her. "If you can move your head, nod for yes, and shake for no. Understand?"

She nodded.

"Are you in pain?"

A shake.

"I'm going to check your reflexes."

Selyn watched him with unease that bordered on alarm. Deidre put her hands over her mouth to keep from squealing and stepped back to give Wynn room. She met Selyn's confused gaze as the girl looked around the room.

"Some muscular atrophy. She's malnourished and dehydrated," Wynn said. "Deidre, the notebook on top of my desk."

Deidre whirled and went quickly. She read through the notes on the first page as she returned, unable to make out Wynn's medical jargon and short hand. She gave it to him, and glanced up, feeling Selyn's eyes.

The girl appeared stunned.

"You're going to need some serious physical therapy," Wynn said and took a few notes.

Selyn's squawked once more and pointed.

Deidre looked behind her, expecting to see Darkyn behind her and relieved that he wasn't. The girl continued to stare at her.

"Your back, Deidre," Wynn supplied.

Deidre twisted to display the tattoos marking her as Darkyn's.

"You've missed a few things," Wynn said with an amused look at Deidre.

"Is she okay?" Deidre spoke finally.

"Nothing rest and therapy can't fix." He sounded beyond relieved.

"We did it!" Deidre exclaimed again in a near-squeal.

Selyn's brow furrowed. She'd yet to look away from Deidre.

"Demons don't act like that," Wynn said then addressed Selyn.

"Your father's mate was human. He turned her recently. She retains many of the less appealing human qualities."

"You're welcome," Deidre said, annoyed at him.

Human. Selyn mouth the word.

"Horrifying, isn't it?" Wynn replied. "Deidre, it's been lovely dealing with you. I'm about to summon Darkyn." He raised his eyebrows in a hint.

Deidre nodded. She smiled at Selyn and left the room.

She'd done two good things today. She walked to her chamber then paused, thinking about the ugly creature that was Zamon. Not wanting to wilt in her room with the energy of excitement in her blood, she padded down the hallway and followed the path she'd taken the other day.

She checked her hair twice to make sure no part of her marks were obscured. Darkyn said Hell would do what she asked, so she willed her hair shorter and blonde. Even demons feared Past-Death; she'd ride on the small woman's reputation. She checked her locks to make certain they turned. Still, her step slowed the first time she crossed demons. To her surprise, they bowed and moved on. The next one to pass her did as well.

Deidre made it to the library a few minutes later. Zamon looked up as she entered.

"Come," he said.

She sat across from him at the large desk. He appeared to be in the middle of recording things again.

Deidre studied him. She tested Hell's powers. Zamon's wings turned pink, and she laughed.

"It is not becoming for a demon," he grumbled.

"You look great in pink."

"The deities," he started, glaring at her. He pushed her a book and opened it. "You are learning about them today."

Cheered by the pink demon, she looked from the unfamiliar writing to him. He frowned at her then touched the book. The words swirled off the page and morphed into images of men and women.

"There are two classes," he said. "The Seen and Unseen. The

more powerful the deity, the more restricted. The Dark One is the most powerful, and he grows more so, as the population of the worlds increase. His power comes from the depraved and the forbidden. There have been two deities in the position of the Dark One, rendering him one of the oldest."

An image of Darkyn appeared forefront before the images swirled and began to play a disjointed movie. It showed him in battle, his hardened body moving with unearthly speed and agility against enemies that were obscured. He went from battle to the halls of Hell to a horse, leading a rebellion of the demon army across the mortal plane. She watched the battle with the Dark One – the one Darkyn lost – and saw him banished to the bowels of Hell. A born warrior, he earned his way out by honing his dealmaking skills. Battle made him ruthless; Hell made him shrewd.

She covered her eyes when she saw him take his demon form.

"To restrict his powers, he can move between Hell and the mortal world but not beyond without the permission of those deities who rule the other domains," Zamon continued. "He cannot enter Death's domain or other areas of the Immortal world without invitation. His magic is limited on the mortal world as well. He must rely upon physical prowess and dealmaking skills to lure Immortals and mortals to Hell in order to tap into the great stores of magic."

Darkyn spent much of his lifetime in battle, she noted. If not with Hell's enemies, then within the ranks of demons. He fought his way from a lowly demon to the position of Demon Lord and finally defeated the Dark One. Merciless, cutthroat, aggressive, he purged the oldest demons from the demon ranks. Any contender for the Dark One position was slaughtered by Darkyn personally. The demons remaining were all young and loyal, trained by him over the years. It made sense he was so skilled a warrior and dealmaker, if his magic was so limited in the mortal world.

Deidre watched the movie in both fascination and fear. Violence and command weren't second nature to Darkyn; they were his first. Her eyes traveled over the image of him training others, his whip-like upper body bare to reveal the roped muscles of his shoulders and chest, the tucked waist and flat abs. He wore black pants that hugged his lower body to reveal the lean hips and long, muscular legs. He was lean and agile. He handled weapons as if they were extensions of his body, never dropping them or misplacing a strike. He was a brutal disciplinarian with no more mercy for his demons than he showed humans who lost deals. He also generously awarded those who helped him win battles. His men were fanatically loyal, revering.

Watching him move made her blood heat. She'd never seen anything like it.

She glimpsed Selyn and even herself in his story. The image of him drawing her blood for the first time on the landing scared her. She'd been terrified that day, unaware she'd be mated to him twenty four hours later.

The images faded and morphed back into words that dropped to the pages. Deidre studied them, pensive. Darkyn dealt with her the same way he did everything else in his life. He allowed no room for error, no alternative but for his victory. He forced her to face her reality from the moment she awoke with his name on her back. He didn't lose at battle. He didn't lose at dealmaking. He was both a strategic thinker and capable of detailed execution. No false hope, no redress, no going back. He fought and conquered.

"Death," Zamon said. He turned the page and touched it. More words leapt from the page. "The second most powerful deity and the second most restricted. His domain extends to the mortal plane. His magic comes from the souls of the dead, which are kept in the underworld. There have been nine deities to serve in this position."

She watched in dismay as images of Gabriel played. The entirety of his history with Past-Death unfolded before her, from the moment Past-Death discovered the seventeen-year-old Gabriel, the lone survivor of demon attacks led by Darkyn. Past-Death adopted Gabriel, trained him, turned him into a killing machine, her top assassin and lover.

Deidre couldn't help staring at Past-Death in the history. Seeing Gabriel was painful. Seeing her mirror image was a reminder that Deidre was created by a goddess with the sole intention of using and discarding the human she made.

Seeing them together made Deidre's chest ache. They did love each other. Deidre watched their history and their love grow then become stale, not because of what they felt, but because of the steps Past-Death began taking to ensure she never lost him. In doing so, she drove Gabriel away.

Deidre's eyes misted over. She swallowed hard. It was a tragic love story, one she knew the end to and dreaded seeing how it came to be that way. By the end of the chain of events that led to Past-Death's rebirth in Hell, Deidre was near tears, hating herself and the woman who destroyed the worlds of all three of them.

Who was Deidre to interfere in something that spanned so long and involved two people who cared so much for each other? Who was Past-Death to create a new life simply to discard it? Deidre never felt she belonged in the mortal or Immortal worlds, because she didn't. She'd been molded to exist for one reason and expected to step aside when her purpose was fulfilled.

It hurt more than glimpsing the one scene the book recorded of her interaction with Gabriel, their first night on the beach, the one that condemned her eventually to Hell.

She couldn't bring herself to see what happened when Past-Death returned to the mortal world five days before. Deidre dropped her head to her arms on the table. She feared seeing them happy again, knowing she really was nothing more than a disposable stand-in until they were able to be together again. Just as much, she feared seeing them miserable, because of her brief involvement in the mix. She wanted Gabriel to be happy but couldn't bear to see it, not when her own world was still so new and frightening.

Deidre's heart felt like it was breaking. She was never meant to outlive meeting Gabriel. From what she saw, Past-Death and Wynn were supposed to make sure of that.

Darkyn claimed there was, but she saw no silver lining to her existence. She was in Hell, because there was nowhere else for her lost soul to go.

Chapter Seven

Deidre.

A vision of the beach where she met Gabriel told her who it was.

Deidre sucked in a breath, torn. Darkyn didn't restrict her movement or who she saw, but the idea of seeing Gabriel again so soon after their meeting yesterday disturbed her.

She didn't want to go, especially with the memories of the movies about his past still fresh. She didn't want to *not* go. Darkyn was right; she still had feelings for Death, and she didn't know what to do about them. After a moment grappling with her mixed emotions, she got up and called a portal.

"I'll be back, Zamon," she told the ancient demon.

"Like I have anywhere else to go," he replied grumpily. His tone made her smile despite her anxiety.

Deidre crossed through the shadow world. She turned her hair back to long pink as she walked, self-conscious about Gabriel seeing her tattoos even though he already knew about them.

Gabriel awaited her on the beach near where they'd first sat together two weeks before. His gaze was on the ocean, his large form tense and still. Stars and a half moon were bright, the sound of the ocean comforting. She didn't realize how much she missed the human world. She ached to be back in it regularly.

"Hi, Gabriel," she called softly.

He twisted, gaze going down her frame. After a moment, Gabriel laughed.

"He turned you into a sex demon!" he exclaimed.

Deidre flushed. The chilly ocean breeze made her dress move as if it was alive, and she swiped at the pink hair blinding her. She crossed her arms, shivering.

"I like it," he added. He patted the sand beside him.

"Of course you do. You're male. Me? Not so much!" she retorted. She hesitated then sat beside him. "This is where we met." She wanted to ask him why he chose this spot but was afraid to.

"I'm surprised he let you come," he said, eyes returning to the sea.

"He says the mate of the Dark One can do whatever she wants. Apparently, evil is equal opportunity."

"Not sure seeing an ex-mate is included."

Deidre glanced at him. The bitterness in his voice bothered her. Gabriel kept his eyes on the ocean.

"Are you really okay?" he asked.

"I think so," she answered. *Given the circumstances.* "He, um, has been very assertive and direct."

"You mean violent and aggressive."

"Not violent," she replied quickly. "Not with me, at least. He leaves no room for failure or my hope that certain things will change."

"You don't think you'll ever leave Hell."

"I can come and go. But he will always be my … mate." It was still an overwhelming idea. Hearing it out loud only made her more confused.

"I'm serious about taking you to the underworld, if he hurts you," he reasserted. "Immortal Laws be damned. If I'd had the balls to …" he stopped.

She rested her temple on one knee, eyes on him. She smiled,

touched by his concern. She almost told him that – of the two of them – she was the one with nothing to fear from Darkyn.

"It's scary to be with him," she admitted. "But … he doesn't mistreat me and there's potential for me to do good from Hell. I helped Rhyn already. We stopped Darkyn's demons from massacring the kids."

"He told me it was over," Gabriel said, gaze intent. "How did you convince Darkyn to stop?"

"I asked him."

Gabriel snorted. "You make it sound easy."

"Well, it was," she replied. "I don't understand his motivation."

"You were right yesterday about saying I wouldn't take a chance," he started. "I want to clear the air, though. There's more to the story than what you know."

"Gabe …" she said, sighing. She hoped he'd drop the subject, that they could start over.

"I have to." He took a deep breath. "I didn't take a chance on you for the reason you think. It had to do with the tumor. Wynn said your happiness made it grow. You were so close to the end, we couldn't take a chance. It had nothing to do with you or how I felt."

"Instead of making my last days happy, you decided to make me miserable in the hopes you could find a solution," she said.

"Pretty much," he replied. "I was going to Darkyn myself to make a deal to save you."

"Really?"

"You beat me to it."

Deidre was quiet for a moment. "I think we both did things imperfectly."

He chuckled.

"Up until today, I wasn't convinced that this might have been destiny from the beginning," she began. "This will sound weird, but bear with me. Hell has a library, and the librarian has been teaching me about the deities through these little video tutorial things."

"You've been sitting in Hell watching movies?" He smiled.

"It's like these books and when you open them, these movies

spring up," she said, motioning with her hands. "I don't know how to explain it."

"It's called an Oracle. Hell has one, and Death does as well. The book houses the spirit of a dead Oracle from the time-before-time that records history, among other things."

"You mean it's possessed?"

"Yeah."

Deidre stared at him, surprised.

"Voluntarily. The Oracles wanted to be put in books," he explained. "Though saying it that way does sound strange."

"It's totally bizarre." She felt bad for the Oracle trapped in a book.

He laughed.

"Anyway, I saw how Darkyn was created from a lowborn demon scorned by others because he was smaller. He had nothing but ambition. I saw how you were created from a seventeen-year-old boy who wanted nothing more than for your mistress to love you." She paused. "I saw what was between you and the original Deidre. Her plan didn't just happen when I was born. She really did *create* me. She waited thousands of years and worked with both Dark Ones to make it happen. Fate played a hand, too, as did Wynn. I don't think she knew they were working as much against her as with her. She had one focus: to be with you in a way you couldn't be together when she was Death."

Gabriel listened, tensing.

"I was meant to be ..." Deidre cleared her throat. The emotions from watching the videos was almost too much. She fought back tears, not wanting to cry in front of him.

He glanced at her.

"Disposable," she managed. "Basically. Or would've been, if Darkyn hadn't decided to honor the informal deal he made with her."

"Gods," he muttered. "You were never disposable."

"Seeing the relative lack of consequence your life has in the grand scheming of deities and Immortals kind of makes you view things differently, Gabe."

"Sometimes when you look at a grain of sand in your hand, you forget that there couldn't be a beach without every one of them."

"That's sweet." She smiled. "I guess what made the biggest impression was watching you and her over the course of thousands of years. There was never a day when you didn't love each other. There were days when you hated the fact you did love her, and there were days when she almost walked away from you for good, because she hated that she couldn't control how she felt," Deidre continued. "But there was a never a day when you didn't love her and she didn't love you."

The truth was so painful. She wasn't sure how she got it out. It made her feel hollow. There was a part of her that wished it had been her she saw in the videos. But thinking it was disturbing. She wasn't certain if she felt guilt because of her relationship with Darkyn or if it was regret. Knowing what she did now about her destiny, would she have sought out a deal with Darkyn?

Her thoughts went to the good she might be able to do from Hell.

"I'm sorry, Deidre," Gabriel whispered. "You gave me hope when I was numb to the world. You don't deserve any of this."

"Silver lining," she said softly. "I helped Rhyn protect kids. I can help others. Darkyn is not an easy person to understand or live with, and I'm still not certain at all what to think of him at times. He's been fair and brutally honest, and he can't hurt me because of our blood bond. I kind of like him, even if he scares me."

"Kind of like him." Gabriel smiled. "Only someone as sweet as you would say that about the Dark One."

"Don't get me wrong. He's not normal. But it makes me think that maybe things happen for a reason."

"What reason is there behind falling for a woman and watching her get shipped off to live with the Dark One?" he asked bitterly.

"You did love me," she said, smiling.

"Yeah."

"I've got news for you, Death," she said in a lighter tone. "What you loved about me is present in your current mate. You just have to give it a chance."

"She sends you to Hell, and you go to bat for her."

"Not for her. For you," she replied. "I want you to be happy. I am out of the picture. I understand this. I also forgive both of you, Gabe. I can't say I want her to be happy yet, but I don't want her to be sad."

He laughed. "That's as spiteful as you get, isn't it?"

"Pretty much." Her face was warm. "I loved you, too, Gabriel. I think a part of me always will. You gave me the strength to take a step I wouldn't have otherwise. You made me want to live when I was ready to die. I'll always be grateful to you for that."

Tears made her vision blur again. As much as it hurt, she knew her place was with Darkyn. Accepting it was difficult – but necessary. Letting go of Gabriel was much harder than accepting her new mate. But neither of them were going to be able to move on, if they didn't both at least acknowledge that she was stuck in Hell – for good.

"You're welcome, I think," he said with a shake of his head. "My offer to hide you in the underworld is always open."

"I won't need it."

They sat in silence, both of them gazing at the ocean. She shivered in the chilly ocean breeze. She was cold but grateful to see the ocean. It always put her at peace. An instinct wriggled, one she didn't want to acknowledge or deal with. Darkyn was always right; the sense he gave her to gauge when someone around her had an ulterior motive was tingling. It made her angrier at her mate, who systematically shut the doors around her and also managed to interfere with her ability to trust anyone else.

"You want something else from me," she whispered.

Gabriel glanced at her.

"Darkyn said my weakness is being taken advantage of by others. He shared some of his power or whatever your deities do. I can sense that you have an ulterior motive of some sort," she explained. "I can't see it, but I feel it."

"Savvy demon," Gabriel murmured. "You needed that."

"No more men like Wynn killing me slowly."

"You're right. I do need to ask you for something."

She focused on him in interest, wondering what Death could possibly need from her.

"I have to get into the underworld. The dealers are rebelling, and they've figured out a way to out me from my position. I have to be there in order to prevent it," he said carefully. "The only way into the underworld is through Hell."

"Darkyn will make you a deal you probably can't live with," she guessed. "I can't make deals."

"I wasn't going to ask you to," he said. "I was going to ask you to help me get home."

Her calm acceptance faded, replaced by turmoil. Gabriel had no way of knowing that Darkyn was in and out of her mind. He was asking for a favor, one Darkyn would discover within seconds of her returning to Hell.

It wasn't fair.

"You're afraid," he said.

She shook her head.

"You're not the only one who can sense emotion in others," he reminded her with a nudge. "It's more than fear. I'd say you're still pissed at me."

"You know what you're asking me to do?" she said at last.

"Yes. I have no other option, Deidre. There's something in my underworld that I have to find before they do."

"What is it?" she asked.

"Only my soul," he replied ruefully.

"Oh, god, Gabriel," she whispered, stricken. Deidre started to panic, not wanting Darkyn to know Gabriel's secret but knowing she wasn't able to hide anything. What would Darkyn do with such a damning secret? Send someone to grab Gabriel's soul?

"Just get me through Hell," Gabriel said. "What happens then won't matter."

"Gabriel ..." She rose and paced, her feet sinking into the soft sand. "You shouldn't have told me that. You shouldn't have asked me." Frantically, she tried to recall anything anyone might've told her about suppressing information from someone reading her mind.

"I have no alternative," he said, rising. "I'm not asking because of what we had. I'm asking because I have no choice. I'll owe you."

"You already do owe me one favor," she reminded him.

"I'll owe you two."

Deidre sighed. "I'll try to help you, Gabriel. God help me, I don't know how."

He watched her, arms crossed. He thought she was being difficult. He couldn't know that she was about to become the only thing standing between his soul and Darkyn.

"I have to figure this out," she murmured. "Can I have a little time?"

"Whatever you need."

"Don't worry. I'll figure it out way before our deal is up," she said, rolling her eyes.

"What deal?"

"The one between me and your Deidre."

"You made a deal." He crossed his arms, wary once more. "Do I want to know what it was?"

She hesitated. "No. Because it doesn't matter."

"Your deal is sealed by the Dark One. Why do I have the feeling he's waiting to collect?"

"I can't talk about it with you, Gabriel. She shouldn't either," she said quietly. "Please just know I bear neither of you ill will, despite the outcome."

"Fuck," he muttered. "That scares the shit out of me."

"It shouldn't. I'm the only one in this mess who isn't out to hurt anyone else," she retorted. "It's strange, but I've learned from Darkyn not to be ashamed of my nature. He laughs at me for being unwilling to hurt anyone else, but he says no one should feel shame about who they are."

"He's a living example of that," Gabriel remarked wryly. "Life lessons from a sociopathic demon lord. I never expected him to be capable of treating you well."

"He does, in his own way," she replied. "Can I get your soul from the underworld?"

"A demon of human origin?" he shook his head. "Neither humans nor demons are permitted entry to the underworld."

She gave a sound of frustration.

"It would take all of five seconds," he said. "I'll accept all risk and if Darkyn is angry, I'll take you with me."

"Let me figure it out," she repeated. "Thank you for checking up on me and for the offer to protect me."

"It's the least I can do."

Troubled, Deidre nodded. She nibbled on her lower lip, thinking furiously.

"Romantic setting for two former lovers." The Dark One's low growl made Deidre blink.

"We're just talking. No need to be jealous," Gabriel said, bristling.

"One might ask why you're distressing my mate," Darkyn said.

Deidre sighed. "I'm not distressed. He didn't do or say anything bad." But she did want to feel him close to her. She had no idea if Darkyn sought her out when she was upset because he thought she might be in danger or because he was concerned about her being with her ex.

She crossed the short distance to her mate and paused in front of him, breathing in his dark scent. Darkyn's frame was rigid and his growl loud. She leaned forward until she was resting against the demon, who didn't move away. His warmth was comforting, his hard body her home. She nudged his chin with her cheek to try to soften his mood. He lifted his head, refusing her.

She nudged him again, this time nuzzling his neck.

"Please don't be angry," she said for his ears only and rested one hand against his heart.

Her mate hesitated then lowered his head, nudging her gently in return in a sign that he wasn't too angry with her.

"This was where we met, Darkyn," Gabe said.

"Thus far, only one of us has managed to hold onto her," Darkyn replied.

"No fighting," Deidre said. "Go home, Gabriel."

She didn't expect Death to listen. To her surprise, he called a portal.

"Always a pleasure, Deidre." She turned to watch him go.

Darkyn's arm slid around her when the portal closed behind Gabriel. Chilled by the cold ocean wind, Deidre pressed herself against his warm body. At the feel of his hot breath on her neck, she tilted her head. The Dark One nipped her.

"What're you hiding, love?" he purred. There was an edge in his voice, one that told her he already knew. "Besides your markings."

Deidre's breath caught. She willed her hair shorter and blonde once again, knowing he'd already read her mind and seen the reason why she changed her hair. His nip made her shiver. No part of her wanted to reveal what Gabriel told her or that she meant it when she said she would find a way to help him. She was still silently cursing herself for asking him why he needed to get to the underworld and him for answering honestly.

She couldn't help thinking it was the first truly honest exchange they'd ever had – and the timing was the worst it could possibly be.

"You always knew when I'm upset," she said to Darkyn.

"I sense your distress, love."

"Darkyn …" she whispered.

"Pleading already," he noted. "That bad?"

"If you already know, why are you asking me?" She gazed up into his dark eyes. His hands skimmed her arms to circle her and rest at the small of her back. One of his nails scratched her rhythmically, sending small streaks of pleasure through her.

"A better question is why you don't want me to know."

"You know why," she said with exasperation. "Because I don't want you to hurt him."

"So you're choosing loyalty to him over me."

"No!" she twisted in his grip to look up at him. "You can read everything about me. I know you know this isn't true."

He wasn't happy. His cold gaze was piercing, his frame tense despite her touch.

"I still care about him, yes," she added. "I'm not choosing

anyone. I'm trying to do what I feel is right, and I'm terrified that you will hurt him."

"You want to lead another deity through my domain without my permission. I've slain demons for far less."

Deidre didn't know what to say. She leaned into him, breathing in his scent.

"Will you give him permission?" she ventured.

"Not unless he's willing to make a deal with me."

"But wouldn't you do whatever it took, too?"

"I would."

"How is this different?"

"If he wants access to my domain, he will deal with me directly, not prey on your weaknesses."

"Kindness and compassion aren't weaknesses," she countered.

"They are when dealing with deities."

She heard the firmness of his tone and understood he was drawing another boundary for her. This one left her saddened and frustrated. It was impossible to help Gabriel without Darkyn finding out.

"I'm sorry," she murmured. "I don't like it when you're angry." She nuzzled his neck, loving the scent of his blood.

Darkyn wrapped both arms around her and lowered his head. His bite was sharp enough to make tears spring into her eyes. The pain melted into hot pleasure once again, and she closed her eyes as he fed long and hard. Rather than incite her, it left her sleepy. She was dozing by the time he finished and nudged her awake.

"Leave the dealings of deities to the deities," he whispered.

"Okay," she murmured.

"Drink."

Rousing herself, she bit him and fed until revived.

"Zamon is waiting for you in the library." Darkyn released her and lifted his chin towards an awaiting portal.

Deidre stepped away, almost crossing into it before she realized he wasn't following.

"You aren't coming?" she asked, facing him again.

"I have matters to attend to."

"You're not going after Gabriel." She searched his hard face, unable to read him.

"Not your concern, love."

She rolled her eyes at him and marched into the shadow world, fed up with all the deities in her life.

Chapter Eight

S he emerged into the hallway in front of Zamon's library. Zamon didn't look up as she entered.

"Maybe we will get through another deity or two more today," he said in a disgruntled voice.

"I'm not having a good day, Zamon," she grumbled back. She mentally envisioned his wings pink again.

They turned colors in response. He gave her a harried look.

"Very well. We are starting with Fate," Zamon said. He tapped the Oracle book waiting where she left it. She sat down to watch, unhappy with how her morning had gone so far.

A familiar face appeared from the words, the golden-skinned deity she nicknamed Mr. Checkmate the first time they met at the Immortal Sanctuary. Fate was as old as Darkyn. Instead of war in his background, there was peacemaking and diplomacy from the beginning.

"Fate has been served by three deities, making it second oldest in existence," Zamon started. "Fate is considered the weakest deity, which gives him unlimited access to all of the worlds. He also appears uninvited in your library at will."

She blinked, not registering the deity was behind her until he spoke.

"I wouldn't say *weakest*," Fate mused. "Perhaps in the histories of the demons. In our histories, I'm king of the universe."

"You again," Deidre groaned.

"He comes here often," Zamon muttered. "Normally to spy upon my records."

"I have no need to spy," Fate replied. "There are a few creatures I've collected over the years that interest me. You are looking well, Zamon, for being a million years old. Pink is a good color on you."

Zamon ignored him. "Weakest, because he has no source of power."

"One might argue that manipulating the Future and unfettered access to the present provides more than enough influence."

"Perhaps he is simply lazy," Zamon answered. "The more freewill Fate allows, the more depravity is created to feed the Dark One."

"It works both ways, demon."

Deidre laughed at the exchange, sensing a quasi-friendship as old as the two arguing.

"I'm guessing Zamon didn't tell you who he was," Fate said, moving around the table. "Darkyn did not slay the Dark One. He simply forced him to retire."

"You?" she gasped, looking hard at Zamon.

"The danger with Darkyn is dealing," Zamon said.

"And fighting. He's the most incredible warrior you ever trained," Fate added.

"I trained my hatchling well."

As she watched, the ancient demon changed forms, turning into his human form, a handsome man in his prime. He was neither ancient nor ugly, with familiar dark eyes and hair and roughly hewn features. Unlike Darkyn, whose hair was short, Zamon's long hair was captured in a braid. His smile didn't reach his gaze but revealed fangs the size of Darkyn's.

"What's a hatchling and what did you just do?" Deidre asked, standing in alarm. The strange calm she felt around Zamon remained, and she recalled more clearly Darkyn's words about how the original Dark One lured in his prey.

"A hatchling is what demons call their offspring," Fate replied.

"You're Darkyn's father," she said, surprised.

"I am. I simply took on a form that you would not find threatening," Zamon answered. "Would you have entered my library if you saw me like this?" He motioned to himself.

"No way," she replied. "But you sent him into the middle of Hell for thousands of years. Did you want him to die?"

"That was the plan," Zamon replied. "I figured if he survived the worst Hell had to offer, he'd make a worthy successor. If not, no loss."

Darkyn's assertion that demons didn't have emotions almost seemed true. Deidre shook her head, once again feeling too far away from the reality these creatures lived in.

"They are different creatures," Fate said. "Zamon and I have always gotten along. Darkyn and me? Not exactly."

"Darkyn is a poised predator. He strikes where men are weak. He has no patience for your games. I invite them in for tea then steal their souls while they talk about the weather." Zamon winked at her. "If you weren't his, honey, I would've fucked you up the day you walked into my library."

First the videos then the confrontation with Gabriel, now this. It was turning out to be a horrible day.

"Why did Darkyn let you live?" she asked in a strangled voice.

"We made a deal," Zamon replied with a grunt. "You should know the power of a deal with him by now."

"Yes," she replied. "And the strength of a blood bond."

"Good," Fate said, satisfied. "In two days your deal with Past-Death is up."

They both looked at her. She flushed, wondering how many people were interested in her fate. She seemed unable to keep secrets from anyone.

"I know," she said.

"Darkyn loses no time claiming his victory," Zamon said. "Brash young demon."

"You win," Fate told Zamon.

"You had a deal about me?" she asked with a frown.

"Hell runs off deals," Zamon replied. "Fate said he would conquer you, but you couldn't conquer him. I said a creature who has never known peace will surrender unconditionally when he tastes it for the first time. Past-Death offered him a private deal before she died-dead and before my retirement." His dark gaze was steady, cunning.

Her mouth dropped open.

"She offered him something that was never before attainable. He is a fearless opportunist who has always wanted to be a god, and the deal was unofficial. If any part of it displeased him, he was able to cancel it. The terms were right," Zamon continued.

"Past-Death offered him me, the deity's mate she created, the only chance he had for a mate like every other deity," she said.

"Yes," Zamon said. "His lust for blood, war and women is insatiable. It made him powerful but drove him beyond madness and nearly destroyed my domain. Twice, though the first time is not common knowledge. Can you not see the appeal of a source of appeasement to a creature older than time?"

"I can," she replied.

It was hard to imagine something that fed off depravity wanted peace. He'd pursued her with the cunningness he was known for. Their interactions weren't what she'd generally considered normal, but she was able to see the moment Fate warned her of, when Darkyn decided to keep her. It was the night he provoked her and forced her to say the words that brought her world crashing down.

I'm yours, Darkyn.

"You're his father. How did you lose your deal?" she asked Zamon.

"He knew me better," Zamon replied. "He was stronger."

"Wow. Okay," she murmured, alarmed every time she learned more about why people feared Darkyn. "What did you win in your deal about me?"

"Nothing but the satisfaction of victory," Zamon said, grinning. "I am forbidden from creating deals with material outcomes."

"For my part, I simply wanted you to survive," Fate told her.

"Whatever," she said and rolled her eyes at him.

Deidre. The summons made her tense. She didn't recognize the voice, but she saw the shadow world.

"I've gotta go," she said, dreading another interaction that got her in trouble with Darkyn yet grateful to flee the two creatures that were currently terrifying her. She called a portal when she stepped into the hallway to see who awaited her.

Past-Death.

Deidre hesitated then stepped into the in-between place. Past-Death's features were pale, her blond hair pulled back into a pony-tail. She was dressed comfortably in jeans and a light sweater. She looked far different than Deidre recalled. It wasn't her physical appearance; it was the shimmer of uncertainty and worry around her, emotions the deity hadn't been capable of.

"Hello," Deidre said.

"Hello," Past-Death replied. "My gods, what happened to you? Darkyn turned you into a sex-demon?"

"I guess if you give a man the ability to build his own mate, he'll make her a tramp." Deidre rolled her eyes.

Past-Death gave a startled laugh.

"You called me?" Deidre asked. She looked down and crossed her arms, chilled in the shadow world but also uncertain what to expect. Their first and only exchange hadn't been pleasant. She was torn between anger and pity for Gabriel's mate right now.

"I guess I wanted to see how you're faring."

Darkyn's lie detector skill gave Deidre a tingling at the base of her skull that she took to be a red flag.

"Weird, but good," she replied. "You?"

"You're doing good." Past-Death's smile was puzzled. "I'm really glad to hear it."

"You mean surprised?" Deidre murmured.

"No. I mean, yes, I am surprised, but I'm also glad," Past-Death said. "I, uh, know now what I did wasn't the best route to take. You must hate me."

"I don't."

An awkward silence fell.

"How can I help you?" Deidre asked. Past-Death's smile faded. Deidre noticed the circles under her eyes, and her air was agitated. She could almost guess what was wrong but remained quiet.

"I'm pretty sure no one can," Past-Death admitted. She cleared her throat. "I'm failing miserably. Darkyn stripped my power when I left Hell. I thought it'd be easy. I mean you humans ... I guess you make it look simple. You know I couldn't figure out how to turn on the shower? I won't tell you how fascinating I find kitchen appliances."

Deidre smiled. She'd never paid much attention to appliances but imagined they might be intriguing to someone who had never seen them before.

"I'm just not getting some things," Past-Death said. She paused, sighing. "Like emotions. I never knew there were so many. I don't know how to control them or to make decisions when they're always there just confusing me."

"You're starting from scratch," Deidre observed, pitying the woman. "You have to go easier on yourself. Take time to learn the new things and try not be so frustrated with yourself."

Deidre stared at her. "How can you be so ... nice?"

Deidre's face flushed with heat.

"I mean, you're in Hell maybe even being torn to pieces every day and you're being kind to me. I don't understand any of this."

"I guess I pity you."

Gabriel's mate blushed.

"Why did you want to see me now?" Deidre asked, her new instincts warning her of an attempt at deception. "You could've checked up on me at any point."

Past-Death considered.

"I'm not sure," she replied. "I guess I was afraid to see what I'd done. I kept hoping things would just go well. I told Gabe about what I did to you yesterday, and he walked out on me."

"That's rough," Deidre murmured.

"I'm fucking up everything," Past-Death continued. "He came back but he's barely speaking to me. Like he's there but I'm not."

"I remember the cold shoulder. He's good at pushing people away."

"I figured I had nothing to lose now. I might as well see what all I'd fucked up," Past-Death finished. "I wanted to check on you. If you were alive, I wanted to see if you had any ... advice about how to deal with Gabriel."

Advice. Deidre was being asked by the woman who stole her lover and her destiny for *advice.* Was the Dark One laughing at her right now? There were days when she wished she was more like him, capable of great evil. Or at least, capable of revenge. Because she wasn't. She felt too bad for the former goddess to walk away.

She took a deep breath.

"Well, first, you didn't fuck me over. I thought you did at first and I'll admit, I'm not completely certain things might not break bad, but for now, I'm fine. Darkyn hasn't hurt me and won't. Look." She turned to show her tattoos.

"Oh my god!" Past-Death exclaimed. "He *blood*-bound you! That crafty son of a bitch!"

"In case I win our deal." Deidre said without thinking. Embarrassed, she cleared her throat. "Sorry. Seems kinda tacky to bring it up."

"No." Past-Death shook her head. "I knew he'd figure out something. Never guessed that. He's not someone who bows to others, and a blood-bond is pretty serious, considering you were already mates. I can't imagine the impact of both on him when one is more than enough."

Deidre still didn't quite believe the others were right. Rhyn claimed the same thing, but she definitely didn't feel as though she had any influence over Darkyn. She wouldn't be so terrified of him, if she did. Then again, would he tell her, if she did? She had no real way of knowing.

"That explains the fangs. So jealous," Past-Death added. "Sexy."

Damn fangs. She had forgotten not to smile and to keep her lips closed together. Deidre looked away, self-conscious about being turned into a demon.

"Anyway," she mumbled. "I'm glad you told Gabriel the truth. We talked after you told him."

"He came to see you." Past-Death frowned. "I guess I shouldn't be surprised."

"He's always loved you, Deidre. That hasn't changed." Deidre said, sensing the jealousy in the woman before her.

"I don't believe it's possible," Past-Death said. "I've been afraid of losing him my whole life."

You had no trouble ripping him from me or me from my own life. Deidre kept her thoughts to herself, growing more distressed with the visit. She hugged herself.

"I don't know how to help," she whispered. "The bond between mates is strong. Gabriel is honorable. He will do what's right."

"I want to do what's right, too, but don't even know what that is."

"Darkyn's approach to the mating bond was much different than Gabriel's. Gabriel gave me space and a choice. Darkyn ... no way in hell. Relentless." Deidre heard the dreamy note in her voice and blushed again. "Anyway I mean, if you confront something instead of letting it fester, it might be easier to deal with. Instead of waiting for Gabe to come around, why don't you go to him? Try to make things right."

"I've been trying to think of how to do that." Past-Death was pensive.

Deidre couldn't help wondering how the woman was able to ask such favors after hurting her so badly. Grudgingly, she spoke honestly, knowing there was nothing anyone – even Gabriel – could do to break a double bond.

"Remind him why he fell in love with you. He loves ... your spontaneity, your sense of humor." She tapped one of her fangs absently. "He loves ...*you* and always has. He's always loved the side of you that laughs. The part of you that makes him forget how grey his world is." Her throat tightened at the memory of the night she met Gabriel.

"My gods. How do you know this?" Past-Death's words were barely audible.

"I ..." Deidre blinked away her tears.

"You figured that out after a week, and I know nothing after thousands of years," Deidre whispered. "If you weren't blood-bound, I'd give him to you now."

Deidre was silent for a moment, wrestling with herself. Several days ago, she would have jumped at the chance. She let herself think what she'd do, if she had the choice between the two. Seeing Past-Death's desperation made Deidre realize Rhyn was right. The bond brought mates together, but it didn't create a relationship. It didn't create trust or affection or hope or love. Accepting, loving, trusting someone – even if bonded – was beyond Immortal Laws to dictate. There was still a choice.

What she started to feel for Gabriel had been real; what she felt for Darkyn was real. It gave her a little bit of peace, knowing she wasn't solely at the mercy of the Immortal Laws and Fate.

She shook her head in response to Past-Death.

"If I can win over the Dark One, you can win over Death," she added. "You have the advantage that he already loves you."

"Not sure why you're trying to help me," Past-Death said, tears sparkling in her eyes.

"I want to see Gabriel happy," Deidre replied honestly. "You are the only person who can do that."

"You really believe that?"

"I do."

"It's not going to happen in a week," Past-Death said, pacing.

"No."

Past-Death waited for her to say more.

Deidre hugged herself, hearing the unasked question about their deal. Darkyn said even if she won, Past-Death could live an eternity. Deidre had no idea what to say and even less of an idea what exactly happened when the deal was over.

"Are you allowed to leave Hell?" Past-Death asked.

Deidre nodded.

"If I don't fuck up everything and wipe out the world or die-dead in two days, I think I'd like to talk to you more," Past-Death said. "If you're interested in being the friend of someone like me."

Deidre heard the pain in Past-Death's voice and felt sorry for her. Emotions warred within her. She wanted to say no and walk away. She wanted to make sure the woman whose gaze had gone from confident to sad ended up okay. She never expected Past-Death to seek her out. All along, she'd hoped some part of the former deity was able to appreciate Gabriel as only a human lover could. But it didn't make it any easier for Deidre to deal with.

"I might need some time for that," Deidre responded at last. "I can forgive you, but I'm not sure I can ever trust you."

"Trust must be earned," Deidre said. "I get it. I'm learning that with Gabriel. I thought this was the first step. I'm just asking for the chance, from both of you, to make things right. If I even can."

"I'll think about it," Darkyn's mate said. "I'm gonna go. Um, I guess you know how to call me if you need anything."

"I do, thank you. Deidre, I really am happy that you're okay."

Deidre nodded. She turned and padded back to the portal to Hell, resisting the urge to run. She stepped through and emerged on the landing overlooking the desert. She slumped against the low wall, propping up her elbows and covering her face. Did she want to cry? Scream? She didn't know. Her eyes were warm with tears and her heart racing from the unexpected confrontation with the distressed ex-deity who viewed her as expendable less than a week before.

She was close to hyperventilating, overwhelmed by the visit from Gabriel and Past-Death, the images she'd seen in the videos in Zamon's library, the revelations from Zamon and Fate ...

Deidre tried to suck in deep breaths. Her body trembled from emotion. As she stared out at the deserts of Hell, she figured out what she felt. She was *furious* and so hurt, she wished she'd jumped into the Grand Canyon like she originally planned.

"My mate, helping someone win a deal against her." Darkyn was amused.

"I need to be alone," she said with more sharpness than she intended.

"Maybe I should say, my mate, facing reality." His touch on her bare shoulder made her angrier.

Deidre moved away.

He touched her again, cold energy spinning through her. Deidre swiped at his hand. She knew the danger of letting him provoke her, but she was too overwhelmed to handle him calmly. He'd been orchestrating everything, always aware of what he did to her without being able to care how hurt she was.

Darkyn took her arm. Deidre snapped.

She whirled and slapped him hard.

"Stop. Please," she said with effort. "I can't think when you do that!"

The demon smiled. Her slap didn't even faze him. He took a step closer. Claustrophobic, Deidre backed away. A flare of interest was in Darkyn's black gaze, one that made her realize he wasn't leaving until he was finished with her. Her throat was tight, her eyes blurring from tears. Her heel hit the solidness of a wall, and she tried to bolt.

Darkyn caught her easily and pushed her back in front of him, her back to the wall. Deidre shoved at him unsuccessfully. The demon lord took her wrists and pinned them above her head. He leaned into her, lowering his eyes to her level.

Deidre heard her own harsh breathing. Unable to look away from him, she couldn't fight the sense she was about to have a total meltdown.

"Please, please let me go," she choked out. "Please."

"No." The low purr was firm.

She pulled at her trapped arms, hating the feeling of being vulnerable to him.

"I can't do this. I can't be here. I … just … can't …"

"You can," he replied. "I know every part of your soul. I know exactly what you are and what you're capable of. If you weren't capable, you'd be dead."

She shook her head, struggling not to cry.

How the fuck did she live with being married to the devil? She'd given relationship advice to the woman who condemned her to Hell, advice meant to help snag the heart of a man she hadn't stopped loving.

Yet this was the way it was always supposed to have been. The histories and their relationship were destined to end this way.

Deidre hated that Darkyn was right. There was one place for her in this mess, and it was with him. It was a truth acknowledged by the primal instinct drawn to the scent of his blood and invigorated by his touch. She'd spent five days with him, silently fighting him, only to realize there was nowhere else to go.

"There's only one door open now," he continued.

The truth of his words made her last meager attempt at resistance melt. Deidre stopped trying to control her tears.

Darkyn's grip loosened. She tugged her hands free and leaned into him, sobbing and shaking, unable to support herself. Of all the emotions running through her mind, the one that hurt the most was knowing that everyone outside Hell had already written her off as a goner. She was the last to lose hope, and it was being forced to see how out of place she was in Gabriel's equation that finally broke her resolve.

He held her for a moment then swept her up in his arms. Deidre clung to him, no part of her capable of resistance. After a moment, she felt him place her on the bed. She rolled onto her stomach, weeping. Her heart hurt too much for her to stop. Even the scent of his blood barely impacted her senses.

The bed shifted under the weight of Darkyn's frame as he settled in beside her. Deidre was rolled onto her side. He placed the bloody thumb to her lips. Its effect was immediate.

She swallowed the few drops. She was able to breathe deeply again and her weeping turned to a trickle. Too exhausted to move, she closed her eyes as he pulled her into his body. He was warm and solid at her back, the only thing capable of grounding her in the nightmare of a world she lived in.

"Drink," he ordered in the low purr.

Deidre opened her eyes. He'd torn his wrist for her to feed. His other arm wrapped around her while his breath was hot against her ear. She fed, ensnared by his scent, until she was soothed then tucked her head in the crook between his neck and shoulder.

"I'm yours, Darkyn," she said the words in a hushed voice. This time, they felt true. This time, there was nothing else standing between her and her destiny.

"You accept your place by my side."

"Yes," she murmured.

He nudged her onto her back. She went, meeting his dark gaze. The soulless, ancient intelligence there as fathomless as the night sky. Even if his features were young and his body lean, he wasn't able to hide what he was.

"You feel pain," he said, studying her features.

"Yes. I hurt." Tears raced from the corners of her eyes. She didn't try to hide them this time; Darkyn had stripped her bare. There was no hiding from her mate.

Deidre touched his face with trembling fingers. His jaw was roughened from a five o'clock shadow. The quiet purr that only emerged when they were alone rumbled gently in his chest. He seemed content to study her. She was afraid to know what he thought, if he was counting the ways he could manipulate her now that there were no more barriers.

"You have always been vulnerable to me," he said, amused by her thought.

She sighed. "You don't understand."

"I have studied human nature for the entirety of my existence. I cannot exploit it, if I do not understand it."

"You want me to hurt. Isn't that what you do?" she asked, wiping her tears.

"I want your pain to be of a physical kind that I cause when we fuck like demons," he replied. "I do not wish you to feel pain otherwise."

"Are you trying to be nice?"

"I do not *try* at anything I do," he said with some irritation. "I conquer."

"So I'm a conquest."

"Without a doubt, love," he said without hesitation. "You are also my mate. I see weakness and vulnerability as I do everyone. But I see more."

"What?" she asked.

"I see beauty."

She gazed at him, puzzled. When he said no more, she smiled slightly. "What does that mean?"

"I see a conquest that gives me pleasure to think of as mine."

Deidre laughed. The demon lord had just admitted to being happy, in his own way. Her hope had been crushed in every other way – except that it stirred once more at the idea there was more to him than she knew. Though she doubted he was capable of emotions like she was, he was capable of more than he claimed, too.

"I'll never tire of conquering you, either," he said and nuzzled her neck. His hand circled her neck to release the clasp of her dress.

Her desire stirred, aided by emotion and hunger for him. Deidre pulled his head to hers and kissed him long and hard. Within seconds, their petting grew frantic, and she shimmied out of her dress before pushing off his shirt.

She groaned at the sensations he caused, soon drowning in the scent of blood and need to feel him inside her.

Chapter Nine

They wrestled, fed and fucked until sheer exhaustion overtook her, and she slid into a short doze. She awoke to the sensation of him drinking from her. Darkyn wore her out enough to where her thoughts no longer spun out of control. Calm, she was able to focus. The image of Past-Death wouldn't leave her mind. She'd felt that level of desperation before and didn't wish it upon the woman meant to be with Gabriel.

"Is it wrong for me to want her to be happy, too, even after all she did?" she whispered.

Darkyn withdrew from her neck.

"I cannot see humans or Immortals or deities as you do. I see only the parts of them that hold depravity, weakness. I do not wish them well or *happy*. I evaluate them for opportunities," he said. "I understand pleasure, not happiness." As he spoke, he slid a nail down her hip, drawing blood. She shivered at the sensation.

"I know," she murmured. "You see me differently now, but did you when we met?"

"I saw what I do with everyone: what it would take to bring you here," he said. "You feared death, and I dangled hope in front of you. You made up your mind to deal with me, even if Gabriel was not part of your future."

"When did you figure out I was your mate?"

"In the shadow world when you told me about your tumor. As soon as I touched you, I knew," he said. "You remember what you were thinking when you turned down my offer the first time?"

She was quite for a moment, thoughtful. It was difficult to hear how easily he'd evaluated and cornered her to get her to Hell.

"You were the first person to give me a choice," she murmured. "You've been reading my mind from the beginning, haven't you?"

"From that moment, off and on. I had to be sure I even wanted you here."

"You let me go the first time because you knew I was your mate. You could've killed me and taken the soul out of my head at any point."

"Yes."

She shivered, unaware just how close she'd been to dying by his hands.

"Is this what all demons do?" she asked.

"Love, what I do to you would kill a demon many times over."

She gave a startled laugh. "Are you serious?"

"Yes."

"A blood bound, deity's mate is the only person who could keep up with you," she guessed.

"Eternity is a long time to go unsatisfied."

It was almost an admission of loneliness, if a demon had feelings. She understood a bit more why a mate might appeal to even the Dark One. Darkyn was ancient, according to the tutorial she'd watched, from the time-before-time. He'd never had a partner in all his time alive.

"Are you satisfied?" she asked.

"Very."

"You aren't going to ask me?"

"I already know you are," he replied. "I see your thoughts like mine."

"*All* of them?"

"Even the one where you planned to lie to me about Wynn healing Selyn."

"Ah. Okay." She waited for some sort of reaction. He was quiet. "Did I make a good deal?"

"You did," he said. "Carte blanche never breaks bad for me. You were emotional, though."

"Yeah. I forgave him, but I just …I think I'm angrier at myself for falling for all his lies than I am at him for lying," she admitted.

"It will become second nature to know when one lies to you."

"I felt it," she said. "I was able to hear when he lied."

"Private deal," he said. "You make no deals with anyone aside from our private deals."

"In exchange for…" She frowned, reluctant to give up the ability.

"A favor of your choosing, so long as it pleases me to grant it."

Deidre sat up, staring at him. His cold gaze was calm and steady, his long fangs resting on his lower lip. The sight of them thrilled and scared her. He was relaxed, and it struck her how different he was with her in bed compared to outside their room.

"You're serious," she murmured. "You would do that?"

"Deal?"

"Yes."

"I am physically satisfied for the fifth day in a row, for the first time since I was hatched," he said. "I feel generous. Use it wisely, love. You may never get another. You can try by pleasing me every night."

"I will try, and I'll use it wisely," she said. "You can trust me." She looked at him curiously. "Do *you* trust *me*?"

"You have yet to be tested."

"But you sense depravity and weakness," she said in a mocking tone she hoped was similar to his.

"You are challenging me already." He flicked his nail against the pad of his thumb. "I am always ready for a fight. Are you, mate?"

Deidre groaned. She wasn't, but she doubted she'd have a choice. As if sensing she was tired, he didn't tease her when she reached for his hand. She sucked his blood clean from his thumb.

The demon purred, watching her. She settled beside him again, comfortable in bed with him.

"Selyn has asked to see you," he said.

"I'll be happy to talk to her," she said. It was the first time Darkyn ever brought his daughter up. "Is she well?"

"Yes."

His voice never conveyed emotion. Deidre wasn't certain if there was any affection for his daughter, though his persistence in healing her was a sign of either care or obligation.

"Obligation," he replied. "She is mine. You are mine. Hell is mine."

"But you went to great lengths to help her. Isn't there some part of you that can care?" she asked, troubled again.

"Not the way humans do."

His quiet statement was difficult to swallow.

"Demons show affection. We are not capable of more," he added.

She shifted to see his face, surprised by his confession. Days before, he'd claimed nothing existed beyond physical pleasure for a demon.

"I can live with that," she said. "You show me affection in your own way, don't you?"

He nuzzled her neck in response.

"Did you ... can I ask if you sent Wynn home?"

"I keep my terms," Darkyn replied. "He went home."

"I don't know how to feel about that," she said, chewing on her lip. She was almost angry enough with Wynn to wish he'd stayed here just a little longer.

"A man like that will find his way back here," Darkyn said.

"Probably. Speaking of difficult Immortals ... what was Past-Death looking for?" she asked, puzzled. "I know there was more to why she sought me out but I don't understand what."

"Weakness. Willingness to negotiate. She knows she's lost and is desperate. It's common among those who deal. Another reason you won't deal without me. Your heart is too soft."

"I wasn't too soft on Wynn!" she exclaimed.

"You offered him a deal when none was needed, love. You could've waited a day for him to fail then cured Selyn."

"The thought occurred to me."

"Yet you offered him a deal. Lesson five: when you have the advantage already, don't deal. You will never deal outside of those we make in private. Your nature is too … pure."

"Like I couldn't …" she placed a hand over his heart "…even the first day, when I thought I had a chance to leave. You knew that though, didn't you?"

He tipped her chin up. His dark gaze gleamed.

"Without a doubt," he said with a cold smile. "I know what you are."

"It's not fair. It's way too easy for you to read me," she complained. "Don't you like a challenge?"

"You fight me where it counts. I look forward to great battles with you over the fate of the humans and fucking you into submission afterwards."

She blushed. Her breath caught at the idea of what he did to her, her blood quickening. He kissed her before pressing his bloody thumb to her mouth. Her body calmed instantly.

"You take no satisfaction out of seeing your enemies defeated?" he asked.

"Wynn and Deidre are not my enemies," Deidre replied. "But no, I take no satisfaction out of seeing someone hurting."

"They went to great lengths to hurt you."

"I know," Deidre whispered, frowning. "You and I are very different."

"We are," he agreed. "I do not understand how you feel as you do."

"Sometimes I don't either," she said, mentally evaluating the discussions she'd recently had with Wynn, Gabriel and Past-Death. "Everyone has something to say about you turning me into a sex-demon. I wish you hadn't done that."

"For my pleasure, not theirs," he replied, unconcerned.

"So you turn me into a seductress who isn't allowed to seduce anyone," she said.

If his sudden stillness wasn't a warning, his purr turned to a low, lethal growl.

"Only mine."

Deidre jumped. The sudden shift of power around him made her uneasy. She nudged his chin, partially to keep him from seeing her smile. He really did feel affection for her, if he was jealous. He lifted his head in blatant rejection.

"Don't be angry," she murmured. "I meant to tease." She nuzzled his neck the way he did to her when she was upset. He didn't move away this time, and she nipped him.

"Not about that," he said after a tense moment. His hands moved down her body, and he nudged her head aside.

"Okay," she said, relieved the danger was passed. He was irked. She wondered if it was because of the thought of her seducing someone else or because of her triumph at winning his affection, even if he beat her at every other thing. "That makes me happy."

Darkyn was silent. She assessed that – for the first time – he wasn't entirely certain how to react. His features were emotionless, his body not yet relaxed completely again. She took his face in her hands and traced his cheekbones and jawline with her fingers.

He kissed her then rolled away.

Deidre watched him, brow furrowed. He wasn't angry, but he wasn't himself either. She heard the rustling of clothing as he dressed. The light of the black fire was too dim for her to see much more than the outline of his form. Her eyes fell to the shape of the hourglass on her nightstand. With a glance at the demon lord, she stretched to grab it and rose.

He started to the door.

"Darkyn," she called softly.

He paused. Deidre approached him until close enough to feel his body heat. She held out the hourglass. Her heart beat rapidly at what it meant to surrender what had been her one hope to leave Hell.

"I don't need this," she voiced quietly.

He accepted it. It dissipated into black smoke in his hands. Her breathing quickened as she realized what she'd done. She felt his gaze on her but couldn't see him in the dim lighting of the room.

The demon lord gripped her neck. The action that once terrified her now made desire bloom in anticipation of what he'd do. Deidre waited.

The fire flared brighter, lighting up his body. When she looked up, he was watching her. He made no move to bite her or kiss her, simply studied her, his thumb stroking the pulse in her neck.

"You're not changing your mind, are you?" she asked uncertainly.

His slow, cunning smile was not what she wanted to see. His hand dropped. He peeled off his shirt. Instinctively, she reached out to feel his warm skin and trace the ridges of his abdomen. Darkyn turned his other side to her, and Deidre stared.

The familiar demon blood bond script ran down one arm from his shoulder to his elbow. Except that, on his body, it was *her* name written in black.

D

E

I

D

R

E

Speechless, she traced her fingers down the letters then looked into his eyes. She had been over every inch of his body numerous times without seeing the marking. He held her gaze without speaking.

"How long has it been there?" she managed.

"Under a day."

"So at any point up until then, you could've …" She swallowed hard.

"You were mine the night I let you drink from me. This is a formality of unwritten terms only," he said.

Stunned, she was silent, trying to digest what he was saying. He was serious when he claimed to want her. She was more than an obligation, if he chose to keep her when he didn't have to. She didn't exactly feel grateful to him, though, not with the emotional trauma he put her through. But the idea he did want her was almost a relief, another sign he was capable of providing at least some form of affection. She wasn't going to spend her eternity with someone who didn't care for her.

Darkyn replaced his shirt. When he was finished, he pulled her into his body and bit her hard.

Deidre winced. The pain soon turned to pleasure, and she melted against him. He didn't drink long, and she nuzzled his neck then found his lips with her own. This time, there was more than insatiable lust and need in his kiss. There was passion and a deep longing she innately understood only she was able to fill. Deidre felt tears on her cheeks once more. Incapable of human emotion, Darkyn was nonetheless expressing what demon emotions he had. His hands ran down her naked body possessively.

He withdrew and pressed his cheek to hers.

"Will you stay?" she asked, touched by the change in him.

"I cannot now. Later," he promised. "You can run for me."

She smiled. "Alright. I will."

He sidled away. Deidre watched him leave. She wiped her face then dressed, too distracted to feel the warmth of a certain deity as he appeared.

"How is my little fruit bat doing?"

She turned. Fate lit up the corner in which he stood brighter than the black fire could her room. He wore jeans and a t-shirt that outlined his lean frame.

"I don't know," she said, a familiar tremor of uncertainty fluttering through her. "I'm trying to figure out how I can want to be with *him* but not stomach what he does as the Dark One. Why are these Immortals and deities so messed up?"

"Imagine all the baggage a human has after one lifetime and multiply that by a few thousand," Fate replied. His multi-colored eyes swept over her. "You wouldn't believe the amount of repressed anger most Immortals have."

"I suppose. Why am I stuck in the middle?"

Fate glanced at her, amused. "Do you really want to be elsewhere?"

No. As much as it didn't make sense, as much as his day job terrified her … She wanted Darkyn, more so now that she knew he had a side – however tiny – that was capable of caring for her and only her.

She shook her head.

"By the way, I'm mad at you," she warned him. "You tricked me! Completely, totally, irrevocably *tricked* me into staying here to further your agenda and then lied about how I was safe when I had the demon marking."

"No, I tricked you into staying *alive* to further my agenda," he corrected her. "If Darkyn didn't want you, he never would've let that mark form on you. His mark is inconsequential."

"Then why not tell me that?" she asked.

He shrugged.

"You play with people's lives every day. But this is *my* life, and I'm sick of it!" Her face felt hot at his nonchalance. She approached him, glaring up at him.

"You can hit me." Fate gazed down at her, smiling. He opened his arms wide. "I don't mind. It's impossible to be angry at a seductress."

She planted her hands on her hips, tempted but not about to do it, now the she knew he wanted her to.

Fate laughed.

"You are the soul to a creature who had none," he said. "It's the only deal I ever lost that I didn't mind losing."

Deidre's anger deflated at the confirmation of Darkyn's thaw.

"You people have such a warped sense of … everything," she said.

"You're one of us now."

"Physically, maybe, but that's it. Are you here for any reason?" she asked suspiciously. "You always appear when something bad is about to happen."

"Keep that in mind," he said wisely. "I brought you something." He reached into his pocket and held out his hand. In it was a green soul, glowing faintly like an emerald under a jeweler's lamp.

"Omigod. Whose is that?" she asked, stepping back.

"Let's just say, you're going to need this," he replied. "When the time is right, you'll know what to do with it."

She almost refused but something about the look on his face made her hesitate. Cringing, she held out her hand. The only other soul she'd touched had told her its life story in a blink of the eye, terrifying her.

Fate deposited it into her hand. Nothing happened. She released her breath and placed it in the small pocket of her dress.

"I'm still waiting for my love tap. Or a bite," Fate said, winking. "Darkyn's not the only one who likes it rough."

Deidre shook her head and spun away, fed up with deities for the day. She didn't wait to see if he stayed or went but walked out of her room. Darkyn had mentioned Selyn. Curious to see how the girl was, Deidre walked three doors down and paused.

Her palms were sweaty at the thought of seeing Darkyn's daughter, but she wasn't certain why. Maybe because it made her stay here feel more permanent. Selyn was now a part of her world, her warped family.

She knocked. After a moment, the door cracked open. Selyn peeked out from the two inches she'd opened the door, her dark eyes identical to her father's.

"Hi," Deidre said awkwardly. "I, um, just came to –"

The teen's face lit up. Selyn wrenched the door open fast enough to startle Deidre. She motioned for Deidre to enter then closed the door and locked it as soon as she did.

Deidre stayed by the door, uncertain. Selyn hurried across the room to a pad of paper and pen that Wynn had clearly left behind, if his tight writing on the back cover was any indication. Carefully, Selyn wrote out something then passed it to Deidre.

"I can't really read … demon," Deidre said, staring blankly at the geometric writing.

Selyn's face fell.

"Is this how you talk to your father?" Deidre asked curiously.

The teen shook her head then tapped her temple.

"He reads your mind. I should've known." Deidre smiled. "Can you do that?"

Another shake of her head.

"Did Wynn say if you'll be able to talk again?"

Selyn nodded then blew out a breath. She pressed her hands together then pulled them apart about a foot.

"Um, after a while?" Deidre guessed.

Selyn nodded once more. She lowered the pen and paper, thoughtful gaze on Deidre. She nibbled on her lower lip with her tiny fangs. She was still too pale and her frame slender enough to indicate she needed some food to bring her back to a healthy weight. Deidre's gaze fell to the table in the corner. She didn't feel able to handle knowing what kind of food sat under a domed tray or what half-demons like Selyn did for blood.

Just the thought made Deidre feel ill.

The teen took Deidre's arm and circled her. Her cool fingers ran across Deidre's markings. She made a sound like a squeak.

Deidre faced her curiously. Selyn's smile was lopsided because of the unresponsive, scarred half of her face. Her eyes, however, glowed.

"You're happy about this," Deidre said.

A look of pained yearning crossed the girl's face, as if she wanted badly to speak but couldn't.

"I can see that. Your daddy can be scary."

Pride crossed Selyn's face. Deidre gave an unsettled laugh. How long would it take her to adapt to a culture where the ability to cause fear and pain was so revered?

Deidre. She was almost grateful for the summons then anxious in the next breath. It wasn't Darkyn, and the vision accompanying it was from the shadow world. Like when Past-Death summoned her.

She wasn't ready to face the former goddess again.

"I have to go," she said grudgingly. "Someone is summoning me."

Selyn frowned. She tapped her chest. Deidre looked at her quizzically. The teen took her arm then nudged her to walk.

"You want to come?" Deidre asked.

Another nod.

"Okay. Are you allowed out of Hell?"

At the look of offense, Deidre almost laughed. Instead, she called a portal.

Deidre stepped through just as Past-Death did. Selyn crowded her, almost tripping them both by how close she was.

Past-Death didn't look in any better shape than when Deidre saw her last. Her intent gaze was inquisitive, her eyebrows raised in a silent question. Deidre had the sense the woman was surprised to see her.

"Hi, Deidre," Deidre said, puzzled. "I wasn't expecting to see you so soon."

"Um, I thought you summoned me," Past-Death replied.

Deidre shook her head. She was almost relieved. Maybe someone had accidentally summoned her, and she wasn't about to have yet another confrontation today.

Past-Death had frozen. A flicker of alarm went across her features, warning Deidre something was wrong.

"Deidre, I think we need to –" Past-Death started, backing towards her portal.

Alerted by Past-Death's sudden tension, Deidre turned and took Selyn's arm. She didn't know what the former deity sensed, but she wasn't going to stick around too long to find out. She pushed Selyn towards the portal to Hell.

Two forms stepped between them and the portal, blocking it. Deidre gripped Selyn's arm more tightly, fear spiraling through her. She didn't recognize the two men before her, but they were dressed much like the two death dealers that tried to turn her over to Harmony in her old apartment.

Deidre glanced over her shoulder and froze. Two people stood between Past-Death and the yellow portal leading back to the human world.

"Harmony," Deidre said at the sight of the female death dealer.

It was a trap. Suddenly, Deidre wished she'd left Selyn in Hell. The girl had started to tremble, no doubt reminiscing about the last time she'd dealt with Immortals. Deidre squeezed her arm in reassurance, not at all certain what Harmony wanted. Last time, the death dealer wasn't interested in her.

"What do you want?" Past-Death demanded of Harmony.

"You aren't Death anymore." Harmony punched Past-Death hard.

Deidre flinched as the small blonde woman went down. Harmony bent over her, saying something Deidre wasn't able to hear. Gabriel's mate was struggling to sit up.

"Deidre, are you okay?" Deidre called.

"Yes." The response was more of a grunt. Past-Death managed to stand. She faced Harmony. "What's going on?"

"Simple. Because of Darkyn's bitch, I've got a price on my head from the Dark One. I didn't betray Gabriel to be stuck in the human world," Harmony said. She snatched Past-Death's arm and hauled her closer to Deidre. "Who is this?"

All eyes fell to Selyn, who was shaking. The growl low in her chest sounded more like a rattle.

"A servant," Deidre said, not wanting them to hurt the poor girl.

"Kill her," Harmony said, motioning to one of the other dealers.

He grabbed Selyn and hauled her a few feet away. The panicked teen stared pleadingly at Deidre. She started forward when the dealer pulled out a knife.

"No!" Deidre cried, heart racing. "I lied. She's Darkyn's daughter."

Harmony stared at her then at the teen girl. Suddenly, she smiled.

"Perfect. Even better," Harmony said. "Darkyn's bitch will get us into Hell. Gabe's will get us into the underworld. Once we're there, we'll have all the leverage we need."

Deidre looked from Harmony to Selyn, wishing she knew how to diffuse the situation in a way that Selyn was able to escape. The girl didn't need any more trauma, and Darkyn would unleash Hell if one of them disappeared and the other was dead. Her thoughts went to what Darkyn taught her about dealing.

"Will you leave her?" she asked. "I have the power of Hell at my back. I can grant you almost anything in exchange for her life." She spoke carefully, aware no one knew about her private agreement with Darkyn that disallowed her ability to make deals. She didn't know what happened if she tried to make one, but she'd do what it took to protect the terrified teen.

"I will, too," Past-Death added. "Any deal I make will be sealed by Death's magic."

Harmony was quiet for a moment. Deidre exchanged a look with her look-alike.

"Darkyn made a deal with Gabriel for your soul, Harmony," she said. "Whoever finds you first, Darkyn keeps you."

The death dealer paled. Deidre guessed the death dealer knew enough about Darkyn to fear him. She definitely feared him, and she was shown mercy by the Dark One.

"Let the girl go, and I'll make sure your soul goes where it should, right beside mine," Past-Death said with calmness Deidre envied.

"Or you can risk an eternity with the Dark One personally over-seeing your day-to-day … activities," Deidre seconded.

Harmony appeared indecisive.

"The soul of a deity or former deity has special standing," Past-Death continued. "Yours will remain right beside mine."

Deidre studied her, hearing the carefully chosen words. Seeing Past-Death, it was hard to remember that the human with the mussed hair and tear-reddened eyes had spent thousands of years cultivating deals. She probably knew many of the same rules Darkyn did about creating terms.

Harmony couldn't know that Past-Death's soul was destined for Hell in a matter of days, or more specifically, to Deidre herself. Darkyn had bargained with Gabriel for Harmony, and Past-Death just sealed the deal for her soul. Deidre waited apprehensively. Right now, no part of her was willing to protect Harmony's soul from Darkyn the way she planned to Past-Death's.

Harmony tossed her head towards the death dealer holding Selyn. She held out a hand to Past-Death. Deidre took it, and they shook, the deal sealed with the magic of Gabriel. Deidre stared at Past-Death, wondering why the former goddess was trying to help the daughter of the Dark One that meant to crush her.

Whatever Past-Death's reasoning, Deidre was grateful. She couldn't stand the thought of seeing Selyn hurt, as much because of everything the girl had been through as the thought of hurting Darkyn. Even if he was incapable of feeling real pain.

The death dealer tossed the teen demoness through a yellow portal, onto the mortal plane rather than into Hell. Deidre gasped, stunned. She was about to demand to know where the girl was sent when Past-Death's words jarred her.

"She's alive."

Deidre swallowed hard and nodded, reining in her panic. Selyn could find her way home. Nothing else mattered except that she was alive.

"If either of you summons your mates, I'll kill the other. If you try to alert anyone or escape, I'll peel your skin from your bodies and watch you scream," Harmony warned. "Got it?"

Deidre nodded. So did Past-Death.

"Now, we're going to Hell."

One of the death dealers took Deidre's arm and waited. After a moment, she realized none of them could see the portal to Hell the way she could. She pointed and started forward. The death dealer yanked her back against him, his one hand roaming down her side.

With a sickening feeling, she realized she'd never asked Darkyn what she meant to: how to turn off the seductress or at least, defend herself against those drawn to her. She gave a sidelong glance to Harmony as the death dealer joined them.

All of them had to know they'd just sealed their own fates. No matter what happened from here on out, neither Darkyn nor Gabriel would ever let them live after this.

For a moment, Deidre pitied them. As noble as Gabriel was, he wouldn't hesitate to turn over anyone who hurt his mate to Darkyn. This much she knew.

She prayed for Selyn to find her way home safely then led them through the portal into Hell.

The Underworld

Book Four

Chapter One

For the first time in far too long, Death stepped from the portal room in Hell into his own domain. A towering, muscular form dressed all in black, he surveyed the world that was his with eyes darker than night. Power swept over him then retreated, lingering in the forests of the underworld, a sign he had not yet won the right to command his realm.

But he felt the tension around him. His magic recognized its rightful master and was struggling not to come to him. He was meant to be here, to break down the dam between him and the magic of the dead that was rightfully his. The souls were calling to him in a faint, mournful wail, their peaceful existence threatened by his weakness.

Hang in there, Gabriel urged them silently. *I'm one step closer.*

He had never been as relieved to be home as he was this moment, standing beneath the milky grey skies where even the weak midday sunlight never matched the power of the setting sun on the mortal plane. He found himself no longer squinting the way he did in the human world.

The trees moved, leaning away from him while their branches

slithered like snakes far above his head. Shrubberies and other small plants scurried out of the way of the three invaders. The air was cool and light. It grazed his skin, bringing with it the familiar mossy scent of the forest.

Home.

"You know where we are?" Rhyn, his best friend and closest ally, asked from behind him. The silver-eyed half-demon was radiating a different kind of tense energy, probably as a result of their trip through Hell to get to the underworld. The power of Hell clung to him.

"Always." Gabriel knew his home better than he knew anything else. "But my magic is still blocked. I'm not going to know if we're in danger."

The thick forest was too dense for him to see beyond the first layer of trees.

"We have two choices. We go Rhyn-style and smash everything in our path to get to the palace. Or, we take our time to scout and plan for a day or so," Gabriel said, turning to face the others with him.

"I think Darkyn needs to make that call," Rhyn responded.

The smaller, lean Dark One, the third member of Gabriel's rescue party, was taking in his surroundings with a sharp gaze.

"How long does she have, Darkyn?" Gabriel asked gruffly. He wanted nothing to do with the demon lord. The only reason he allowed the Dark One to be there: the woman-turned-demon that was trapped somewhere in the underworld. They had no choice but to work together at this point.

Darkyn's fists clenched. Unreadable, the lethal, youthful demon was glaring at him, his long fangs resting on his lips.

"Don't be a dick, Darkyn," Gabriel snapped. "We have the same goal. If we need to act fast, then tell me."

"My mate is newly blood bound. She will weaken quickly," growled the Dark One. "She doesn't have more than three days."

As usual, the demon's candidness left Gabriel a little surprised. When Darkyn had no reason to lie, he was almost trustworthy. The problem: figuring out if this was one of those times, because trusting a lying demon almost always ended in someone losing his soul.

The only leverage Gabriel had was that Darkyn was also blood bound, meaning he'd need the blood of his mate or spin out of control with unquenchable bloodlust. And … he had begun to think that the ruler of Hell had a soft spot for the mate he claimed.

"Rhyn, go on ahead and scout. We'll move fast," Gabriel said.

"I'm going with the half-breed," Darkyn replied.

"No. You're staying with me."

Darkyn faced off with him.

"Neither of us has any magic here. We have a better chance together, especially since the underworld hates full demons," Gabriel said. *And I'm not letting the Dark One loose in my fucking domain.* "Rhyn, go."

Rhyn drew a knife and trotted off, his thick frame disappearing into the thick foliage.

Gabriel half-expected Darkyn to trail, but the Dark One remained.

Breathing in the humid air, Gabriel assessed their location and the best way to approach the palace at the center of the underworld, where they needed to be. He had spent long enough repairing the defenses of the underworld to know where the best places to place scouts and sentries were. Common sense told him to go the path of least resistance.

The instincts of a master denied his place, however, wanted to chop a direct route through the forest and to slaughter those involved in betraying him and kidnapping his mate. As much as he hated agreeing with a demon, Darkyn was right. Gabriel needed to conquer his world once and for all.

Once he figured out how to do it without getting everyone around him killed.

"You up for a fight?" he asked Darkyn.

The demon drew two blades and spun them deftly in his hands.

"Thought so. No mercy, demon."

"It's not in my nature to grant such a thing." Darkyn almost spat the words.

Gabriel chuckled. *You really fucked up this time, Harmony.* Betraying one deity was worthy of a sentence in Hell. Betraying two?

If his own mate wasn't involved, Gabriel might've felt some remorse at the thought of turning over the traitorous death dealer to Darkyn.

Darkyn whirled the blades. The black band around his wrist caught Gabriel's attention. "I didn't know demons wore watches."

"It's not a *watch*. Why would an immortal give a shit about the passage of time?" Darkyn replied.

"So you're just accessorizing?"

The Dark One pinned him with a glare.

Gabriel almost smiled. Poking the lethal demon was dangerous – but entertaining.

"It's connected to Hell. Time passes differently in your under-world," Darkyn explained. "This tells me how much time my mate has left before starvation or bloodlust take her."

At once Gabriel felt guilty.

Sensing it, Darkyn offered a cold smile. "It also tells me how much longer your mate has until she loses her soul. That deal was made in Hell on Hell time."

Note to self: never talk to this bastard again.

"At least it matches your outfit," Gabriel managed.

The Dark One scowled. "Ever find the instruction manual you were looking for? The one to tell you how to do your job as Death?"

"Fuck you, Darkyn." Gabriel had forgotten the demon was able to read the mind of human-Deidre – and knew every secret or thought he'd ever shared with the woman who had once been his mate for a few weeks.

Gabriel's instincts were humming with warning. Everything from his heart to the human world was at stake, and he had nothing but his intuition, pure strength and flickers of mostly denied power to wrest back control of his underworld.

He couldn't let himself think about the two women whose lives hung in the balance or the fact that no Death in history had allowed the Dark One access to his realm. Likewise, he wasn't going to consider how many souls the rebelling death dealers had compromised or how much suffering the newly dead and supposed-to-be-dead were going through. He wasn't even going to *acknowledge* the stifling Immortal Code or how many rules he'd broken.

He was here to reclaim what was rightfully his, no matter what the cost. Only then would everything else fall into place.

"Mates, blood, fate," Darkyn's growl was quiet as he recited the only sacred rules the deities were expected to follow. "In the time-before-time, that's all there was. Right now, that's all there is."

Gabriel glanced at the demon. A full head smaller than his almost seven foot frame, Darkyn was deceptively underwhelming in person. But Gabriel knew how ruthless, aggressive and cunning the master strategist really was. With no conscience and battle prowess forged in the depths of Hell, the lean demon was one of the two greatest allies Gabriel could think of wanting at his side, and the greatest enemy he'd ever face.

I have a feeling he'll be both before we leave here, he thought.

Despite knowing Darkyn wasn't one to miss out on an opportunity to try to usurp the authority of a fellow deity, Gabriel almost felt a connection with the creature from the time-before-time, a demon hatched before any of the current realms existed. He wanted to think it was their mutual connection to the women trapped in the underworld, and ignore the fact that he'd begun to regard Darkyn in a different light since becoming a deity himself.

"Is this what the time-before-time was like?" he asked, unable to help his curiosity about the mysterious era.

Without answering, Darkyn started forward, towards the living forest of the underworld.

"How did it end?" Gabriel pressed.

The demon lord paused and faced him. The slow, evil smile on his face told Gabriel he didn't really want to know.

"The Dark One won," Darkyn replied.

You'll have to get through me first, Gabriel vowed silently. It wasn't the right time to let Darkyn provoke him, not when Gabriel wasn't able to access the power of the dead.

The stakes were higher than ever before. He pointed in the

direction they needed to go and breezed by the bristling demon, determined to take back what was rightfully his before anyone else lost their souls.

Chapter Two

The former goddess of the underworld, known as past-Death, crept down the corridor leading through the dungeon. It was the most ancient part of her palace, all that remained of the original structure created in the time-before-time. The rest of the palace had been rebuilt many times over, but the worn, uneven stones lining the floor, walls and ceiling here had seen the passing of every age since Death first began ruling its domain.

With her memories stripped by the Dark One, she found herself pausing every few steps, listening hard, concentrating harder, knowing there were memories being whispered by the walls, secrets she was no longer privileged enough to hear. The dungeon had remained intact for millions of years, rendering it the most powerful stronghold in the underworld.

It should mean something to her, something important. Something she'd know if she were still a deity or if the damned Dark One hadn't taken her memories.

The yellow-grey flames of ensconced torches located every ten steps or so along the corridor provided some light. Even weaker than the daylight in the underworld, there was more darkness in the hall than light despite the many torches.

She reached the end of the hallway and gazed at the solid wall. It was a dead end. This much she recalled when she set out walking. While concerned about escaping, she was more worried about knowing whether the death dealers had freed …

Them. She racked her mind once more and rested her fingertips on the stone wall. There was danger here, emanating from the two cells nearest the dead end, those with powerful wards capable of imprisoning a full deity. Gripping her head, she tried hard to recall why this was more important than escaping, whom she should fear more than the death dealers likely to kill her.

Why, as one of the most powerful deities in the universe, she had once felt threatened enough to lock up these two prisoners and leave them to rot for eternity in her dungeon.

"HOW THE FUCK did you do that?"

Past-Death's eyes snapped open, and she stared into the darkness overhead until she recalled where she was. Her head throbbed from the rough treatment of Harmony's loyal death-dealers. The dream of walking down the hallway remained vivid in her thoughts.

I'm lucky to be alive. She didn't know why she was. Becoming human had keyed her in on a few things she never knew as a deity, and one of them was that her death dealers despised the fact they were conscripted into working for her for millennia. Many of them didn't simply resent her; they *hated* her with a passion she'd never felt for anything.

Except maybe for Gabriel.

Despair and sadness spiraled through her at the thought of the man she'd always loved. By now, he had to hate her as much as any other death dealer. He'd been willing to give their relationship another chance, but this latest ordeal had to be one too many. No one could go through what she put him through and still love her.

The idea hurt her physically. She didn't understand her human body enough to know how that was possible. She'd never had aches and pains as a deity, either, and those made her feel even worse than the knowledge she was locked in her own dungeon.

She pushed herself up, not registering there was someone else in the dark cell until he spoke again.

"Really," came the male voice.

"Really what?" she responded, squinting into the corner from which the voice came.

The tall, lanky frame of a demon emerged into the weak light cast into the cell through the single window. His hair was blond, his teeth sharpened to points. He appeared gaunt. If the glow in his eyes was any indication, he was also half-starved.

Her whole body went rigid in fear, until she heard the rattle of the chains trapping him in the corner.

"Oh, good," she sighed. She hadn't realized how sore she was. It was the uneven stones she'd been passed out on as well as the mistreatment by Harmony's death dealers. "You can't eat me if you're chained."

The demon growled.

She propped herself up against the wall and relaxed, assessing her human body. Nothing hurt too badly, aside from the ache of her muscles and the grumble of her stomach. As much as she loved food, it was becoming really annoying to be so dependent upon it, more so here, where there was no ready supply.

"You can get out," the demon said. "How?"

"What?" She leveled a look on the disgusting creature. "You think I'd be sitting here if I could?"

"I saw you, Lunchmeat. You faded until you weren't there then came back."

Frowning, Past-Death reviewed the dream. She'd been walking down the hallway, but it obviously wasn't real if she was trapped in a cell.

"You have some sort of magic?" The demon was eyeing her in a combination of hunger and suspicion.

"No," she said with a snort. "You must've been hallucinating."

"I know what I saw."

I hate demons. She didn't respond. She'd tolerated demons as a deity, but being attacked by one as a human made her regret not permanently eradicating the vermin when she was a goddess. Unlike the demon, she wasn't chained and stretched to try to alleviate the cramping of her muscles.

There was a chance she was able to access some of Gabriel's magic. As the mate of a deity, she was supposed to have that ability. The only problem was that Gabriel wasn't able to access his own power consistently. The chance she could? Probably none.

The creature was staring at her with such longing, she stifled a tired laugh. He was clearly hungry.

"How long have you been here?" she asked.

"Forever," he replied angrily.

"No, really."

"In human time, perhaps a week. But time here is different. A month?"

"Could be a month or a second, depending," she mused, accustomed to the way time changed in the underworld. "Too long, either way."

"Long enough to know you have fallen from favor, cupcake." There was satisfaction in his voice.

"I'm not the one chained to a wall and left to starve," she shot back, irritated.

Another growl.

"Did I really disappear?" Past-Death rested her head against the wall and closed her eyes.

"Yes."

The idea was ridiculous, but humoring it, talking to the demon, kept her mind off the pain burrowing into her heart and her physical discomfort. The dream was solid in her mind. She was almost able to recall the feel of cool stone beneath her hands when she'd touched the dead end.

It was real enough. Then again, she'd been Death for thousands of years and had known every part of the palace at one point. How much was a dream, and how much was a memory resurfacing from wherever the Dark One had cast them?

Her thoughts returned to the two cells at the end of the corridor, and her frown deepened. The cells were aligned based on their ability to hold prisoners. Immortals and death dealers being punished for various reasons were kept in the cells nearest the entrance, those cells with the least amount of magic binding them. The cells at the end of the hallway contained the most powerful magic spells, capable of imprisoning full deities forever.

Behind doors made of colorful petrified wood, there were prisoners important enough for her to almost remember, even after having her memory wiped.

"Keep quiet, demon. I'm going to take a nap," she ordered.

"If you go again, bring me a snack. I'm starving," the demon added. "I'd settle for a child or really short person. I don't need a full meal."

"That's not going to happen."

He muttered under his breath.

Past-Death focused hard on imagining herself in the hallway once more. If she was able to leave the cell, she could find something equally as important: the soul she'd left Gabriel when she turned over the Underworld to him.

His soul. Stuck somewhere in the palace, because he hadn't known how important it was.

She started to doze and let herself fall into sleep, the thought of the demon in her cell disappearing.

Chapter Three

The human-turned-demon, Deidre, awoke groggily. Her fangs had dug into her lower lip while she slept, and she tasted blood. The light, metallic scent made her stomach roar in a way that left her a little ill at the reminder of her newfound status as a demon bride. Pushing herself up from the cold, uneven stone floor, she struggled to see far into the cell in the dim light streaming in from the single window overhead.

Harmony and her cronies had knocked them out upon entering Death's underworld. She assumed they were in a prison somewhere. It was impossible to see how wide the room was through the darkness, but it was shallow, with the back wall about ten feet from a door that looked like wood and shone like polished stone.

Petrified wood. It was beautiful, or would be, if she were anywhere other than a dungeon. She shifted to lean against the back wall of the cell. Her head was pounding and her stomach cramping. With a small groan, she wrapped her arms around her belly and leaned over.

"Cramps are the first sign."

It took her a moment to process the male's voice.

Deidre straightened and squinted into the dark side of the cell.

She heard chains rattle a moment before a lanky figure emerged far enough for her to see him. Tall and blond, the steely-eyed demon had fangs little longer than hers.

"Of what?" she asked.

"One of two things. You're either starving or spinning into bloodlust madness." He squatted, his distance from her enforced by the chains at his wrists and ankles. "My guess is starvation. You're a ... new demon."

"How do you know that?"

His gaze swept over her. "Let's just say I know who you were." He motioned to the side of the cell opposite him.

She looked, noticing the jeans-clad legs for the first time.

"We can eat her," he offered, licking his lips.

"No," she replied with a glare.

"Shame. I think a former deity would taste good. Like chicken. Or cake."

"If you'd ever eaten either of those, you'd know they're too different to be compared."

He shrugged.

"Who are you?"

"Jared. Humble servant of your mate." The demon shifted to sit on his knees and haunches. "*Hungry* humble servant of your mate. I was supposed to be keeping an eye on a certain death dealer and ended up getting caught."

The cramps subsided. Deidre released her breath then crawled on her hands and knees to the unconscious woman whose looks were identical to hers. With hands that shook, Deidre checked the pulse of the woman who put her smack dab in the middle of Hell.

"She's okay," she murmured and pushed blonde hair out of the sleeping woman's face.

"Mostly bruises."

Deidre felt for the trickle of magic belonging to her mate that was always present. For the first time since entering Hell, it was gone. Any connection to Darkyn was severed.

"I felt the door to Hell open," Jared said. "Someone came through."

Darkyn. Her breath caught. "Are you sure?"

"Yeah. Probably not the boss," Jared added glumly. "Death would never let him into his realm."

Not even to save me? She didn't want to know that answer. Gabriel was devoted to his duty, and she didn't think she was ready to know just how far from helping her that put him. Deidre shivered in the chilly air.

"I'm hungry, too. No one will know if we eat her," Jared tried again. "She'll be a delicious chicken cupcake."

"Chicken and cupcakes do not go together!" she snapped.

"What do we care? We drink blood."

"We're not going to eat her!"

"You're blood bound. If you're not out of here in a day or two, you'll be dead. Just a sip."

"That's Gabriel's mate!"

"She doesn't have to know if we have a little snack while she's out."

Darkyn won't leave me. Gabriel won't leave us. Deidre wrapped her arms around her knees and buried her face into the crook of one arm. There was no denying her hunger. The Dark One had turned her into a demon, though she retained the heart and mind of a human. Sucking blood from someone who was not her mate was completely out of the question.

"Don't count on it, demon," came the voice of Gabriel's mate. Past-Death moved away from the wall. She held her head.

"You okay?" Deidre asked.

Past-Death nodded then grimaced.

"Do you know where we are?"

The woman across from her lowered her hands and gazed around with pale blue eyes. "Dungeon under my palace. At least we're where we need to be."

Deidre raised an eyebrow. "You want to be here?"

"We have to find something before the death dealers do."

"We aren't in any position to escape, cupcake," Jared observed. "You weren't able to leave. It didn't work this time."

"No, it didn't." Past-Death sounded frustrated. "I think you're too hungry to see straight."

"You can fix that."

Deidre listened, not certain she wanted to know what they were talking about.

Past-Death glared at him before turning her attention to Deidre. "I do agree with him. You need blood. Darkyn wiped most of my memories before turning me loose in the human world, but I do know that a blood-bound demon won't last long without her mate."

"What about him?" Deidre asked automatically in concern. "Will he be okay?"

Past-Death eyed her. "Do you really care?"

Deidre rested her chin on her arms. When she arrived to Hell, she would've given anything to escape Darkyn. But he'd changed that over the course of a week, shown her that even the devil had the smallest capacity to care. He terrified her – and was the first Immortal or deity in the sick world she'd entered that showed her how to survive.

How can I love the devil? She caught herself thinking the question once more. It was baffling – but she couldn't deny what she felt every time she saw him or how much she ached for him. She'd fallen as much for him as for the sake of humanity. She had what no one else did – the ability to influence the devil into giving some kind of mercy, however small.

She was also the one person in the universe that he couldn't kill.

She breathed in the scent on her skin. She still smelled of him from their last round of lovemaking, and the memory of how he tasted made her stomach cramp up again.

"Owww," she mumbled, gripping it.

"You need blood," Past-Death advised.

Deidre shook her head. "I'm not a monster."

"Not a monster, but you *are* a demon," Jared pointed out. "If not the blood of a former deity, how about a demon's?"

"You're volunteering?"

"Let's just say, when your mate finds out about this, he'll be less likely to kill me for fucking up and ending up in prison."

"No. I just … ugh! I can't do it!" Deidre said. "I'll be fine. He'll find us or Gabriel will and then we'll go home."

Past-Death and the demon exchanged a look.

"Actually-" Jared started.

"Yes!" Past-Death all but yelled above him. "You're right, Deidre. They'll find us."

The way she said it made Deidre wish she had her magic, so she could tell if the former goddess was lying or not. Darkyn had assessed her greatest weakness to be that she was too trusting of others who lied and manipulated her. He gave her the ability to know when someone was trying as a defense mechanism.

That, too, was gone. She never thought she'd miss demon magic or blood.

Nibbling on her lip, she got as comfortable as possible with her back to one wall. Her gaze strayed to the demon, who was restlessly jiggling his chains. She'd seen the damage a creature like him could inflict and how even teenage demons like Darkyn's daughter were addicted to blood.

As far as she'd come with Darkyn, as much as she wanted to be with him, it scared her to think of a lifetime surrounded by demons.

"So … do you *have* to eat people?" she asked Jared.

"No. They taste the best, though, and Dark One doesn't give a shit who we eat."

Ugh. There were moments when she wasn't able to reconcile her lover with the devil. "What about kids? How are demon babies raised? On blood?"

"Kids?" Past-Death echoed. "You want to have kids with him?"

"I want to spend my life with him."

"So you think you can do the whole house, kids, college shit with the devil?"

I don't know. Deidre craved him, but she also feared what it meant to be a demon. She hadn't thought twice about having children. The idea was unusually … natural. As if it was supposed to be this way with her mate. But demon children and raising them on blood? *I can't do that!*

"Half-breeds can eat humans or human food," Jared supplied.

"I can barely think about tomorrow let alone what happens if things work out," Past-Death admitted.

Deidre wrapped her arms around her legs and rested her chin on her knees. She'd been thinking a lot about what life with the devil really meant since realizing she no longer had the urge to leave her mate.

"Maybe that's best," she murmured. "I mean, we don't know if I'll ever see him again. Thinking that far ahead … confuses me."

"Let's focus on getting out of here," past-Death rose and crossed to the door. "We have to find it." She pulled at the door then pushed before squatting to study the hinges.

"Find what?" Deidre asked, watching.

"Something that belongs to Gabriel. We have to get it before … they … do." Past-Death grunted as she pulled at a hinge.

"What could be … oh." Deidre recalled the last conversation she'd had with Gabriel. His soul was here somewhere, and if the traitors found it …

She didn't know what happened but assumed it was really bad.

"I know where it is," past-Death said. She straightened. "Dammit! They must've fixed the cell doors. I hadn't used this damn dungeon in forever, except for …" She cocked her head to the side, pensive.

"Except for what?" Jared asked warily. "What kind of beast would someone like *you* keep down here? The legendary underworld ogres?"

"They wouldn't fit in a dungeon."

"We've heard all kinds of rumors about the creatures of the underworld. Your trees are possessed, and most the animals are poisonous to demons." The demon sounded uneasy.

"Can't be worse than the monsters in Hell. Anyway, I can't remember. You can thank your master for that one, demon. But I kept something really bad down here." Past-Death blew out a frustrated breath. "Deidre, if either of us gets out of here, you need to go to the top floor, center wing. In my bedroom is a jewelry box. It's there."

Deidre glanced at the demon. He was listening too closely. "Umm should you say that in front of him?"

"It has a protective spell on it. Only a deity or his mate can see the box," Past-Death explained.

"Sweet, succulent human cupcake," Jared purred. His gaze was on past-Death, the light in his eyes inhuman.

"Wait a minute!" Deidre exclaimed, hopping to her feet. "I *know* you, don't I?"

Jared shrugged.

"You were in my apartment. With the demon pretending to be my ex …" she trailed off, recalling the night that changed her life. She'd been nearly eaten alive that night, only to be saved by Gabriel when she tried to jump off the building and landed in the Caribbean Sanctuary belonging to the Immortals. "That was one of the worst nights of my life." She blinked away tears. Even if she'd begun to tentatively accept her place in the mess past-Death created, she still hurt when she recalled how rocky her journey had been.

What was worse: where that journey ended. In a dungeon.

"Just doing my job," Jared said. "C'mere, cupcake. I'll make everything all right."

Past-Death rolled her eyes. "Can this get any worse? Stuck in a cell with a hungry demon."

"At least he's chained up," Deidre said, recovering. "They don't want us dead, or he wouldn't be."

"There are worse fates than death."

"No shit. I think I've seen that first hand!"

To her surprise, past-Death laughed.

The sound of the lock's bolt being drawn back made her scramble away from the door and join past-Death in the back of the cell. Deidre took her hand uncertainly, fearful of what was going to come through the door.

It swung open to reveal five forms, all of them she assessed to be death dealers.

"You. Come with me." The one in front ordered, pointing at her.

Deidre's breath caught. She glanced at past-Death and was more unsettled to see the fearful expression on the face of the woman who used to rule over the death dealers. Her heart pounding, she stepped forward to obey. The long, Grecian style dress she wore in Hell swished silently around her legs. It was held in place by a collar, the black material light as air and softer than silk. It brushed the tops of her feet.

She crossed her arms as she moved, glancing at the two in the cell behind her as she reached the door. Past-Death appeared scared, and the demon was frowning fiercely.

Both seemed to be aware of some danger Deidre couldn't even imagine. She was too new to the world of Immortals and deities to know what to expect or even why they wanted her, if not to manipulate Darkyn.

Can't be worse than Hell.

A death dealer snatched her arm and hauled her into the hallway. The door closed, and she looked at the fireless torches lining the hallway.

"Sexy," one of the death dealers purred.

New fear flooded her at the whisper. Darkyn had not only turned her into a demon, but into a sex-demon, one who didn't now how to control her power over men. Even Rhyn had warned her about being careful outside of Hell, where her influence was no longer dampened by the magic of Hell.

It's present here, like it was in the human world. Dread sank into her stomach. One of the two death dealers who cornered her in her apartment had been affected while the other was not. She didn't want to think about how much more danger she was in here, if half the death dealers weren't able to control their reactions to her. *Dammit, Darkyn! Why did you do this to me?*

She kept her eyes down and her senses as alert as possible.

One of them was bleeding. She smelled the blood, and it sent a tremor through her, along with another pang in her stomach.

"Come on," the death dealer holding her arm growled when she slowed.

Deidre gritted her teeth. Her mouth was watering. She could almost taste the blood in the air.

I'm not a monster. She was blood-mated to one demon only, and only his blood would satisfy her.

They led her into a room at the end of the hallway, at the base of the stairs. It wasn't a cell, but maybe a break room for guards. There was a petrified wood table in the middle, a few books, a vase of grey flowers. It was better lit by a combination of torches and windows. The guard released her. She rubbed her stomach and looked around.

"What am I doing here?" she asked. She half expected to see Harmony waiting for her.

"Stay here. Harmony wants a word." The door behind her closed.

Deidre faced it. She sat on the edge of the table. There was nothing she could eat or use for a weapon. She pulled her pink dyed hair over one shoulder, running her fingers through it nervously as she waited and poking her lower lip with her fangs.

Not two minutes passed before the door opened.

Deidre put the table between her and the entrance.

The moment Harmony set foot in the room, she felt a surge of both fear and anger rip through her. The beautiful redhead was flanked by two massive death dealers. She was armed, her green eyes piercing and her lean body that of a warrior.

"Darkyn's mate," Harmony said, studying her. "Never thought he'd want someone like you. Cowardly, mousy. Can't even fight."

I'm not a coward. Deidre was quiet, not wanting to provoke the death dealer.

"I need a blood sample," Harmony said. She motioned to the men beside her and withdrew a small vial from her pocket.

Deidre backed away from the large men but had nowhere to go. One grabbed her and wrapped his beefy arms around her, while the second positioned her arm and drew a knife. He cut across the vein in the underside elbow.

Expecting them to hack her to pieces, Deidre flinched and

watched the thick rivulet of her blood start down her arm. "Why?" she asked, confused.

"There are certain defenses in the underworld that only the invasion of demons can trigger." Harmony sat on the table and positioned the vial to collect her blood. "You being here isn't enough, so we're going to provoke them."

"And then what?"

"Don't worry, demoness. I'll keep you around as a bargaining tool. A little bit of pay back for that fucker of a mate of yours," Harmony responded.

"Darkyn will find a way to come for you, and Gabriel will never let you keep the underworld."

Harmony met her gaze, stiffening. "I'll just have to make sure they're both dead-dead before this is over."

Deidre debated responding then decided she didn't have much to lose. "That's the stupidest thing I've ever heard. *You* can't take down Gabriel and Darkyn."

Harmony slapped her.

Deidre licked away the drop of blood from her lips, head ringing and cheek hot.

"Look at what I've done, little demon. I've taken over the underworld. A human like Gabe can never become a god, or this place wouldn't be falling a part! I'm making things right. As soon as I'm Death, the Dark One will have to bargain with me as an equal. If there's anything left of you, I'll use it to bring him down," Harmony said, agitated yet resolved.

This is madness. Deidre listened, aware of how precarious her situation was.

"Once I kill Gabe, things will calm down. You'll see," Harmony added.

"So he's here?" Deidre asked.

"What do you think?"

I think he'll kick your ass.

Harmony sealed the vial and handed it to the death dealer who cut Deidre. "Take this to the ogres. See if it works." She moved towards the door. "Stay here, Deidre. I need a bucket of blood for the next one."

"Want a guard posted?" one of the men was looking at her a little too eagerly, a familiar glow in his gaze.

"This little mouse is too scared to run," Harmony replied.

Deidre's heart fell to her feet. She was already suffering from hunger; she didn't think losing half her blood was going to make it easier to escape. She wasn't a coward, either. How was a human supposed to act when she was alone and vulnerable in the world of Immortals and deities who didn't think twice about killing and harming those weaker than them?

All three left, and she sat on the table, fingers pressed to the wound in her arm. When the bleeding stopped, she stood and paced.

Five minutes passed then ten. Too anxious to sit still, she went to the door and placed her ear to it. She heard no sounds from outside that indicated Harmony had left a guard.

She tested the door. To her surprise, it opened.

"I'm not a coward, Harmony," she murmured, face warm with the idea she was trapped in a room that hadn't been locked.

Deidre peeked into the hallway. She heard and saw no one. The doors lining the dungeon were all closed, and she mentally kicked herself for not paying attention to how far they went. She wasn't able to trace her way back to the cell where past-Death and the demon were.

... go to the top floor, center wing. In my bedroom is a jewelry box. It's there.

What were the chances she'd make it out of the dungeon, let alone to the top floor of a place she'd never been before? Deidre debated, her heart racing at the thought of being caught.

Then again, what did she lose if they threw her right back here in a cell?

There are worse fates than death.

For once, she was grateful for her ignorance about the Immortal world. Something told her she didn't want to know what those fates were or how bad it could get. She definitely didn't want to be there when Harmony returned to drain the rest of her blood.

"I can do this," she whispered. "Find Gabriel's soul then come back here and rescue Deidre." *Not sure what to do about the demon, though.* Was she obligated to help him, because they were both demons? Or did she just leave him to his fate, knowing he'd probably end up trying to kill someone on the way out? "First things first. Up."

Choosing a direction, she crept down the hallway then jogged. At the end was a stairwell. She saw no guards but heard people talking in a room near the end of the hallway on the basement above the dungeon.

Lifting her skirts, Deidre ran on tiptoes up the winding stairwell. She paused at the first landing leading to the upper level of the two subfloors to peer down a long hallway before continuing up. The voices came again, this time from the stairs behind her.

She ran faster, bypassing the second landing without bothering to look for any sign of danger. The stairwell dead-ended at the fourth level, indicating the palace was three stories tall. The voices drifted off, as if the dealers had exited on the second floor.

Deidre crept down the hallway. There were muffled voices from behind the closed doors of the room nearest her, and she hurried by them and trotted down the hallway. Light poured in from windows in the center of the hallway, and she paused, startled by what she saw outside the palace.

The forest was alive. Deidre stared at the trees with snake-like branches. They hissed rather than rustled in a chilly breeze, and some large creature with six legs was disappearing into the brush. She'd thought it early morning by the weak sunlight and was surprised to see the two suns full up in the grey sky directly overhead.

And I thought Hell looked weird. She couldn't take her eyes off the tree branches. The sound of some strange birdcall came from the forest.

"I need to get out of here." She eased back from the window and started down the hallway again. There was only one intersection on this level in the middle of the long corridor.

Deidre turned down it, hoping she was following the directions.

This hallway was much shorter than the other, but it was lined by two doors on either side, spaced far a part, and one door at the other end.

She paused to listen then opened the door closest to her. It was a guest bedroom with everything covered in white sheets. Uncertain what past-Death's room would look like, she decided to open all the doors before beginning to search in depth.

The other three on either side were identical: massive chambers with sheets covering all the furniture. Deidre hurried to the door at the end of the hallway and opened it.

This one *felt* different, as if she should know it.

It was completely trashed, the petrified wood and stone furniture shattered, the white drapes and bedding shredded. Souls littered the floor, and she closed the door behind her, not at all certain what she sought.

Deidre nudged green gems aside with a grimace, guessing Gabriel's wasn't among them, or it would've been picked up already. She sought out the jewelry box. It was nowhere in sight. Deidre walked carefully through the soul-covered room and searched it once.

"Under the furniture?" She eyed a massive stone block that appeared to have formed the base of a dresser. There was no way she'd be able to lift the destroyed pieces of furniture.

Determined to find the soul before someone found her, she circled the room again, this time pausing in front of a door in the corner. A crumpled letter lay a few feet in front of it.

Come on in and meet me.

Her eyes went to the door. Was it just her or did the edges of the door glow unnaturally? What was behind it? Who was the note for?

"Not me," she said. She knelt to get a better look at the floor.

Jammed under a piece of stone that used to form the bedframe was a plain wooden jewelry box.

Deidre crossed to it. Dropping to her knees, she pushed and pulled it until it began moving then worked it free.

She opened it. The contents were simple: a green soul and a

tarnished ring, the only treasures the former deity had found worthy enough to safeguard.

"You've always loved him," she murmured with a touch of sadness. "I hope you can earn his love, Deidre." For a moment, she was struck by deep sorrow. There was a time when she found herself falling for Gabriel, too, only to have the rug yanked out from under her.

Darkyn was a different kind of man, a hard one to understand, and an almost impossible one to love. Yet she found herself yearning to be in his arms again, to see the look on his face she'd witnessed only once, when he last made love to her. He did love her in as much as a demon could. She was as much a part of him as he was of her, and the absence of his magic and presence made her ache with hollowness.

And hunger. The cramps were getting worse. Grimacing in pain, Deidre doubled over and gripped her stomach. She waited for the pain to pass before breathing deeply.

Voices in the hallway made her gaze fly up. She listened, assessing this was a search party by the shouts going back and forth. Deidre snatched Gabriel's soul and closed the box. She pushed it under the bed and rose, tucking the soul into the small pouch hidden in her dress to join the green gem Fate gave her before she was snatched by death dealers.

She went to the door and pressed her ear to it.

The shouts grew quiet. She waited a moment then eased the door open.

The large form of a death dealer was on the other side.

Deidre panicked and tried to slam the door closed.

He jammed his foot between door and frame then shoved it open.

Deidre stumbled back.

Darkyn! She screamed silently, knowing her mate wasn't able to hear her this time.

The death dealer snatched her arm and yanked her into the hallway.

"Got her!" he shouted, hauling her to the main corridor. "Tell Harmony!"

Three other death dealers were in the hallway lined with windows. One darted away at the order while the other two lingered, eyes on her.

Deidre saw the flare of lust in both their gazes. She dropped her gaze, trying to be as still and quiet as possible to keep from drawing more attention.

"This is Darkyn's little demon," one said. "Where were you going, little demon?" He lifted her chin to see her eyes.

The light of lust burned brightly.

Deidre swallowed hard. "Nowhere. Just looking for a way out."

"Pretty little thing," the other said, joining them. "Looks like she needs a lesson in not running from us."

"Harmony wants her alive," the man holding her said.

"Fucking scum of the earth demons." One spat.

The man holding her chin was peering at her with an unhealthy level of curiosity. "This is the mate of the Dark One. If she can handle him, she can handle us."

Shit. Deidre glanced up at the man holding her arm, expecting him to be somewhat immune.

The same gleam was in his eyes.

"Harmony won't want you to hurt me," she managed.

"Listen to that purr," one said with a grin at the other.

"My mate will slaughter you," she added with more firmness. "Do you want to know what he did to the last man who touched me?"

The three glanced at one another.

"You really think you'll leave this place, little demon?" the first asked. "Death can't even get into the underworld. He'd never let the Dark One in."

This statement seemed to help them make up their minds. The three shifted closer.

Deidre wrenched away from the man holding her arm and began backing away. "Do you really want to take the chance he never finds out? It's only an eternity of your souls in his hands."

"I'll take that chance for a taste of you."

Deidre's heels hit the wall. Panic flared within her. Darkyn wasn't able to help her this time, and neither was Gabriel.

"Don't do this," she whispered. "Please."

"She's begging for it." One of them laughed. "Your wish is about to be granted, little demon. We'll do you up right then throw you to the beast."

God, please, if you're there. Save me, just this once.

Chapter Four

"Time does not pass in Hell as it does here."

Gabriel glanced over his shoulder at Darkyn, who was eyeing the sky with suspicion. The suns had gone down and popped back up in less than two hours only to remain in the same place in the sky for over ten hours. The night − if it could be called such − lasted less than forty-five minutes. A full day had passed while a second day seemed stuck.

"You get used to it." Gabriel almost smiled at the demon lord's discomfort and faced forward again, focused on the trail at his feet. The Underworld wasn't resisting his plunge into the forests, but it wasn't exactly helping much, either. As he expected, branches and bushes shifted to create a path for him to walk.

But they moved so slowly, he'd thought twice about abandoning the path and using his sword to hack through the trees.

"These are not real trees," Darkyn added, smashing the hilt of his dagger into a snake-like branch that got too close.

"The trees are a defense mechanism. Normally, they tear demons a part, limb from limb," Gabriel said. "Show a little respect, Darkyn. They're being relatively civil with you."

The demon lord growled from deep in his chest. He was a

generally tolerable companion, one who remained quiet, for the most part, and helped push stubborn bushes or branches out of the path when needed.

In truth, Gabriel wasn't certain why the trees hadn't attacked the demon. It was nothing he had done. He'd tried asking the trees for help getting to the palace. The most they were willing to do was grudgingly move out of the way – and it was clear they weren't happy about it. If they wanted to tear Darkyn a part, they weren't about to listen to Gabriel telling them to stop.

As if aware of his resentment, the path disappeared.

Gabriel looked up and froze.

The trees had formed a wall before him, blocking the direct route to the palace completely.

"You –" Darkyn started.

"Don't say a fucking word, demon," Gabriel snapped, frustrated. "How the fuck do I get to where I need to be when my own underworld won't listen to me?" He placed his hands on his hips, unable to imagine his predecessors running into any sort of problems like he had since taking over as Death. "Is it because I'm of human origin? Are you working for Harmony now?" The words were directed at the wall of foliage before them.

Darkyn's dark chuckle was amused. "Baby god, can you not see what is before you?"

Gabriel clenched his teeth, resisting the urge to smash a fist into the face of the creature who had helped upheave his life.

"Your domain lives. It talks, and when you fail to listen, it will demand," the Dark One said. "This path is not the right one."

"It's the most direct route!"

"You misunderstand. This path is not the one your underworld wishes you to take."

Gabriel absorbed the words, not wanting to listen to the latest deity telling him he was doing it wrong. No part of him wanted to ask Darkyn of all creatures to help him understand.

Facing Darkyn, he was about to pull his sword free and start hacking, when he saw the Dark One studying him.

"What?" he growled.

"I have an observation to make about you of human birth." Darkyn tilted his head to the side. He was pale beneath his tanned skin, a sign of the strain he faced without his bloodmate. "Your ego is that of a god while your understanding is that of a child."

"Great. Thanks." Gabriel blew out a breath. "You're saying I'm too stubborn to ask you for help."

"Correct."

Gabriel turned his gaze to the sky, thinking hard. It was hard to deny that the Dark One had been around longer than any deity or Immortal Gabriel knew, and even harder to admit that he might know a thing or two that Gabriel needed.

"I don't trust you," he said.

"It is not about trust. It is about winning. You do not owe me trust, and I do not owe you assistance. But right now, we have somewhere to be and no way to get there, if you do not use what I know."

It felt like a trap. Given what Gabriel knew of the Dark One, he doubted any information was going to be provided free of charge, even if Darkyn didn't ask for anything in return.

Yet.

"Okay. What am I missing?" he asked grudgingly.

"Your underworld is telling you something. Ask the right question, and it will answer."

"You think my underworld is … what? Going to talk to me?"

"In its own way, yes. Every deity with a domain has a bond to his realm. It's what allows him to reign," Darkyn said. "You clearly have no bond, and yet, your underworld is trying to guide you."

"It's not this way with Hell?"

"Hell is strictly won or lost, passed from victor to victor. Your domain has patience. Almost like it chooses you, instead of you winning the right to rule." Darkyn was eyeing another branch that snaked too close.

"I imagine it would've chosen someone not of human origin, if what everyone keeps telling me is true," Gabriel grunted.

"Does that matter now?" Darkyn snapped.

No. Gabriel faced the wall of branches and trees. He'd spent millennia in the underworld among the trees beneath the grey sky. He existed as another living being among the forest and now, he was the master. His relationship with his surroundings had changed. The trees realized it long before the idea occurred to him.

Your domain lives.

He knew there was life in the underworld, but he'd never quite thought of the collective life as being one large, living creature, one capable of *choosing* who ruled it. It was almost too farfetched for him to accept.

Then again, Fate had claimed the same about the Immortal Codes that were flexible to deities and no one else.

"Sometimes the souls best equipped are those of human origin," Darkyn added. "Frail creatures whose lives are over in a blink. Nonetheless, your kind has its occasional uses."

Gabriel regarded the Dark One with quiet amusement. "She surprised you. You didn't expect to keep her around, did you?"

"Not at first." Darkyn was licking one of his fangs almost absently. "She is like your underworld. Different."

"That they are."

"Ask it the right question."

"The right question." Gabriel faced off with the wall of foliage. "You don't want me to take this path," he said. "What path should I take?"

The trees and three-winged birds overlooking him went still. An eerie silence fell, and he sensed the magic of the underworld around him, shifting and moving, even if it remained out of his reach.

It's talking. Or maybe, thinking. His underworld was debating what to do and what to tell him.

Gabriel shivered. He'd never looked at the underworld the way the deity Fate taught him to view the Immortal Code: as a person, one that could be negotiated with. At most, he'd thought of his home as being something obligated to obey him, because of his position as Death.

The silence passed, and a trail opened to his left, cutting through the forest for at least a mile.

"It's not the way to the palace," he murmured, frowning.

"Your domain will not betray its master."

Gabriel took a step towards the new pathway, his insides twisting in concern for those trapped with the death dealers. "I'm trusting you," he said under his breath to his surroundings.

Gabriel quickened to a trot and then a run. The forest made no move to stop him again, instead opening the trail far ahead, a sign he was meant to go the way it wanted him to.

Darkyn trailed, running at his heels.

The trail wound through low hills and dips that ran along the eastern floor of the forest, through small fields and larger clearings, in a direction Gabriel soon recognized.

The forest was taking him to the Lake of Souls, located not too far from the palace. His pace quickened when he realized where the underworld led him, and he began to worry something else had gone wrong with the souls that hadn't yet bled through to the lakes in the human world.

The green glow above the lake – visible during daylight or night – was soon ahead.

Branches snaked into his path and blocked the trail, a sign he needed to slow.

Gabriel did so and unsheathed his sword. The branches left the path.

"I smell them," Darkyn said quietly, drawing abreast of him. His long daggers were drawn. "Four."

"Easy. Where are they?"

The demon lifted his nose to the air and breathed in deeply. "Three right, one left at the mouth of the trail."

"I'll take the three," Gabriel said, cold fury resurfacing at the idea of confronting those who betrayed him and put the entire world in danger.

Darkyn slapped the flat of one dagger across his chest as he started forward. "I need the food."

Gabriel hesitated at the ragged note in the demon lord's voice. Unwilling to pity the source of evil in the universe, he at least acknowledged that he needed the Dark One at full strength if they were to take on a few hundred death dealers.

"Bon appetit," he responded.

Darkyn started forward at a trot.

Gabriel gave him a head start of a few feet, not about to cross swords with the blood maddened demon yet. Darkyn launched out of the forest without a second look, throwing himself into the midst of the three death dealers huddled together, talking.

With a quick glance at his surroundings, Gabriel ignored the sounds of a demon slaughtering and eating his prey and instead, faced the remaining death dealer.

The man's eyes widened, and he raised his sword too late.

Gabriel severed his head with one stroke of his massive sword and sheathed the weapon before kneeling beside the body.

"One fate for traitors," he said, feeling no sympathy whatsoever for the betrayer.

Green fog lifted from the dead dealer's body, swirling and snaking towards Gabriel.

He held out his hand. A small emerald – the Immortal's soul – formed in the palm of his hand. There was a time when he'd regret having to punish a traitor, when it hurt him as much as the soul to crush it and send it to an eternity in Hell.

That time was gone, another shred of his humanity taken when his mate and Deidre were kidnapped. If anything, he hesitated only because he doubted he had too many threads of humanity left in him.

I never want to be the Death she was. Yet the more he learned, he more he realized why she'd done some of what she did, and how little alike they truly were. Past-Death had known no mercy or kindness as a goddess and viewed his as weaknesses. She executed her duty with cold devotion. While he recognized her effectiveness, he also knew that she lacked empathy and respect for those she served.

It was human to provide those that failed the first time a second chance to make things right. Deities didn't understand the concept. He was a mix of both, capable of giving second chances or stripping that right away.

Gabriel debated for a moment. He'd shown leniency on the human plane to those death dealers that sought to betray him. A quick death and not sending their souls to Hell was the only second chance he'd offer.

But here … in his underworld, knowing what he did about Harmony's plan to kidnap his mate and Deidre, he didn't feel anywhere near as generous. There were times when second chances weren't warranted, and the heartless wrath of a god was.

Protecting those who deserved his compassion from those who did not was his priority now. The lines were more cleanly drawn in the underworld. He could no longer view punishing his former colleagues with regret for what they'd done to disrupt the balance of life and death and endanger so many innocent souls.

He roused himself and stood. The sounds of Darkyn gorging on the bodies of the Immortals ceased, and Gabriel turned.

Looks like someone exploded. None of the remaining pieces of the three men were in chunks larger than the size of his hand, and blood was splattered everywhere, dripping down Darkyn's chin and coating the ground at his feet.

"This is yours," Gabriel said and tossed him the soul.

Darkyn caught it.

Gabriel went to the edge of the Lake of Souls and crouched beside it, gazing into the waters. Souls rested in the bottom or floated in currents – billions, perhaps trillions, of them. The leaking of souls into the mortal plane was unprecedented. While the relative percentage was small, it never should've been possible for the souls to bleed over in the first place. He risked the souls being captured by the Dark One or other souleaters who might want the emeralds for reasons other than to protect the dead.

The waters were still. The last time he'd been here, the Lake was bubbling and boiling, in clear turmoil.

Wind swept through the trees. Rather than the slithering of snakelike branches, he heard something different, faint, sad. A mournful call, the unified sorrow of the trees and millions of life forms that existed in the underworld.

"You're in pain," he whispered, startled to realize his home was capable of emotion as well as communicating with him.

Gabriel shifted to his knees, concerned, and placed his hands in the shallow waters nearest him. The suffering was here, too, and he closed his eyes to listen.

The Lake's murmur was soft and just as sad, the currents tickling his fingers and conveying tiny shocks of pain. He struggled to understand fully what the Lake wanted him to know, why the underworld had brought him here. The heart of the underworld, the Lake was the source of Death's power and magic. Its walls were cracked, and it was losing souls daily, despite his efforts to seal the cracks in the human world.

Help. The Lake mourned the loss of its souls and experienced pain at the cracked plane between the underworld and mortal realm.

Gabriel withdrew his hands from the waters, overwhelmed by the emotions of his underworld. He sat for a long moment, raw and desperate, not at all certain what to do to comfort the heartbroken lake and troubled souls it contained or even if he could do anything.

Darkyn knelt beside him and stretched for the water.

"No." Gabriel caught his wrist. "The trees may not object to you being here, but the Lake will fuck you up. It does not tolerate demons, even now."

Darkyn growled but lowered his hand, his hungry gaze on the souls in the waters.

Gabriel knew Darkyn's intention of stealing souls to make an army of undead. They'd been competing at finding souls in the mortal world for weeks now. He reminded himself to be careful about how much he revealed to the demon with neither morals nor empathy.

"Why did it bring us here?" the Dark One demanded. He stood and began pacing restlessly.

"Blood didn't take the edge off?"

"No matter how much I drink, I will still starve."

Gabriel said nothing, attention returning to the lake. The demon's words stirred his sense of urgency, the one he was trying hard to repress so he could think clearly and understand the message his home was trying to give him. One thought didn't allow him to dismiss the demon the way he wished to: that of the human Deidre starving alongside her mate.

"It's hurt. Sad. Broken," he responded. "Does Hell have a heart?"

"Heart?" The Dark One snorted. "Hell has a source of power, one that must remain intact."

"How does it work?"

Darkyn stared at him. "How? It simply does. It's the origin of my power, a gathering of all the depravity that exists in the universe, like the lake is yours."

"What would you do if it cracked?"

"Fix it."

Gabriel suppressed his sarcastic response. The demon was agitated, as if realizing how fucked he was now that normal blood didn't quell his appetite.

He's not the only one fucked. Gabriel wiped his face. "The harder I fight, the worse things get."

"Then stop fighting."

"And what? Watch the world crumble?"

"You don't get it, baby god." There was a mocking note in Darkyn's voice, one that made heat climb up Gabriel's neck. "How do I explain to someone with your puny, human understanding of the world?"

Gabriel shook his head, ready to ignore whatever the Dark One planned on saying to bait him next.

"Your mate. Would you talk to her or treat her the way you do the underworld?"

Gabriel twisted, eyeing the creature.

Darkyn was licking one of his fangs again, focus on the forest, his head tilted as if he was listening.

"No," Gabriel said after he assessed that the demon wasn't fucking with him. "Would you?"

"A mate has to be won over and then, there is nothing she won't do for you."

"You said she had to be conquered before."

"Same thing."

"You see only the end game, don't you? I'm looking at the how."

"If you do your part, you only need be concerned with the end game."

I know I fucked that part up already. Gabriel grimaced. "So do your part and talk to the domain like it's a partner rather than a servant."

"Just a suggestion. I don't give a fuck what you do, except that the end game here concerns me."

"Can I ask you something?" Gabriel stood.

"I grow tired of this."

"I know. One question and I'll stop talking to you. Trust me, I'd rather not fucking deal with you, either."

Darkyn waited.

"Do you care for her?" Gabriel asked quietly. "I know demons can't love and human emotion is very different. But in as much as a demon can, do you care for her?"

"I think my mate is the least of your concerns, Gabriel." A dangerous note was on Darkyn's tone.

Gabriel nodded. Given what he knew of the Dark One, he sensed it was the only response he'd ever get from the demon on the topic. He'd hit a nerve, which was enough to tell him that what he suspected was true. Some part of Darkyn was here for a reason other than he was hungry.

The knowledge soothed away some of Gabriel's lingering guilt about Deidre ending up in Hell. He knew what she felt, that she had fallen for her mate. Now, he was certain it wasn't a one-way road.

The sound of someone making his way through the forest broke the tension between them.

Darkyn whirled, and Gabriel drew a dagger.

Rhyn emerged, sweating and grinning, his cheek slashed from a weapon's strike. Darkyn replaced his daggers and paced. Rhyn trotted towards them.

"Good news and bad news," the half-demon said cheerfully. "Good news: we've got allies here. Not many, but they might help."

"Good," Gabriel said, pleased to know he had some loyal dealers left. "Bad news?"

"There are about three hundred dealers in the palace." Rhyn

swatted at a branch that got too close. "More in the barracks and scattered in the forest."

"I'm ready." Darkyn started towards the trees.

Gabriel shared a glance with Rhyn. "Darkyn, we need a better plan than taking on three hundred trained death dealers."

The Dark One ignored him. The trees separated for him, creating a path in the direction of the palace.

"Guess we're doing this the demon way," Rhyn said with a wink. "We got this, Gabe. Easy."

Gabriel said nothing, unable to shake the sense he needed to figure out something more about the Lake, like how to help it. He was missing the key to unlocking his power. Was it here?

"We need to return here once we've got things under control," he said, walking with Rhyn towards the path.

"Darkyn's not gonna last too much longer without going crazy," Rhyn said softly, eyes on the demon ahead of them.

"I know." Gabriel's hands twitched with the instinct to grab his sword. "He'll probably explode and take everyone with him."

"That'd be my guess."

"We'll be ready. As long as his mate is —" Gabriel smashed into a sudden wall of foliage and stopped, staring up at it.

"What the fuck?" Rhyn asked from the other side. "You there?"

Gabriel cursed and wiped his face. "Go with Darkyn," he snapped. "Apparently, the Lake has some business with me."

"Hmmm."

Gabriel didn't need to see his best friend's face to know Rhyn was likely plotting a few different ways to take out Darkyn. The two had a brittle relationship, mainly because Darkyn had tried for months to kidnap Rhyn's mate and steal their unborn daughter.

"Play nice," Gabriel called. "For my sake. When this is over, you can go back to trying to kill each other."

"All right." Rhyn didn't sound pleased. "Find us when the trees let you."

Gabriel glared at the foliage. The sounds of Rhyn moving away faded, and Gabriel retreated back to the lake, furious.

"Tell me what the fuck you want," he ordered the Lake. "You know we don't have time for this shit!"

The moment the words escaped, he recalled what Darkyn had said.

There were days when he wanted to talk to past-Death like this, but he never would. He didn't quite feel calm enough to take a gentler approach.

Gabriel tried to leave by a different direction only for the wall to pop up again.

Reining in his anger, he went back to the Lake and sat beside it. It took a few minutes for his frustration to subside, and he shook his shoulders free.

"I'm here and I'm listening," he said with difficulty. "Right now, my friends are in danger. I need you to talk to me. Somehow."

He waited.

The Lake said nothing.

Gabriel sat back against a boulder. Every part of his being screamed at him to leave, to help Rhyn and his mate and Deidre.

But he stayed. Darkyn's wise words circulated through his emotions, assuring him that his domain was trying to work with him, not make his life worse. The underworld wanted to show him something, and he was going to figure out what.

Hopefully without losing those I care about.

———

"THERE'S over a ninety nine percent chance that you'll need a succession plan before this is over."

Darkyn ignored the deity Fate, intent on getting as close as possible to the palace to assess what it'd take to conquer Harmony's forces. He had nothing but cold dispassion for the living forest and its lost master. With a healthy respect for Gabriel as Death's top assassin, Darkyn was waiting for the newly turned god to realize his power and end the disorder of his domain.

A rebellion in Hell would be met with nothing short of the

crushing might of Hell. It would *never* be permitted to grow this far out of control.

"Same chance I gave you of ever getting your mate," Fate added.

"So clearly you've been wrong before. You will be again," Darkyn snapped.

"Except you knew coming here that something was going to happen."

Darkyn paused and turned to face the deity with golden skin and eyes of ever-changing hues. "It's always a risk."

"There's more to lose this time."

"I don't lose."

"Except for the first time you tried to takeover Hell and then the human world," Fate pointed out.

Darkyn had never understood how his father, Zamon, was on such good terms with a creature that knew neither discipline, war nor self-sacrifice for the sake of victory. He barely tolerated the godling and did so only because it was generally expected that deities gave each other the courtesy of speaking before acting. He'd seen how his own mate was played by Fate and had more reason not to trust the youthful deity.

But they were at odds over more than his mate. Fate had Sight much deeper than Darkyn's, which meant the plans the Dark One had been hatching since he first emerged from the bowels of Hell were a matter of record with Fate rather than speculation like they were with the other deities.

"I may have sensed it," he allowed. "What is it to you, Fate, if I die-dead here?"

"Just looking at chains of events. I would like very much for it to stick, for you never to return," Fate replied. "No chain of events supports that, unfortunately."

"Good."

"Not good. Some of these chains leave you ... and us ... worse off."

Darkyn spun and began walking once more. The urge to decapitate the deity was unusually strong, a sign of how affected he was by his hunger. Self-control and limitless violence were two of his trade-marks. Anywhere else, he'd remind Fate of the latter. Here, his energy was better saved and spent where it was needed, not wasted on Fate.

"Do you trust her?"

Fate's question made him halt once more.

There were two things Darkyn knew better than the twisted depths of his own soul: one, that he was meant to become the most powerful ruler Hell had ever known. The second: his mate was meant to rule at his side, despite being the opposite of him in every way. Deidre was his, even more so than Hell, their bond unbreak-able by any force in the universe. The human with the pure heart and soft voice had started out a novelty, one he hadn't planned on keeping around. That changed the night the marking of their blood bond appeared on her, when he realized there was something he wanted more than he'd ever wanted Hell.

Born into a time of chaos and after hundreds of thousands of years of unrest, he'd found something he never fathomed existed: a home. A partner. A moment of peace. The only place and time in all of the world where he didn't have to carry weapons, because there was no threat, no danger, nothing but her soft skin, complete submission, blood of honey and the stamina of twenty demonesses.

"A creature like you does not deserve to discuss her," he growled, edgy and restless.

"I ask, because you need to give some serious thought about succession. Things can get bad, if you don't. Or they can get terri-ble. Not your kind of terrible, I'm afraid."

"I trust no one."

"Wrong answer. Pick someone. Anyone. Because you may make it out of here in some form, but you'll lose Hell in the process, if you don't think this through."

It almost sounded like Fate was doing him a favor. Yet Darkyn new better than to assume this was the case. If anything, whatever it was that Fate Saw warranted a warning to the creature Fate liked least.

It wasn't a good omen.

"I didn't spend my lifetime conquering Hell to surrender it now," he said.

"As always, I respect your decision."

He sensed Fate disappear without looking. Darkyn started forward again, shrewd mind working quickly. Wisdom honed over thousands of years knew better than to ignore the advice. His priority, however, was his mate. It wouldn't matter who took over Hell, if she died before he reached her.

He glanced at the countdown displayed in the hourglass strapped to his wrist. He was running out of time. Worse – so was she. His bloodmate was strong, but nothing would prevent her from falling into the madness of bloodlust, if he didn't find her soon.

Darkyn quickened his pace to a run through the possessed forest of the underworld. The underworld and human realms would never recover from the wrath of his demon mercy if he returned from the underworld alone.

Chapter Five

Past-Death walked down the hallway once more and paused between the last two doors in the dungeon. She looked from one to the other. There was no way to know what was behind them without opening them.

Which she wasn't about to do. The deity in her had been scared enough to lock these … creatures up. With no power whatsoever, she wasn't stupid enough to open the doors.

Then again, she wasn't convinced this wasn't a dream. What harm might come of opening a door in a dream?

She pressed her hands to one of them, willing the dungeon to tell her its secrets.

Nothing.

At least they're still locked. It was the best sign she was about to get on this trip.

If this was real, she needed to find Deidre, who had been taken from their cell. Past-Death didn't want to guess what grudge Harmony bore the Dark One or his mate, but she didn't think Deidre's treatment here was going to be handled with kid gloves. The fear and urgency she'd experienced watching Deidre being taken was strong in the dream, the urgency real.

She owed it to the woman to try to help her.

Turning, past-Death made her way down the corridor and paused in front of the door to the cell she shared with Jared. The petrified wood was cool beneath her fingertips, and she dwelled on the sensations, not understanding how this was neither a dream nor reality. It wasn't possible for her to be outside her cell, and yet, it felt so real …

Shaking her head, she continued down the corridor, feeling the familiar sense of safety granted a person who knew they were in a dream. Most of the cell doors were open, the depths empty. A few closer to the entrance were closed, a sign Harmony had tossed others into the dungeon.

Past-Death hesitated at the bottom of the stairwell ascending from the dungeon into the newer of the two basements. There were guards there, she knew, or should be. There had always been guards stationed on the subfloor between the palace proper and the dungeon during her time. If there were keys, she'd be able to find them.

Like this is real. She hesitated, not convinced there was any use in tracking down keys or Deidre in a dream.

The demon seemed to think she was capable of leaving the cell. Not that she'd ever trust the word of a demon but …

Stranger things had happened. Being alone in her dream was rather peaceful, the stressors of her human life absent.

No harm in looking, especially if I find Deidre. Past-Death trailed one hand against the wall of the stairwell the way she used to whenever she visited the dungeon.

Back when the palace was hers.

She paused halfway up, remorse and longing settling deep inside her, along with a sense of loss. She'd given up everything to become human and then fucked it all up. If she hadn't left her position as Death, the underworld and all its souls would be safe. Gabriel wouldn't be locked out.

They wouldn't be a part, and she wouldn't be sad, because she'd lost him.

Anger flared within her, and she shook her head to clear the emotions. She wasn't certain how to handle the human feelings. Lately, they'd imprisoned her as much as the death dealers, made her incapable of acting, left her spinning out of control.

As a deity, she had never experienced these sensations. As a human who recalled what it was like to be an all-powerful deity, she hated being … vulnerable. Weak. Emotional.

Past-Death continued up the stairs to the second subfloor. It was lined with a few more rooms, some used by her predecessors as torture rooms, as well as guard quarters and supply rooms.

Voices drifted from a doorway on her right, and she stopped at the edge of the door, fear fluttering through her at the thought of discovery.

It's just a dream, she reminded herself.

With a deep breath, past-Death entered the room boldly.

The three death dealers acting as guards didn't look up at her entrance, and she relaxed. They certainly appeared to be very real, but they weren't able to see her.

Are all human dreams like this? Past-Death studied the three. She knew them. They were junior death dealers, from the same crop as Harmony, who hadn't been around for more than five hundred years. She had hand selected every grim reaper she ever conscripted.

How had she missed the warning signs that these particular trained assassins wanted to usurp Death? She'd read their souls when she brought them in. They at least started out as loyal. Was it simply what Gabriel had tried to tell her on many occasions? That compelling the elite killers to work for her was wronging them? The duty was an honorable one, to claim and protect the souls of humans, Immortals and other deities alike. Who would not want to perform such a sacred duty?

Not that it matters now. She looked away from the three. Whatever mistakes she made in the past, they were done with. Not only that, but Gabriel was smart enough to avoid the same issues she'd somehow created over the years.

Past-Death's gaze fell to the ancient keys to dungeon cells that hung on one wall. They were in two rows, arranged in the same order that the cells were in, with each key having a duplicate. Doubting anything she did in a dream was going to carryover when she awoke, she plucked up two keys: one to her cell and the other to one of the two cells at the end of the hallway.

Now to find Deidre. She clutched the keys in her hand, wracking her thoughts to figure out where Harmony might've taken the mate of the Dark One.

Two dealers passed by the doorway. One called a greeting into the three and ducked inside, snatching the key to a cell before leaving.

Past-Death stepped away to give him room, unable to shake the instinct that tried to tell her once more that this dream was too real. She trailed the death dealer into the hallway and caught a glimpse of the second one carrying a limp body dressed in black.

Human Deidre. The woman was bloodied, bruised and unconscious, her pink hair spilling over the arm of the death dealer carrying her.

Past-Death gasped, at once swinging to the other end and gratefully reminding herself that this was a dream and nothing else. Because human Deidre appeared dead, or close to it, and the guards had grabbed the key to one of the two cells past-Death knew contained something very dangerous, very wrong.

She started to follow them, a sense of dread heavy in her stomach.

"HEY, cupcake. You're doing it again."

Past-Death was jarred awake. It was a little easier this time, though her headache was worse. She pushed herself into a sit, uncertain how she slept at all on the uncomfortable floor.

"Where did you go?" Jared asked with too much interest.

"Why does it matter?" Past-Death grumbled. She glanced towards the corner where the human Deidre had been. "How long was I out?"

"Time here confuses me."

The weak light of the sun was still visible through the window.

Reassured no more than a couple of hours had passed, she wiped her face and went over the dream in her head once more.

Something terrible had happened to Deidre. The idea of the human suffering even more made her nauseated, guilty to the point she wanted to cry.

"I smell blood," Jared said, tilting his head. His eyes flared with light. As if able to see through the walls, he followed the movement of someone by the cell with his gaze. "Demon blood."

Weird timing. If she were still in her dream, she'd be following the death dealers past the cell right about now. Past-Death listened hard for the sounds of someone moving down the hallway. The walls were too thick.

"You're certain?" she asked.

"I'm starving. I know food when I smell it."

Past-Death rose to cross to the door and see if she was able to hear anything. The moment she stood, the tinkle of something falling from her lap onto the floor drew her attention.

"You did bring something back," Jared said, interested. "Keys?"

"Don't be ridiculous," she snapped. She squatted beside the sounds and reached down.

She gasped.

"What?" Jared snapped.

"It can't be." Past-Death picked up the two keys from her dream. "It just … can't be."

"Keys." Jared laughed.

"If these are real …" Past-Death's gaze went to the door and what she knew was beyond.

The death dealers were throwing a near-dead human Deidre into a cell with a creature past-Death didn't remember.

She crossed to the door with the keys, only to curse. The door could only be opened from the outside using the key.

"I have to get out of here!" she said, slapping the door with her hands.

"*We*, cupcake," the demon corrected.

"No way in hell, demon!"

"How far do you think you'll get on your own, even if you leave the cell?" he challenged.

Past-Death paced, half-listening. Her mind was reeling with the idea of human Deidre being fed to some sort of beast, overwhelming her ability to think about what to do.

"If your demon friend is hurt, I can give her my blood," Jared added.

"Shut up!" she snapped. "You're a demon! You'll kill me and then her!"

"I can't kill her, or the boss won't be happy," he replied. "And I'm willing to make you a deal."

She rolled her eyes and sat down, needing to calm her soaring thoughts in order to make sense of any of them. Another drawback of being human: emotions had a way of clouding every logical thought she had.

She needed to escape, grab Deidre, find Gabriel's soul and leave. There were so many obstacles between her and those simple goals: finding Gabriel and Deidre, the death dealers, the fact she had to calm down considerably if she wanted to disappear into the dream state again and unlock her own door.

"I can fight," Jared said. "I will slaughter any death dealer in our path. Free me, and I'll help you get out of here."

"I can't leave her." Past-Death struggled with her thoughts and feelings. Her head was pounding harder, and she didn't understand why.

"Then we escape with her," Jared said easily. "I collect a bounty for returning her to the Dark One, and you don't get eaten."

It was bad when a demon started making sense. She debated his offer, knowing how demons revered deals and the power of bargaining among the deities.

"So you don't eat me - ever. You help me escape and rescue Darkyn's mate," she said, thinking carefully. "I'll free you in exchange for your help."

"I get to eat the death dealers."

"I don't care, Jared. As long as you don't hurt or eat me and

Deidre. No unwritten terms. No modifications or substitutions or creative execution of timeframes."

"Very well." He didn't sound pleased.

She didn't care. Clutching the keys in one hand, past-Death rose and approached him, hand outstretched.

"Deal," she said.

"Deal." He touched her fist with a fingertip, the only part of him capable of reaching her while chained.

"Okay. Now to get out of here. I need to sleep again." She paced instead. "My head just won't stop!" Frustrated, she gripped her temples.

"I'd be happy to knock you out."

"Is it painful?"

"Hopefully."

"No thanks. I've got to do this. I ruled over the Underworld for tens of thousands of years. I can will my stupid human brain to let me think." With a deep breath, past-Death stretched out on the uncomfortable floor. "Don't wake me up this time, demon. If you see me fade, leave me alone."

"Just bring me an arm or leg. I'm so fucking hungry."

She ignored him and closed her eyes, her thoughts going to the soul in her bedchamber first. She needed to secure Gabriel's soul, before it was too late, and then find the keys to Jared's chains.

Come on! Dreamwalk.

"Cupcake, should that be happening?" If not for the odd note in the demon's voice, past-Death would've ignored him.

She cracked open one eye to see what was going on. He was pointing at her feet. She checked to make sure the keys were in her hand still then lowered her arm and looked around her.

A faint grey haze had begun to engulf her, starting at her feet. It didn't touch her skin but snaked up her body, swallowing her in a soft fog. It was clingy and cool, like walking through the shadow world that existed in the place between portals.

"Oh, fuck," she mumbled. Her heart felt as if it stopped, and she forgot to breathe. "I was out more than two hours, wasn't I?"

Jared shrugged, unconcerned. "The suns went down and came back up, but not much time passed."

"Another day in Hell time must've passed." Past-Death closed her eyes.

"What is it?"

My soul. She didn't answer him out loud. The one-week deal she'd made with human Deidre was over.

She'd lost. Gabriel didn't love her, and time was up. Her soul belonged to the Dark One's mate, who lay dying in a cell down the hall.

Tears rose, and past-Death swallowed hard. If she'd been outside of the underworld, there would be no problem. Her soul would become Deidre's only upon death.

But here, in Death's underworld, there were no barriers between living and dead like those that existed in the mortal plane. She was able to live here eternally – with or without a soul.

The process of her soul leaving was painless. It was the realization that she'd failed to win over Gabriel that felt like it was killing her from the inside out. For a moment, she wasn't sure why she needed to leave the cell at all. She'd failed to win the man she loved, failed as a human in every way possible.

She'd once retained the knowledge of the universe, the secrets of deities and stories of every life that ever existed. She'd given up everything, her power, her control – and lost everything she cared about. Nothing prepared her for being human.

Nothing prepared her for failing.

Past-Death leaned against the wall. Tears trickled down her cheeks. Rather than the emotional mess she expected to be, she was numb.

She'd risked everything and lost. The hole growing inside her ached, and she stared blankly into the dark corner opposite her. What did humans do when they ran out of options? Die-dead? Run away? Try again? How did they live like this? What purpose was living in the shadow of someone she loved and spending the rest of her long days knowing she'd driven him away?

How much worse was she as a human that Gabriel had been able to love her when she was a goddess?

Trust. He'd told her it took time to build. Humans by nature didn't have as much time as others in the universe. How much time was required? Two weeks? A month? She'd never bothered to count months before, because they passed in a blink to a deity.

But now, a month seemed like forever, if it mattered at all at this point.

Without the one week bet hanging over her head, she doubted there was any need to rush. If trust took a month, then she only had to figure out one thing: How did she wake up each day knowing she'd lost Gabriel?

Or … did she wake up each day hoping to win back a small part of him?

Or was it simply too late?

Desperation made her hurt from the inside out.

It was the most painful thing she was able to imagine. She'd reached a dead end, one that none of her manipulations and power could help her walk away from.

She had to earn her way out of this mess the way a human did, and she didn't know where or how to begin.

Maybe by saving Deidre. I owe her that much.

Her life as a human may have been wasted, but she could still do whatever was possible to help those she'd wronged. It meant putting aside her agony and despair to save the woman she'd condemned to Hell a week before and expecting the world to continue to hate her, no matter what good she tried to do now. It was too late for her. It wasn't too late for Deidre.

Past-Death drew a shaky breath. Tears leaked from the corners of her eyes, and she focused on calming her mind enough to put herself into the strange sleep, the only way to reach Deidre.

It didn't matter what happened once they escaped. She had nothing to look forward to, and her soul officially belonged in Hell.

I'm not meant to live through this ordeal. The stark realization made her sick to her stomach. Deidre deserved better. Gabriel deserved better. Past-Death caused chaos and hurt everywhere she went.

The cool stone felt good against her hot head, and she focused on falling again into the vivid sleep. It was getting easier to enter it, and she gripped the keys tightly as the sense of floating into darkness returned.

When she was able to register where she was, she stood facing the doors of one of the two cells she knew should never be opened.

This time, she had no choice. She had to save Deidre.

Past-Death shook the thoughts free. She turned to face one door, safe in her dream-like state from whatever was inside. If the death dealers weren't able to see her when she stood in front of them, she was able to take a peek at what horrible monster she'd imprisoned before surrendering her position as a deity. She could free Deidre and then run back to her own cell and open it.

Not like I have anything to lose at this point. Her heart fluttered fast. Unlocking the door, she pushed it open only far enough to peer into the cell.

It appeared to be empty.

Surprised, Past-Death pushed it open a little farther until she was able to see three of the corners.

Nothing.

She entered the cell and looked around critically. There was no sign of Deidre or anyone else. A thick, undisturbed layer of dust coated the floor.

"It's the wrong fucking key." Past-Death's panic stirred. She'd grabbed one key but not the other, which meant Deidre was in the other cell.

Why would she have secured a cell with no prisoner? Especially one of those at this end of the hallway? Or had the death dealers freed the occupant?

"I know someone was here," she muttered.

Past-Death opened the door wider to illuminate the cell as much as possible. A small, blue gem winked as the faint light from the hallway caught it. Sensing no one in the cell, she crossed to the flicker of light and was able to make out something else.

Bones. Whoever had been in the cell was long dead.

She picked up the blue gem. The emerald-shaped gem rested in a band of metal that appeared to be a cross between brass and gold in color. By its size, it belonged to a man. It seemed rather plain and like it could use a good cleaning. If it held any sort of magic, if it was more than a trinket, she wasn't able to tell.

"I guess you're no longer a threat," she said, uncertain if she should be relieved or disturbed to know she had unwittingly left him to die. "Rest in peace, whoever you are."

It didn't seem right to take away the only possession belonging to the dead man. Past-Death set the ring down and left, locking the cell once more.

Sensing someone behind her, she whirled.

No one was present. She stood perfectly still, waiting for some sign that someone else was there, perhaps someone as invisible as her.

She thought she saw the flames of the nearest torch flicker, as if someone had passed by it, and the flicker of blue. A full minute passed with no other sign.

"I really hope I didn't just let something out," she murmured. Her gaze fell to the door across the hall. With a jolt, she realized she needed the other key in order to rescue Deidre.

Past-Death hurried down the hallway towards the stairs, intent on grabbing the key and helping Deidre before something worse happened.

Chapter Six

Deidre hit the cold stone floor and heard the cell door slam shut. Too weak to move, she lay still. The world was one of haziness and blood – her blood. She smelled it, and it rendered her hungry and made her want to sob. But her energy was gone, along with her voice, depleted after all her screaming and struggling.

Her lower body was shredded from what the men had done, her upper body bruised and broken from their blows when she'd tried to fight them. Her head had a gash in it, her vision blurry and her nose broken and streaming blood into her mouth and down her throat.

No more pain. It was there, at the corner of her mind, waiting for the barrier that left her numb to fall. After a lifetime with a brain tumor and more surgeries than she cared to count, she'd learned how to separate herself from the pain.

As long as she didn't move. Agony would tear down the brittle wall between her and her sanity if she did. Tears trickled out of her eyes to the cold floor.

What did I do to deserve any of this? It wasn't the first time she'd thought such a thing, but it was the first time she wasn't able to find any sort of silver lining in her situation. There was no demon lord to save her, and no matter what she said, she hadn't been able to convince her attackers to take mercy on her.

It was light outside. She'd spent several lifetimes screaming or so it felt like, but she was able to see the suns through the window, high in the sky. Either little time had passed at all or an entire day had.

Chains rattled from one side of the cell, drawing her attention away from her thoughts. Even if Jared wanted to eat her, she wasn't able to move. From her peripheral, she glimpsed a dark shape inching towards her cautiously from the direction of the corner.

She closed her eyes, destroyed by the idea that she was about to be eaten by a demon after the disaster that was her life. A sob escaped her, and it hurt so bad, she swallowed the next one.

"Demon?" It was a woman's voice that came from the other prisoner in her cell.

Deidre opened her eyes and blinked way tears.

The face that hovered over hers wasn't anyone she recognized. The young woman had long, curly dark red hair, skin made pale from her imprisonment, and a round face. Her eyes were those of a deity: flashing black then white then every color in between. They stopped at dark purple and stayed that color.

"Are you a demon?" she asked in a rough whisper, as if she hadn't spoken to anyone in a long time.

"Yes." Deidre mouthed the word, unable to talk.

"You are hurt."

"I want to die."

The woman raised an eyebrow. "That is not for you to decide."

Deidre started to cry again, and pain filtered through her. "I can't live ... like this ... anymore. My life is hell."

"Then you want her to balance you," the redhead murmured. "If you are worthy of death, you will die. If you are worthy of life, you will live. If you are worthy of some other state, you will have it."

I don't care anymore! Deidre wanted to scream.

"Do you wish to be balanced?"

"I don't understand."

"Just say yes, and it will be over, in some form."

"Yes."

"Take her hand."

It took all of Deidre's resolve to raise her hand to the one the redhead held out. Deidre took her soft, cool hand and closed her eyes, unable to help the sobs that escaped her. She went over the past few weeks in her mind, from finding out she was terminal to meeting Gabriel to entering the sick world of the Immortals. One choice, and she'd ended up in Hell, the mate of the Dark One, and a demon. For a split second, she'd found a place at his side, only to end up here.

My life was a waste.

"Please let me die!" she begged again, body seizing uncontrollably from pain and sorrow.

"Almost done," the woman replied.

Deidre clenched her hand. The wall between her mind and the pain slipped away, and she started to slide into dark agony. Just when she thought she was about to lose herself for good, the pain stopped. Broken bones grew together and the tears and bruises in her skin healed themselves. The inhuman movement of her body fixing itself scared her as much as the pain.

The woman released her.

Deidre lay still, terrified to move in case the pain returned.

"It is not your time to die," the woman said.

The scent of blood was on her clothing still, and she was weak. She examined the forearm that had been broken in the light. It was healed, along with every other part of her. She gazed at herself, unable to recall fully what happened to her. She'd been taken out of the cell with past-Death, wandered up to discover Gabriel's soul and then … blank.

Without the memories, she no longer had the urge to jump off a cliff and end it all.

Deidre pushed herself up, beyond relieved when the movement caused no pain whatsoever. "This is amazing. How did you do that?" Deidre asked.

The woman had crept back into the shadowy corner of the cell. She settled, the rattling of her chains quieting.

"*You* did that," came the quiet response.

"Pretty sure I would've killed myself, if I had the ability," Deidre said. She wiped tears from her face. "How can I heal without my mate?"

"The Dark One." It was a scoff. "The Great Imbalance!"

Deidre shifted to sit comfortably, exhausted. Her stomach was hurting again, and she gritted her teeth until the discomfort was gone.

"You had the ability to heal but slowly. I sped it up," the goddess said, calming.

"You're a deity, aren't you?" Deidre asked. "Fate has eyes like yours."

"I know. My brother comes to visit me sometimes."

"He's your brother and won't help you out?"

"Long story," the deity in the corner sighed.

I guess I shouldn't be surprised, Deidre thought. If Fate was one thing, it was unpredictable. "Why are you locked up down here in the first place?"

"Deity business is messy."

Deidre smiled faintly. "I know."

"You are the first demon she hasn't killed."

"She?" Deidre's brow furrowed. "You mean you?"

"Yes."

"I'm not a ... well ... I wasn't *born* a demon."

"They're hatched. You were born," the woman corrected absently. "She saw that, though. You were turned."

"Saw?" Deidre waited.

"When you are balanced, all is revealed, from the moment you entered the world until the moment you take her hand. The content of your soul is hers to examine."

Deidre shivered at the explanation. "Who are you?"

"The Great Balancer, the scales of justice in a world that does not like it."

"Do you have a name?"

"Karma." The word was a grunt.

Oh, shit. Deidre didn't speak for a long moment. She'd met the devil, Death, and Fate. Never in her imagination did she believe Karma was real, too.

"Your scales are severely off balance. You have experience such evil and so little joy." Karma's voice grew soft. "Karma cannot let that injustice stand."

"So you didn't kill me because I've been tortured and killed a couple times over?" Deidre asked, recovering herself. "Kinda seems like ending it all would be a better alternative."

"Not the way it works."

Deities and their bizarre rules. "I never thought I'd like ... I mean, meet ... um, like to meet Karma."

"No one *likes* Karma, but everyone is supposed to meet her."

Deidre felt a little bad at the quiet note in the deity's voice. "They can't if you're here. Why are you in prison?"

"Immortals and deities don't like Karma either."

Deidre gave a husky laugh, startled by the disgruntled note in the woman's voice, as if the deity was truly hurt that no one liked her.

"Who put you here? Harmony?"

"*You* did. At least, your deity form did. Captured Karma a thousand years ago. Karma has been forgotten here and Immortals and deities have run amok, doing as they please."

"Wow." Deidre's thoughts went to the Dark One. "What do you do to those who are securely on the side of evil?"

"She can do little to deities, aside from a temporary re-balancing. Immortals and humans, Karma can balance as needed. Whatever they have earned, she delivers."

"And I earned being healed?"

"You have nothing to fear from Karma. You cannot commit the amount of evil needed to balance your scales in your lifetime."

"That's good. Just confirms what I know about my life." Deidre drew her knees to her chest. "It's fucked up, isn't it?"

"Yes."

At least in Hell, she had Darkyn, and no one would dream of fucking with him or his mate. Deidre felt tears rise for a different reason. "I miss him," she murmured. "I shouldn't, but I do."

"He's your blood mate. You *should*, even if he didn't earn you."

Who knew she'd find Karma supportive? There was a time when she'd cursed the deity several times a day.

"He will come for you," Karma added. "He is already here."

"What?" Deidre's breath caught. "Is that possible?"

"She can always feel great imbalances from a distance. He is here."

Hope bubbled within her breast. Deidre wasn't certain what she felt at the news: relief, exhilaration, fear.

Hunger that made her mouth water and the furnace at the pit of her stomach blaze to life.

"We need to get out of here," she said and stood, pacing.

"*We?* You would take Karma?" Karma asked curiously.

"Yes, I would take Kar – you. I would take *you*." Deidre caught herself. "Any reason why you refer to yourself in the third person?"

"Bored. Karma started it to entertain her and then forgot how not to talk about Karma like that."

We'll fix that later. "Where do you want to go? Do you have a … uh, domain or home like Death and the Dark One?"

"No. She has nothing."

"Okay then. Let's focus on leaving."

"She needs out of these." The chains rattled. "You need to avoid the death dealers, lest you end up half-dead at Karma's feet again."

Deidre shivered. "Not that I want to, but why can't I remember what happened?"

"You earned peace of mind. Karma can separate the memories that cause you the most pain."

Do I thank her or freak out she messed with my mind? Deidre shook her head. "We need keys."

"Or … search the corner opposite her. They toss Immortals in every once in a while for her to balance."

Deidre's gaze lingered on the dark shape of the deity. She'd learned a lot about how shifty the gods and goddesses of the universe were. She'd learned never to trust them, too.

She saved my life. After a brief hesitation, she went to the corner and knelt, feeling around with her hands until she found something.

Deidre leaned back and moved it into the light, dropping it with a startled yelp.

"That's a femur!" she exclaimed.

"Should be femurs for five over there. Not that they'll help," Karma said, unconcerned.

"I'll never understand how dismissive you deities are of life!"

"Not dismissive. We understand it differently."

Whatever that means. Cringing, Deidre patted the ground delicately. Her fingers grazed another bone, then a pile of them. She ordered herself not to get sick and sorted through them. Bile rose in her throat at the thought of the dead Immortals piled like rocks in a corner of a cell.

She began to understand why the Immortals and Deities didn't want Karma loose, too. If this was evidence of what she did to most …

"Anything?" Karma called.

"Bones mostly."

"Knives, tools, belt buckles?"

Deidre grimaced then grabbed an armful and moved to the lighted part of the cell. She deposited it.

"I think I'm gonna be sick," she said, gazing down at the bones. "You did this?"

"They earned it."

"They hurt people or something?"

"These were death dealers who didn't obey Harmony. She tossed them down here. They hurt many people outside the confines of their sworn duties. When they were balanced, they were found lacking. It cost them their lives and souls."

Unwilling to dwell too long on what Karma did to them, Deidre drew a few deep breaths then knelt and began searching for something the deity in the corner could use.

"What happens if we run across someone once we escape?" she asked.

"They must agree to be balanced."

"Or … what?"

"Karma kills."

Her eyes flew up. She could almost see Karma shrug.

"Okay. Let's just try not to kill anyone helping us escape. Can we do that?" Deidre asked.

"If you help Karma out of here, she will be indebted to you."

Don't sound too disappointed. "I don't know about a tool, but this um, bone looks like it was fractured to a point. Will that work?" She had no idea what part of the body the bone in her hand came from.

"She can try it."

"*I* can try it," Deidre corrected absently.

"I can try it," Karma echoed.

Deidre walked to Karma's corner and handed it to her. "I'll keep looking."

She continued searching and listened to the sound of the deity jamming and manipulating the chains. Deidre brought another two piles of bones to the center of the room. The effort – and idea of touching human-like remains – left her lightheaded. She took a break for a moment before sifting through the remains.

"Karma freed one lock!" Karma said in excitement. "But the bone is broken."

"I think I found another." Deidre pulled free another one with a jagged point. She slid it across the floor to the deity. "I'm not seeing tools."

"We need more bones," Karma said with a grunt. "Karma can make that happen."

"Um ... I don't think that's the best alternative. I'll keep looking for bones."

"Half the Immortals in this palace have it coming."

"Do you and Death ever scuffle over territory?"

"Sometimes, like when Karma balances someone whose name hasn't been written on the list. Past-Death put her ... me here for it."

"Who did you judge?"

"Gabriel."

Deidre gasped. "But he's ... *Gabriel.* You wanted to kill him and past-Death wouldn't let you?"

"Kill? No. He didn't earn death." There was a silence as Karma worked on her bonds. "Past-Death pissed off Karma again. Karma figured out how to get back at her and was going to tell Gabriel what past-Death was doing to manipulate his future."

"And she imprisoned you." Deidre grew thoughtful.

"My brother turned me in. Said I needed to learn not to fuck with deities."

"That sucks. So you knew exactly who I was when I was brought in."

"Yes." The sound of something snapping drew a curse from the deity.

Deidre flinched at the thought of desecrating the remains of anyone, even an Immortal serving Harmony.

"More bones," Karma ordered.

Deidre sought out two more and took them to the corner. Suddenly, Karma's movements stopped.

"They're coming," she whispered. "They want to see what Karma did to you."

"No!" Deidre said, starting to panic. Her eyes went to the bones in the center of the room. "I'm not going with them again!"

"Toss your clothing on the bones. They won't dare come close enough to be balanced."

Deidre obeyed without question and went to the dark corner with the rest of the bones.

"Three." Karma's count was accompanied by the snap of another bone.

Deidre heard the sound of a death dealer rapping on a door nearby. Huddled in the corner naked, she prayed he bought their bait. She didn't remember her last run in with them, but she could guess what happened by the blood on her body and where the dress was torn.

"Keep silent," Karma warned. "Karma is almost free."

I'm not sure that's a good thing, Deidre thought. Was she unleashing a plague of a different kind by freeing Karma?

The door creaked open.

Deidre held her breath and prayed. Karma's rattling stopped.

A death dealer entered, his gaze on the pile of bones and the black dress in the middle of the cell.

"Shit," he muttered. "Harmony needed her alive."

"You should've thought of that before you tossed her in here," Karma said calmly. "Karma saw what you all did to her. If Karma knows, the Dark One will."

There was a pause then an alarmed, "He'll know you killed her, too!"

"Well … maybe Karma didn't."

The death dealer froze in place, gaze riveted to the corner where Karma was. "Is she alive or not?"

"She's in the corner."

"You don't let anyone live."

"Then go tell Harmony she's dead."

The death dealer shifted feet. Deidre could almost see his thoughts: face certain death here or certain death if he disobeyed Harmony. Who did he fear more?

He took a step into the room.

"If you're alive say something," he ordered.

"I am," Deidre said quietly.

The death dealer inched forward then stopped and retreated to the doorway, leaning out to reach the nearest torch in the hall.

"Come here," Karma whispered. "Quickly!"

Deidre scampered across the bones to the corner where the deity was. Karma took her hands and pulled her closer. Deidre dropped beside her, noticing how warm she was compared to the cold air and stone floor of the dungeon.

The death dealer stepped back into the cell. She covered her chest self-consciously when his torch lit up the corner.

"Close your eyes," Karma said for her ears only. "Demon or not, Karma has seen your soul. You are not ready yet to see this."

The words filled Deidre with fear. She hugged her knees to her chest and squeezed her eyes closed, ducking her head.

"She is alive!" the death dealer exclaimed. "Come with me, demon!"

"Come and get her," Karma challenged.

He said nothing.

"What can Karma do? She is chained, remember?"

The sounds of the dealer's feet scuffing on the stone floor started then stopped. Deidre's jaw clenched. She waited to hear the sounds of his horrible death or for Karma's manacles rattling.

The silence stretched on. Deidre resisted the urge to look, afraid of what she'd see if she did.

"Here." Karma's word was accompanied by the brush of the Hell dress across Deidre's arms. "You can look now."

Deidre lifted her head tentatively. She saw nothing of the death dealer. The door to their cell yawned open, and Karma stood in the middle of the cell.

Pulling on her clothing quickly, Deidre hurried to the door. She didn't look too hard at the rest of the cell, not wanting to see what her newest ally was capable of.

Peering around the corner, she stepped into the vacant hallway.

Karma followed. Deidre faced her, startled by the woman's appearance in the full light. Her dark auburn hair fell almost to her waist. Her eyes were large and deep set, her taller, fuller frame gaunt and dressed in a worn gown from an era Deidre wasn't able to iden-tify. Karma was beautiful in an earthy way and innocent looking, her appearance nothing like what Deidre expected. Like every other deity she had met, Karma appeared deceptively young, in her early twenties, aside from her inhuman eyes.

"It's nice to meet you," Deidre said. "And thank you."

"Her inevitable pleasure."

I'll never get used to dealing with deities.

Karma offered Deidre her hand. Deidre took it, and the deity whirled and ran down the hallway in the opposite direction that Deidre had gone earlier. She was about to object and tell Karma about past-Death being imprisoned when Karma gasped.

"Be still!"

"What? What's wrong?" Deidre started to turn.

Karma yanked her to face her and released her hand. "Be still!"

Deidre froze, listening, afraid there were guards sneaking up behind her or some other danger she couldn't sense.

"You have a new soul." Karma appeared puzzled, her gaze

taking in the space around Deidre.

Confused, Deidre looked down. She saw the strange fog form at her feet and frowned. "I don't understand. What is it?"

She took Deidre's hand and held it out, palm up. "Look."

The fog snaked around Deidre's hand and centered in her palm, coalescing and solidifying until it took on the shape of an emerald with the coloring of smoky quartz. There was no mistaking what it was despite the unusual color.

Uncomfortable with the idea of holding souls, Deidre hesitated then closed her fist around it. Once, a soul had spilled out its story all at once to her, terrifying her at the intensity and tragedy of its tale. She braced herself for a similar experience, only for the soul to remain quiet.

"Whose is it?" she asked.

An image of past-Death formed in her head briefly before sliding away.

"Oh, god," she whispered, looking again at the smoky gem. "It's been a week."

"You have more." Karma was eyeing the pouch at her waist, the one protected by magic that kept the death dealers from seeing it. "Karma senses souls, one her brother gave you."

Deidre opened the pouch and dropped past-Death's soul into it. She stared at it, bitterly realizing Gabriel's soul rested beside his mate's. The third gem was given to her by Fate before she was kidnapped by the death dealers. She didn't know whose it was, but Fate seemed to think she needed it.

"I guess I'm collecting them." A pang of hurt went through her at the thought of past-Death losing her soul. It meant Gabriel wasn't the only person who was heartbroken. *At least I have it and not Darkyn or someone who won't protect it.*

"Karma thinks we should go."

"I have to free my friend."

"Karma thinks this isn't a good idea now." The deity's gaze was on the cell across the hall from hers. "She –"

"I," Deidre corrected again.

"– I thinks we should go quickly."

Deidre roused herself from the sad thoughts about the gems in her pouch. She tied it closed and wiped her eyes.

"Is there something wrong?" she asked, following Karma's look.

"Very." Karma rested a hand on the petrified wood of the door of the closed cell. "Karma ... *I* feels a great imbalance."

"Darkyn?" Deidre's hope surged.

"Not *the* Great Imbalance. Karma thinks ..." the deity drifted off.

"Does Karma ... I mean, do you know what it is?"

"No." Her tone was softer. "Karma feels sad. You are sad?"

"I am."

"Karma reflects the emotions of those around her. Sadness is Karma's least favorite feeling. Please refrain from sadness."

Deidre managed a smile at the note of pleading in the deity's voice. "I'll try not to, if you can stop referring to yourself in the third person. It's kind of weird."

"Very well. Karma ... I will tries. We need to escape."

"No. I have to help someone," Deidre said firmly.

Karma cocked her head to the side. "We cannot stay in the dungeon."

"This place is huge. We can hide somewhere, find the key to my friend's cell and free her."

"I thinks your plan is not thorough enough to be successful."

"Do you have a better idea?"

"Not yet." Karma's gaze went down the hallway. "There is someone else here."

Deidre spun, panic flying through her at the thought of being cornered again by death dealers. She almost sighed. There was no one in sight. Spooked anyway, she let Karma take her hand and start down the hallway.

"Come on. I'm not being trapped again. We are both in rags and we need to rest before we face death dealers for keys to the cell," Karma said firmly.

Deidre went, her gaze lingering on the cell she'd shared with past-Death.

Hang in there. I'll be back.

Chapter Seven

T*hey're leaving without me.*

Past-Death watched the two women race down the hallway towards the stairs. Not that she expected Deidre to come back for her after all they'd been through, but ...

It stung knowing she was being left behind by everyone. She hadn't been able to find the key to the other door and had stalked a few different death dealers to look for it only to come up empty handed.

Everything hurts. Past-Death stood frozen in the hallway for a long moment, until they disappeared up the stairs. She blinked away tears that shouldn't be possible to feel in a dream.

Trudging down the hallway, she traced their steps, this time stopping in the room with the guards to find the key to the demon's chains. After grabbing it, she continued into the main palace. Deidre was safe and well, and there was nothing past-Death was able to do if she didn't escape her cell first.

The path was so familiar, her feet went where they needed to while she spent time in her thoughts, trying to quell the pain of betrayal and loneliness.

Only when she stood outside her old bedchamber did she blink back into reality. Opening the door, past-Death paused to take in the destruction with no small amount of horror. This room had been hers for thousands of years. Seeing it in such disarray weighed her heart down even more.

She made her way around the mess, seeking out the jewelry box where she knew the soul she sought was located. Her gaze strayed to the door in the corner, the one containing secrets only the deity Death was permitted to know. The sight of it made her think of Gabriel, which made her even sadder.

Pushing away the emotions, she focused instead on doing what little good she was able to. Kneeling beside the jewelry box, she opened it, only to find the soul gone.

"Shit!"

The dream began to wobble and fade. If the soul wasn't here, who had found it? How did she recover it, before Harmony figured out how to fuck over Gabriel for good?

How did she tell Gabriel she'd failed him yet again? Frustration and sorrow made her eyes water. She was turning out to be the worst human ever.

Past-Death snatched the content of the box, a tarnished ring, before she was yanked out of the dream once more.

"HEY, CUPCAKE."

She groaned, gripping her head hard. The headache was pulsing, her general fatigue adding to the discomfort. She expected to feel the same sense of betrayal she did in the dream and was relieved that she was … numb.

"You were out for another day," Jared called. "I'm tired of this fucking place!"

"If you were more patient, I might've brought you a snack," she retorted.

"Really?" he asked. "What was it? A head? Goblet of blood?"

Past-Death rolled her eyes and sat carefully. "Shit. I gotta go back under to get us out of here."

"This is taking forever. Why didn't you just free us last time?"

"Shut up, demon." She gripped her temples. "You're not the only one who's hungry and sick of this cell." She slid the ring she'd grabbed onto her finger and placed his keys beside her, unwilling to reveal she had them until they had a way out. It was suicide to be stuck in a cell with a starving demon.

"Don't wake me up this time," she ordered and lay back down again. "Got it?"

Jared grumbled in response.

It was easier to fall into the dream state this time, possibly because she was too exhausted to resist it. Standing outside her cell, she drew a deep breath and paused before unlocking the door.

Was she really going to trust a demon to get her out of here? True, demons were sworn to uphold their deals. But since becoming human, since taking on the frail body of a mortal, she'd found herself hesitating when she never would have as a goddess.

I'm afraid of almost everything. She hated that about herself. As a deity, the universe had feared her. And now the reverse was true. She was sick of it yet too aware of how vulnerable and weak a human truly was.

"If my twin was brave enough to make a deal with the Dark One, I can work with a demon," she murmured.

Past-Death unlocked the door and pushed it open.

Almost immediately, she was sucked back into her body.

"EXCELLENT, CUPCAKE!" Jared all but shouted.

Past-Death took a minute to assess her headache and decided she'd just have to deal with it. Jared was rattling his chains, and she feared what happened if Harmony's men were drawn by the demon's noise.

"I need funnel cake," she mumbled and sat up.

Her head pulsed, and her stomach growled.

"Free me!"

Past-Death eyed the demon as she rose. "You better not make me regret this, demon."

"We have a deal," he said. "Stay out of my way until I find a snack."

It wasn't the reassurance she sought, but she tossed him the keys to his chains. "There are at least two death dealers on the floor above us. Is that enough to keep you from gnawing off one of my arms?"

"Maybe."

She heard the chains fall to the ground. Despite his hunger, the demon moved faster than she could track with her human eyes.

He gripped her neck and shoved her into the wall behind her, the dark depths of his eyes boring into hers. He was salivating, his fangs dripping, his lean body pressing her into the wall.

Past-Death gasped, too startled by his speed and burst of strength to move.

"Do not forget this, human," the demon growled. "If you think to betray me to your mate, I will -"

"I ... won't!" she gasped.

"I know who you are and what you've spent the past thousands of years doing."

"I swear it. No harm will come to you from me or my mate, so long as you keep your word about helping me."

The demon studied and then released her, stepping away.

"If you hadn't noticed, I'm not who I was anymore," she added with some bitterness.

"You are always who you are," he scoffed. "You just aren't immortal anymore." He faced the door. "Stay here."

Past-Death released the breath she was holding. For a split second, she'd seen her death at the hands of a hungry demon. Adrenaline managed to clear most of her headache, and she sagged against the wall.

Despite all the sleep, she didn't feel rested, perhaps from the effort of dreamwalking. Or maybe, it was fatigue, another experience she never knew the meaning of before becoming a human. She was tired and hungry, and for some reason, that was making her angry.

She waited for the demon, too tired to do more than hope he was serious about returning for her.

You are always who you are. His parting words played over and over in her thoughts, and she chewed on them. He hadn't meant it as a compliment; that much she knew. The idea behind his words intrigued her tired mind.

Was it true she was the same person she'd always been, just in a new body?

Or did being human change the essence of who she was?

She still loved Gabriel and her underworld. But her life was so much more confusing now. She'd never had to think twice about right and wrong, about emotions or life and death.

Sooner than she expected, she heard someone hurrying down the hallway.

Past-Death crept away from the door, in case it was one of Harmony's sentries. A moment later, Jared poked his head in.

"Come with me, cupcake," he ordered. "I've had my fill for now."

I don't want to know what that entails. Past-Death moved into the hallway. She tried not to look at the newfound slickness on his clothing that gleamed in the torchlight. The faint scent of metallic blood was in the air around the demon, and the glow of bloodlust remained in his gaze.

"You know this place. Where do we go?" he asked, starting towards the stairs.

She considered. "We have a few options. If the dealers haven't found the passages hidden in the walls, we can use those to move around. There are safe spots where we can hide, and of course, the armory has the thickest walls and doors of the whole palace."

"Armory?" Jared stopped and turned to her. "That's where we need to go."

"You realize that's the most dangerous place to go, right? Harmony will have it well guarded, and it's on the main floor," she said skeptically. "I can't imagine a demon like you has a plan."

"I don't need a plan. I need weapons."

"To do what?"

"Find the other cupcake and leave."

Past-Death said nothing, uncertain what to feel. Deidre had run off with someone else and left her. Even so, she didn't think she had it in her to abandon the human-turned-demon once more. "She doesn't know the palace. It'll be hard to find her."

"We'll use your secret tunnels." Content with the solution, Jared started forward again.

I owe it to her to try. Not much else worth living for now. Past-Death trotted after him. "I need food, Jared."

He lifted a bag she hadn't noticed he carried. Blood dripped from its soaked bottom onto the stone floor. "I saved you a hand."

"Human food."

He gave an exasperated sigh. "What does that consist of? Wood?"

"They eat a lot of bread, vegetables. Funnel cakes. I miss funnel cakes so much," she replied.

"What is a funnel cake?"

Past-Death debated for a moment, uncertain what it was. "It's a vegetable," she decided. "Not sure what kind of tree it grows on."

"Fucking plants. How can you people eat leaves?" Jared grumbled.

"We eat cooked animals, too. Never raw humans like you savages."

"You just capture and put an animal in an oven?"

"Sort of, yes."

"How can you enjoy the taste that way?"

"I've never seen the full process but it comes out good." She shrugged, admitting silently it did sound strange. "I'm sure the dealers have food here somewhere."

"It would be much easier if you'd just eat this hand."

"I'm not going to eat a hand, Jared."

They started up the stairs.

"How do we get to the armory?" he asked. "Where are these hidden tunnels?"

"Relax, demon. There will be one about halfway down the hall-way." She slowed as they approached the room where the guards had been. Blood was splashed into the hallway, a sign of how frenzied Jared had been when he claimed his meal.

He walked by the door without a glance.

She paused in the doorway to survey the mess, expecting to feel upset by the sight of the ravaged remains.

She didn't. If anything, there was a small sense of satisfaction at knowing those who betrayed her and Gabriel had been served their justice by a demon.

As Death, she'd seen every kind of death possible, from the peaceful passing of a human in its sleep to the slaughter of genocide and the remains of a natural disaster.

This … this didn't bother her. What bothered her: feeling as if it should. Wondering how long she had until she ended up torn into pieces like those in the room. Suspecting no one would mourn her, once she was gone.

"Cupcake!" Jared called.

Past-Death moved away from the doorway, uncertain how she was supposed to think about her world. "It's on your right, Jared."

He turned to face the wall and stared.

"Maybe you can't see it because you're a demon," she explained.

"Very well. Open it."

"Grab a torch." She went to the door only she was able to see and tugged it open. Taking his arm, she led him into the narrow tunnel and closed the door behind them. "See?"

"Where does it go?" Jared asked, looking around.

"It used to go wherever I wanted it to. Hopefully it still does," she replied. Releasing him, she rested a hand on the wall. "To the armory, please."

The sound of stone shifting and grating reached them as the palace responded. Pleased to know she had some influence still, Past-Death smiled at the darkness before them and waited for the sounds to stop before starting forward. The small gesture did little to soothe the gnawing despair at her core, but it was something.

From the corner of her eye, she caught a spark of turquoise, like the glow of a tiny lamp, or the gem she'd seen in the ring in the dungeon.

"Come on," Jared said when she lingered.

Nothing was there. Shaking her head, past-Death trailed him.

They walked in near darkness for close to ten minutes before light edging a doorway appeared ahead of them. They reached it and paused.

Jared handed her the torch and bag.

Past-Death stood back as he opened the door and leapt into the room, ready for a fight.

He straightened, looking around. "This is not the armory. This is ... awful."

She followed him into the room. Before she set foot into the bright space, the overwhelming scent of food reached her.

"Thank god!" she gasped, breathing in the scents of savory pies and sweets. "I guess I was more interested in food than the armory." She shoved the torch and bag at him.

The massive kitchen took up half of one wing and was empty of cooks. Meat pies cooled on stone shelves while various kinds of pastries and dried fruit tarts rested on a long counter.

Jared scowled, his nose wrinkling. "You prefer this to blood?"

"Absolutely!" Past-Death hurried forward. Not caring what the demon thought, she stuffed a meat pie in her mouth and several more in her pockets before scooping up as many pastries and tarts as she could carry. The flaky, buttery crust of the pie hid tender meat and flavorful gravy, and she scarfed three of the palm-sized portions before letting out a deep sigh.

Her headache and anger receded, and she felt more solidly a part of the world, less like she was going to pass out.

"This is the best part of being human," she said with a groan, taking a second bite of a fruit tart.

"Is our tunnel still there?" Jared asked impatiently.

A glance at the wall confirmed it was. With some regret, Past-Death dropped more food into a small sack and closed it, her stomach straining but her hunger still present.

"Okay. To the armory," she said, striding forward. "Come on, demon." Taking his arm again, she led him into the dark tunnel.

"Can you lift a sword?" he asked.

"No."

"Ever used a dagger or knife?"

"No."

"Axe?"

"I don't know anything about weapons," she snapped.

"How about a shield? Can you *not* get killed on your own, or do I need to stand in front of you?"

Past-Death ignored him and walked through the darkness, feeling more confident than she had in a long time, despite not knowing how to fight. The underworld had always been her home, and the fact it was helping her navigate the palace made her think things weren't quite as bad as she thought.

"They're much worse," she muttered under her breath.

The outline of another door appeared, and they stopped before it once again.

"I'll go first." Jared shoved his food supply and torch at her.

She accepted both and stood back obediently.

He whipped the door open, and she trailed. The sounds of movement and talking in the armory ceased.

Past-Death peered around the corner and took in the fifty death dealers lined up to check out weapons. They were staring at Jared and her in surprise.

Jared, too, was frozen, staring back at them. Past-Death glanced from him to the dealers and back, waiting for the demon to do something.

"Go on, demon. Eat them," she said, nudging Jared forward.

"I have a new plan, cupcake," he whispered, taking a step back.

"What?"

Jared snatched her arm and dragged her back into the tunnel, sealing it closed. "Run. Now." He started down the hallway.

"That's your plan?" she demanded, surprised. "What happen to the demon who can handle anything?"

"Demons are not stupid, human. We know when to run."

Someone slammed something against the door, and she jumped, dropping the torch. After a split second longer of hesitation, Past-Death turned and ran, following him into the darkness. They had to go somewhere safe, a hiding place only she knew about, and she racked her brain before deciding to trust the passageways to take them to safety.

Chapter Eight

Hours passed. Gabriel tried to leave the Lake several more times before giving up and lying back on a boulder to stare at the grey skies.

Mates-blood-fate. Darkyn had said this was all that mattered now, and he had been dwelling on the lessons he'd learned since becoming Death. He'd learned to track souls without the innate soul-radar granted to every death dealer brought on board. He'd discovered and healed most of the cracks allowing souls to escape to the human world. He'd found his mate, lost her, then found her again, met a couple of deities and learned too much about how little he was able to trust those he once viewed as colleagues.

The flexibility of Immortal Code, the need to respect the original three laws, decoding the ancient soul compasses, tracking demons in the mortal world ...

He'd learned so much the hard way, the result of avoiding the first step he was supposed to take: placing his soul in the sacred room off Death's bedchamber.

What if he'd done that first? How many of these trials might've been avoided? How many death dealers would've been saved going to trial for their rebellion?

"You've got my attention." He spoke again to the Lake of Souls. "I understand your pain. I don't know what to do about it." He ignored any self-consciousness he experienced at the thought of talking to an inanimate object. He'd last swum through the lake to find the soul of the Ancient Andre, an expert demon tracker and half-brother to Rhyn, and resurrect him.

Shortly after, the underworld locked him out. Fate claimed it was for his own good. Gabriel hadn't felt … whole since then. He'd struggled to figure out who he was supposed to be, and worse, doubted he was the right person for the job, once the troubles began.

"Just when I feel like I'm getting somewhere …" Gabriel sat back, suppressing the urge to lose his temper. "I guess technically, I never got anywhere, if I'm stuck here. I'm failing you, and I don't know how to make things right. I thought cleaning up the souls on the human world was what I was supposed to do, especially after you locked me out."

The Lake didn't respond.

"Now, I think …" His gaze went to the grey heavens. "I don't know anymore. Do you remember when the sky cracked open? That's when she dropped you into my lap and told me to take care of you. It's when I started failing at being who you need me to be, when I started to *feel* too much again."

The trees and animals fell silent for the first time since he'd intermittently begun talking to the Lake hours before. Sensing they were listening, Gabriel reviewed what he'd just said to see if he could pinpoint what they were responding to. He sat up.

"I went to the human world to try to fix things, and you shut me out."

The world began moving again.

"Okay. That wasn't it." He drew a calming breath. "Deidre would know what to do."

Silence.

"So you're … what? Interested in hearing about her? Sad she's gone? As furious as I am with her?"

The animals and trees remained quiet.

"The heart of the underworld is broken. Because you miss her?" Gabriel rested his elbows on his knees, sensing he was close to whatever it was the Lake was waiting for. He shifted to peer into the water and gazed at his reflection, gazing back at him. He appeared worn and frustrated, the skin around his eyes tight, and sorrow in the depths of his gaze.

Souls glowed like tiny lanterns beneath the surface of the water, and he heard the sad song again from the trees and lake. They felt much like he did. As he watched, a scene began to play out on the surface of the Lake, one of the day where he'd felt pain after a lifetime without it.

The day Past-Death turned away from him. He watched himself storm off. She had seen him go. When she turned away, there were tears on her face, and he saw for the first time what he'd never known about the goddess who held his heart.

She'd loved him enough to be hurt, too. Deities were immune to emotions, sociopathic liars out to protect their domains. The traits were needed, because they never let anything else come between them and their duties.

"Except something did," he whispered. *Shit.*

For a long moment, he sat in the silence, allowing his thoughts to return to where he hadn't wanted them to go: to the past he wanted to forget but couldn't.

"Because I miss her," he whispered. He racked his brain to recall when exactly the underworld had begun failing, before the demon invasion and the cracking of the sky that occurred before he was appointed as Death. "This started before Rhyn came to the underworld to find Katie and was followed by the demons. It began ..."

The moment Death made me give up my soul and then dumped me.

Gabriel dwelt on the unpleasant memory of trading his soul to Past-Death in exchange for her allowing Rhyn the time he needed to save his mate. The only freelancer among the death dealers, he'd volunteered to stay with Past-Death for tens of thousands of years, after falling in love with her when he was a foolish seventeen year old mortal.

Shortly after demanding his soul, she banned him from her bed.

He'd thought her callously uncaring at the time, but the vision replaying on the surface of the water told him otherwise.

"That's it, isn't it?" he murmured. "She was hurting, and the skies cracked. I'm hurting, and the Lake cracked. I am hurting, and so are you."

Mates-blood-fate. Pre-destined to become mates, he'd gotten close to breaking two of the three original laws governing the universe: one when he walked away from past-Death and the second when he refused Fate's advice about accepting his Future.

Worse – his human emotions were out of control since he'd met her again as a human. They were wreaking havoc on the under-world. He wasn't in control of his world, and he wasn't in control of himself.

"In my defense, there are two of her, and there weren't exactly instructions," he said with a snort. "How does this help me fix all this? Or ..." He fell quiet, not liking the solution drifting into his mind. "I help you by fixing *me*. How do you expect me to move on, after all the pain she's caused? I don't want to become what she was." He shifted restlessly. "I don't want to treat her the way she did me."

The longer he thought, the more challenging the idea became. How did he cut the string tying him to the emotional baggage built up over tens of thousands of years? How did he heal wounds that had been opened so many times, they no longer healed?

How did he rein in emotion he hadn't experienced since he entered the underworld as a teenage boy?

"You are the Keeper of Souls, a compassionate Death of human origin who understands life better than a deity ever could. If you cannot remember how to forgive, who can?"

Gabriel twisted, not realizing how deep in thought he was until he saw Andre, the eldest of Rhyn's brothers who sat on the Immor-tals' Council That Was Seven. The night-skinned Immortal was dressed practically for the often-stormy underworld in cargo pants and a windbreaker. His tanzanite colored eyes glowed brightly. Andre rarely appeared anything other than polished and put together. He offered a small smile.

"How long have you been standing there?" Gabriel asked.

"Long enough to hear you figure out what's wrong."

"When I became a deity, I never expected to have to bare my soul to so many people. Fate was one thing, but I'm even taking advice from the Dark One now."

Andre chuckled and drew nearer. The peacemaker among the constantly fighting Immortals, he had a calming influence even over a deity like Gabriel. "It's not a bad thing, Gabriel. If I learned one thing over the years, it's that everyone has some unique knowledge that can help you somewhere along the line."

"You're being the diplomat."

"Not at all. It's true."

"I wish I had your patience and understanding of the world, Andre."

Andre was quiet for a moment, and Gabriel assessed he was debating how to respond. "Gabriel, what you call patience and understanding were honed out of a great deal of pain. You do not want to go through what I did in order to gain this level of patience and understanding." The quiet note in the Immortal's voice was like the man himself: much, much more than what was apparent.

"I know much of your history, Andre," Gabriel said. "I mean no disrespect for what you've been through. Someone like you seems more capable of handling all this. I seem to be failing."

"It's a matter of perspective, Gabe. I see you as succeeding in every challenge you've faced."

"It's not enough. The underworld is reflecting my pain. I'm destroying it by not knowing how to be the man it needs me to be," he said in a hushed tone. "It's a lethal cycle."

"Fix it," Andre suggested. "You alone have that power. Stop the cycle, forgive yourself for your past and move on."

"Is it that easy?" Gabriel gritted his teeth to hear the Dark One's advice echoed by someone he respected so much more.

"I imagine it's the hardest thing you've ever had to do, which is probably why the underworld is requiring you to do it," Andre said. "You must prove you can overcome anything, even your past, your emotions and the hold they still have on you, in order to be the deity the souls need you to be."

Your past, your emotions and the hold they still have on you. Gabriel mulled on this phrase, the truth in the words touching him to his core. He'd done his best to change his view of his duty and world, to shift from loyal soldier accustomed to taking orders to the commander giving them. To an extent, he felt he'd succeeded. He was used to controlling every part of his day and world, within the confines of his duty.

Since becoming Death, he'd felt like he and his world were spinning out of control.

Andre was right. The souls and underworld deserved someone better than he'd been. Someone selfless enough to walk through the door in his bedchamber that he'd avoided out of resentment and fear of becoming someone he hated. Someone who wasn't trapped by his past.

How he felt no longer mattered, not when the souls were suffering as they were.

"When you say it, it doesn't sound that bad." Gabriel flashed him a half smile and rose.

"I imagine you already know what to do?" Andre asked curiously.

"Stay out of my head, Immortal. I raised you but can render you dead-dead just as fast," Gabriel growled in warning.

"It was a guess only." Andre sounded entertained. "Whatever it is, I suggest you find a way to knock it out before things get worse."

Gabriel's thoughts went first to his estranged mate and then to the door he was supposed to walk through in order to become a true deity. Of the two of them, he'd rather take a chance on the door. It was much harder for him to determine how to handle his anger and hurt, let alone cut that emotional baggage out of his life completely.

Putting aside his emotions, he refocused on what they needed to be doing. "You alone or is Tamer with you?"

"He'll be along shortly, I believe."

"Wait here." Gabriel strode to the edge of the forest and paused, not about to smack into another wall of branches, if the Lake wasn't done with him yet. "The only way I can fix things is if you let me through," he whispered to the forest.

He waited. The forest sounded normal. Taking one step then a second forward, he almost sighed. Nothing moved to block his path. It was one thing to know what was wrong, quite another to understand how to fix it.

Human emotions weren't that easy to manipulate. The resentment he felt towards his mate seemed too much to overcome, and yet, he knew he'd never stopped loving her, either, no matter what she'd done to him over the course of tens of thousands of years. No matter how many other men she fucked in the bed she shared with him or how she constantly manipulated him.

The problem was human Deidre. Sacrificing an innocent woman, one Gabriel had started to fall for, only to have her ripped away and the greatest lie in the universe revealed. He was able to forgive almost anything his mate did to *him*, but to forgive Past-Death for hurting Deidre …

His feelings became a jumbled mess whenever he tried to process it. Deidre had found a home with the Dark One, but that didn't alleviate the guilt and responsibility Gabriel felt.

How do you let go of the past that easily?

How did he accept his fate when it meant being okay with what past-Death had done?

Because the goddess who did those things is not the same as the human that replaced her. The thought wasn't new, but it was getting easier to swallow.

As if hearing the thought, a path cleared before him, leading towards the palace.

"That's the key, isn't it? It's not just whatever is in that room. It's taking a chance on someone I already love."

The trees went silent for a split second then began to move again.

"You're a shitty matchmaker," he told the underworld. "You ready, Andre?" he called over his shoulder.

"I am."

"Come with me." Gabriel started walking. "There's something I have to do at the palace. I've been fighting my fate since the first day and unknowingly made things worse. I've gotta fix it."

"Gabriel."

"I know. I should've –"

"Gabriel. The trees don't want me following you."

He turned to see the path blocked once more, dividing him from Andre.

"I guess I need to do this alone," he said under his breath. "Andre, find Rhyn and Darkyn. Make sure they make it to the palace without gutting each other."

"I will do my best."

"I'll see you all there." Gabriel shook his head, amused at how vocal his underworld was being after shutting him out for so long. He needed all the help he could get right now, if he was going to make things right once and for all.

The pride of a master who wished his domain to acknowledge him stirred once more, and he considered how to handle his challenges. Smashing everything between him and the palace sounded fantastic.

Except he'd never make it in one piece. Not only that, but every time he tried to fight to get somewhere, he ended up knocked on his ass. No, he'd have to take a much more subdued approach to execute his priorities. First the door he'd feared entering, then his mate and finally, the rebelling dealers.

I was ready to forgive her. The thought dragged his focus from the underworld into his thoughts once more. He'd been ready to move on with past-Death despite her admission of how she condemned Deidre to Hell.

She'd one time despised the human side of him. She'd not only gotten over it, but became what she hated most in order to be with him. Likewise, he'd have to accept the ugly side of who she had been if he was to fall again for who she'd become.

He dwelled on it, instincts monitoring his surroundings for any sign of danger. Content to let his mind think, his innate abilities warned him, and he whirled. One of his death dealers, a man built like a bowling ball, stood a safe distance behind him.

"Tymkyn," he said, straightening out of his fighting stance.

"Hey, boss. You're hard to track."

Gabriel eyed him, aware he didn't know which death dealers he was able to trust yet. "Mind check," he said, referring to the method he used to ravage a dealer's mind to make sure he was loyal.

Tymkyn bowed his head without hesitation.

Gabriel rested a hand on his head briefly before removing it. "I thought we'd lost you. You went silent."

"I couldn't get out!" Tymkyn exclaimed. Short, wide and ugly with a bulbous nose, the strong death dealer was Gabriel's best tracker, capable of navigating the changing landscape of the moody underworld. "Wasn't going through Hell again."

Gabriel smiled at his trusted hunter's distraught tone.

"Rhyn told me to find you." Tymkyn's expression changed, grew proud and beaming. "There are sixty death dealers here who refused Harmony's takeover. They're all that remain of the hundred that are loyal to you. She's been systematically tracking them and killing them."

"Sixty." Gabriel kept his tone even.

The number made some part of him weep. There were over a thousand death dealers in existence. About forty were trapped in the human realm, another few picked off by demons. Only sixty in the underworld remained loyal.

Tymkyn waited, excited by the news that filled Gabriel with sorrow.

Because, when this was over, those rebelling would be killed, which meant he'd experience another crisis trying to collect souls. It was more than that, though. It was the knowledge he'd have a hand in killing seven to eight hundred of the men and women who had become his colleagues over the years.

My duty is to something much higher. The souls, he reminded himself.

"That's good, Tymkyn," he said. "Great job locating them."

Tymkyn's smile widened. "I will take you to them!"

"No," Gabriel said quickly. "I cannot stray from my path right now."

"But you're headed to the palace with all of Harmony's dealers. Alone."

"I'm Death."

Tymkyn snorted. "You can still take a sword to the heart. Let me go. It would be the greatest honor to become a member of your vanguard."

Gabriel clapped him on the shoulder, the man's earnestness touching him. "You will, when this is over. For now, I have a matter I have to take care of before I attack them outright. Can you bring the others to my cabin?" he asked, referring to the tiny, wooden home where he'd lived, outside the palace, for hundreds of years. "Stay hidden and await my signal."

"I'd like to object, boss."

"I know, and I thank you for your concern. Consider this an order."

Tymkyn frowned. "I'll gather them now. What will your signal be?"

"I have a feeling you won't be able to miss it," Gabriel said with some humor, knowing how big of a bang he'd make when Harmony's men realized he was in their midst. "Quickly."

Tymkyn nodded and dashed into the brush.

Pleased to have one dealer remaining as his ally, Gabriel started towards the palace once more. There were secret passages only Death and her lover of a few thousand years knew about. He'd take them to reach the closet where his magic lay waiting.

And then he'd issue an ultimatum to Harmony and her dealers: lay down their arms or face the wrath of Death and Hell.

Chapter Nine

ndre walked for three hours along the trail leading from the Lake of Souls in the direction the demons had gone. With a knack for tracking the creatures, he knew when he was close, even before the two appeared on the path before him.

Darkyn and Rhyn were in the middle of a stare down with one another, growling and poised as if for a fight, despite the fact they had neither the time nor luxury of postponing their real mission to see which creature was stronger.

Andre wasn't surprised by the scene. Demons were temperamental creatures, prone to acting out of instinct primarily and viewing the world and everything in it as either belonging to them or beneath them. They were hardest to deal with when hungry, agitated or hunting, circumstances when their emotions were rawer than usual, and logic was generally lost on them. These two in particular were immensely powerful – and stubborn.

Andre's urge to calm those around him was born more out of necessity than anything else. A powerful empath, negative emotions clung to him like his shadow. He picked up on the feelings of others even without diving into their minds, and their instability managed to disrupt his own inner peace. It was like swallowing poison.

The eldest of the Immortals on the Council That Was Seven, Andre had honed his ability and self-control over thousands of years. What once drove him over the edge was now simply a nuisance. He hadn't dulled his sensitivity, simply learned to bear the fruits of feeling what those around him did with patience and compassion.

But never weakness. Inaction and fear were never part of who he was, even when facing down two demons strong enough to crush him.

"Does winning the Toughest Demon Award somehow transport you out of here?" he asked calmly of the two bristling demons.

Rhyn's jaw ticked, a sign he'd heard, while Darkyn remained motionless.

"You're right. This is a much better use of your time than rescuing Darkyn's mate or preventing the world from collapsing when Harmony succeeds in her mission."

That did it. His casual tone drew both of their hostile gazes.

Andre smiled gently, ignoring the anger he sensed directed now at him. Just as their emotions had an effect on him, his had the same effect on those around him. Another reason to always remain calm and open.

"Are you ready to do what we're here for?"

Neither responded.

"The trees want us to go west. If they have a west in the under-world." He glanced at the suns that had been frozen in the sky for a few hours before starting forward. "I'll be at the palace, whenever you all care to join me."

Stepping by them, he started into the forest, confident they'd follow.

"No offense, Andre, but you can be a real dick." Rhyn was the first to trail him. "You know I'd chop off your head to claim the Toughest Demon Award, don't you?"

"I know there's no love lost between you and any of your broth-ers, Rhyn," Andre replied. "But also that you are duty bound and will honor our shared blood even if you dislike me for who I am."

"A weakness I do not share," Darkyn growled. His voice was

close enough to assure Andre he, too, followed. "The Toughest Demon Award doesn't exist. If it did, it'd go to the Dark One by default."

"I am so fucking ready to take off your head after what you tried to do to my Katie!" Rhyn snarled.

"Focus, Rhyn. And Darkyn, you're weakening quickly," Andre said carefully, aware of how little he wanted a long lasting grudge from the Dark One when they left the underworld. "Your strength is better spent not fighting my shit head of a brother."

"Shit head? Really?" Rhyn grumbled. "I think Andre just called you a pussy, Darkyn."

"Hush, Rhyn," Andre chided. "We have more important issues to deal with."

"Harmony, death dealers, and two powerful deities about to lose their shit."

"There's something else here, too. Something I can't figure out."

"What can *you* sense, demon hunter?" Darkyn demanded.

"He can track your ass even in Hell," Rhyn replied, bristling once more.

"Be calm, Rhyn." Andre shook his head. "Darkyn knows one of my gifts but perhaps not the other."

"What is this gift?" Darkyn asked.

"Andre can suck up your emotions then crack your head open with them," Rhyn summarized. "He can read minds sometimes, too."

"Empath," Darkyn supplied.

"Exactly," Andre said.

"You knew about Sasha."

Another thing that always surprised Andre about demons: their candidness was never curbed by diplomacy or politeness or proper timing, the way his was. Andre and Rhyn both stopped and faced the Dark One, who ceased surveying their surroundings to return their looks warily.

"If he knew, he would've stopped him, before he almost destroyed the human world!" Rhyn snapped.

The name of the betrayer from the Council stirred up memories

— and regret. Andre had known what his half-brother was long before Sasha openly declared his allegiance to the Dark One.

It didn't help that Sasha had had Andre rendered dead-dead several months before. Andre hadn't yet reconciled his emotions about that incident, despite the knowledge his half-brother paid the price with a painful death.

Darkyn was gazing at him, and Andre reminded himself that the Dark One was not just another demon. Darkyn had been around longer than even Wynn, the father of the Councilmembers.

Darkyn was from the time-before-time. For him to be one of the only remaining survivors from that era indicated he was far more cunning and dangerous than Andre was able to assess from their very few interactions. Which meant Andre had to always err on the side of caution: not giving the demon lord a reason to track him down later.

"I did know, Rhyn," Andre said softly. "I knew the secrets of everyone around me. It's the nature of who I am."

Rhyn frowned at him.

"You follow the empath code," Darkyn said with a cold smile. "I like that."

Andre smiled politely and turned to begin walking once more. He didn't particularly like the way Darkyn said it, but he wasn't about to engage the demon more than necessary. Aside from their purpose there, he firmly believed in not giving power to ideas and motivations that did not benefit him.

They walked in relative quiet for a while, and Andre took in the grey underworld. He found himself missing the sun from the human realm and hoping he saw it again and had a chance to help his brothers.

Rather, had a chance to figure out what their father was doing, before he fucked up everyone again. The brothers still bore the scars of the twisted psychopath that raised them. Andre had originally sent Rhyn away when he was a child as much to save him from the Immortal world as to subdue the powers he couldn't control. He'd done what he could to help the rest of his brothers.

He hadn't done enough to save Sasha or Kris. Their fates and deaths weighed heavily on him despite the wisdom of knowing they chose their own paths. He hoped he had another chance to save the rest of his brothers or at least, to do what he could to help them this time around. Being dead-dead gave him time to think while resurrection provided him a second chance to act differently than he had before.

"Time's up. Hell has a new soul," Darkyn's low, quiet voice tugged Andre from his thoughts.

That doesn't sound good. Andre exchanged a look with Rhyn, not wanting to humor the demon lord. He willed his half-brother not to ask.

"Just one new soul?" Rhyn asked.

Rhyn was always Rhyn. Andre listened, not eager to hear the exchange.

"The soul of a former deity."

"Past-Death?"

"Yes."

"Will fit in well with your Army of Souls."

Darkyn didn't reply, and Andre frowned. He'd known about the deal the two Deidres made from diving into the mind of past-Death a few days before. It was one thing to lose a deal with a demon.

It was an entirely different thing to lose a deal sealed with the Dark One's magic. The chances of past-Death ever leaving the underworld were now gone, if she wanted to stay alive.

"The deal was between the Deidres," he found himself saying. "Hell may own her soul, but you don't, Darkyn."

To his surprise, the Dark One didn't respond with any sort of confirmation that he believed his mate capable of turning over anyone to Hell. Andre risked a glance at the creature and saw his features were pensive.

"It belongs to Hell. This is all that concerns me," Darkyn replied with a shrug.

"A woman clip your wings, demon?" Rhyn taunted.

"She did not clip my wings, half-breed. She makes matters more interesting."

"Wait until there's a hatchling involved." Rhyn grimaced. "That's when things get *interesting*."

"What else did you dig from past-Death's brain, Immortal?" This was addressed to Andre.

"Empath code," Andre replied calmly.

"Which is what?" Rhyn questioned.

"It's fairly simple. Empaths are forbidden from interfering in the natural course of a person's life without an invitation and must treat secrets like they're sacred," Andre replied.

"So you couldn't tell people Sasha was going to fuck up the world, and that I wasn't a threat. You let everyone believe I betrayed the Council, too."

"I sent you away to protect you from the fucked up world our father created. With respect to the Council, have you seen how your brothers turned out?" Andre explained with mild humor. "Before Katie, there was no one in the universe able to keep you from destroying everything you ran across, outside of Hell."

"You're welcome, half-breed," Darkyn said.

"Fuck off, Darkyn." Rhyn grunted.

"Just because I keep secrets doesn't mean I can't help those who need it," Andre added, as much for Rhyn as Darkyn.

"I wouldn't call it helping," Rhyn replied.

"Hell kept you alive. Sasha went mad within a decade of his time there and was rendered nonlethal relatively quickly. Andre would've known that as well," Darkyn said. "It was a shrewd, strategic move. Hell resolved both of his issues."

"Correct," Andre replied. It was unnerving to agree with the Dark One. It took a great deal of effort for him to turn his back on his brothers, even knowing it was for the greater good. Hearing the Dark One agree with his decision was disconcerting at best.

"That makes you sound cold, Andre," Rhyn observed. "More like something Wynn would do."

"Wynn would've destroyed you, not protected you," Darkyn replied. "He has the backbone Sasha never did."

"What a fucked up family."

"I was sorry to hear about your daughter, Darkyn," Andre added. "I had no way of knowing he'd harm her."

"I have plans for Sasha's soul, when I find it," Darkyn replied. "I have plans for you, too, empath."

Andre let the quiet threat slide over him. He had more important issues today. Whatever came tomorrow, he'd handle when it did. If anything, he was grateful that both demons seemed to be responding to his attempts to calm them down.

It gave him a chance to redirect their restless energy towards the people following them.

"Can either of you use your demon senses here?" he asked.

"Not fully," Darkyn replied.

"Mostly no," Rhyn echoed.

"Then I suggest you get ready to fight." He stopped walking and closed his eyes, using his empath radar to pick up the emotions of everything around him. "There are five at least."

"Where?" Rhyn drew his sword in response. "I can't smell them."

"That way. About twenty meters." Andre pointed. "I'll wait here."

The two turned to face the direction he indicated.

"First one there gets the Toughest Demon Award," Rhyn said and pushed the smaller Dark One out of his way.

"No half-breed can take what belongs to me," Darkyn snapped.

Never should've mentioned the Toughest Demon Award. Andre thought ruefully. He'd forgotten another trait of demons: they were territorial predators. Hopefully, they stayed focused on competing rather than defeating one another.

The demons melted into the forest, leaving behind a few waving bushes.

Andre waited until certain they were gone before facing the direction they'd been headed. "I know you're there," he said quietly into the forest.

Nothing but the natural sounds of the forest filled the air. Whatever stalked them didn't seem … solid. It was more like an echo of a person, a reflection perhaps, conveying parts of someone without the depth he was accustomed to feeling from someone else's presence.

"Whoever you are, I will not hurt you." He tilted his head to listen and focus his senses. Whatever it was, it was slippery, rendering it hard for him to track consistently. "My name is Andre. If you can hear me, give me some kind of sign."

The presence fled, but not before he caught a strange flash of blue-green light.

"That's a sign, too," he murmured, blue eyes taking in his surroundings.

Unable to explain the odd encounter, he oriented himself and began walking towards the palace. Time was running out. He was able to track the demons down if the forest decided not to lead them to him when they were done.

The ghostlike presence returned, fled, and came back once more to stalk him, each time accompanied by a spark of turquoise light. He didn't address it this time, instead cueing in his gift to study it.

Occupied in isolating what it was, he didn't heed his instincts until he was almost upon the ring of death dealers acting as scouts.

He froze, focused on his surroundings once more. He'd barely stopped in time and took a moment to assess them.

Chances were, he wasn't going to slip by them, and he knew better than to take on fifty death dealers without the help of the demons.

Andre retreated a short distance and chose a place to meditate, settling onto a rock to await Rhyn and Darkyn.

The presence had vanished once more.

What are you, and what do you want from me? He asked silently.

Chapter Ten

Deidre wished she'd been anywhere else, where she was able to enjoy the hot spring bath in the chamber adjacent to past-Death's bedchamber. There were three round, deep, hot tub type baths, and steam rose from each. As it was, she bathed with such speed and worry, she dropped two bottles of oil into the springs before wrestling the third open and pouring soap into her palm.

If not for the blood caking her, she would've skipped a bath.

I'm glad I can't remember. She shuddered, breathing in the steam deeply. It calmed her, and the hot water soothed her achy body. Karma had healed her, though her muscles remained sore from the trauma of her body breaking and healing itself. Scrubbing blood off her, she dunked her head into the water quickly before climbing out and hurrying to the thick towels stacked in a wardrobe by the door.

Karma was on guard in the bedchamber, but something told her the long-imprisoned deity didn't really understand the purpose of watching without engaging. Wrapping the towel around her, Deidre emerged tentatively from the bathing chamber into the destroyed master suite, uncertain what she'd find.

The redheaded deity had changed clothing and captured her

thick curls at the base of her neck. She sat with a book on an over-turned trunk.

Deidre crossed to the wardrobe whose door was still open, and she surveyed the clothing critically. Everything was in white or shades of cream. The material of the clothing was rather coarse, woven to withstand time rather than provide comfort to a goddess unable to feel it.

"Never thought I'd prefer a Hell dress." Deidre sighed. She pulled out what appeared to be the most comfortable of the clothing, a long dress, and then tugged on leggings beneath it. Knowing the boots would fit, she quickly pulled them on, tied them and straightened.

When she turned, Karma was standing directly behind her.

"Oh, god!" she gasped. "You shouldn't sneak up on people, Karma."

"Karma thought only water nymphs had pink hair," Karma said, studying her pink-dyed hair.

"Someday, someone is showing me what a water nymph is," Deidre replied. "Did anything happen?"

Karma raised an eyebrow in polite offense. "Yes, and Karma … *I* took care of it." Her eyes were blue this time, her round face lightly flushed.

"I'm guessing you didn't hide until they left."

"Karma doesn't hide. She needed clothes that fit. You are too small."

Deidre took in the new clothes. Karma wore all black, like a death dealer. "Okay. We should probably move on."

Karma started towards the door, and Deidre followed, strapping the velvet purse containing souls to her belt.

"We can go back to the dungeon," Karma told her.

"I think we need a plan."

"Karma … I heard the death dealers talk before they found Karma. There was a prisoner that escaped. The dealers are searching the palace, except for the dungeon. It's safe."

"Did they mean us?" Deidre asked.

"No. A demon."

"Jared got out?"

"Is that what they're called now?" Karma sighed. "Karma has been in prison too long."

"No, I mean, the demon in my cell was named Jared. But if he got out …" Either Past-death did, too, or had been eaten. Deidre didn't want to dwell on the glimmer of satisfaction she experienced at the idea of the woman who fucked up her world getting what she deserved.

She shook her head to free her mind of the bad thought, aware she felt bad for past-Death being eaten by a demon, no matter what the former deity had done to her.

Her stomach seized, and she dropped to her knees, clutching it. The hunger pangs were getting more frequent, more intense. Pain pierced her abdomen and radiated outwards into the rest of her body. She closed her eyes.

"Come, Deidre," Karma whispered, tugging at her arm. "There are people coming."

Deidre wasn't able to move. She huddled, nauseated, in silent agony. Her chest was too tight to breathe.

The door to the bedchamber burst open. She lifted her head, gaze blurred. There were four death dealers in the room and at least twice that in the hallway.

"The little demon is alive."

She recognized the voice, even if the accompanying memory was gone. Deidre shuddered. Sheer terror gave her the strength to move despite the pain, and she pushed herself to her feet. Her pulse raced with adrenaline, and Karma wrapped an arm around her, steadying her.

Together, they moved away from the door, putting the trunk between them and the death dealers.

"Karma can take … four, I think," the deity whispered. "How many can you fight? Five? Six?"

None. I'm too weak. Deidre's eyes watered, and she drew a shuddering breath.

"Oh, no. Karma does not like that emotion," the goddess snapped. "You're a *demon*. You can fight."

"I can't," Deidre said in a cracked voice. "I tried before!"

"You tried to fight them like you're *human*."

"Ready for round two, little demon?" one of the death dealers taunted. "I brought more friends this time. Good thing, seeing as how quickly you recovered the first time."

Deidre squeezed her eyes closed, fear paralyzing her. Maybe if she passed out first …

I'm tired of being the victim of the Immortal world. The thought crystalized, along with a sense of helplessness to know she didn't have the ability to prevent her fate at the hands of the death dealers.

"No!" Karma grabbed her arms and shook her hard. "No! You're a demon. Fight them how a demon fights!"

"I don't … know … how!"

"Where does the Dark One get his power?"

"What?"

The dealers entered the room cautiously, weapons drawn.

Karma snatched her arm and all but dragged her into the bathing chamber, barring the door. Deidre sagged to the floor, already trying to make her mind numb.

Not again. I can't go through this again.

Spinning, Karma grabbed Deidre's arms again and hauled her up. "Look at me!" The deity's eyes were piercing green, her curls gone and her hair straight standing on end, as if she'd stuck her finger in a light socket. "You are a demon now, and you can draw power from the same thing the Dark One does. I *know* you are tired of this, and I know you can do this. There's lots of power here for one such as you."

"Depravity?" Deidre asked uncertainly.

"Evil. Hatred. Pain. Resentment. Betrayal. Whatever emotion it is that makes them hurt you. You can use it against them."

"I don't know how."

"How?" Karma echoed, astonished. "You just use it! Did the Dark One teach you nothing?"

Deidre drew a few calming breaths and forced her panicking mind to focus. "Y… yes. He did. How to kill."

"Then do it!" Karma released her and took a hand. "Look.

You've got small claws. When demons are threatened, they grow claws and fangs. Make them grow more."

Something smashed into the door, and the bar across it cracked.

Deidre looked at it fearfully then at her hands.

Karma was right. Her nails had grown to short points and turned black, the same way …

"Wait a minute. They do this when I'm in bed with Darkyn," she murmured.

"Defense mechanism. What he does should probably kill you."

"That's what he says."

Karma grinned suddenly. "Then pretend you're in bed with him."

Desire shot through her at the thought, pooling at her belly. As Deidre watched, her nails grew longer, until they were thick and pointy enough to look threatening even to her.

"You can kill with them," Karma told her. "They are like tiny swords. They will go through anything."

"I'm like Catwoman." Deidre studied the lengthened nails in a cross between revulsion and intrigue. "Or maybe Wolverine." Her nails stopped growing at about two inches long. "Umm … definitely Catwoman."

Karma appeared confused. "Yes. Whatever it takes. How does this Cat-wo-man act? Afraid of death dealers?"

The door splintered.

"She's not afraid of anything," Deidre said.

"You can be that! You *are* that inside."

"He taught me another way to kill," Deidre continued, flipping over her hand to study her palm. "I couldn't do it to him. Karma, I don't know if I can kill." The demon way of killing usually involved a lot of blood and pain, from what she'd seen. Neither was natural to her.

"You can kill, or you can watch Karma get killed, because we won't make it out of here otherwise. Karma is weak right now, too."

Deidre looked up, startled, and met the deity's grim gaze.

"You have to be a demon now," Karma said firmly. "You are the mate of the Dark One, the most powerful creature in the universe. The power is in the men who want to hurt you. Use it."

I'm tired of being the victim. Deidre studied her hands once more and then nodded. She clung to the idea she already had the power within her to defend herself and Karma this time. After a fatal brain tumor, the list of deities and Immortals trying to use her for their means, the loss of her life, her mortality, her human boyfriend ...

This ends now. No more Immortals fucking up her life and body, no more deities trying to control her. Anger trickled into her, and the black fingernails grew longer.

Karma moved away from her and faced the first death dealer hacking his way through the door.

Swallowing hard, Deidre watched Karma duck the blow of a sword and grab the dealer's arm. He froze, his mouth opening in silent horror. Karma's hair lengthened and whirled around the both of them with the tangibility of smoke and the eerie writhing of a snake, her eyes flashing white then black and settling on red, while her features grew stony.

She, too, appeared frozen, absorbing the man's vitality. He grew pale, gaunt, and mummified so quickly, Deidre would've missed it, had she blinked. His hair and skin were the last to fade away, revealing a skeleton. Karma's hair returned to normal, and she released him.

The bones and clothing fell at Karma's feet, and she readied herself to face the next man. Red hair remained straight, the tendrils stretching out towards the next dealer through the door.

The rest of the door exploded, knocking both of them back. The dealers kicked aside the bones and charged into the room.

Karma moved to the side opposite Deidre, forcing the dealers to split up. Their effectiveness was further whittled down by the narrowness of the path around the round baths.

"Hello, little demon." The death dealer approaching Deidre had eyes that glowed with lust. His dagger was raised. "Ready to scream for me again?"

Deidre retreated, struggling to focus on Karma's words to keep from losing her angry edge.

… you can draw power from the same thing the Dark One does.

Deidre glanced at her fingernails. She doubted they'd do much against a sword, but she already knew from fucking Darkyn that they could slice through skin easily. He loved pain, and she began to realize that he'd been quietly teaching her how to be the demon she really was, using his body as her scratching post.

Depravity. Evil. How did she channel what was clearly in front of her? How did she draw on Darkyn's power when he was cut off from her? She had never thought to seek the bad out in anyone, but the large death dealer looming over her made her want to give it a go.

"I'm unarmed," she whispered, holding up her hands. "I … know how this went last time. I just want it not to hurt."

The death dealer considered her then sheathed the sword. "No promises."

"Better your hands than a sword, right?"

He snatched her arm hard enough to hurt. Deidre grimaced, fighting away the frantic urge to curl up in a ball and sob. She rested a hand against his chest to steady herself and focused hard on feeling the parts of him that would attract her mate.

I am the Dark One's mate. If there is evil here, it will obey me. Closing her eyes, she chanted the words over and over, trying not to notice that the death dealer was ripping her dress to get to her skin with the haste of a man not fully under his own control. He grabbed one breast and squeezed too hard, shoving her into the wall behind her and rubbing his erection against her hips.

This ends now.

The scent of blood was in the air, thick, rich and compelling. Deidre's mouth watered, the demon side of her responding to its food source.

A whisper reached her, something dark and cold, emanating from deep within her attacker and tingling through the hand she held over his heart. The cool energy went up her arm, tickling her from the inside, and she redirected it, willing it to do to his heart what she never thought herself capable of before.

The dealer hesitated and started to pull away.

Keeping her hand rooted to his chest, Deidre focused harder, tears on her cheeks.

"Stop," she whispered to his heart. "Now."

The dealer dropped.

Gasping, Deidre's eyes flew open, and she stared down at the body at her feet. She had no time to dwell over her first kill but was confronted by a second dealer. This one paused, glancing at the dead man, before he stepped over him and took her arm.

"Claws!" Karma shouted with a grunt from across the room.

A quiet, quick death was one thing, but Deidre wanted nothing to do with blood. It was drowning her senses already, pulling at a part of her she didn't want to acknowledge existed. One that lusted to gorge itself on the coppery rivers of blood pulsing through the body of the man before her.

Coupled with her hunger, the thought of tasting him was overwhelming.

The cold flow of energy was stronger from this man, and even stronger from the man behind him. Her demon senses were opening, and she drew in the evil with less effort than before, collecting it with some bafflement, and then readying it to defend her.

Driven beyond emotion by hunger and fear, Deidre didn't wait for the next man to grab her but gripped his arm, unleashing the cold energy into him.

He fell instantly.

The man behind him drove her back with a slash of his sword. Deidre jumped away, uncertain what to do against the weapon, and concentrated on sucking in more of the cold energy circulating in the room to use when she had the chance. Slipping on the tile, she landed hard on her knees, barely avoiding another blow.

He hauled her up, and she slashed his forearm, forcing him to let go.

The dealer bellowed, and the scent of blood filled her nose. Deidre barely had time to move before he wrapped his hand in her hair and wrenched her head back, knife at her neck.

"Got one!" he shouted behind him.

His blood dripped down his arm, and she found herself unusually fascinated by the trickle of maroon droplets towards her.

Deidre licked her lips. Horrified by her body's response, she steeled herself, touched his forearm and released the cold energy.

Man and knife fell.

Her hand was covered in his blood. She stared at it, resisting the need to lick it clean. She wiped it on her dress instead and rose.

"Deidre!" Karma's choked cry drew her gaze.

With her hand around the neck of one man, Karma was immobilized while her magic wound around him, unable to fend off the second death dealer with a sword at her throat.

This ends now. Deidre chanted silently, gaining strength from the fury behind the words.

The dealer raised the weapon to strike off Karma's head. A flare of fear drove away what little thought Deidre could muster. Demon instinct, intoxicated by the scent of blood, compelled her forward, a black fog wrapping her in its embrace as she all but flew over the ground.

She felt it more strongly then, the flow of evil emanating from the man. Betrayal, malice. He'd done bad things and betrayed Gabriel, and his depravity called to the demon in her like a siren song.

Deidre let go of the human side of her, knowing it wasn't strong enough to do what the demon side of her needed to do and save Karma. She closed her eyes and let her senses take her. Vaguely, she registered slashing someone's body with her claws not once, but three times.

Warm blood sprayed her, and someone screamed. She tasted blood in her mouth, its sweet, rich flavor making her human instincts clamor.

But god, was it so good! She drank deeply before her emotions caught up with her. A combination of disgust and hunger filled her.

Deidre opened her eyes and released the body of the man much larger than her. He dropped to her feet, and she stared.

His neck was ripped out, the way she'd seen Darkyn do before to his demons when they tried to attack her during her second day in

Hell. The dead man's exposed skin showed the signs of being shredded by her nails. Blood dripped from her fingers and mouth.

Staring at the damage she'd done, she wasn't able to decipher exactly what she felt. Shock that she'd taken out someone so much bigger than her, disappointment the blood did nothing to whet her appetite and horror that she was losing the part of her that was human.

Satisfaction that she'd just proven beyond a doubt she was the wife of the devil.

The bathing chamber was silent, and her demon senses told her the only other living life was Karma.

"You did it!" the goddess cried, startling her. Her features glowed, her eyes white-grey and her hair slowly settling.

"Yeah," Deidre managed, staring at the bodies at her feet. Her head was pounding, her internal war to keep from diving into the blood pooling beneath one of the dealer's absorbing her concentration. She wiped her mouth on her sleeve and grimaced at the amount of blood covering her white clothing.

The deity was smiling, any judgment Deidre feared absent from Karma's whirling eyes and possessed hair.

"You get to claim their souls," Karma said cheerfully.

"I don't think I can do that."

"It's simple. Touch one and tell him to come to you."

Deidre shook her head, uncertain if she wanted to weep at what she'd done or wallow happily in blood. Her body trembled, and she regarded her bloodied clothing briefly. "I need to change," she whispered. "I feel dirty."

"Karma thinks you should wear black. We might have to kill more. Blood won't show up on black as much."

Deidre nodded and fled through the dead to the bedchamber, at once relieved by the absence of heavy, humid air and scent of blood. She went to the wardrobe and started to pull out more clothing, when it hit her.

She'd killed four men, using the devil's magic, and even drunk the blood of one. Her adrenaline faded.

What if, one day, the demon side of her replaced her humanity? What if she slid into the depths of Hell and lost herself?

She barely spun in time to vomit outside the wardrobe. Stomach heaving, Deidre dropped to her knees once more and held her midsection, tears rising with the reality of what she'd done. She threw up the blood she'd just sucked down, her stomach cramping for Darkyn.

Karma approached quietly. Deidre ignored her, struggling with her own inner agony, until the urge to purge receded.

"I've never … I can't …"

"I understands, remember?" Karma said. "She … I can feel what you do."

Deidre nodded, somewhat relieved not to have to voice her tangled feelings out loud.

Karma crouched beside her, peering into her eyes. The deity's hair was in tight curls once more, her eyes faded green. "Karma is proud of you." She pushed hair out of Deidre's face.

"I'm not … sure what to … feel."

"Happy to be alive. Happy that Karma is alive. Happy to know you never have to be hurt again."

Deidre drew a shaky breath. "Okay. Are you docking me Karma points for this?"

"Karma has points?" The goddess smiled, puzzled.

Deidre shook her head. "It's, um, a saying. I guess I want to know if it's okay that I killed four people."

"You saved Karma the effort of doing it."

"That's not exactly what I meant." Deidre debated silently for a moment. She had proven to herself that she was no longer the victim. But at what cost? "Am I a bad person now?"

"No." The resolute response was quick, firm.

Deidre studied Karma, not entirely reassured that the woman who had just killed ten men was the best judge of character.

Then again, she's Karma. She'd know if I crossed the line. Except Deidre didn't know how slashing someone's throat open was not crossing the line.

252

"Could you be biased since I did it to save your life?" Deidre asked doubtfully.

"I am not biased!"

Deidre straightened and managed a wan smile. "You said it right first try."

"We are both learning today." Karma appeared pleased with herself.

Deidre wiped her mouth on her sleeve, stomach steadied.

"You do not act with malice," the deity added gently. "Karma has no problem with those who act justly."

Deidre sighed, uncertain why hearing the words meant so much. "I guess I'm afraid of turning into the devil or losing *me*."

"Trust yourself. It's not possible for you to be anyone but who you are, even if you are half a demon," Karma said wisely. "Karma can see your soul from the inside out, remember? It is pure, even now."

"Darkyn said the same."

"Dark One." Karma growled, the way she did whenever talking about the Great Imbalance. Her eyes flashed black.

Deidre smiled despite herself.

"Change. We must go," Karma said and stood.

With effort, Deidre rose and went through the wardrobe quickly. She was feeling even weaker after the incident in the bathing chamber. Her fingers had trouble gripping anything on the first try, and her movement felt labored. Her vision was growing fuzzy around the edges, her ability to concentrate long gone.

The sensations were familiar – those she'd begun to experience when she was dying of a brain tumor.

"Karma … I think I'm going to be in trouble soon," she whispered. "I'm dying, aren't I?"

"Yes." Karma's tone was sad.

Again. It didn't seem possible that she'd evaded her fate once only to run into it again as an Immortal. Deidre changed as fast as she was able to.

"Only the blood of your bloodmate can save you," Karma said.

"We need to find the other Deidre and leave," Deidre murmured. "Soon."

"Then come. They will send more dealers soon when they see these have disappeared."

Deidre took a moment to center herself and then strode forward, joining Karma at the door.

Karma took her hand, and they entered the hallway together.

Chapter Eleven

Barreling through the dark passageways of the palace, Jared hit the brakes when another door appeared before them.

"What're you doing? Go!" past-Death urged, pushing at him.

A flare of blue-green behind her made her turn. As before, there was nothing there. She stared into the darkness, not understanding why she kept seeing it.

"You go first, cupcake. I'm not getting my head chopped off."

Rolling her eyes, past-Death maneuvered by the demon, fearful of being followed. She'd never been concerned about such a thing before and wasn't certain if it was even possible for the death dealers to find her in the walls.

She opened the door into a dimly lit room with no windows. It was small, and she recognized the same ancient, quiet magic that resonated in the dungeon. Recognizing the pedestal in the center of the room, she started to retreat. The tunnels had indeed taken her to the safest place in the palace.

"Shit," she muttered. "You can't be here."

"What?" Curious and assured no one was waiting to attack, Jared shoved her hard enough to knock her into the room.

"Really. We need to go!" past-Death said, taking his arm.

"Stop." He gripped her neck in response. "What is this place?"

Past-Death said nothing, aware no demon in history had set foot in the sacred room. Only the two Deaths preceding her had ever been here. Even if her blocked memories didn't let her recall what she'd done in here, she innately knew this sacred spot and its power.

"Are those … souls?" Intrigued, Jared released her and strode towards the pedestal. A caldron sat on top, the glow from the souls in its waters the only light in the room.

Past-Death heard the sounds of distant pursuit, confirming the dealers had found a way into the passageways, and reluctantly pushed the door closed. "Only Death or Death's mate can find us here. We're safe enough for now. But we can't stay long."

Jared's growl was low and deep as he took in the contents of the caldron. He reached into the caldron.

"Don't touch!" she shouted. "The water is demon proof. It'll kill you instantly."

Jared hesitated.

"On second thought, do touch it. You're a pain in the ass," she added.

He lowered his hand without moving.

Past-Death stepped beside him and peered into the caldron. There were only a couple hundred souls in its depths, but they ranged in color from the large black one to different shades and sizes of red, blue, green, yellow, purple, and orange. The gems glimmered and winked.

"Death is guardian over the souls of the deities," she whispered. "It's why no one likes to fuck with Death."

"Good trump card." He pointed to the black one. "Dark One?"

"Darkyn's predecessor. As soon as Zamon lost Hell, I collected his soul and brought it here," she said. "It's not the same with all of them. Some just appear when the deity dies-dead." She closed her eyes, trying to recall the exact importance of the closet. The sacred room was hidden behind the door in her bedchamber, a place every Death must first go and place his soul in with the rest of the deities.

"Death's domain extends beyond what most think of it. I just can't remember what else is here."

Lifting her eyes to the entrance, she shivered as the cool magic humming within the room grazed the back of her neck. There were two dozen smaller bowls along one table, and she paced to it. Each one was filled shallowly with water and contained flickering images.

"Sanctuaries and the shadow world," she murmured, studying each. "Portals maintained by Death for use by deities and Immortals."

Jared said nothing and walked the perimeter of the closet, trailing his hand along the wall, as if he were looking for other hidden doors.

Past-Death returned to the caldron, a sense of longing and uncertainty floating through her as she took in the souls once more. Her past was erased, the entirety of her reign as Death missing. She recalled the last twenty-six years only. They were like distant memories, with the human memories of the past week all that seemed real.

They'd know what I can't remember. She studied the lantern-like souls in the bowl. Did she want to recall everything she'd ever done? By the reactions of those around her, she wasn't certain.

Gabriel knew what she was and was willing to take a chance on her. If she didn't want to do it for her, didn't she owe it to him to see if there were any secrets she should've known as a former deity to help him?

"Jared, you said I will always be who I am. What did you mean?" she asked. "Something more than a philosophical outlook? An Immortal secret I forgot?"

"I don't give a shit about your self esteem." He was in front of the door, his ear pressed to it as he listened. "Something happened out there. I smell food."

"Are there dealers waiting for us?"

"No. Nothing living."

"Good. Now, I want to know what you meant, seeing as how you've never met me before."

"Come with me to Hell, and I'll tell you."

"Damn demons. You can't just answer this one question?"

"Does it matter to you?" he asked, facing her.

"Yes."

"Then no, I won't. You can make me a deal."

I really hate demons. "Never mind." She took a deep breath and let her hands hover over the waters of the caldron.

Fear floated through her. She wasn't so sure she was ready to see who she was, or at least, who others thought she was. But she needed something to jar her memories more now than before.

"You think you should do that? It's not human-proof?" he mocked.

"I may be human, but I'm also the mate of a deity."

"Hasn't done you any good so far," he pointed out. "If you could access Gabriel's magic, wouldn't you have been able to get us out of here?"

"I got us out of our cell." She eyed him. "Why are you so concerned for my safety now?" He had a point, even if she didn't like it. She didn't remember enough about the souls or closet to know whether or not a human mate of a powerless deity was able to talk to the souls in the caldron.

"I like not being dead-dead, and you are the best way to ensure I stay that way."

A tear she didn't feel dripped into the waters beneath her hand. Past-Death wiped her cheeks, uncertain why her human body thought now was a good time to cry.

Because I can see everything I gave up. The knowledge of the universe. The power of a goddess. The only thing missing from the closet: Gabriel.

The tears came too fast for her to prevent them, and sobs wracked her tiny frame. Past-Death sank against one of the walls and drew her knees to her chest, burying her face in her hands. She wept for all she'd chosen to give up. She wept for what had slipped through her fingers. Her future was bleak, lonely and depressing and she was helpless to change it. Even if she was able to earn back the trust of good people like Gabriel and Deidre, did she deserve it? Was she worth the time and effort it'd take them to forgive her?

Or was she better off leaving their lives for good? Gabriel was her mate by Immortal law, but she wasn't going to spend a lifetime with someone who didn't want to be with her and could never love her, even if he stayed.

The idea she'd truly lost him had never seemed real before now, and it was a thought she didn't think she could live with. She'd risked everything to love him the way she thought he deserved – and lost.

Past-Death cried until she was too tired to continue then pulled out one of the meat pies from her pocket to nibble on. There was some relief in sobbing, but it hadn't helped her resolve any of her issues.

How did someone like human Deidre handle a situation like this, where there seemed to be no real hope?

Silver lining. Past-Death dwelled on the thought she'd heard others use when talking about human Deidre. The Dark One's mate had managed to make a relationship with a demon work, had spent years with a terminal brain tumor and almost died several times when she entered the Immortal world.

She did it by looking for the good in everything, and Past-Death closed her eyes to think hard. Where was the good in her situation?

"I have nothing else to lose," she said for her ears only. She could start over, prove to herself and Gabriel that she was capable of being a better person. If there was one thing she learned from Deidre, it was that the human-turned-demon never lost hope.

Gabriel had loved her for so long, wasn't it possible he might one day love her again? If she became the person he deserved, the kind of human she needed to be?

Jared was pacing, his attention on the door. "Before you start that shit again, why not come with me to see what's out here?"

"Why?"

"Because I think we will both be pleasantly surprised. And I need you to get back in here."

Past-Death sighed no longer caring whether or not he was setting her up to be eaten or killed. "I doubt there's anything there that will surprise me."

"I bet there is."

"You willing to make a deal?"

"Yes. I bet something out there will surprise you, in exchange for you getting me a snack."

"Is that all you think about?" she grumbled. "Fine. Same small print as before." She climbed to her feet, drained and miserable.

With a nod, Jared opened the door to her bedchamber.

Deidre winced at the sight of the trashed room that had been hers. Seeing the damage didn't sting quite as much this time, though her gaze strayed once again to the jewelry box. Knowing the soul wasn't there, she resisted the urge to check again.

Human doubt. It was worse than pretty much every other emotion she'd learned about so far.

Jared didn't venture too far ahead of her, as if suspecting she was going to make a run for the closet and lock him out of it.

The bedchamber was quiet, the door to the bathing room open. Steam curled out of the door and clung to the ceiling of the bedchamber. The entrance gaped open. There were no sounds of pursuit or death dealers in the hallway outside.

"What is it?" she whispered. "What do you think will surprise me?"

"First, do you have weapons up here?"

She started to answer then stopped and looked around. She didn't – but Gabriel had kept a small arsenal in a wardrobe. "Actually, there might be. Gabe kept some of that ungodly shit there." She pointed then started to make her way towards the wardrobe.

In her path, Jared appeared to be transfixed on something. He didn't move when she approached or respond to her answer. Impatiently, she drew abreast of him and pushed at him, not wanting to venture from the narrow path through the rubble and debris that remained of her trip.

He wasn't moving.

Past-Death climbed over a few chunks of petrified wood to pass him before she, too, stopped to stare at what had his attention.

From this angle, she was able to see the bodies in the bathing chamber and how the hot springs now bubbled red. It wasn't the bloodied corpse closest to the door that caught her attention but the collection of skeletons littering the bathing chamber and even her bedchamber, near the door.

Puzzled, she walked over to the skeleton in front of the entrance and knelt beside it. The man had been reduced to bone and clothing. "I should know what did this," she said, mentally battering at the blockade in her mind that kept her memories from her. "But it's been more than twenty six years ago. I'm not surprised, though, demon."

"What?"

She twisted, glaring at Jared. "What is wrong with you? Help me figure out what this is or go get weapons or something."

He was smiling. "You don't see it."

"The bones?"

"No." He indicated the bathing chamber by tilting his chin towards it. "You know what tears out a man's throat like that?"

She rose and moved to get a better look. One of the death dealers had his throat ripped out, and the deep scratches on his face and arms were visible. "Ugh. Looks like the work of one of you sick demons."

"Only two demons in the palace," he said, satisfied.

"You and ...who?"

"Deidre."

"Oh, no. She's way too ..." Past-Death patted the air, seeking the right word. "Soft. I'd believe me capable of that before I'd consider her."

Jared strode forward, pausing by the wardrobe containing clothing. He fished something off the ground and lifted it.

Past-Death frowned. It was Deidre's Hell dress.

"She's a demon, the mate of the Dark One. I think she's learning her power," Jared said, far too satisfied by the discovery for past-Death's comfort. "Surprised?"

It was hard to deny the idea, especially with Deidre's dress in her bedchamber. Past-Death was pensive for a moment, unable to shake the sense of guilt in her. Her actions had turned Deidre into a demon. Was there any part of the sweet, innocent human that would survive Hell?

Or was it like she was learning: she was still very much herself, just … different in a few ways. Weaker. Less able to control her world. More willing to trust something intangible like hope, maybe even love.

"If true, yes," past-Death said. "So now I owe you what, a hand?"

"Whatever."

"It won't be mine."

"I'm fine with that."

"Well, that doesn't explain the skeletons, unless that's a trick of Darkyn's no one knows about that Deidre picked up?" she asked, turning to the wardrobe with weapons.

Jared shook his head and growled. "No. It makes me think we are better off in the closet."

"I didn't think demons were cowards."

"I'm not a coward. A survivor. You seem to forget you aren't immortal anymore. As a demon in the underworld, I've got the same chance of surviving as a puny human, except I can fight."

"Whatever, demon. Is this what you're looking for?" She threw open the doors of the wardrobe. Gabriel kept a plethora of weapons he'd mastered over the years: swords and knives of different sizes and different blades, axes and maces, whips, bos, nun chucks … There were exotic weapons she didn't know the names of he'd likely found in the fairy realm of Elisia, demons' weapons in black metal, and a few other ancient human weapons.

"I'm in love," Jared breathed. He pushed her unceremoniously out of the way and gazed at the collection, wide-eyed and drooling again. "Most of these are collector's pieces."

"Pick what you want," she said, unconcerned. "If we don't make it out of here alive, it won't matter what those things are worth."

He murmured and marveled, needing no audience, as he picked up a weapon to study it, replaced it with reverence demons showed only for tools of killing, and moved to another.

Past-Death returned to the pile of skeletons. "I know what did this." But thinking about it made her head hurt.

She'd seen Deidre run away with a young woman, no doubt a deity. One capable of doing *this*.

"C'mon." Jared gripped her arm and hauled her up. "You need to practice."

"Practice what?" she grumbled.

"Killing." He pushed her arms up and wrapped a leather belt with delicate filigree around her waist, this one containing sheathes for a few weapons he'd lined up on a chunk of marble.

There was a time when a single touch caused men to drop at her feet. Past-Death had never feared taking a life; it had been a sacred duty, one she performed up until the day she left. Death was sacred, as was life, though she doubted she was going to like the way demons killed.

"Short sword, axe, and knife. These are Elisian, made for the fairy warriors who are about your size." Jared held up each one as he spoke before placing it in its respective sheath. "You're in luck, cupcake. There are a few dead dealers in the bathing chamber waiting for you to practice."

He wore his own collection of weapons, much larger than hers. Sheathing the last, he pushed her towards the bathing room.

"So barbaric," she complained. Past-Death stepped over rivulets of blood, disappointed by the amount of blood that tainted the hot springs pink. "It'll take a lot of work to get the blood out of there."

"The Elisian metal is light enough for someone as weak as you."

She glared at him.

"We've got a few bodies. Try chopping off arms or something," Jared suggested.

"Really? This is your plan?"

"Listen, cupcake, it's easier to do when someone is already dead-dead. You can make mistakes here. You can't when they're alive." He drew a dagger as he spoke and bent down, slicing off the ear of a dead dealer. "Lots of skeletons. Whatever did it works fast."

"I noticed that, too." Past-Death took in the death. "Ten skeletons, four other. Only one looks like a demon did it. These three look like they just fell over dead."

"A demoness learning her magic. She can kill with a touch. This one was personal," he assessed, standing over the dealer with the ravaged body. "Maybe this skeleton-maker was in danger."

Past-Death wasn't certain how to explain it. Until she saw Deidre again, she wasn't about to assume the sweet girl could do anything like this.

"Me, however …" She gazed down at the body at her feet. "I think I can." Death was second nature to her. She understood it differently as a human and had the compelling need not to cause too much pain. She'd never understood the difference between a quick and slow death or why so many begged her for a quick one, when she was a deity.

It was because humans and Immortals were blessed with the ability to feel the softness of clothing, the warmth of sunlight. Their bodies were sensitive and delicate, the sensations so deliciously intense, like the way Gabriel smelled or how his hands felt skimming down her naked skin.

Having been attacked by a demon, it made sense to her now that pain was as powerful as pleasure to creatures so sensitive to their environments.

"Elisian weapons are specially designed … to require less … effort," Jared explained, gnawing on the ear he'd chopped free.

"You're disgusting," she muttered.

"Better his ear than yours."

She grimaced at his display and drew the axe. With a head the size of her palm and delicate designs carved into the staff, it appeared more like a decorative piece than anything else. It was as light as a stick, and she swung it around in front of her face. The blade appeared to be sharpened to the point of becoming translucent.

"You sure this is meant to be used in battle?" she asked.

"Positive. Test it. Hack off that one's foot."

Her attention went to the dealer nearest her. She bent over, raised the axe, and drove it downward. Expecting to feel resistance, she braced her body and almost fell over when it sliced through the ankle with no effort.

"Wow." Past-Death regained her balance and straightened, hope blossoming. "You're right. I can defeat an army with this. We may not die here after all."

Jared snorted. "If they were already dead, maybe. But you have to not get killed first in order to take out one of your trained killers."

"There's no Elisian armor?"

"None. Toss me that foot and we're even."

With a grimace, she picked it up by the big toe and threw it to him.

"How 'bout its head? I'll keep it for later."

"Chop off your own head," she snapped. "I'm not supporting your filthy demon habit."

"You who shoves a whole animal into an oven find my habit filthy?"

Past-Death replaced the axe at her waist and drew the sword, intent on trying out all her new toys.

"Someone is coming."

Her gaze flew up.

Jared had gone rigid, clenching the ear between his teeth as he reached for a dagger.

"Back to the closet," she said and hurried out of the bathing chamber.

Whatever Jared sensed, she did not, but demons had the instincts of animals, not humans.

Jared was quick to follow, and she opened the door to the secret room, leading them in.

Only when it was closed did she relax. "Did the death dealers find us?"

"Maybe. I'd rather meet them on neutral territory than risk fighting in that mess."

Past-Death returned to the caldron, wishing she knew what was supposed to happen in the sacred place. "I guess we wait them out this time."

Chapter Twelve

"Okay, so no one is here," Deidre stood in the doorway of the cell she'd shared with past-Death and Jared. There was no blood in the air, a sign past-Death hadn't been eaten before leaving the dungeon.

He got his fill of the guards on the floor above. She'd stopped to look too long, drawn by the delicious scent of blood and the eerie, nauseating acknowledgment she had the same ability to disassemble a human body as Jared had.

"I don't know where to start looking. I could search this place forever." Troubled, she moved away from the cell. Past-Death had the advantage of knowing the palace, whereas Deidre was easily lost and running on fumes.

Karma had drifted down the hallway and stood halfway between Deidre's old cell and her own.

"Karma, are you ready to go?" Deidre called as loudly as she dared with a worried look over her shoulder.

The deity's hair had gone straight, a sign Deidre took to mean she was upset. Approaching, Deidre reached out to touch Karma's arm.

"Whatever it is, it's okay," she said. "We'll get out of here together."

"This does not worry me," Karma replied.

"What's wrong then?"

Without replying, Karma turned away and started down the hallway, towards the exit. Deidre followed, concerned as much for her new friend as she was being discovered.

Or being forced into a position where she had to kill again.

"Your friend is not here," Karma observed. "We should leave the palace. Find those seeking you."

Deidre's heart skipped a beat. "Darkyn."

"The Great Imbalance and others."

"They aren't here for me," Deidre said. "But he is. You think we can evade the dealers long enough to reach the forest?"

"Karma isn't sure." The deity studied her. "You are very weak."

"I know." Deidre swallowed hard. "I don't have a choice though, do I?"

Karma shook her head. "And if you die-dead, Death or the Great Imbalance are the only who can raise a soul."

"So we need to find them no matter what." Deidre chewed on her lower lip. "What about my friend? What if she's in trouble or worse?"

Karma rested her hands on Deidre's shoulders, and her hair instantly tightened into spirals. "You are in trouble now. You will not live long enough to help her. We must go to the forest and save your life."

Deidre managed a smile. "Why do people hate you? You're so sweet."

Karma's eyebrows quirked. "I am sweet because you are. I reflect those around me, remember?"

Deidre nodded, not wanting to think about how Karma was going to react when she ran into the Dark One.

"We will fix you then come back. Come!" Karma took her hand and took off at a quick trot, jarring Deidre out of her spot. "It will be dark soon. We can escape then."

"Really? It looked like noon to me."

"I has been here long enough to understand how time passes. Night is coming."

Deidre said nothing, focusing her remaining energy on fleeing.

"Once we leave the palace, don't let go of my hand, until we reach safety. No matter what."

"Okay," Deidre replied. Reluctant to leave past-Death behind, she also suspected she wasn't going to last long enough to make a difference in helping her quasi-friend, if she didn't find her mate in time.

The idea he'd come to the underworld to find her – that Gabriel let him – filled Deidre with an emotion so happy, it gave her strength when she feared hers was almost gone.

Together with Karma, she ran.

Chapter Thirteen

G abriel checked the sky once more. The two suns were up
in the position of midday, but the forest animals had
grown quiet, preparing for the night they knew was
coming.

Calculating how long he had before someone noticed the scouts
missing on the eastern side of the palace, he determined he had
enough time to await nightfall. There were hundreds of death
dealers in the palace. He didn't need to go in, just make it to the
wall where he knew there to be an entrance to one of the secret
passages past-Death taught him about.

He settled back into the brush and withdrew a rag to wipe the
blood from his weapons. Steadying his breath, he focused on
grounding himself in the short period of time he had between day
and night.

"Are we not charging full speed to take the palace?"

Tensing, Gabriel twisted to face the speaker without raising his
weapons.

Fate crouched a few feet away, dressed as if for a safari, down to
his round hat and the binoculars dangling around his neck. The

stunning deity was lean and toned, his eyes swirling every color and no color at all. Brown hair peeked out from the hat.

Gabriel wasn't entirely certain how to take the deity's visit. "You come when no one wants you and don't come when I could use insight. You are brilliantly inconsistent, Fate."

"As are you, Death." Fate smiled, flashing white teeth. Ostensibly open and friendly, he was nonetheless devious in the way of a powerful, bored god. He settled onto a stump near Gabriel. "But I'm happy to say you're getting better."

Gabriel continued with his weapons, debating what to say to the deity who had proven to be both the best mentor he'd ever had and the greatest liar he'd ever dealt with.

"Did you figure it out?" Fate asked at his silence.

"Figure what out?"

"What's wrong with the underworld. Why it locked you out."

"*You* locked me out."

"Semantics. It would've done the same if it could. A domain is vulnerable to its master, even if he doesn't intend to hurt it."

Gabriel eyed him. "Maybe I did. It was broken, because I came close to breaking two of the three original laws, thanks to human emotion."

"Terribly romantic, isn't it?" Fate grinned. "The great deity Death suffers from heartbreak and turns away from his destiny, and the universe crumbles."

"Terrible, yes." Gabriel sheathed his weapons. "What's worse: why you couldn't just tell me what to fucking do."

"It's complicated."

"No it's not. Just say, hey, Gabe. Stop being an ass and be a good Death."

"I think I did try that approach." Fate grinned. "I told you a lot, Gabriel, but you weren't ready to hear it or didn't understand it, if you did."

Gabriel shook his head, sensing it was probably the truth.

"You needed to learn a few more important lessons first," Fate said simply. "I can't force feed outcomes, Gabe. I may egg along chains of events from time to time, but if I am to respect free will, I need to show you the road without necessarily telling you where it goes."

Gabriel swallowed the retort he wanted to give.

"And then there was Deidre," Fate added a bit more sadly. "Every once in awhile, the plight of a human makes me almost-feel something."

"That's the problem," Gabriel seconded. "I can't get over it."

"You must, if you are to heal yourself and the underworld."

"You have no fucking clue what it's like to feel. Not *almost* feel but really experience emotions."

"I don't," Fate agreed. "But maybe you should look at it the way Deidre does. As a silver-lining. If past-Death hadn't done what she did, Deidre wouldn't exist."

"She wouldn't hurt or spend eternity in Hell, either."

"She wouldn't have reached the part of you and Darkyn that can feel."

Gabriel was quiet, considering. "I'd rather spare her the misery of her current life than letting worthless gods *feel*."

"Gabriel, you are missing the point. You are Death, the Keeper of Souls, Guardian of the Dead, Master of the Underworld, the first ever human-turned-deity. Your very existence was destined to start a new era, rewrite the Immortal Code, and create billions of new chains of events."

"I think you're exaggerating," Gabriel said with a chuckle. He moved onto his belly to peer through the brush and monitor the movement of dealers to and from the palace.

"If you being *you* has resulted in this, then what do you think Deidre being Deidre will do? You are both anomalies, created at just the right time, and given just the right power you need to forever alter the Future." Fate crawled down beside him.

"To prevent another upheaval," Gabriel guessed. "To stop Darkyn from raising his Army of Souls."

"What're we looking for?" Fate had his binoculars out.

"You blind, old man? We're barely thirty meters away."

"They came with the outfit. There must be a reason to use them."

"Look for anything that might prevent me from reaching the palace." Gabriel rolled his eyes. "Am I right? Are the two super important humans coming into play on your chessboard right now to counter Darkyn's plans?"

"Yes."

"So this is less about helping me and more about some danger only you can see," he surmised.

In that light, Fate's explanation made sense. Unfortunately, it came from the mouth of a known liar.

However little he trusted fate, Gabriel understood that Deidre was as special as he was. She was first human to become a deity's mate – twice even! – and the first and only mate of a Dark One. She'd already displayed her ability to influence Darkyn, to protect the innocent and therefore limit the reaches and power of Hell.

"It's both," Fate replied. "I'm ninety percent more likely to succeed now. Besides, everyone needs a favor from Death at some point."

"You plotting against me?"

Fate smiled without answering.

Gabriel fell quiet, dwelling on the explanation while also scouring the tree line for signs of activity. Fate had a way of softening horrible events, of making them sound manageable, if not necessary. If it weren't the fact he was also an untrustworthy, lying asshole …

"I can see the appeal," Fate said. "These are effective."

It was hard to stay upset at the low-key deity who appeared impressed by something as human as binoculars.

"You swear on what horrible, corrupt, shriveled up soul you have that Deidre was not created simply to suffer?" Gabriel asked.

"I do swear it. You were both created for reasons greater than you know. Besides, the past is done, Gabriel. Hanging onto it is what got you into this mess. It'll kill you, if you don't let it go."

Gabriel relaxed. The assurance eased some of his concern while making the hair on the back of his neck raise in alarm at the smug note in the deity's voice.

"Speaking of Darkyn," Fate murmured. "He and Rhyn are smashing through the forest."

Gabriel looked in the direction Fate was peering. Without the precision of the binoculars, Gabriel saw the forest's frantic movement and the darting of dealers in the direction but was unable to identify exactly what came.

"Good timing for a distraction," he said and pushed himself up.

The suns had begun to drop rapidly towards the shifting horizon of the underworld. In a matter of two minutes, it'd be sunset.

"What's the plan?" Fate asked, standing as well.

"You can see the Future," Gabriel said wryly. "Why don't you tell me?"

"It's more fun when you don't look." The lean deity clapped his hands and rubbed them together. "I'm ready." Dressed in his safari clothing and matching wide-brimmed hat, Fate was armed with binoculars and his grin, about as far from ready as Gabriel could imagine.

"You're really coming with me?" Skeptical, Gabriel started to smile.

"Until things get bad, at which point I'll leave," replied the deity.

"Appreciate the honesty." Gabriel growled. "So I should assume you don't have my back."

"That's not how this works."

"It never is."

"This adventure isn't going to wait long for us." Fate faced the palace.

"Did you peek at the future and know it's safe to go or are you a fucking lunatic as usual?"

Fate stepped from the forest.

Gabriel drew his weapons with a muttered curse and followed, lifting his weapons into ready positions, in case Fate was fucking with him.

The raucous from the southern approach drew his attention briefly. The forest appeared to be boiling with activity, and dealers swarmed like ants over the two demons. For a moment, he hesitated, compelled to help, especially knowing Darkyn was far weaker here without access to his power. If Rhyn or Andre were killed, Gabriel was able to raise him. He didn't feel quite so generous towards the Dark One.

The demon had to stay alive, for Deidre's sake.

"Come on, Gabe. They're fine," Fate called.

"You're sure?"

"Compared to our issue, yes."

Gabriel returned his focus to the palace and trotted after the fearless deity ahead of him. Fate reached the wall and waited.

"This way," Gabriel said, motioning towards the north. "Secret passages. And what do you mean by *our* issue?"

"There's an eighty percent chance that a certain prisoner in the dungeon got loose. I want to assess the damage, if so."

Gabriel said nothing, uncertain what past-Death might've kept in the dungeon, but understanding Fate's sudden interest in doing something that might get his hands dirty.

Sticking to the side of the palace, they hurried down the north side, until Gabriel reached the entrance to the secret passageways. The door was where he expected it to be, and he opened it, motioning for Fate to enter with him.

The inside was dark and quiet.

Death's bedchamber, he willed the stones.

A few seconds passed before he heard them begin to shift. Gabriel waited in the darkness until they had settled once more, listening absently to Fate's restless movement behind him.

"Watch your step," he whispered and started forward.

"I don't like the dark, Gabe."

He said nothing.

"I would go so far to say it scares me, if I felt such a human emotion," Fate added, crowding him.

"You're scared of something?" Gabriel asked, amazed. "You're a god who taunts deities and can access the Future. How can you almost-fear anything?" More comfortable in the darkness and night than out in the sun, Gabriel trusted the palace to take him where he needed to go and strode confidently forward.

"It is frightening not to be able to *see*."

"I doubt a dark hallway is the worst place you've ever been."

"True. But this is how I imagine the lives of everyone else to be."

"You fear losing your Sight, not the dark," Gabriel clarified. "You think we wander around in the darkness trying to stick to some path you put at our feet and hoping not to hit a brick wall?"

"It definitely looks that way from where I sit. You have no idea what you're doing."

"It's not about *knowing* what we're doing. It's about experiencing. It's what we call living. You fucking deities will never get it. Past-Death is the only one of you brave enough to try it while the rest of you look down on the human experience," Gabriel said, irritated. "I can tell you one thing, Fate. You'd never get bored as a human."

"Perhaps. It's a little too limiting for my taste. Though I sometimes do things like this to see what I almost-feel. I'm not sure I could spend a lifetime like this." Fate was quiet for a moment. "I could create a theme park for deities. Being Human, the Ride."

"Make sure it randomly jackknives into brick walls in the name of establishing new chains-of-events."

"That can be arranged."

The outline of a doorway appeared ahead. Gabriel slowed. "I need to do something I should have my first day," he said. "I need some space. You want to go to the dungeon?"

"Yes."

"After I step through the door, tell the passage where to take you."

"Are you excited?"

"About?"

"Everything you need to become the most powerful Death ever is behind the door you've been avoiding since you took your throne."

Gabriel's heart quickened. Past-Death had once told him he'd become like her, when he walked into the closet in the corner of her bedchamber. He'd avoided doing it for that reason. No part of him was ready to give up what remained of his humanity to turn into the manipulative sociopath that preceded him.

It seemed … petty now to avoid doing his duty, because he resented her. However lacking she was in the emotional area, however cruel she was capable of being, she'd been an effective and devoted Death, her first priority always the souls she safeguarded, even if she fucked up everyone else around her.

In contrast, emotions had clouded his judgment, and he'd left his home vulnerable and the souls exposed to those who wanted them for nefarious purposes.

"Now you are afraid," Fate whispered.

"I won't fail this time," Gabriel said firmly. "Safe travels to the dungeon."

Without another word, he opened the door and left, closing it behind him.

Death's bedchamber was trashed. It wasn't the rubble of his bed and walls alone that made his brow furrow, but the evidence of a small massacre in the wake of the destruction. With a deep frown, he took in everything then decided not even the bizarre scene before him was going to deter him.

Gabriel strode to the door in the corner and balled up his fists. His heart raced, his emotions flickering between regret and resolve.

If I have to give up what it means to be human to protect everyone, I will. But it was hard. So hard. He'd held onto his soul for tens of thousands of years and managed to keep the piece of him that made him empathize with those whose lives he took. It wasn't easy. He'd almost lost himself a few times, only for his best friend, Rhyn, to bring him back and remind him why a world filled with emotionless gods and goddesses was wrong.

Human life was sacred – and so was human death. The Immortals and deities never understood either as such, but humans were special. Delicate. With the shortest life spans of all the creatures in all the realms, they were also capable of so much: of love and loss, of great accomplishments and harrowing disappointments, of beauty, no matter what their circumstances. They did more in their short years than a member of any other race of creatures did in millennia.

He wasn't ready to lose that connection, but if he didn't accept his fate fully, the underworld and everyone he cared about would suffer. The souls would suffer, too, the selfish decision of one man plunging billions of innocents into eternal despair.

Whatever lay behind the door before him, it was the key to stopping the underworld from its downward spiral, the key to establishing control.

Gabriel drew a calming breath, opened the door to his future – and froze in surprise.

Staring back at him from the middle of the most sacred place in the underworld was a demon.

"What the fuck?"

"Before you –" The demon started.

Gabriel had whipped out a knife and snatched the familiar demon before it finished. He slammed him into the ceiling, blade biting into the skin of the creature.

"-do that." The demon squirmed.

"Gabriel!" It was past-Death's voice. "Stop!"

More surprises every day. Unable to explain what was going on, he went perfectly still, ready to snap the demon's neck or release him, depending on how well he understood the explanation that came next.

"We're helping each other escape," his mate said. "He got us out of the dungeon. I promised him neither you nor I would hurt him. So put him down now."

Her cool command had no effect on him this time. "Are you hurt?" he asked her without releasing the demon. "Are you saying this under duress?"

"No, Gabriel," past-Death sighed. "He's like my pet ... sorta. Smelly, disgusting and always hungry but basically harmless. Release him. Please."

"I know this demon," Gabriel said, peering more closely at the blond creature. "You've alternately helped then betrayed then helped Rhyn."

"Yes," the demon hissed. "Friendly pet."

Gabriel lowered him from the ceiling, struggling to digest how he'd entered the most sacred place in the underworld only to find a fucking demon there ahead of him. He ventured a glance at his mate, and his gaze stuck, the way it always had whenever he saw her.

Beautiful, if tired, deity-Deidre's large eyes were the purest blue, her wispy blonde hair swept back and tied at the base of her neck. She was pale enough to be a ghost, and her clothing was rumpled and bloodied. His protective instinct prodded him, and he found the resentment he normally experienced whenever they saw one another slipping away at the sight of her state.

The pulse of their bond shimmered between them for a split second, his attraction to her as strong now as it had been when he first fell for her so long ago. He wanted to sweep her up in his arms, make love to her until the sad look on her face disappeared, and then conquer his world with her at his side.

We aren't ready for that yet. Frustration of a different kind left him more wired, but he restrained the urge to touch his mate, to feel her warm skin and hold her while gazing into her eyes.

"Hey," he said.

"Hey," she answered with a small, shy smile.

"Hey," the demon said.

Gabriel eyed him and strode to the door, tossing him out. He closed the door behind him.

"I swore to help him, Gabriel," his mate reminded him.

"If something happens, we'll hear him scream." Gabriel was transfixed by her once more.

She folded her arms across her chest, appearing as apprehensive as he was frustrated. He wasn't certain where to start and had completely forgotten the sacred surroundings.

"See? Nothing bad happened by coming here," she started. "I don't know what you thought this was, but it's not bad."

Gabriel took in the subdued room. Drawn to the souls at its center, he peered into a large bowl of multi-hued gems.

"Deities," he said, surprised. "This is where I was supposed to put my soul?"

"Yeah."

Fuck. She was right. There was nothing in the room trying to change who he was, only his fear.

"I'm a fucking fool," he muttered.

"Not for that reason." Past-Death rested a hand on his forearm then withdrew quickly. Her cool touch sent relief spinning through him. "I'm afraid I can't help you figure out what's supposed to happen next. Memory loss."

"I don't care," he replied. Turning to her, Gabriel swept her small frame into his arms and squeezed her hard. She molded against him, resisting no part of his hug. "You're safe. That's all that matters. Though I can't believe you're hanging out here with a demon."

Gabriel held her, his body instinctively relaxing the way it did every time his mate was in his arms. It took all his concentration to keep his hands from wandering the way they wanted to.

Her arms circled him, and she squeezed. "I'm resourceful." She lifted her face to rest her chin on his chest. "Aren't I? Am I resourceful? I know I *was*."

"Yeah," he said with a chuckle. "You're definitely resourceful."

"Am I better this time than last?"

At the mournful note in her voice, he looked down at her. She appeared distraught or at least, overly concerned about his response.

"I've always loved you," he replied, brushing hair from her face. "But yeah, you're much more likeable this time around."

The sadness didn't leave her features. She ducked her head and pressed it to his chest. He held her quietly. Before her abduction, they'd reached a truce, willing to try to rebuild the trust between them. Losing her again had cemented his determination but also his fear that they were destined to continue hurting each other, whether by choice or not.

Somehow, he had to get past that fear and uncertainty, had to accept his mate and any baggage that came with her.

"I don't like losing you," he told her.

"You won't again. I can't leave the underworld for one," she replied. "Second, I'm ready to be a better person, whether or not you want to be in my life. Losing your soul because your mate doesn't love you enough kind of makes you rethink who you are."

Gabriel said nothing, squeezing her more tightly against him. He hadn't asked about the deal, uncertain what good it'd do. There had been too much anger for him to love her unconditionally, the way he once had.

What he did know: she belonged where she was, in his arms, her warm, feminine body pressed close enough that he was able to smell her familiar scent. He filled his senses with her, a tremor of resentment and anger lingering despite his attempt to push their rocky history out of his thoughts. He'd vowed once not to let his past rule him. He thought he'd been relatively successful, until the Lake showed him images that made the intense emotions bubble up again.

There were no more lies between them, no more secrets. Knowing this did little to ease the ache he experienced whenever he thought of her. There was so much damage and history between them …

Unable to dispel his troubled thoughts, he simply held her, grateful to know she was safe and in his arms once more.

"Did you retake the palace?" she asked, voice muffled against his chest.

"No. I came with a few Immortals and a particularly hungry Dark One."

"That's it?" she pulled away to stare at him, startled. "Gabriel, how can we take back our home?"

"I have a plan. Trust me," he growled, irked as much by her critical tone as he was her too accurate question.

She studied him briefly. "Okay. I do." Without another word, she moved away from his embrace towards the souls.

"That's it? You'll trust me?" he echoed.

"Yes. Without question."

Impressed, he joined her at the pedestal. "I've never heard those words from you."

"I figure it'll soften the blow when I tell you the demon and I are using the weapons you kept up here."

He hissed. "Those were rare, collector's items in mint condition spanning several millennia of search efforts."

She held up an Elisian knife proudly. "I can almost use it, too."

"That's … good," he managed.

She went to sheathe the blade and dropped it, point down, on the floor.

"Oh, gods, woman, be careful with that shit," he grumbled.

"I got it." She lifted it to show him then put it away carefully. "Jared was teaching me how to hack off limbs with them."

Gabriel glanced at her.

"Barbaric." Her features skewed. "But I'll do it. I'll defend you and the underworld, even if I must behave like a savage."

He hid a smile. She was uncertain but determined, her arrogant edge dampened by sorrow. The mix was enchanting, her honesty, absentminded humor and dedication to her duty reminding him why he'd fallen in love with her long ago in the first place. There was a new, raw edge to her as well, one he didn't know how to read. It was neither despair nor vulnerability, and for the first time since he'd known her, she was completely, utterly open to him.

"We'll be alright," he promised her, wrapping an arm around her once more. "I really expected more of this place."

"Maybe there is more," she said, frustrated. "I can't remember. You can monitor the Sanctuaries and in-between places from there." She pointed to a low table lined with bowls. "Your soul goes here, whenever you find it."

He grimaced. "You searched?"

"Of course. It's the first thing I did," she said, gazing up at him. "You can't love me yet, but I love you, Gabriel. I wouldn't let them hurt you. I've never let anyone hurt you and I never will. You may not have known that, but it's true."

"I think that's my job now."

"Oh, no. I'll always take care of you," she replied archly.

He'd spent his life feeling the emotion that was displayed on her face. She wasn't the woman he fell in love with. She was becoming the woman he'd wished she'd been.

"But yours wasn't here," she added and returned her attention to the souls.

"Harmony has it."

"No." At the odd note in her voice, he waited. "I almost think … Deidre has it. I told her where it was, and she was taken away." She drifted off. "They returned her to the dungeon, to the cells at the back, and she escaped with … someone. I didn't see her again after she left our cell to ask her about your soul."

"If you didn't see her, how do you know this?" he asked.

She hesitated. "It's hard to explain. I was able to dreamwalk. No one could see me, but I could go anywhere and even get the keys to our cell."

"You were always good at being a ghost in your realm and spying on your dealers. Maybe you retained the ability."

"I was spying on you to make sure there was no one else."

"That's not creepy," he replied wryly. "There never was. Only you."

She ducked her head to hide a smile, face growing pink. "I know."

"About Deidre …" he started and then stopped.

She tensed. "They did something horrible to her, before she escaped."

"Horrible?"

"There was blood everywhere."

Gabriel's stomach filled with the weight of dread, but he didn't let himself dwell long on it. If he hadn't restricted the Dark One's magic in the underworld, there would be no underworld left when Darkyn found out.

"She's okay?" he asked.

"She seemed to be."

"Darkyn won't flip out then."

Past-Death stared at him. "I can't believe you brought that thing into my underworld."

"*My* underworld," he corrected. "He wouldn't let me access the portal through Hell otherwise."

"I hope you have a plan with how to deal with him!"

"I do. Trust me."

It took longer for her to say the words this time. "Okay. I do."

Maybe she's serious. "You said she escaped with someone from the dungeon? Fate went down to look for other occupants. Any idea who he wants to find?"

Past-Death shook her head. "I can't recall. There were two. One is dead, the other a female deity I felt the need to lock up for some reason. I hope Fate finds her and gets his ass kicked."

"And you don't know where Deidre is?"

"No. The demon wanted to find her, too, but we don't know where to start looking here."

She looked at him, a little too long, and Gabriel lifted his eyes to hers.

"It kills me to see you sad," he said, softening.

"It's deserved."

He took her hand and squeezed it. "I don't think it's as bad as you think."

Past-Death arched an eyebrow at him.

"Aside from losing your soul and the underworld being ready to implode, I think things between us are better than they've been," he said with a touch of his dark humor.

"That's awful, Gabriel." Her features skewed, as if she wasn't certain whether she wanted to cry or laugh.

"There are no more secrets."

"No, there aren't," she agreed. "Why did it take the world crashing down around us for us to really see each other?"

"Because you're the most stubborn fucking person in the universe."

This time, she did laugh.

Gabriel gazed at her, the thrum of his mating bond to her strong and sure. He always struggled to keep the distance he thought was warranted between them, aware that trusting her was how he normally ended up fucked up. Her laugh melted the iciness around

LIZZY FORD

his heart, made him yearn to take a chance on the partner he
believed her capable of being.

Human Deidre had called them both selfish, and he realized
how true it was. Obsessed with one another, he and past-Death both
had blinders on when it came to dealing with anything that got
between them.

"Are we still dysfunctional?" past-Death asked somewhat sadly.

"A little, yeah."

"Did you ever think maybe that's the way we're supposed
to be?"

Gabriel chuckled. "As long as we can trust one another, I don't
care what shade of dysfunction we are."

"I promise never to lie to you again, Gabriel. Or deceive you or
to twist the truth or manipulate you," she said solemnly. "Does
that help?"

"It's a start."

Past-Death sighed. "Humans are so fucking slow at everything."

Gabriel smiled. He loved her spirit as much as her laugh, but
nothing yet had proven to him that she was worthy of his trust. "If
there's something you want to say, I'm listening."

"Like … what?"

"Anything. What's making you sad."

Past-Death appeared torn for a moment before she nodded.
"Maybe there is."

Gabriel leaned back against the wall, getting comfortable.

"I've had nothing but time to think here. I'm pretty sure I owe
you an apology," she said quietly. "Probably more than one. For
lying and everything."

"I'd say so."

She rolled her eyes.

"I need to apologize, too," Gabriel said. "This entire thing with
the underworld is my fault. All I had to do was walk in here, and
everything would be mostly fine."

"I told you to," she reminded him.

"And that's why I couldn't do it."

Past-Death frowned.

"I may have loved you my whole life, but I hated you, too. I think you know now as a human how not to deal with another human, especially one you like?"

"Yeah." Disappointed, she stared at the floor. "I hated the human part of you, because I felt like it came between us. I couldn't control it or you completely. And I couldn't understand it."

Gabriel listened.

"I did a lot of really stupid things." There was pain in her voice. "I don't … regret becoming human, though, Gabriel. I've learned more about you in the past week than I ever knew in all the time we spent together. I'm only sorry that I lost you in the process."

"You say it like there's no second chance," he said quietly.

"I've got nothing else to give, Gabe, and I don't know what to do."

"I swear to you, Deidre. I'll do everything I can to get your soul back. On my heart, on my soul, on the souls in the Lake. Whatever it takes, I'll get it back," he said.

"You can't promise me that, Gabriel. Your duty is to the underworld and its souls."

"And to my mate. You know how importantly I take that."

She studied him for a moment then looked away. "I do. I also think you let your feelings for me prevent you from being Death."

"Not my feelings. My past," he said, hearing the truth in the words. "But that stops now. We're doing this together."

"You're so sweet, Gabriel," she whispered. "You're such a better person than I am."

"Stop, Deidre. Today we're starting again. Think we can do that?"

She nodded, though he saw the doubt on her features.

"It'll work. It has to. We care too much about one another for it not to," he added softly. "Trust me?" He took her hand and squeezed it.

Past-Death lifted her gaze to his. "Always."

He smiled, a flicker of hope flaring to life within him. With nothing else between them and the door closed on their past, they had a shot at making it. He felt it.

She turned her attention to the caldron. "Your underworld needs you, Gabriel."

He shifted closer to her, and they both puzzled over the caldron. "You don't remember what should happen next?"

"No. But it can't be that hard." She frowned. "Maybe this is all there is? You put your soul here and it's done?"

He said nothing but peered more closely into the caldron, releasing her hand to lean forward. "There's writing around the inner lip of the bowl."

Past-Death leaned forward as well. "Definitely ancient Immortal script."

Gabriel ran his thumb over the geometric writing to loosen the grunge of time that had sunk into the grooves. "Finally. Maybe someone else left me instructions." Whoever carved the wording into the bowl had been kind enough to use Immortal script rather than the script of the deities, which originated from the time-before-time.

He searched until he found the start of the sentence. "*Death must swear to the deities by one of The Three Laws to protect all souls and to perform his sacred duty until the underworld chooses another.*" He reread it to ensure his translation was generally accurate. "The underworld chooses another. So you didn't pick me?"

"Missing memory." Past-Death tapped her temple. "But it definitely signaled to me I was out when the sky cracked. I trusted you above everyone to take my place. Whether I was influenced by something …" She shrugged. "No way for me to know."

Gabriel dwelt on the revelation. "This is why a boy of human origin was permitted to enter the underworld in the first place without being dead or losing his soul. It chose me the day you took me in, didn't it?"

The idea his appointment was planned from the day he entered Death's service at the age of seventeen and not a knee-jerk reaction by a manipulative, vengeful goddess made the world around him seem to stop.

I've been waiting for someone to say they made a mistake. He hadn't realized it until this moment, that his frustration and resentment with the overwhelming job were born as much of self-doubt as they were feeling ill-fitted to the position of Death. Some small part of him believed what every other Immortal and deity told him about no human belonging in the seat of a deity.

He hadn't been able to trust past-Death's judgment enough to believe that maybe there was a greater plan in motion, hadn't believed that not only was he the right person for this job but the *only* person the underworld would accept.

You are both anomalies, created at just the right time, and given just the right power you need to forever alter the Future. Fate had said. The deity was known for being melodramatic, but Gabriel saw his words in a new light.

Like Deidre, he hadn't been *born*. He'd been *created* by some deity with a higher purpose. His battle wasn't with the underworld but with himself.

What if this chain of events hadn't started when he was a teen but before that – at his birth? What if he had always been destined to become the first ever Death of human origin that ever existed?

"I think I understand now," he said in a hushed tone, humbled by the idea that his life meant so much more than he ever knew.

"I can see it on your face." Past-Death smiled. "I really want to take credit for this moment." She took his hand again.

"Me, too," Fate said from behind them. "In fact, I think I will."

"You," Deidre growled, facing him.

Gabriel took another moment of peace, before he, too, confronted Fate. "That's why you wanted me to come here first," he said.

"One of the reasons," Fate admitted. "The other was so I can see you take the oath."

"By one of the three original laws from the time-before-time."

"Yes. It's a historical moment, or will be." Fate smiled. "The first human to become a deity. Don't frown, honey."

Past-Death was scowling at him. "I don't remember why, but I know not to trust you."

"You'd be right," Gabriel replied firmly.

Fate winked at past-Death. "No hard feelings, as long as you acknowledge that I won."

Gabriel said nothing, studying the god. He thought twice about asking the question he wanted to ask. Namely, if past-Death had created Deidre, who created him?

But he didn't think the answer was going to be one he liked. Deidre had gone through nothing but heartache since discovering she was made to be a stand in by a goddess with one purpose. He didn't want to think about what went into making him a possibility.

"You find who you were looking for in the dungeon?" he asked instead.

"Yes, who is in the dungeon?" past-Death seconded.

"No one now."

"Don't be an ass," she snapped.

"Two deities you locked up, one with my help. The other ... even I don't know what your vendetta might've been. No one picks a fight with him, except for the Dark One."

"Aaaaahhhh," Past-Death murmured. "I bet that's why. Some part of my elaborate deal with the past-Dark One or Darkyn."

"Who were they?" Gabriel asked.

"Karma, who escaped, and Peace, who appears to be dead-dead," Fate replied.

"Karma," past-Death repeated with a shiver. "I remember not liking her either."

"You picked a fight with Peace?" Gabriel demanded.

"I'm sure I had a reason." She shrugged. "When you hold the souls of the deities in your hands, you really don't care who you fight with now, do you?"

"Death killed Peace, fittingly enough." Fate grinned.

Just when I think she can't surprise me ... Gabriel eyed her. "Is Karma dangerous?"

"Very. My sister has none of the restraint I do in general," Fate replied.

"Sister. She'll be thrilled to see you again." Gabriel drew a deep breath. "Okay. First things first: the oath. Second, I'm going to give the death dealers a chance not to spend eternity in Hell."

Past-Death gave him a long look, and Fate raised an eyebrow.

Gabriel pulled a knife from its sheath. "How does this work? I cut myself and say the words?"

"Cut, immerse your hand in water then say it," Fate directed. "You'll be introducing yourself to the gods and goddesses of eras past, sealing your commitment with two of the three laws."

"Three," past-Death corrected him.

"Whatever."

Mates-blood-fate. Gabriel shifted back to the caldron, his heart pounding as he realized he was about to take the final step to seal his position as Death. His mate flanked him on one side while Fate went to his other.

With a deep breath, he sliced his hand with the knife and lowered it into the water. Souls rose up to greet him, caught in invisible currents, while his blood twisted and twirled like red ribbons into the depths of the bowl.

"I swear by the Three Laws to protect all souls and perform my sacred duty until the underworld chooses another," he repeated quietly.

More souls rose up. As each brushed his hand, a flurry of images crossed his mind, before the soul floated back to the bottom of the bowl.

He closed his eyes, unable to register exactly what it was they were sharing with him. The visions were too fleeting, the messages too faint, but he watched and listened anyway. As he did, he became aware of something else: the quiet flow of knowledge from a second source.

Names, faces, histories ... they washed over him, hundreds of thousands a second. The souls in the Lake were eager to tell him their stories as well, their tales conveyed through the bond the Lake shared with the water in the bowl. Ever reverent of the souls, he couldn't help but feel humbled at the secrets they shared, the hopes, dreams and disappointments of each of them.

It was an honor even greater than the one he considered serving Death in the capacity he had before. Trillions of beings were trusting him to keep them safe, and the intensity of such a realization made him want to weep at the enormity of what it truly meant to be Death.

Clenching his jaw, Gabriel took it all in, unable to stop the flood of knowledge and unwilling to disrespect the souls he protected by trying. Instead he did what he always did and let the souls speak. The knowledge of eras past raced past his eyelids, the whispered secrets of every age pummeling him.

And then it hit him like a punch in the stomach. With a grunt, he bore the familiar sensation, his astonishment soon replacing discomfort.

It was the feeling of a bond, like that to his mate, being formed between him and the underworld. The missing link, the confirmation of the incredible secret he'd learned in the short time he'd been in the sacred closet.

The underworld had chosen its master and was officially, eagerly welcoming him.

Just like Darkyn said. He didn't want to guess if the Dark One had purposely told him or guessed right. With knowledge from the time-before-time, there was a chance Darkyn knew.

The only thing he was concerned about: letting the souls speak.

Chapter Fourteen

For someone who never left the dungeon, Karma seemed to know where to lead them. Four times they evaded discovery when the goddess ducked into a room or around a corner suddenly, and twice, Deidre thought they had been discovered, only for the death dealer to walk right by them.

Karma had some sort of magic about her, though Deidre wasn't able to pinpoint what. It wasn't pure invisibility, or they'd run straight out. It had to do with the individual death dealers they passed, as if Karma knew how to evade the senses of some but not all.

When the deity stopped in a quiet alcove of a hallway, Deidre released her breath. Her stomach was cramping once more, not enough to cripple her, but bad enough that she wasn't able to stand straight. Focused on the pain, she gritted her teeth and waited for Karma's next move.

The pain faded once more. Deidre straightened. "What're we waiting for?" she asked.

"For you to be ready to fight, if we must," Karma answered. "This way leads out." She pointed towards a hallway swarming with death dealers.

"Oh, god." Deidre's heart quickened. "That's a lot of people."

"We are both in black, and they are incensed already."

"Is that why the other two didn't pursue us?"

"Eh." Karma shrugged. "Karma can hide herself. I reflects emotions and also sometimes the faces of others."

"Like a chameleon," Deidre said, impressed.

"Maybe. How many legs does it have?"

"Four, I think."

"Maybe not like a chameleon," she said. "You will have to stay close. It takes more effort to hide both of us."

"If we go with the flow of dealers, we'll be less likely to have our faces seen," Deidre said, observing the foot traffic. Most were headed in the same direction while the occasional dealer appeared to be going against the flow. "Are they headed out?"

"I thinks so."

Deidre glanced at her newfound friend and noticed how pale the deity was. The skin around her eyes was tight. "Are you okay?" she asked.

"I derives my strength from balance. There is so little here. I hurts, too," Karma said softly. "But you derive your power from imbalance. Can you fight?"

Deidre's heart jolted, her stomach turning at the memory of what she'd done earlier. While scared, she knew she had no choice, if they were to escape. "Yes," she replied. "I can fight."

"Claws."

Deidre released the deity and looked down. This time, her fingernails lengthened and turned black instantly. Her gums itched, and she instinctively breathed deeply, seeking out the faintest hint of blood.

Her hands trembled, as much from physical weakness as fear. The resolve and anger she'd experienced in the bathing chamber returned, and she shook out her shoulders.

Whatever it took, they had to make it out alive.

"I'm ready," she said.

"Pull up your hood."

Deidre stretched back and reached for the hood, tore it with her claws, then gripped it between her fingers and yanked it up.

Karma took her hand again, this time more carefully, before they started forward at a quick walk. Reaching the intersection, the two of them waited for an opening then plunged into steady stream of death dealers headed outside.

Bombarded by scent, Deidre's nose wrinkled, and she finally covered it with her hand, not about to sneeze and draw attention to them in the lethal situation they were in.

The corridor spilled out into the dark night, and standing just outside was the redheaded woman Deidre hoped never to see again.

Harmony. The leader of the rebelling death dealers was taking in the face of every assassin trotting out of the palace and assigning them to a direction.

Deidre squeezed Karma's hand and all but yanked the deity closer. "Use your power for Harmony!"

"For harmony? What else is balancing for, if not to establish universal har-"

"No! I mean the redhead there sorting dealers!"

"Ah. Karma will do so."

"We can't be holding hands or she'll know."

"But-"

Deidre yanked her hand free. Karma started to turn. Deidre pushed her forward again. The two men separating her from Harmony were soon gone. The underworld night was chilly, a humid breeze smelling of blood, battle and the forest washing over Deidre as she waited anxiously.

The scent of blood made her drool to the point she had to wipe her lips. Disgusted, she tried to breathe through her mouth to keep from smelling anything.

"Palba, I thought you were already assigned," Harmony said, taking in Karma's features with a sharp gaze.

"Not yet," Karma replied.

"Squad A." Harmony pushed the deity out of the way and focused on Deidre. "Tensur, I *know* you were assigned."

Deidre froze, afraid to move, afraid she might say something to

Harmony about how fucked she was when Darkyn or Gabriel cornered her. The green-eyed, traitorous beauty was examining her more critically.

"Something's not right here." Harmony lifted a lock of pink-tinted hair.

"Run!" Karma hissed.

Deidre bolted.

Harmony snatched her with reflexes too quick to follow. Deidre reacted just as quickly, slashing the death dealer across the face with her fingernails.

Wrenching loose, Deidre held out her hand to the awaiting deity and ran into the night, towards the smells and sounds of battle.

Harmony's shriek of anger and pain was followed by a flurry of orders directed at finding the two who slipped by her.

Heart pounding in her ears, Deidre ran as hard as she could, clutching the soft hand of the panting deity towards the dark blob she knew to be the scary forest she'd seen from the windows of the palace.

Karma angled them away from the battle. It was too dark to know what was going on for sure, though Deidre caught the flashes of blades in the light of the two moons and saw what looked like an anthill forming in the center of the battle.

Fear shot through her at the idea of Darkyn being at the bottom of that dog pile, beneath dozens of dealers, and she slowed, squinting to see better.

They drew parallel of the mess, and the deity slowed when she noticed the growing mountain in the center of the milling figures.

"What is that?" Deidre asked.

A shout behind them reminded her of what pursued, and Karma jerked her forward.

"Come ... on!" she gasped.

Deidre fled.

They reached the forest when Deidre smelled it: the rich, over-whelming, powerful scent of her mate's blood.

Her stomach seized, and she dropped, torn from Karma and her senses by the pain twisting her insides.

"Deidre!" Karma sounded panicked.

Vaguely, Deidre heard the sound of flesh meeting flesh as their pursuers reached them. One of them careened into her and tripped, landing on the ground ahead of her.

This ends now, she chanted again. She wasn't weak, and she wasn't about to be captured or killed when she was so close to her bloodmate.

A sob escaped her, but Deidre forced herself to her feet. "Karma?" she asked shakily, struggling to determine which of the blurry figures near her was her friend.

"Here!" came the grunt.

Deidre leaned against the tree nearest her heavily, righting her senses and quelling her urge to vomit. She closed her eyes to identify the cold flows marking the sources of power radiating off the death dealers. They were heavy here, the thick ribbons of magic emanating from the writhing mass of the main battle swept through her. She shivered from the combination of night and magic then opened her eyes.

Unable to balance more than one person at a time, Karma was fighting off three dealers with a knife and her hands. She ducked and wove among the trees to keep them from ganging up on her at once. Even so, Deidre guessed the dealers were under orders to bring them in alive – or they'd both be dead.

After another second to ground herself, Deidre pushed away from the tree and lunged at the death dealer nearest her. Her claws tore into the flesh of one of his arms, and she discharged the cold power curling within her.

He dislodged her with a shove, only to drop to the ground immediately after.

Karma gave a muffled cry.

Deidre struggled to her feet, driven by the scent of blood and the cold power within her. A dealer snatched her, and she careened into him, slashing at his throat and yanking back simultaneously. He gave a gurgled shout that alerted the five shapes rushing towards them from the palace.

With a second slash of her claws, she finished the job and spun to face the dealer that had Karma pinned to a tree. Deidre grabbed and pulled him away to give Karma the chance to escape. Karma whirled and snatched him, her hair going straight and eyes glowing eerily as she drained his vitality.

Deidre took a moment to catch her breath, unable to get the scent of blood out of her nose. She pinched it closed and faced the direction of the palace.

The five attackers were at the tree line.

"We have to go!" she shouted and darted forward frantically to grab Karma.

The deity released the bones she held and stumbled after her.

The scent of Darkyn was growing stronger, driving her closer to madness, making her stomach scream out of hunger and blinding her to anything but the need for blood.

Not two steps later, Deidre was yanked backwards, as one of the dealers caught up with Karma. She released the deity and caught her balance before turning. Karma was screaming, but it seemed like the sound and scene came from far, far away and was in slow motion.

Anger, hate, betrayal, revenge ... Deidre let the cold power fill her, too physically exhausted to support herself without it.

And then she let go, the same way she had in the bathing chamber when Karma's life was in danger. The demon side of her stepped up, better equipped to protect her than the human side.

Deidre dived into the melee, shredding every inch of skin that came near her and sending death charges through those she touched for too short a timespan. Magic swirled and gathered around her, through her, and blood rained down on everything like honey falling from the sky.

Lost in the bloodlust, she didn't stop, until someone snatched her out of the blood-fueled trance.

Jarred back to her senses, Deidre blinked and tried to pull away, looking up into the eyes of the one creature able to stop her.

The Dark One was a head taller than her, lean in the way of a warrior, with eyes that appeared to be sinkholes at night. A low growl emanated from his chest, while his direct stare sank into her mind. His body sucked up the excess magic, freeing her from its hold. His scent, warmth and the nearness of his strong frame brought her back from the blood-infused haze, made her body tremble once more as it recalled how weak she was.

The scent of his sweet blood intoxicated her, the compelling need to taste her bloodmate making her stomach cramp and her heart flutter in her throat. But it was the ferocity of the bloodlust in his eyes, coupled with the way the Dark One was always a little more terrifying during the dark of night, that made Deidre hesitate to touch him or pull away from his tight grip.

"You came for me," she whispered breathlessly.

"You're my blood monkey," he replied.

"That's it?" she asked, disappointed.

He pulled her roughly into his hard body, his fangs lengthening the way they did when he was preparing to feed. "I surrendered my power at the gates of the underworld, and I haven't eaten or fucked in three days. What do you think, blood monkey?"

Deidre hid a smile. "I think this just might work out, Darkyn."

The hunger pangs returned stronger, and she gasped, clutching at his bloodied shirt and pushing her face against his warm chest. The scent of his blood was strong.

"You're hurt," she murmured, disturbed.

"I like the pain," he reminded her.

"Can't you heal?"

"Hush," he ordered quietly and pressed a thumb to her lips.

His rich taste was like a drop of heaven. It soothed her in a way nothing else ever had. The world outside of them was forgotten for a split second, and she rested her head on his shoulder, wanting to weep and drink, to lose herself in his blood, scent and body.

"Now drink, love," he told her.

She wanted to refuse in case he was weaker than he was letting on, but the compelling urge was too much.

Deidre dug her teeth into his neck and sucked down his blood hungrily, not caring who watched her. Slowly, the cramping ceased, and her hunger disappeared, until she was so full, she was almost drowsy.

LIZZY FORD

"You learned to defend yourself," he whispered, nudging her head.

She dislodged her teeth from his neck and nudged him back, the familiar, subdued display of affection making her eyes water. Any doubt she'd experienced about where she belonged vanished. "Yeah."

"Did they hurt you?"

Her split second of hesitation was enough to answer his question.

Darkyn lifted her chin. "Did they hurt you?" It was a warning growl this time, the inquisition of a deity, not the inquiry of a lover.

"Yes," she said in a choked voice. "But I'm okay." She nuzzled his hand. "I'm okay, Darkyn."

It didn't take him stiffening for her to know that no one got away with threatening the bloodmate of the Dark One. Tears spilled down her face, and he caught one on his finger, gazing at it briefly.

"Who the fuck is this?" Rhyn's question jarred her out of the intimate moment.

Deidre twisted without leaving Darkyn's arms.

Rhyn's sword was pointed at a shivering body in the hollow of a tree. The half-demon was bristling, his chest heaving from fighting while his liquid silver eyes glowed. He nudged Karma with his foot.

"Don't, Rhyn! She's a friend!" Deidre exclaimed. "She helped me escape the dungeon."

Rhyn bent down and gripped Karma's arm, pulling her to her feet.

Deidre's mouth dropped open, and her gaze flew to the goddess. Both Karma and Rhyn had gone completely still.

"Oh, no!" she breathed, tugging at the hold Darkyn had on her.

"Let it run its course, love," he whispered, tightening his grip.

She rested back against him, praying Karma remembered she wasn't supposed to kill anyone who helped them escape.

Karma moved, and Rhyn stepped away, shaking his head as if to clear it.

"Oh, thank god!" Deidre exclaimed.

Karma was eyeing Rhyn, her hair in long, loose curls, her eyes black. Before Deidre could warn the dazed half-demon, Karma drew back and punched him in the nose.

"Careful, little girl," Rhyn snarled, grabbing her arm. "I'll break you in half."

"You had that coming," she growled in return.

"Okay, let's just … calm down," Deidre said. She moved away from Darkyn and paused beside the deity. "Are you okay?" she asked.

"Rhyn is almost balanced. The Great Imbalance …" Karma whispered. Her hair darkened and darted around her head like snakes around her head, while blackness had swallowed her eyes.

"Are you hurt?"

"Minor."

"Take my hand. I can help you, can't I ?"

Karma hesitated then stretched out to her. With some embarrassment, Deidre realized her own hand was covered in blood. She wiped it on her pants then took Karma's hand and tugged her out of Rhyn's grip.

The deity ceased shivering.

"Your allies always amuse me, love," Darkyn said. "I had begun to wonder where Karma went."

"Karma?" Rhyn repeated and stepped back. "Not just a scary story Immortals tell their kids to make them behave?"

"She's not a scary story," Deidre replied and pulled the woman into her arms.

Almost immediately, Karma's hair tightened into ringlets again.

Deidre met Darkyn's gaze and was unable to look away from the demon that traveled to the underworld to save her. Her body churned with both desire and hunger, his blood calling to her in a way that made her want to leave everything and melt into him for good.

"Cute claws," Rhyn said, assessing her. "Can you use them?"

"She did." Darkyn nodded his head to the side to indicate the dead.

Deidre didn't let her gaze stray, just focused on her bloodmate, whose presence made her feel like she wasn't about to die for the first time since entering the underworld.

"Great fucking work, mini-demon," Rhyn exclaimed. "Not to break this up, but we gotta retreat. They're going to figure out what we did soon enough. Anyone else with you?"

"No," Deidre replied.

"Congrats, half-breed," Darkyn purred. "To touch Karma is to be judged. She's of the soul-eater class of deities, meaning if she doesn't like what she finds, there's a chance she'll make you dead-dead."

Rhyn eyed the goddess.

Soul-eaters? Deidre said nothing.

The goddess was not quite normal yet, with half her hair in tight, cheerful curls while the other was in long, snakelike threads. One eye was human and a pretty shade green, the other filled with black.

"I take it you and I were judged to be ... normal? Not worth eating?" Rhyn asked awkwardly.

"Somewhat balanced," she supplied.

"Lead on, half-breed," Darkyn ordered.

Rhyn shook his head but obeyed, striking off in a direction leading deeper into the forest. Darkyn motioned for Deidre to go ahead of him, touching her cheek lightly as he did, and trailed, daggers drawn.

"It's okay, Karma," Deidre whispered as they walked. "Unless you implode or something from Darkyn being too close, you're safe."

"Not implode," Karma replied in a tight voice.

Deidre glanced back at Darkyn, whose attention was on their surroundings. They were in the middle of the underworld with countless foes pursuing them and her top thought was alone time with her ferocious bloodmate.

Karma giggled.

"Sorry." Deidre blushed, aware the deity was able to feel her thoughts. "Are you really okay?"

"As much as can be. Karma has been weak for so long ..."

Karma drifted off. "You help me, but I fears what happens when word gets out she's alive, and she's not yet recovered."

"Because you're a soul-eater." Deidre chewed her lip.

"Death, Dark One and Karma are all soul-eaters. We don't necessarily *eat* them. We just take them."

"What do you do with them?"

"I eats them." Karma giggled again. "But it is a better fate than they'll face in Hell."

Evil has too many layers to these people. They walked in silence, Deidre's stomach growling loudly while she kept a hold of Karma's hand.

They didn't go far but stopped when a death dealer popped up in their path.

Deidre froze, not ready for another battle so soon. To her relief, the half-demon ahead of her greeted the man with a wave of his hand.

"Landon! We found one. Two. Well, one and a half. Not sure what the half is yet," Rhyn said with a wary glance at Karma.

"Temporary allies." Deidre didn't hear Darkyn move behind her, but she sensed his body heat and instinctively leaned back.

"Imbalance," Karma hissed.

Deidre broke contact, disappointed but aware she was keeping the two from trying to kill one another.

"Take her to Andre. He's balanced well enough," Darkyn instructed her. "Then return to me, love. We need to talk, after I fuck you fast and hard."

Deidre shivered at the husky note of hunger in his voice, her body crying for the Dark One. She moved forward with more haste than she intended, causing Karma to trip.

The goddess giggled again.

Flustered, Deidre said nothing but followed Rhyn, her blood humming with the idea she was about to taste and fuck her blood-mate after far too long. Only one uneasy thought remained from her uncertainty about an eternity in Hell, one she didn't know how to bring up to him.

Later. She promised herself.

Chapter Fifteen

W ith some apprehension, she trailed Rhyn past two lines of death dealers that eyed her suspiciously before they reached a small cottage.

Rhyn pushed the door open, and she entered, tugging a reluctant Karma with her. She recognized the familiar, dark-skinned Andre instantly from the time he'd poked and prodded at her mind to determine how bad her brain tumor had been.

He smiled and stood from a small desk where he was writing with the help of a lantern, his genuine warmth and relaxed air reassuring her they were safe despite the leery death dealers.

"Deidre," he said with a polite bow of his head. "There is not much here in the way of modern conveniences, but you're welcome to have a seat."

Karma was peering at him curiously.

Deidre sat on a bed, the only other place to sit in the one-room cabin, and the deity sat beside her.

"You are?" Andre asked, pulling his chair closer to them before he, too, sat.

"You may not want to get too close," Rhyn warned from the doorway.

"Karma," the deity answered.

"The Great Balancer," Andre said. "A pleasure."

"She's really sensitive to those around her," Deidre said. "I think because she's relatively weak right now. Can't really manage her … uh, reactions to people."

"I take it you passed her test." Andre offered a friendly smile. "I have nothing to fear." He held out his hand.

Deidre's breath caught at the blatant display, while Karma perked up.

"You wish to be balanced?" the deity asked.

"I do." Andre appeared confident, his gaze steady and features warm.

"You sure?" Deidre asked. "Not that I know anything bad about you, but she has a way of turning people into skeletons and eating their souls, if you fail."

"I'll take my chances."

Deidre released her grip on Karma, cringing when the deity took the Immortal's hand. While she knew little about him, it was hard to think of a creature that lived thousands of years would be balanced.

Karma closed her eyes, and Andre did the sane.

Deidre exchanged a look with Rhyn, who appeared interested but unconcerned. "He's the only one of my brothers who stands a chance at passing," he explained.

The ground beneath the cabin trembled suddenly, the windows creaking.

Deidre looked down then at Rhyn. "Earthquake?"

"I don't —"

Another quake.

Rhyn straightened. "You hear that?"

She cocked her head to the side. What sounded like the splintering and crashing of trees reached her. Confused by the sounds, she waited for Rhyn to say something else.

"It sounds like footsteps," he said, turning to face the world outside the cabin.

Another tremble, more crashing.

"Footsteps?" she echoed and rose, crossing to the window. "It'd have to be the size of a dinosaur or something."

"Giants."

She sneaked a glance at him. By the severity of his features, he wasn't joking.

"What kind of giants?" she whispered.

"The kind that want to fucking crush us."

"This place is like a nightmare." She shuddered, thoughts on the snake-like branches of the trees.

"Could be worse. Could be Hell." He winked at her. "Stay here. I have to get to the ogre before Darkyn." Rhyn threw open the wardrobe next to the door and pulled out a sword as long as her leg.

"Why?" she asked anxiously, heart flipping in her chest. "Is he that hurt?"

"Andre is giving out a Toughest Demon Award. I aim to win it." Snatching a knife, he strode out of the cottage.

Perplexed, Deidre followed him with her gaze.

"There's no such thing," Andre said from behind her. "It was my attempt to keep the two of them focused on their mission here and not killing one another. Unfortunately, they took it a little too seriously."

She turned, sighing with relief to see him alive. Karma's hair was in tight, cheerful ringlets, her eyes green. Her features glowed.

"He's balanced!" The deity all but shrieked.

"And you are a very young goddess," Andre replied. "You'll need to learn some self-control."

Karma rolled her eyes at the brotherly tone.

"I'm glad you're getting along," Deidre said, amused.

Another tremble of the earth beneath her drew her attention to the wardrobe. She didn't know how to handle any of the weapons on display there and wished she did.

"Are there enough people on our side to handle a giant?" she asked. "And where is Gabriel?"

"The forest sent him a different direction," Andre explained. "The answer to your first question is no. We aren't currently equipped to face ogres or the amount of death dealers allied with Harmony."

"Is there a plan?"

"Not to get killed before Gabriel gets this situation under control."

Worry for her mate made Deidre step out of the cabin. The earth tremors were getting stronger, the sounds of crashing trees closer. The giants came from the direction opposite of the palace, and she saw the loyal death dealers scrambling to form two fronts.

Dread sank into her stomach, heavier than ever. Fully sated after her meal, she nonetheless knew Darkyn had to be all the weaker for not having a chance to drink her blood. He was the most incredible fighter in the universe, but if he was truly cut off from his source of power and injured, he was also vulnerable to fatigue or being mortally wounded.

"Andre, you all need to be ready to move." A death dealer ducked into the doorway behind her and called. "There's no guarantee we can hold this position."

"Understood."

Deidre looked up at the dual moons of the underworld hovering far overhead. If she was able to fight so well when weak, what could she do now that she'd fed? The steady thrum of depravity was around her, waiting to be tapped into.

Cries of pain came from a short distance behind the cabin, and she whirled.

"Deidre, come with me," Andre said calmly, joining her.

Karma, too, was transfixed by whatever was attacking from the rear.

"We need to move, ladies. There's a rendezvous point in case we get separated. The Lake of Souls," Andre said.

Deidre listened. Darkyn's faint scent was in the air. He was somewhere near the attacking giants. The fact she as able to smell him so easily made her stomach churn. She'd been too hungry to assess the state of her mate, to understand exactly how injured he was.

"I have to go, Andre," she said, starting forward.

"Deidre-"

"Take Karma. I'll be fine." This time, she knew it to be true. With a newfound confidence in her ability to take care of herself and a full stomach, Deidre didn't think much of anyone was going to stand in her way of reaching Darkyn.

Andre's words were lost as she broke into a run. Deidre raced towards the sound of fighting, adrenaline filling her ears with the sound of rushing wind while her fingernails grew. She battled the stubborn forest on her own, and then stumbled upon the path being used by death dealers headed towards the fight. The forest made way for them.

The closer she got, the more blood was in the air, a sign the battle was not going well. She sought out Darkyn's scent, veering from the cleared path when the shifting winds brought his trail from a new direction.

Her pace slowed considerably as she fought the brush and trees, but she didn't have to go far. The shadows of some great, ancient creatures soon fell over her, and she froze, staring ahead of her with fear.

"Holy hell," she whispered, stricken.

The two giants were a head taller than the tallest of the trees, great, ugly creatures headed in the direction of the cottage. One swung a sword large enough to cut a path through the trees while the other wielded a club made out of stone.

Deidre considered turning back, until she caught the scent of Darkyn once more.

He'd come this far to save her. She wasn't going to abandon him to face these … things alone.

Starting forward again, she soon reached an area where the giants had cleared of trees. Bodies and pieces of bodies littered the forest area and the battleground. Someone had started a tree on fire, and the writhing branches screamed, adding to the sounds of booming footsteps and shouts of death dealers.

She ducked down, searching the chaotic scene for her mate. Her nails were long, her mouth watering at the thought of drawing blood. A look up at the nearest of the two giants reminded her there was no way she'd be able to inflict any sort of damage on a monster that size.

The giants walked slowly, each step making the ground rumble and shake. She shifted to maintain her balance, uncertain how she'd find her mate in the mess.

Deidre bit her thumb and then held it up, letting the wind take the scent of her blood towards the battle. She crept forward and ducked, horrified to see a giant's sword cleave the five new dealers on the scene in two the minute they stepped into the melee.

One of them dropped a torch, and fire spread slowly around the giant's shoe. His bellow made her cover her ears with a wince.

"Deidre?"

It wasn't Darkyn's voice but Rhyn's.

"You here?"

"Yes." She stood carefully, balancing herself against a tree.

The large, half-demon left the cover of a thatch of bushes and ducked behind the tree beside her.

"You shouldn't be," he said.

"I came for Darkyn."

"You plan on rescuing him?"

"Maybe," she said archly.

"That right there disqualifies him."

She rolled her eyes, recalling what Andre had said. He was a shrewd motivator, given the combative, competitive nature of the demons she'd met.

"You need to get the fuck out of here," Rhyn said firmly.

"I'm not leaving. I know he's hurt, and I know he needs to –"

"Sssssshhh. Get back and don't move." The half-demon had gone rigid, his back pressed to the tree.

Deidre sucked in a breath and stood still, peering through the branches of the tree she was behind to see what was going on.

The giant with the shoe on fire was kneeling, batting out the flames. His head was a little too close for her comfort, a mere ten feet away.

"When I say, run that way." Rhyn pointed to the side of her opposite him.

"Run?" she echoed. "Won't he come after me?"

"That's the plan." He whirled his sword and gripped it with two hands. "You're bait."

"Great." She frowned, her nails digging into the tree.

"And Deidre?"

She looked over at him.

"When I say run, I mean run *fast*. Just in case."

With a shake of her head, she straightened and readied herself to run. She sniffed the wind and was somewhat relieved to realize Darkyn was in the direction she would soon be headed. She'd seen him fight in the video tutorials his predecessor, Zamon, showed her in the library in Hell. Nothing in the universe was able to match Darkyn's agility, cunning and lethality. If anyone could defeat a giant, it was him, assuming he had access to his magic or regeneration ability and wasn't already severely injured. The reminder of all he'd given up to find her was disturbing. Even without his power, he was a formidable foe.

"Ready?" Rhyn hissed.

She swallowed hard and balanced herself.

"Now!"

Deidre darted and immediately toppled to the ground when the giant took a step. Scrambling up with a curse, she took off, leaping and slapping brush away, staggering each time the giant stepped.

Another pain-filled bellow split the air.

"Duck!" Rhyn shouted.

She dropped to the ground without hesitation, squeezing her eyes closed. The sound of metal smashed through trees not far above her head. Trees groaned and crashed to the ground, and she twisted to see behind her.

The giant had Rhyn's sword sticking out of one eye and was pursuing somewhat clumsily, blood streaming down its skewed face. It crashed to its knees, and Deidre flinched, waiting for the trees it hadn't chopped down to fall over.

"Plan B!" Rhyn grabbed her arms and hauled her up. "Run like fuck." He pushed her in one direction then took off in another.

She ran hard, following the scent of Darkyn.

The giant stormed off after Rhyn, and she caught herself against a tree, pausing to catch her breath and assess her situation.

The other giant was under attack from a handful of death dealers and a familiar shape she'd know anywhere: Darkyn. He was moving effortlessly, striking at the monster's tendons and the sensitive parts of his feet and legs, his daggers whirling too fast for her eyes to follow. He clambered up one leg as if gravity had no hold on him and slammed a sword deep into the giant's thigh.

The monster bellowed, and Darkyn leapt to the ground, sword in hand. A thick rivulet of blood spurted out of the giant's thigh, and she guessed he'd hit the main artery.

Teetering, the giant swung wildly at the surrounding forest with its club, taking out one death dealer and half a dozen trees.

The wind shifted, taking her scent towards her mate, and Darkyn signaled her back without turning, his focus between commanding the few death dealers willing to face the creature and the furious ogre.

Deidre saw the club move towards him in slow motion. A scream stuck in her throat. The massive stone club smashed into the back of the Dark One with a sickening crunch and threw him twenty feet into the air. As if one blow wasn't enough, the ogre hit him again mid air, driving him straight into a tree.

She stared, not believing what she saw to be remotely possible.

Deidre stumbled forward, jarred back into the moment by the sound of her own scream. Oblivious to the dangerous battle so close to her, she darted across the cleared area to the still form of her mate.

"Darkyn!" she cried, dropping onto her knees beside him.

The scent of his blood was thick in the air, the sources too numerous for her to identify.

"Darkyn!" she said more softly, rolling him onto his back.

He was alive and growling. His skin was warm, and she wiped blood from his roughly hewn features. His chest appeared to be crushed, along with most of his body.

"Oh, god!" she gasped and bent over him, fluttering kisses over his bruised face. "You can heal. Feed and heal." She sliced her wrist for him, placing it to his lips.

He twisted his head away.

"What're you doing? Drink!" she insisted.

"Can't heal fast enough … here."

"Of course you can!"

He lifted an arm. Even with a bone protruding from it, he seemed oblivious – and determined. Gripping her neck, he pulled her face to his.

"Kill me," he said, his lips brushing her ear.

Deidre stared, uncertain she'd heard right. She cupped his face gently with both her hands, desire and hunger spinning through her again. "Darkyn, you need to feed."

"It's too late for that. Kill me, quickly."

Her eyes watered, and she shook her head. "It's not too late. You just have to do it."

"Love, if you don't take Hell, that fucking giant will."

Her brow furrowed.

"Whomever defeats the Dark One, the last to strike, the last to deal, takes his place," he explained, rasping painfully.

"No, no, no!" she whispered frantically. "Darkyn-"

He squeezed her neck, silencing her. "Quickly. I am dying." He pulled her to his neck. "Drink until I am dead."

Deidre's body shook, and tears blurred her vision. She pressed her mouth to his neck, unable to resist the intoxicating scent and taste that was him.

"I'm giving you Hell, love."

"I don't want Hell. I want you!"

"I know. This isn't the end." He was fading, his voice distant, his effort to fight his death clear. "You … remember what I taught you of … deals?"

"Y…yes."

"Make it good."

Deidre wanted to scream at him and demand how he was able to think of deals at a time like this.

"Take Hell," he whispered again. This time, his strain was clear. "Quickly."

Tears raced down her face, but she focused on obeying him, praying this was part of some great plan of his. He hadn't won Hell after a lifetime of battle only to give it up. There was more; there always was with him.

"I love you, Darkyn," she whispered in a choked voice. Deidre closed her eyes and bit him, sucking his thick nectar into her mouth.

This isn't the end, she repeated to herself over and over, taking some solace in the words.

She drank until his body went limp and the rattling of his breath stopped. Deidre withdrew and sat back.

"Please don't leave me," she whispered in a choked voice.

A cold breeze whipped by her, and she shivered. Lightning arced overhead, the explosion of its accompanying thunder making the ground rumble. Deidre instinctively moved closer to Darkyn, wanting to protect his broken body from further harm.

She rested her head on his chest and willed him to take another breath, to tell her this was some twisted joke of his. Her insides knotted and her heart felt as if it were shattering. Fresh pain pierced her hard enough to take her breath away.

This isn't the end. She breathed in his smell and wrapped her fist in his bloodied fist, comforted by the feel of his warm body beneath. "I don't understand, Darkyn. What am I supposed to do?" *And why couldn't you just tell me you cared about me?* Was it that hard? He lied for a living. Even if he wasn't capable of true emotion, he could've said the words, for her sake.

Suddenly, her concerns about being in Hell for eternity, about losing the human side of her, no longer mattered. Holding her dead lover in her arms, she realized there was really only one thing that did, and he was gone, killed trying to save her from Harmony in a domain that wasn't even his.

Another crack of lightning made her jump.

Deidre twisted to see the sky, stunned. Clouds darker than night had begun to amass directly overhead and swirl steadily, the way they did before a massive tornado. Branches flailed in a wind strong enough to bend trees.

The wind touched everything except for her and Darkyn. Deidre watched it, not understanding what was going on. She was in the eye of the forming tornado, in relative calm while trees bowed to the gales around her. Smaller trees and bushes were uprooted and thrown into the forming funnel.

The giant was huddled against the ground, the death dealers taking shelter in the trees. Her heart fluttered with fear, but she didn't move, not caring what happened now that Darkyn was gone.

Lightning struck closer, causing the tree nearest her to explode. The debris was swept up by the wind before it reached her. The storm took on a more ominous look, that of a black hole sucking up everything in its path.

Tears flowed down her face. Deidre watched the world being ripped a part around her and hunched over Darkyn's body, waiting for the storm to take her as well.

I'm giving you Hell, love. No part of her cared to run Hell, but she couldn't help wondering what he meant or why it filled her with doom.

Lightning smashed too close, and she closed her eyes once more, praying she went quickly.

One moment, the storm raged around her. The next, her body was pierced by light and pain so intense, she was thrown away from Darkyn. Hot electricity paralyzed her while the cold fire of the Dark One raced along her nerve endings, torturing and teasing, intense and overwhelming. Frozen in agony, she stared at the sky above, watching as bolts of lightning smashed into her and the clouds grew darker, larger.

Just as abruptly as it started, the sensations left. The lightning retreated to the sky and ceased, while the gathering storm remained, swirling around the black hole at its center.

Deidre gasped in breath, the hot-cold power racing through her body. She sagged, uncertain if she was grateful to be alive or disturbed she hadn't joined Darkyn in death. The thrum of cold power she'd sensed before was stronger, wrapping around her, flowing through her, tugging at her to rise.

With some effort, she did so and stared up at the horrifying tornado forming above. The cold tendril of power was like smoke extending from the dark clouds in the sky. It wrapped around her shoulders, and she began to comprehend.

I'm giving you Hell, love.

The storm wasn't a threat to her. It was an extension of Hell, created by the depravity existing in the underworld and feeding her power and strength.

Deidre looked down at her hands, not wanting to believe what had happened. Her nails were long and black, her hands still small and delicate like a human's. The pouch at her waist caught her attention, and she pulled it free. Inside were the souls of Gabriel, past-Death and one more that Fate had provided her.

Gabriel and past-Death.

She looked up at the sky again. Darkyn's soul had to be here, in the underworld.

Make it good. She'd thought he was talking nonsense in his last moment, but Darkyn was giving her a roadmap.

Hope trickled within her, along with the strange urge to level everything before her. The demon half of her step forward, the side that understood what was happening. After her experience in the underworld, there was no denying she was more than human.

A roar from behind her made her spin.

The giant had regained his sense of balance and rose out of the forest, while the rest of the death dealers clung for their dear lives to trees or boulders to keep the storm from taking them.

Deidre gazed up at the creature raising its club to crush her the way it had her mate. Cold fury unfurled within her, feeding the darkness gathering around her, and she glared at the monster.

I'm giving you Hell, love.

"There's only one way to find out," she said, hating the monster that took her mate from her. Uncertain how to call the power out, she pointed at the creature.

The dark smoke hovering at her feet darted after it, wrapping around its legs, while tendrils of clouds broke off from the black hole and bound the creature's upper body. Power pulsed through her, the ecstatic experience second only to fucking Darkyn. It rendered her giddy, thrilled her, made her want more and more of the intense feeling to ease her pain.

"Time to feel the wrath of Hell," she told the giant, watching with some fascination.

The tendrils grew thick and began to tighten, squeezing the life out of the monster. It bellowed and writhed but wasn't able to break free. Finally, it gave a pain-filled scream and went limp.

Deidre braced herself against a tree to keep from being knocked to the ground by the force of its fall. The tendrils dissipated instantly, leaving behind the dead ogre.

She glanced a little uneasily at the storm overhead, wondering how she was able to control it, before turning her attention towards the palace. Squeezing the souls in her hand, she realized she now had two reasons to go that direction. The first: to destroy Harmony and seek her revenge against the death dealer responsible for taking away her bloodmate.

The second: to bargain for Darkyn's soul.

She was tired of pain, tired of bearing the brunt of the Immortal world. This time, there was nothing to stand in the way of what she wanted, not when she brought with her the might of Hell. And there was nothing she wouldn't do to get Darkyn back.

Deidre started forward, the storm moving with her.

This ends now.

Chapter Sixteen

You can't leave me.

Gabriel's eyes snapped open as the latest soul brushed his fingertips. Deidre's voice was clear and loud compared to the whispers of the other souls. The images that passed were of the underworld ogres, allies of Death from a different era placed in hibernation long ago. Gentle giants, they were nonetheless deadly, if they chose to be. He'd met them several times during his travels, before Death gave the dying breed a permanent home in the underworld in exchange for their periodic protection.

"Something's wrong," Gabriel said and shifted forward. It was difficult for him to sort through the sheer volume of information entering his thoughts, the stories of souls, the images of deities. Somewhere among the voices was the steady stream of the underworld's soft voice, a bond as strong as his was to his mate, yet subtler, quiet.

At his fingertip was the second black soul in the bowl where there had been only one before.

"Really wrong," he whispered and picked up the soul of Darkyn. He stared at it, marveling and horrified simultaneously. "Darkyn fell."

"What?" past-Death crowded him. "What about the others?"

"Someone freed the giants," Gabriel said. "Poor souls aren't smart enough to know what's going on."

"Cupcake!" the muffled shout came from the direction of the bedchamber.

"I think we've got more than one issue," she added, eyes going towards Jared.

Gabriel dropped the soul of the Dark One back into the bowl. "Stay here. I know what I need to do."

Fate was conveniently gone, he noted when he turned. The deity had a knack for disappearing when circumstances went from bad to worse.

"Um, no." She followed him.

"Deidre, you aren't immortal anymore. You'll be safe here," he said, facing her. "I won't risk losing you."

She rolled her eyes. "Yeah well, I don't care. I belong at your side, fighting our enemies, not stuffed in a closet." She gave him a look of cold defiance, the kind that made his blood quicken and desire eddy through him.

"I'm serious," Gabriel said.

"So am I." A tortured look crossed her features before she drew a deep breath and threw her shoulders back. "I've been a selfish being my entire life. I need to make amends where I can."

"Your soul belongs to Hell. If something happens ..." He wasn't able to finish the thought. It was more complicated with Darkyn gone, especially since the Dark One had been cut off from Hell when he entered the underworld. How succession worked wasn't clear to Gabriel.

"I'm willing to take that risk to help you and the others," she said firmly. "It's not a request, Gabriel. You can take me with you, or I'll follow you anyway."

Gabriel studied her, sensing her resolve while also experiencing a tremor of fear. He wasn't able to read her mind to know exactly what she was thinking, but he suspected she'd reached close to rock bottom. It made him want to take her in his arms and hug her, to assure her everything would be okay.

But that wasn't the right approach with past-Death. She was far too independent and obstinate enough to prove whatever point she felt needed to be proven, at any cost. Whatever amends she wanted to make, she wasn't going to be dissuaded. This much he knew.

"If you're doing this to prove to me that you can be trusted, please reconsider," he said.

"The world doesn't revolve around you, Gabe," she said with a faint smile. "I'm doing this for me. I already lost my soul and your love. I have to prove to *me* that I'm worthy of being with you." The words were spoken with her normal calm confidence, but he heard the effort that went into them. "I want to be the person I know I can be. I just need this chance, Gabe."

Familiar unease went through him, a combination of frustration and resentment. Gabriel debated silently, aware the former goddess was hurting as much as he once had. His pain and anger had lessened, and he suspected it was because of the same reason she appeared distraught every time she looked at him.

She'd learned her lesson the hardest way possible, and at the cost of her soul. Any anger he felt towards her melted knowing she was in the kind of pain he went through at her hands when she took his soul months ago. No part of him was able to feel satisfied at the tables turning.

If anything, he had the urgent need to help her, to soothe away her suffering. No one deserved that kind of suffering, even someone who hurt him the way she did.

Since discovering her deal with human-Deidre, he'd been trying to figure out a way to barter with the Dark One to regain her soul and come to one conclusion: Darkyn knew how much Gabriel wanted it and would put a price tag on it that Gabriel wasn't able to pay.

But with Darkyn gone … Gabriel ached for Deidre, hearing her heartbreak in the memories shown him by Darkyn's soul. Yet the Dark One's demise might give him the opportunity he sought to get his mate's soul back.

The answer was somewhere within the knowledge pouring into

his thoughts. He just had to isolate it. In the meantime, past-Death stood a better chance of surviving with him at her side than alone.

It went against every bone in his body, but Gabriel nodded once. "I don't like it, but I understand and respect your decision," he said at last.

"Thank you." She drew a dagger. "Let's go save our pet demon, shall we?"

Gabriel snorted and rested his hand on the door. "Ready?"

"Partners?"

He nodded.

"Then, yes."

Wrenching the door open, he saw the demon braced against the door of the bedchamber, which was bucking beneath the weight of death dealers trying to get in.

"C'mon, demon," Gabriel called gruffly. "We'll take the secret passages." He stepped outside the secret room to ensure Jared was able to see the entrance.

The demon bolted towards him. He was halfway across the bedchamber when the door burst open.

Gabriel waited until Jared was in the room before closing the door. Past-Death stood at the back of the closet at the opening of the passageways.

"Thank you, cupcake," Jared said and hurried forward.

"Go, demon."

They plunged into the passage, and Gabriel gave the stone walls silent instructions of where to take them. As he moved, he considered the immensity of what he'd learned in the sacred closet.

He was *chosen*. The underworld wanted him as Death, and he didn't have to lose the last fragment of his humanity. The streams of knowledge continued to flow into his mind, the pieces of an ancient puzzle falling into place. He began to see the bigger picture, the history of the realms and of humanity, the rise and fall of deities, Immortals and humans.

Acknowledged history, forbidden history, secret history as told by the deities flowed into him, while the souls filled in the details, like sand sliding between boulders. He grappled to understand knowledge far surpassing anything he'd ever uncovered in the Oracle's book at the Caribbean Sanctuary.

While those pieces fell into place, so did a few more, outside the streams he was being force fed.

His mate had given up all this knowledge, all this power to be with him. Hers wasn't just the power of a deity; it was the power of the goddess who ruled over the rest of the deities. The Keeper of Souls was imbued with knowledge and information from across time and realms, from the lowliest human to the loftiest of the gods.

For a woman who craved control and loved power, it was a lot to sacrifice for a shot with a mere human. It soothed the remaining feelings he had about her, the ones based on memories of how cruel she'd often been to him.

Even that part of her was gone, dissipated when she realized what it meant to be human, when she began to comprehend what made him resist her attempts to strip him of his human decency over the years.

Past-Death had fucked up many times, but in the end, she'd tried to get it right. It was this thought that led Gabriel to one that banished any lingering anger.

The goddess hadn't had the capacity to understand what some of her actions, like creating Deidre as a stand-in, truly meant when she did it. She came from a place of absolute power and control, crippled emotionally and incapable of true compassion.

She went against her nature when she fell in love with him and again when she destroyed the sanctity of souls to create Deidre's. Just as Gabriel wasn't able to see the world as the chessboard she did, she hadn't been able to see it through the eyes of a human.

But she tried, because he meant more to her than all the power and knowledge in the world. She gave up being a goddess to become someone new, someone she thought he deserved.

Which is a lot. He had a headache already from downloading the information.

There was too much to sort through, especially now, and he dug through the chaos of his mind to find the bond to the underworld.

The underworld – his underworld – needed him. It was the first and only logical place to start.

"How long does this take?" he asked, touching his head, somewhat off balance with the activity in his mind. It was distracting his senses, turning his attention inward when it needed to be focused on the threats he faced from the external world.

"I'm not sure," she replied.

Gabriel shook his head and realized they'd stopped walking and were waiting at a door. Drawing a knife, he took her hand and squeezed, then opened the door. "Stay here. If anything happens to her, demon, there is nothing the Dark One can do to you that will be worse than what I do," he warned.

"Very well," Jared said unhappily.

He stepped onto the flat roof of the palace, not surprised to see four death dealers pacing around the perimeter. With the buzzing in his mind, it was harder than usual to focus. He tried to recall the names of the sentries and shook out his shoulders, aware he was about to make his first move as the official ruler of his domain.

The sky was cloudy, the wind cold and stiff. Gabriel sheathed the weapon and approached the first guard, who froze the moment he caught sight of him.

Gabriel kept his distance. "You get one shot at this," he said calmly. "A quick death followed by mercy. Or –"

The death dealer drew his weapon and charged with a shout.

"– we can do it this way." With a grunt, Gabriel whipped out his daggers and threw up a block deftly, aware of the other sentries running from their positions across the roof towards him. With two strikes and a block, Gabriel beheaded the first man and knelt, calling his soul to him.

The green gem materialized in his palm, and he rose to confront the three attackers hovering a safe distance from him with raised swords.

"Everyone gets a choice," he boomed at the three and held up the gem. Was he shouting because of the stiff wind or to hear above the buzzing in his head? "To reaffirm their allegiance to me and be granted what mercy Death is willing to offer. Or ..." He crushed the soul in his hand, the green powder turning black as it was picked up by the breeze. "… continue down the path leading to no mercy and a special place in Hell."

Two of them sized him up while the third lowered his sword and appeared ready to run. Gabriel guessed who would do what a moment before the two attacked, their swords flashing in the weak sun. Trained and honed for fighting over thousands of years, his powerful body responded instinctively, and within seconds, both men were dead.

Gabriel eyed the third man, who was close enough to strike him, if he bent to collect the souls of the others. "Made your choice?"

"Mercy." The man placed his sword on the ground and knelt.

"Good." If one of every four laid down their swords, he had a slim chance of taking back his palace. Gabriel sheathed his knives and withdrew his sword. With a single blow, he removed the death dealer's head and then knelt, collecting the soul. This one he tucked in his pocket to toss into the Lake, then shifted over to the other two.

The buzz was maddening. Gabriel closed his eyes for a moment of relative peace. The flow of knowledge was waning, turning from a flood into a stream. It was almost over.

He rose, did away with the souls of the remaining dead assassins, and then turned to face the direction he'd come.

"Harmony," he growled.

The redhead was flanked by no less than two dozen loyal dealers, all armed to the teeth. There were slashes across one of her cheeks, as if she'd gotten into a fight with an animal. Gabriel studied her before letting his gaze drift over the others gathered. He recognized nearly every one of them. This time, instead of regret, he experienced only a flare of anger at those who chose to betray their sacred duty to the souls.

I was chosen. He repeated silently. In all he'd ever done, he'd never abandoned the souls the way they had.

Without a shred of fear, he approached the death dealers, stopping when the two on either side of Harmony drew their swords. Harmony appeared hard, cold, her pretty features unyielding.

"This is the end, Gabriel," she started.

"It is, Harmony," he agreed. "I am the rightful master of the underworld. I know you've been operating under a lack of faith in me as the underworld's choice of Death. Because of who I am and the relationship I shared as a colleague with you, I want to offer you and your dealers a final chance to stand down."

"Mercy is a human trait," Harmony replied firmly. "You lack the strength and the mindset required to be Death. I'm going make things right."

Gabriel didn't let her words sink in. After many lifetimes as the top assassin for Death, he knew better than to believe such nonsense. "I'll take that as a no," he said. Raising his voice, he addressed those with her. "Does she speak for all of you? If not, step forward."

He was greeted by silence.

Harmony started to smile. "My turn for an ultimatum."

Gabriel waited, making a show of shifting his armament around to prepare for a brutal battle with those before him. He'd faced down more than this before, demons even. His reputation was known far and wide, and he was going to use every ounce of it to dissuade those he could from fighting him.

"You stand down. Hand over the title of Death, and I'll let you leave this place alive," she said.

Gabriel hefted the long sword strapped to his back and gazed at the blade. "No can do, Harmony."

"There are over six hundred of us!"

"Not a problem."

Harmony frowned at him. "If you think your friends can help you, Gabe, think again. No, in fact, *look* again." She pointed.

Gabriel glanced where she indicated, and his gaze stuck. "You awoke the ogre?" he demanded. "There's a reason past-Death didn't wake them when the demons invaded. If you brought them out of hibernation to take care of a few men ..." He shook his head.

The massive creature gradually moving towards the palace wasn't all that that caught his attention. It was trailed by a storm unlike anything he'd ever seen. It appeared to be uprooting and swallowing the forest as it grew nearer. The sky at its core was black, the swirling clouds and dark fog enveloping everything in their path. Tendrils of blackness shot forward to grab trees and haul itself closer. It was neither a true storm nor a true monster, but some kind of twisted hybrid, something that didn't belong in the underworld. Gabriel faced the direction fully, unable to explain the horrific sight.

"What else did you wake up, Harmony?" he asked, his concern for his safety eclipsed by the storm that looked powerful enough to shred the underworld.

With the flow of knowledge lessening, he was able to make out the faint cry of alarm of the Lake of Souls echoing in his thoughts. The storm came from the opposite direction, but if it wasn't stopped, it'd suck up the Lake and its souls easily.

"Harmony, what did you do?" he demanded.

"Take it or leave it," Harmony said, ignoring him.

Gabriel faced her, disturbed. "There won't be an underworld to rule over, if you don't stop whatever it is you did!"

"I need an answer, Gabriel."

"I will hand deliver the soul of anyone who raises a sword to me to the Dark One," Gabriel replied. "That is my answer."

Harmony lifted her chin to the man beside her. He signaled the largest men among her loyal flock forward. Gabriel stretched his neck and lowered himself into a fighting stance, ready to knock the head off of every man they threw at him.

I am Death. No one takes what's mine.

Suddenly, Jared appeared, shoved out of the invisible doorway leading to the secret passageways that Gabriel had come through as well. The demon landed hard on his knees in the space between Harmony and Gabriel then bounced up, looking around.

"What the fuck, Jared?" Gabriel snapped.

"Just thought you might need … back up," the demon said, gaze settling on the death dealers.

Gabriel snatched him and dragged him close. "Where's my mate?"

"Relax. She's safe in the walls."

Gabriel sought any sign the demon was lying. His instinct told him Jared wasn't. "Try not to damage my extremely rare weapons, asshole."

Jared offered a grimace and pried himself loose, stepping aside to draw his weapon.

"This is your plan?" Harmony looked between them, amused. "A cowardly demon and a former human to take on the might of Death's army?"

"Death's army has been disbanded," Gabriel replied. "You all are traitors now. I'll rebuild after I collect everyone's head and soul."

"Have it your way." Harmony turned away. "Bring in the rest!"

The entrances to the roof opened in unison, and death dealers spilled out, surrounding Gabriel and Jared.

"I'm really not much for fighting. At least, not when they have weapons and can fight back," the demon said. "If they're alone in a dark alley with no weapon, it's different."

Gabriel glanced at him, none too pleased at his choice of companion, before finding Harmony again with his gaze. "You're not staying for the victory, Harmony?" he called after her.

"No need. We've caught your friends. I'm going to personally render them dead-dead then come back for your head."

Gabriel's jaw clenched. It didn't seem possible that Rhyn would be taken alive, and he didn't know what damage the ogre might've inflicted on the handful of loyal death dealers that remained. His mate was safe, but he didn't know what had happened to human-Deidre, Andre, Darkyn, Rhyn …

"You have a plan, right?" the demon asked.

"Can you shapeshift?"

"Not without the portal to Hell being opened."

"That's not happening." Gabriel whirled his sword and took a step towards the death dealers inching closer. "The plan is to not get killed until I come up with a better one."

"This is a good plan."

Sensing the creature was mocking him, Gabriel glanced over.

The demon appeared as sincere as a demon could, and it dawned on him there was probably a reason Jared routinely ended up in dungeons.

Figures I got the shittiest demon in Hell at my back.

Chapter Seventeen

"Something's wrong," past-Death said moments earlier, pushing away from the wall in the dark passageway. "He should've been back by now."

"Stay put, cupcake. I like my head where it is," Jared growled.

She fingered the hilt of the knife at her waist. A familiar, blue-green glimmer caught her attention, and she peered into the darkness. It was leading away from the roof, back down the hallway. The glow had tried to lead her somewhere before and appeared to be waiting for her again.

Fate had identified the deity that died in the dungeon as Peace. Since entering the cell, she'd been haunted by something, perhaps the deity itself in some sort of dreamwalk form. If there was one deity that could end this chaos, it was this one. How was it possible for it to be alive when she'd seen the bones?

"Will you at least peek out and check on him?" she asked.

"I did a moment ago. He was killing the sentries. He should be done and the roof clear by now."

"Look again."

The demon grumbled something.

"Please," she added.

Jared opened the door. The relative brightness of the underworld blinded her.

"Take care of him, demon." Past-Death closed her eyes and shoved him out of the passageway. "I need to do something." She slammed the door closed and stood blinking until the sunspots left her vision.

Turning, she spotted the green-blue glow once more and strode after it. The stones scraped and groaned as the passageway molded into a new direction, one she wasn't dictating. Past-Death drew a dagger and continued into the darkness, heart pounding.

A doorway appeared. She slowed and approached it with some angst, uncertain how much to trust the spirit of a deity she accidentally killed in the dungeon. With a deep breath, she stepped through …

… and into the hallway of the subfloor above the dungeon.

The burst of color was halfway down the hall already, past the room teeming with death dealers where Jared had slaughtered several earlier. If they noticed her, if any one of them decided to leave the room before she passed them and reached the stairwell … her hands shook and she wiped sweat from her brow.

For Gabriel.

Steeling herself, past-Death moved quickly down the hallway on tiptoes. She sucked in a breath and held it as she darted by the open doorway packed with death dealers. A quick glance made her think they had recently returned from the battle outside.

She raced down the hallway and caught her small frame against the wall of the stairwell before descending fast. Past-Death waited to hear the sound of pursuit, for someone to figure out she was there. None came, and she stopped at the bottom of the stairs, scouring the area for any sign of the glow.

The sound of a cell slamming made her gut twist. She ducked into the nearest open cell and pressed herself against the inner wall, out of view of anyone passing. Three death dealers trotted by her. She waited for their footpads on the stairs to cease before easing out of the cell.

The glow was in front of the cell the dealers had just closed. It disappeared through the petrified wood door. Past-Death went to it and stopped.

"Hello?" she called, hitting the door with the flat of her hand. "Can anyone hear me?"

A muffled sound came from the other side.

"I can't hear you!" she said more loudly, gaze darting towards the direction the dealers had gone.

"Yes." This time, the voice was clearer. "We're here." It sounded like a woman's voice, and her heart soared at the thought she'd found Deidre at last.

Past-Death leaned back and pulled the keys she'd kept from her pockets. She tried both of them without success and cursed.

"Just ... wait," she said lamely and took a step back.

There was no way she'd be able to get the keys, unless she dreamwalked. But doing so meant she wasn't able to control how long she was out. Worse, she'd be exposed, if the dealers returned.

"There must be some benefit in being the mate of a god!" she complained, pacing. Hearing the words aloud, Past-Death whirled and faced the door.

Gabriel had officially taken his place as Death. By all rights, and from what she knew of Immortal and deity mates, she should have access to some of his power.

"When I was Death ..." she trailed off and placed her hand against the petrified wood of the cell door. To her delight, she heard the sound of the lock being drawn. Past-Death pushed the door open. "Hello?"

There were three forms in the cell, two of which she knew. Andre the Immortal, and Tymkyn, once her best tracker. The third, Karma, was the woman she'd seen Deidre leave with, a creature that made her retreat farther into the hallway.

They were staring at her in different levels of wariness. Tymkyn appeared disbelieving, Karma distrusting and Andre's brow was furrowed. He sat with his back to the far wall, blood drenching his clothing.

The glow she'd followed to the dungeon was perched on Andre's shoulder. In the silence that followed the door opening, past-Death gazed at it hard, not quite understanding why it had led her to the prisoners when she was looking for Peace.

"Where's Deidre?" she asked, pulling her focus from her mind.

"Gone," Karma said sadly.

"Not dead!"

"No," Andre said and got to his feet with some difficulty. "She went after Darkyn."

"So there are two demons loose somewhere in my underworld," past-Death said, uncertain what to think. *Gabriel's underworld. Whatever.*

Tymkyn started to smile then ducked his head. He moved towards Andre and wrapped an arm around the Immortal.

The blue-green glow was sticking with Andre, at least until he stepped foot outside the cell, at which point it darted down the hallway.

Past-Death moved for them to exit the cell, puzzled. She turned to follow the glow with her gaze and saw it disappear into the cell that once held the deity.

"Where's Gabe?" Tymkyn asked.

"Roof. Fighting sentries," she replied, distracted. "Wait here for a moment." Past-Death trotted down the hallway towards the locked door. She placed her hand against it and waited for the lock to click before pushing.

The glow was settling back where she'd originally found it, on the ring located at the center of the pile of bones. Crossing to the remains, she bent to retrieve the ring and straightened, peering at it.

"You've been following me around, haven't you?" she murmured. "You led me to them and back here again. Any chance you'll just appear and fix everything?"

Nothing happened.

Was it possible a godship could be passed through a relic such as the ring? She didn't have the memories to know for certain, but something about this ring had gone out of its way to find her, take her to the three in the cell, sit on Andre's shoulder and bring her back here.

"Deidre?" Karma called. "We must leave."

She pocketed the ring and left. The three waited in the hallway, and she hurried to them, thoughts racing with options on how to help them leave.

Footsteps and the sound of rustling weapons and armor from the direction of the stairs made them freeze. Past-Death tried to determine how many came. It sounded like much more than the four of them could face with no weapons and one wounded.

"Hide," she whispered. "We have to hide. Maybe we can throw them off and run."

"Better idea," Tymkyn said and motioned her forward. "I will not face Gabriel's wrath if you get hurt on my watch. Take the Immortal." Carefully, he helped stabilize Andre while past-Deidre replaced him supporting the wounded man. "I've seen what this little girl can do." Tymkyn motioned to Karma. "You two hide, and we'll take care of them."

Past-Death hesitated but nodded, sensing how badly injured Andre was. She hobbled with him to a cell several down from the one where she'd found them and maneuvered him inside, gasping as she rested him against the wall. He sank to a sit, and she glanced at the door. If anyone made it down this far, they'd be found for sure. Closing the door would tip off the dealers who knew the cells were supposed to be open when not occupied. After a moment of internal debate, she pulled out a dagger and sat beside Andre, ready to defend them if needed.

"My apologies," Andre whispered. "If it's easier, leave me here."

"Don't be ridiculous," she replied.

He was wheezing, another tip off any death dealer that made it this far wasn't going to miss. Past-Death resisted the urge to shush him. Her side was wet with his blood. He wasn't going to last long as it was.

"Darkyn and Deidre," she said softly. "You don't know where they are?"

"Fighting ogres. Same as Rhyn."

"Whose bright idea was it to let the giants out?"

Andre gave a hoarse chuckle and rested his head back against the wall.

She studied the blood covering his upper body in the dim light from the hall. "Can I help you? Somehow?"

"I don't think so, but thanks," he replied. "I'm fine with this, really. Been dead-dead once. I know it's nothing to fear."

What felt like a bite on her thigh drew a curse from her, and her attention went down to her lap.

The ring was glowing through her jeans. Leaning to the side, past-Death pried it out and stared at it. The light was greater than that of the hallway, the gorgeous shade matching Andre's eyes.

Andre.

"Hey, you ever want to be a god?" she half-joked.

He shifted his head towards her, peering at her through his eyelashes. "Not especially."

"How badly do you *not* want to be one? Because I think maybe someone chose you for a spot."

Andre lifted his head, quizzical turquoise gaze on her.

"Long story short: I locked someone in the dungeon who then died. Not my intention," she said and then paused, considering. "Well, it might've been. I really can't recall. Anyway, something's been haunting me since I returned."

"A presence. Sometimes there, sometimes not," he guessed. "Accompanied by ... a flash of blue."

"Exactly. You felt it?"

"Yeah."

"I think this is why." She held up the ring for him to see. "I think I'm supposed to give this to you."

Andre's eyes settled on the glowing gem. "No part of me wants to ask, but who or what god is it?" By the reservation in his voice, he had the same opinion of the inconsistent deities that she'd started to understand as a human.

A shout came from too close, a sign the death dealers had discovered the empty cell.

She rose. Leaning against the doorframe, she risked a peak out and bit back a curse.

An unarmed Tymkyn and Karma were able to fend off several attackers, but probably not the ten lingering in the corridor.

Her gaze went back to Andre, who was bleeding out quickly.

He wasn't going to make it long. The others didn't have a chance of surviving, either, if they decided to challenge the dealers. Discovery was imminent, and Gabriel would be all but alone to take the palace.

What would Gabriel do to save those he cared about? Past-Death thought for a split second. Dread sank into her stomach. "Whatever it took," she whispered.

"Pardon?" Andre asked, a little too loudly.

"Hush!" Crouching beside Andre, she shoved the ring into his hand. "Take this. Learn to use it fast. Get the others and help Gabriel!" She rose and crossed to the door.

"Deidre, wait!" Andre called in a rough whisper. "What're you going to do?"

"What I should have long ago. Something I never would've done as a goddess." If ever there was a chance for her to help, it was now. These were the kind of people Gabriel needed with him, if he was going to succeed. She had nothing to offer in the way of Tymkyn's fighting skill or Karma's balancing judgments or Andre's peace-making efforts. The best she could do: become a distraction. Give the rest of them a chance.

Show Gabriel I can be human, too. Her lover and mate had sacrificed so much for her over the years. She had the chance to even the score, or at least, take the first step in that direction.

With a deep breath, she threw her shoulders back and stepped into the hallway. "Hey. I think you guys are looking for me!"

The death dealers whirled to face her. None of them moved initially, unease on their features, as if they still feared her, even knowing she was no longer a goddess.

"Where are the others?" one demanded, starting towards her.

"In the secret passageways, where idiots like you can't reach them," she said in the haughtiest, most goddess like voice she was able to muster, the tone that made Gabriel growl. "I want to see Harmony. Now."

"That's good, because Harmony wants to see you." The death dealer stopped before her.

She craned her neck back to meet his gaze, unafraid. "Then take me to her, slave."

"You don't get to control us anymore, bitch." With a smirk, he grabbed her arm and hauled her down the hallway.

Past-Death held her breath, hoping they didn't search the cells for the remaining three. When they reached the stairs, she released it. The nine others trailed obediently. Only when they reached the top of the stairs did she start to wonder what the fuck she was going to do next.

Harmony was outside the room where the guards and keys were kept.

Determined to face her fate without flinching, past-Death reminded herself silently that she still had something to prove: that she was worth Gabriel's love. A thrill raced through her, along with fear. Facing down his greatest enemy was almost as enjoyable as funnel cake, the part of her that relished challenges and mind games intrigued to see what the hell Harmony thought she was doing.

"Not who I was expecting," Harmony said, gaze sweeping over her. "Now that you have no magic, you're nothing but a puny doll."

"And you're a dealer who doesn't realize she's already dead-dead."

Harmony tensed but didn't otherwise react. "By now your Gabriel should be almost dead. I doubt he can face down two hundred men on his own."

"My Gabriel is the rightful master of the underworld. He's also the greatest warrior Death has ever known, and right now, he's pissed off," past-Death replied. "If I were you, I'd send up another two hundred before you set foot on the roof."

Harmony stared at her, and past-Death sensed she'd rattled the woman. Snatching her hard, Harmony dragged her forward. "Where is it?" she hissed.

"Where is what?" past-Death demanded, refusing to flinch despite the pain.

"His soul! So I can end this and take my place as Death!"

"You?" past-Death arched an eyebrow. "You are one of the least impressive dealers I ever brought on board. In fact, I'm not sure why I did."

Harmony's backhand sent her reeling.

Past-Death landed on her stomach, her head ringing. The warm, metallic taste of blood was in her mouth and stars in her vision.

"Where the fuck is it?" Harmony demanded again.

Past-Death laughed. "You will never be Death, Harmony. The underworld chose him, not you."

"Search her!"

She lay still as one of them searched her roughly. She didn't have so much as a hair scrunchie in her pockets, and the dealer rose with a shake of his head.

Harmony was glaring at her from across the hallway, arms folded. The scratch marks on her cheek made past-Death wonder if she'd had a run in with a certain demoness. She said nothing and climbed to her feet.

"I've got another plan," Harmony said and gripped her arm too hard once more. She started forward at a quick walk. "One more likely to make you suffer the way you deserve."

Past-Death trotted on tiptoes to keep up with her. *Remember. Quick deaths are better.* She sought out something to infuriate Harmony even more as they marched through the palace that used to be her home to a central set of stairs leading to the roof.

"You remember the last talk we had?" past-Death asked with what innocence she was able to muster. "The one where my twin and I swore that your soul would go where mine is?"

"Shut the fuck up."

"Mine belongs to Hell."

Harmony missed a step. "You swore!"

"Darkyn's mate swore. I supplied the location," she said, referring to the deal Deidre made with Harmony before the death dealer kidnapped them.

"It won't matter soon. You're going to tell me where Gabriel's soul is, and I'm going to destroy it and then destroy you the way someone should have thousands of years ago."

Past-Death fell quiet. As uncertain as she was about how to be a good human, she was confident about how she had performed as a goddess. The underworld had flourished, and the souls were safe during the entirety of her reign.

Well, until the last few days.

"If you don't tell me, Gabriel will," Harmony added. "There is nothing he won't do for you. I watched him lust over you for years, follow you around like a fairy does flowers. Pitiful. Weak. Human."

Past-Death winced, fearing his devotion was true at one point but fearing more it wasn't anymore. There was a time when she thought the same about Gabriel, that his humanity was a vulnerability.

"You're wrong about him being weak," she voiced. "He's the strongest of you all, the only one who didn't walk away from the souls and lose faith in the underworld the way you did."

The familiar flash of heartache almost crippled her. She didn't want to think about how Gabriel was going to react. Though recalling the way he'd looked at her in the sacred closet, how gently he spoke to her about caring for her, how he'd held her …

He'd cooperate, not out of weakness, but because he did still love her. *Love isn't weakness,* she realized. It was the opposite: a source of strength, honor and self-sacrifice. Secrets Gabriel had known his whole life that she was finally learning.

They reached the roof, and past-Death took in the situation with astonishment. The bodies of death dealers littered the rooftop while a safe distance away, Gabriel and the demon Jared fought the two dozen remaining. Gale strength winds whipped her hair in front of her face, and she pushed it aside, entranced by Gabriel.

She watched her mate move, awed and aroused by his sheer strength. Gabriel swung the sword as if it was an extension of him, his masterful eye, agility and otherworldly instincts making him an unusually graceful, completely unstoppable killing machine. Thick muscles moved smoothly beneath his dark clothing. His biceps bulged beneath the t-shirt he wore, his roped forearms chiseled and rippling the same way the muscles of his back did.

He's so beautiful. Had she ever really noticed it? Or did she see it completely anew each time she saw him? Why did it take her losing him and her soul for her to realize a man as honorable and amazing as he was wasn't going to be manipulated into love?

It was then she noticed how many dealers had already fallen. Past-Death gave a laugh of sheer mockery. "I told you – send two hundred more!"

"I'll do one better. I'll send three hundred more." Harmony tossed her head to one of those following and shoved past-Death forward.

She landed hard on her knees and grimaced, twisting to sit on her backside instead.

The storm approaching from the east drew her gaze, and her breath caught. Past-Death stumbled to her feet and shifted away from the landing of the stairwell crowded by death dealers to get an unobstructed look.

It was devouring everything in its path, chewing a part the underworld and destroying it. She glanced in the direction of the Lake of Souls, whose glow was visible from the palace roof. Panic and fear shot through her at the prospect of what happened to all the innocent souls if they were swept up and crushed by the storm.

Deidre. Past-Death wasn't certain which direction her twin, Rhyn and even Darkyn had escaped in, but she found herself hoping that at least two of the three hadn't gone east.

"Fix this, Gabriel," she whispered, overwhelmed by the sight of the monstrosity headed their direction. "Only you can."

Harmony snatched her arm once more and turned her to face Gabriel once more. Another forty death dealers had moved onto the roof, and Harmony started forward, taking past-Death with her.

When she was close enough, she stopped and shouted, "Gabriel!"

The wind took her words. She released past-Death and moved closer, into his line of sight.

Past-Death shifted away from the dealers, waiting for a chance to run for it to open up.

Gabriel twisted and met her gaze. After a lingering look, he lowered his sword and straightened from his fighting stance.

Harmony waved off those dealers waiting to face him, and past-Death saw Gabriel and Harmony talk for a moment without hearing anything. His dark gaze remained on her, not Harmony.

Past-Death studied him, regret in her gut once more as she realized how bad their situation was. She regretted so much of what she'd done to exacerbate the situation, but there was one thing she began to understand was worth it all: the chance to be with Gabriel.

Harmony strode back to her and wrenched her forward, dagger at her neck. Past-Death leaned back instinctively from the razor sharp blade, not trusting the angered death dealer to keep it steady with the harsh wind.

"One more time. Where the fuck is it?" Harmony growled.

"Harmony!" Gabriel boomed. "If you harm one fucking hair on her —"

"Tell me where it is!" Harmony shouted back.

"I don't know! No one does."

"Bullshit." The woman's desperation was clear in her gaze. "You will tell me!" She turned her attention to past-Death, digging the knife into her neck.

Past-Death met her gaze. "You know what, Harmony? I do know where it is. But I won't tell you. Kill me, and you can rot in Hell right beside me."

"Deidre!" Gabriel called sharply. "Tell her —"

Harmony wrenched past-Death's head back. "Say hello to Darkyn you bitch."

Past-Death closed her eyes. In the moment before death, she was certain of one thing.

She'd never, ever betray her Gabriel, not for power or her life. This was what love was: putting someone else above her own interests, something Gabriel had done to her his whole life. *I understand now.* The realization made her want to sob that it took her death for her to understand what was truly worth living.

Lightning slashed the sky overhead, and a burst of wind knocked her and Harmony to the ground. Stunned not to be dead, Past-Death lay still for a long moment, sucking in deep breaths of air. She started to crawl away on her knees, anxious to reach Gabriel or the safety of the palace.

Harmony snatched her and dragged her back, shoving her onto her back and climbing on top of her.

"This ends now!" the death dealer shouted, knife at past-Death's throat.

"Holy gods and goddesses." It wasn't the infuriated death dealer on top of her or the bite of the blade into her neck that had past-Death's attention, but the sky overhead.

Harmony glanced up then sat back.

Past-Death stared as the inky black tendrils of the storm snaked across the sky, writhing as if they were real. They were followed by clouds too dark to allow the smallest sliver of light through, a black hole devouring everything. Clouds dropped from the sky, snatching up death dealers and tossing them into the center of the storm, where they were completely swallowed.

The form of the remaining ogre whirled round and round in the sky above the palace until it, too, was sucked into the black hole at its center.

"Get the fuck away from my mate!" Gabriel's roar split the air, his sword flying over past-Death's head to impale a nearby death dealer.

Harmony ducked the dagger he threw and rolled off her, yanking more weapons free as she leapt to her feet.

Past-Death scrambled up, was pushed back by the wind, and clawed her way to her feet once more. The storm was snatching dealers off the rooftop left and right, the screams and chaos blinding her as much as the hair she couldn't keep out of her face.

"Gabriel!" she screamed.

"Here!"

Past-Death turned in the direction she thought his voice came from, unable to tell for certain with the wind whipping sound around her. Something hot slid through her, and she touched her abdomen absently, cursing hunger pangs.

Harmony stood half a dozen feet from her, straightening from her throw.

Past-Death's fingers fumbled over the hilt of a knife, and she looked down. The dagger protruding from her upper abdomen didn't seem real, and she stared at the blood quickly soaking her clothing. The pain took a moment to reach her as well.

"Oh, shit," she murmured, comprehension filtering through her. Past-Death dropped to her knees and gripped the hilt with both hands, yanking it free.

Hot pain tore through her, and she hunched over, the roar of the wind fading, replaced with the clamoring of her panicked instincts.

"Deidre!" Gabriel dropped beside her. He pulled her back against him, and she leaned into his strong body, relaxing.

"Is it bad?" she asked. The pain was growing tolerable, and black had begun to line the edges of her thoughts, like it was time for a nap. *I like naps,* she recalled. Another human experience that ranked up there with sex with Gabriel and funnel cakes. "It doesn't feel bad."

Gabriel said nothing, instead focused on applying pressure. Blood spurted over his hands, and she looked up at him, admiring the chiseled features of his rugged face.

"You are incredible, Gabriel," she murmured wistfully. "Why didn't we just ... love each other and be happy?"

His gaze dropped to hers, his dark eyes scouring her face. "Is that really what you want?"

"It's what I've always wanted," she replied. "I'm sorry I made it so difficult." She struggled to sit, wanting to talk to him face to face and suddenly confused as to why she was lying on the roof under a storm. Shouldn't they be inside, talking?

Why did her head feel like it was sinking into sleep when she wanted to be awake?

"Be still, sweetheart. You're hurt bad."

"I am?" she asked, perplexed. She looked down at the blood covering his hands. "Oh, yeah. That's right. Harmony and ... Gabriel! You have to fix this storm! It'll hurt the souls!"

"Hush," he said, holding her more tightly to keep her from moving. "I will. You need to keep still."

Past-Death closed her eyes. "You go do that and I'll take a nap."

"No, honey, stay awake." He nudged her.

She groaned. Why did he sound so upset? She wasn't certain. Something to do with the distant pain in her abdomen and the sound of a storm coming …

Past-Death slid into unconsciousness, content to be in Gabriel's arms again while she slept.

Chapter Eighteen

"Deidre!" Gabriel nudged her again.

The bloodied woman in his arms didn't respond. She was growing pale, her heartbeat slowing while she continued to bleed out. She wore the ring he'd gotten her thousands of years ago, a simple silver band with filigree.

"Stay with me, sweetheart," he whispered, shaking her to try to wake her once more.

She'd been willing to die for him. Until the moment, he never thought her capable of living for anyone but herself, even when she tried.

"Stay with me," he said more urgently, fear, panic and anger coursing through him.

A gust of wind knocked him over, and he rolled with her to keep the storm's long arms from snatching her. Laying her out carefully, he shifted to his side and brushed her hair from her face. The underworld was crashing down around him, his longtime love dying in his arms. For a moment, he wasn't able to think straight or quiet either of the screaming voices in his head stemming from his bonds to the underworld and his mate being under duress.

The woman he'd loved and hated his entire life, the one who

made his blood race and quieted his thoughts, was dying before his eyes, this time for good. He wasn't able to raise someone whose soul was outside his reach. The idea of losing her forever was one he'd experienced more than once. As frustrating as their relationship often was, he couldn't escape the simple fact that he wasn't able to live without her. He'd loved her as a goddess, and he loved her more as a human struggling to figure herself out.

Flying debris knocked him onto his back, and he stared at the black hole, almost fully over the palace.

Gabriel rolled back beside her placed her hands over her wound and pressed down, fury and heartache boiling over.

What good was being a deity, when he kept losing her? What good was being human, when his pain immobilized him? Which part of him took precedence: the one that served the souls or the one suffering heartbreak?

"I am a fucking god!" he shouted into the wind. Blinded by rage and hurt, he rose and raised his hands to the storm. "You can't have either of them!" Cool power swept through him, and he turned to face its source, surprised at the green fog racing towards him from the direction of the Lake. The magic of the souls sang through him in billions of tiny voices, their unified chorus conveying power that made the palace beneath him quiver.

A man-sized tornado broke away from the storm and landed on the rooftop, tearing across the expanse, tossing dealers from its path as it made a beeline for one person in particular: Harmony.

The death dealer lashed out at it with a sword, which the black smoke avoided easily. The fog cleared to reveal the small shape of Deidre, glowing darkly with the power of the black hole overhead, her pink hair tossed in the wind and her eyes swallowed by black.

It can't be possible. Cold realization shot through Gabriel as he suddenly understood why there had never been a storm such as this in the thousands of years he was in the underworld. It wasn't Harmony's doing either, or something past-Death had set loose before she quit.

This was Hell. Forbidden from bringing his magic with him, Darkyn had none, unlike his successor, who faced no such restrictions when she became the Dark One. Horror flew him at the idea of innocent souls being lost, along with the underworld and everyone else he cared about. Harmony was one kind of threat, but with the power of Hell behind her, Deidre was something else entirely.

Deidre brushed away Harmony's attempt to stab her with the sword and strode forward, snatching the death dealer's neck and lifting her off the ground.

The power flowing through him made the air around him sizzle and the winds avoid him. With a tortured glance at his dying mate, Gabriel started forward at a run towards the newly appointed Dark One. If he didn't stop this, none of them would survive.

The black hole was tugging at the edge of the palace, and the stones making up his home shuddered and began to break away. The past few months flashed through Gabriel's mind, his frustration and anger at the challenges of becoming Death, the opening of old wounds when he discovered his mate, the knowledge of all the ages and that the underworld had chosen him.

"No," he whispered, fury and resolve solidifying within him. "I am the Keeper of the Souls, the master of the underworld. You will not harm my realm!"

The moment the words were spoken, the entire world fell silent, still. Gabriel slowed, not understanding. The storm and black hole were frozen, the fleeing death dealers as well. Nothing moved or stirred, except for him.

The eeriness of the sudden quiet made his skin crawl for more reasons than one. Power was thick in the air. His hair stood on end and the movement of his blood felt electrified. He spun completely around, elated to have stopped the destruction and the death of his mate and realm without fully comprehending his next move.

A sob broke the quiet, and he faced Deidre once more, startled when she stepped away from Harmony in confusion. The death dealer remained suspended above the rooftop, stuck in time like the rest of the world.

Deidre reached for a sword at her feet and hefted it up, preparing to lift it and hack off Harmony's head.

"Deidre?" Gabriel approached her cautiously, uncertain what to expect.

The woman faced him, black fog tracing her movements and pooling in the air around her. Her eyes were completely black, tears on her cheeks while her chest heaved, as if she was trying not to cry.

He stopped within arms reach. Whereas Darkyn's magic had been subtle, the woman before him radiated cold power. It was wild, uncontrolled, the opposite of how her mate had handled the power of Hell. Sensing the danger of a Dark One out of control, Gabriel shifted closer.

"This is you." He pointed to the sky. "Isn't it?"

She nodded. "Darkyn … gave it to me."

"So what? You could kill Harmony in cold blood?"

She glanced at the death dealer. "She deserves it." The vehemence in her voice contained an inhuman edge, another sign she wasn't in control.

"But you don't."

Deidre appeared confused.

"Listen. You aren't the kind of person who does things like this," Gabriel said, resting his hands on her shoulders. "Deidre, you aren't in control right now."

"Back off, Death," she snapped and wrenched loose. "I will end this! I must kill her!"

"Are you hearing this?"

Deidre ignored him and lifted the sword with both hands, eyeing Harmony.

Gabriel caught her wrists and twisted the weapon loose, pulling her towards the edge of the roof.

Deidre struggled, and he wrapped both arms around her, stymying her efforts and carrying her.

"Look at what the fuck you're doing!" he snapped. He faced the wide path of destruction the storm had left.

"I don't care!" She thrashed at him, the black fog around stretching for the black hole overhead.

"No!" he roared to the power of Hell trying to evade him. "You *will* obey me!"

The magic froze in midair before retreating back to Deidre. She was fighting him hard.

"Stop, Deidre!" he ordered. "The Dark One doesn't care, but you do! The human side of you. The one mourning the loss of your mate!"

She strained in his grip, and another sob wracked her tiny frame. He held her securely.

"You are destroying my world, Deidre," he said more quietly. "What happens to the souls in the Lake when your storm takes them? Billions of innocent humans? People you've known and cared about?"

She stilled, panting. "I don't care," she said more quietly.

"You do. I know you do," he replied. "You're hurt, Deidre. You lost someone you care about and you're seeking revenge in a way that will leave no one standing when it's over."

The woman was quiet, her breathing growing more erratic.

"I know what it feels like," he added. "I know how dark it can get."

"Stop, Gabriel! Let me go."

"Not until you listen and *see* what you're doing! You're the one who gave me hope, Deidre. Do you remember what you said? On the beach, the first night we met?"

"No." It was a forced whisper.

"Death lets you see the stars and the moon instead of how dark the night is," he repeated. "It gives you hope. You taught me this. After a thousand years of numbness, you reminded me what it means to be human."

"I'm so tired of all of this, Gabriel. So tired of fear and hurt and … everything." She was calming, the inhuman edge fading from her voice.

Gabriel released her without moving away. "Look at what you're doing, Deidre."

She wiped her face.

They stood quietly, observing the large swath of nothingness that remained from her journey through the forest to the palace.

"My mate is dying." He cleared his throat at the rough note that crept into his voice. "Yours is dead. Are you really going to punish the souls of so many? Are we going to make each other suffer more?"

Deidre faced him. Her eyes were blue again, the air around her electrified but calmer. "No, Gabriel," she said. "I couldn't. I won't."

"You're out of control." He pointed to the sky. "Just a little. I have a duty to stop you, but doing so will probably destroy everything. *You* need to stop this, Deidre. You need to keep the part of you that's human. Trust me, I know how hard it is, and there's no fucking instruction manual."

The corner of her mouth turned up in a sad smile. Tears trickled down her cheeks. "I didn't think I could hurt so much, but this is different. It's worse than when I thought I was losing you."

"You really cared for him."

"I do. I thought I wanted out of this horrible world, to be human and forget everything," she said. "But I need him. I don't want to live without him, and I don't know how to …" she drifted off, grappling with her emotions.

"You need balance," he finished for her.

"Yeah. Darkyn and … a weekend house on the beach in my world, so I don't forget what it's like to be human."

"Balance is good," he agreed. "Something I'm working on as well. If you let yourself kill Harmony in cold blood, or you take lives you shouldn't, you're going to regret it. Trust me. There's not enough water in the ocean to fill that void, not for someone as naturally good as you are."

"She has to pay."

"Let me handle that. Her soul is destined for Hell anyway. This is my domain, and I reserve the right to reclaim it, which means you need to stop whatever you're fucking doing and step aside," he said firmly.

She gazed up at him, sorrow in her features.

"As a fellow deity, we are obliged to fuck with each other mercilessly, plot against one another and also to occasionally pretend to be interested in compromise," he continued.

Her eyebrows lifted.

"As friends, I'm asking you to step aside and let me handle this. I understand your stake in this. Trust me please, Deidre. I'll kill her, and you get eternity to fuck with her in Hell."

"That's more Darkyn's thing than mine." Her gaze went towards Harmony. "I want him back, Gabriel."

"Are you wanting to make me a deal?"

Deidre hesitated then nodded.

Excitement flickered through him, and he pretended to consider. "You do have something I want."

Deidre reached for the pouch at her waist and tugged it free. She dumped its contents – two green souls and one the shade of smoky quartz – onto her palm.

Fuck. "You've got two things I want," he said. "Whose is the third?"

"No idea. Fate gave it to me. Said to hang onto it."

Gabriel was quiet for a moment, pensive. Fate had reason to fear Darkyn was going to do something truly horrible down the road regarding the army of undead the demon lord had been building. To resurrect such an enemy was not going to earn him any points with others like Fate, who already liked too much to conspire against one another.

One look at the uncertain hope on Deidre's face, however, made him realize he couldn't say no, either.

"I've got conditions," he started.

"I'm listening."

"Darkyn is hell bent on destroying the human world or taking it over. There are ... people who think he's got a good chance of doing it. Right now, being dead-dead, he's neutralized."

"I won't let him," she said firmly. "I've told him so."

"I believe you, but I need a stronger assurance. He's been collecting souls to add to his undead army. I want those souls back."

Deidre studied him. "Gabriel, I don't know where they are."

"His demons will. When you get back to Hell, you can find them and turn them over to me."

She was quiet.

"Second, I want past-Death's soul and mine." He nodded

towards her palm. "If Fate thinks you should keep the third, keep it. Just don't turn it over to Darkyn."

Deidre blinked back more tears.

"What's wrong?" he asked more gently.

"Darkyn said I was a horrible dealmaker. I think he's right. I know I should have my own conditions, but all I can think about is getting him back."

"You also know you can trust me," he reminded her. "I'm not asking for anything that'll hurt you. Losing the souls will probably piss him off, but you also know it's for the right reason."

She nodded, nibbling on her lower lip with her tiny fangs. "There are two things I want from you, Gabe," she said.

He waited. She appeared to be choosing her words carefully.

"For the first, I want to watch you take care of Harmony and to take her soul back to Hell with me."

"Easy," he agreed.

"For the second … every time there's a full moon, you have to meet me on the beach where we first met," she whispered. "An eternity is a long time. I think we need to remind each other regularly that we're still human. I felt that part of me slipping away today, and I can't … I won't lose it."

"I understand that feeling," he said in a hushed voice.

"If you can't come, send Deidre," she added. "She asked me once if we could be friends. I don't know yet for sure, but I want to give it a try."

The sweet Deidre was back. She had an edge now and a streak of confidence he didn't recall about her, but her heart remained as pure as the storm was evil.

Gabriel glanced up to make sure the black hole hadn't started moving on its own. To his astonishment, it was gone. The skies were cloudy, but this was the normal underworld grey, not the black fog of Hell.

"I really did cause it," she murmured, following his gaze.

"One of the downfalls of being a deity of human-origin: our domains respond to our emotions. A lesson I recently learned," Gabriel explained.

"Darkyn had to know that."

"Oh, he knew. You were the one person in the universe he'd give Hell to, probably because he knew you'd give it right back after you regained his soul. Am I right?"

She nodded. "I don't want Hell."

"There aren't many people who would pass up ruling the most powerful source of magic in the universe."

"I don't care about power, Gabriel. I've never wanted more than a cottage on the beach and someone to share it with me. Oh, and not to die of a brain tumor, which worked out." She cleared her throat. "Sort of."

"He trusts you."

A shy smile slid free. "I know. Don't tell Fate."

"No worries there. That man has issues."

"Definitely."

"We have a deal? I'll go get Darkyn's soul if so."

Deidre held out her hand. "No additional conditions, unwritten terms or creative executions of timeframes."

"Agreed." He shook her hand, and their deal was sealed with a flash of cool magic. She handed him the two souls. Exhilaration raced through him. "Wait here."

Gabriel left the roof, weaving among the statues of death dealers. Once inside, he sprinted towards the bedchamber and ducked into the secret closet, snatching Darkyn's soul from the caldron.

When he returned, he saw Deidre kneeling over past-Death. He quickened his pace, not fully certain he was able to trust the temporary Dark One with his mate, despite their common understanding and generally good relationship.

"What're you doing, Deidre?" he called, nearing.

"Something amazing," she replied, a breathless note in her voice. She leaned back to display past-Death pushing herself into a sitting position. "Look! Good as new!"

Fear shot through him, and Gabriel dropped beside his mate. "Don't move!" he urged, hurrying to cover the wound in her belly. "Dammit, Deidre! If you'd left her frozen, I-"

"She's fine," Deidre replied. She stood and stepped away to give him room. "I don't know how, but she is."

"I'm fine," his mate echoed, pushing his hands away. She met his gaze, and he paused, searching her features. Her cheeks were glowing, her blue eyes bright. She cupped his cheeks with her hands and placed a light kiss on his lips. "You worry too much, Gabriel."

He lifted an eyebrow at the familiar teasing note in her voice.

"Now that I understand why, it makes me happy," she added.

"Because I love you," he said. He gathered her into his arms, not convinced she was healed, and hugged her against him.

"Is it over?" she asked.

"Almost, yeah." Gabriel breathed her scent in deeply, enjoying the feel of her warmth and softness after almost losing her. The muscles of his body relaxed instinctively, the bond between them no longer suffering from pain.

"What happens when it is?" There was apprehension in her question.

"Then we won't have any more excuses not to make this work."

"I like that idea."

"Me, too," he said, chuckling.

She lifted her head from his shoulder and gazed deeply into his eyes. "Thank you for waiting for me for all these years," she said. "I promise you, Gabriel, I will be everything you deserve in a mate and more. I don't care how long it takes for you to trust me. I'll prove I'm worthy of you. I'll work on being a good human every day."

"I do trust you, Deidre," he said softly. "The moment you chose to let Harmony kill you instead of telling them the whereabouts of my soul, I trusted you. The goddess I knew never would've sacrificed herself that way, even for me."

"You mean it? We're not dysfunctional anymore?"

"I don't think we'll ever be normal, sweetheart," he said, laughing. "But we're the perfect kind of dysfunction."

She smiled. Past-Death leaned forward and kissed him hard, her warm lips pressing to his. Gabriel responded with some restraint, recalling how hesitant she'd been when they made love the first time. The sensations and world were still new to her, and he wasn't about to rush when they had an eternity to enjoy one another. Deepening the kiss, he slid his tongue between her lips and tasted her, his blood heating and racing through him at her sweet flavor.

The mating bond resonated inside him, stirring the ferocious need he'd been repressing around her, along with the protective, possessive compulsion to make her his again, to explore her body and its reactions to him until he knew them by heart. The time for restraint would be gone soon, and every fiber in his body sang in anticipation of claiming his mate.

"I did it again!" Deidre's exclamation reminded him of his surroundings.

With some regret, Gabriel withdrew from his mate and rested his temple against hers. Her breathing was uneven, the pliant body in his arms making him want to run away from the frozen world long enough to make love to her.

"You have to ... fix this," she whispered. "Make sure the souls are okay."

"I know." He gave her a quick kiss on the forehead. "It might take me a while."

"I'm never going anywhere again, Gabriel."

The fierce determination on her face pulled a smile from him. "Good. Stick close to me. We've got to take care of a few things. Then, it's just you and me. We've got some making up to do."

She grinned. "As long as you're naked."

"Promise."

She laughed somewhat breathlessly.

He rose and pulled her to her feet. Hand-in-hand, they went the direction Deidre had gone. She'd awoken Tymkyn, who was getting to his feet, his dazed gaze taking in everything around him.

"You alive?" Gabriel asked, slapping him on the arm.

The small man nodded. He picked up his sword.

"Get to work. Every death dealer not allied with us loses his head. They should be easy pickins' while frozen."

Grimly, Tymkyn nodded. "Understood."

"Who'd you come up here with?"

"No one. Andre couldn't be moved from the dungeon. Karma was with me on the stairs and then ... gone," Tymkyn explained.

Gabriel frowned at the news about Andre. "Before you start, go check on him."

"I'll go, too," past-Death said. "He was pretty badly injured."

Gabriel gave Tymkyn a long look and nodded towards his mate.

"With my life, boss," Tymkyn said solemnly.

"Hurry back," Gabriel told past-Death.

She smiled. Her features were radiant, and there was a spring in her step he'd never seen before. He watched her trail Tymkyn into the palace.

Gabriel turned his attention to the chaotic scene on the roof and in the sky. A dozen dealers were stuck in the air above the place, having been snatched by a now non-existent storm. Hundreds littered the rooftop, and he scrutinized them as he wove among them, uncertain which were dead-dead and which were frozen.

He'd seen past-Death claim souls en masse before. Closing his eyes, he envisioned the souls leaving the bodies of the dead-dead and depositing themselves at his feet. Cool power unfurled within him. The souls began to tell their stories in faint voices. He listened until the flow stopped and then opened his eyes. A pyramid of souls was at his feet.

The sheer number saddened him. While traitors did deserve Hell, he wasn't able to get over the amount of colleagues who chose to turn away from their duty and him.

It'd be easier if the dead-dead were all on one side of the roof, he thought absently.

Deidre gave a startled cry, and his gaze flew up.

The bodies of the dead-dead were being lifted by green fog and deposited on one side of the roof.

Slowly, Gabriel smiled. The power that refused to listen to him before was growing more responsive. "Bring any allies to me," he directed the magic.

The fog brought him two dozen bodies, some of which came from the surrounding forest.

"So few," he whispered, shaking his head. He scoured the faces until he saw Rhyn and relaxed, thrilled to see his best friend among the living. Kneeling beside him, Gabriel envisioned the half-demon and the others awakening. Seconds later, the men on either side of him stirred.

"What the fuck?" Rhyn sounded groggy.

"Guess who figured out how to be a god?" Gabriel asked.

"'Bout fucking time, dude."

Gabriel helped his friend up. "Got a mission for all of you," he called to the group. They were bloodied and injured – but loyal. "Every dealer in the palace and on the roof, aside from those on that side, are to be beheaded and their souls deposited into the pile in the middle."

He watched the expressions of the men as he spoke. Not one of them flinched or appeared taken aback by the order.

"The only exception: Harmony."

"Got it." Rhyn swung his sword free and strode towards the first. "Good to see you, Gabe!" he called over his shoulder with a grunt as he decapitated the first dealer.

"You, too, Rhyn." Gabriel hid a smile and faced the direction where Deidre stood.

The death dealers nearest her had moved away uncertainly, as if sensing her power but unwilling to challenge it.

She was watching him. Gabriel waved her over. He strode towards Harmony and stopped, gazing at the death dealer responsible for the events of the underworld.

The Dark One joined him, her power making the air around him uncomfortably cold.

"Stay calm," he reminded her with a glance at the sky. The clouds were darkening once more, the wind picking up. "Got it?"

She nodded.

"You sure you want to see this?" he asked, withdrawing the long sword from his back.

"Yeah." There was no hesitation or remorse on her face. Hell and the underworld had hardened her enough that he believed her capable of standing up to Darkyn the way she claimed she would to protect humanity.

Gabriel touched Harmony's shoulder and envisioned her unfrozen.

She dropped to the ground again and caught her balance, staring at them.

"Let's keep this clean," Gabriel said. "On your knees, Harmony."

The death dealer looked around, confusion on her features. She grabbed a knife like the one she'd used to try to kill past-Death.

Gabriel didn't give her the chance to strike but swung the sword once, taking off her head with a single blow. He lowered the weapon and watched her body drop. It was a kinder death than she deserved, but Hell would make up for that.

"It's over," Deidre whispered.

He said nothing but called the soul to him. When the emerald had formed, he handed it to her.

"For Darkyn," he said. Reaching into his pocket, he retrieved the onyx soul of her mate and passed it to her. "For you."

She held the soul up, peering at it with mixed emotions.

"You've got the power of the Dark One, one of the only two entities that can raise men from the dead," he explained. "Do me a favor and wait until you're home to try it."

"Will do." She pocketed it. "What happens next?"

"The Dark One gets the fuck out of my domain," he said, smiling.

Deidre offered a small smile in return. "Sorry about the damage."

"Could be worse."

"I don't want to know. Tell Deidre farewell for now. And if you find that demon, can you send him back? I think he belongs in Hell's prison. I owe him for killing my ex."

Gabriel laughed. "It wouldn't be his first time."

She held his gaze a moment more before turning and stating away. A portal appeared before her.

"Deidre," he called. "One more thing."

She faced him.

"When you raise someone from the dead, they owe you a favor.

No conditions, no restrictions, no questions asked," he said, grinning evilly. "Just, you know. In case you need some leverage with him."

A slow smile spread across her face, and her eyes flickered black before retuning to their normal hue. Without another word, she disappeared through the portal.

"Gabe, there's no one in the dungeon," his mate reported breathlessly as she trotted up to him. "Andre isn't anywhere to be found." A flicker of something went through her gaze. He wasn't certain what exactly.

"Shit," he muttered. "I'll let Rhyn know."

She took his hand with both of hers, gaze going to Harmony's body. "I am so sorry, Gabe."

"I'm not," he said firmly. "It's a new era, a new way of doing things. We'll rebuild the army and clean up this mess."

"Fresh start?"

"Yep."

Past-Death smiled and wrapped her arms around him. He enveloped her in a hug, tension easing from his frame.

"Yo, Gabe!" Rhyn called, approaching. He wiped his bloodied sword on one leg. "Good news: mind-to-mind communications are back. Bad news: something happened at home. I gotta go back." There was concern in the half-demon's silver eyes.

"Katie okay?" Gabriel asked.

"Yeah. Not sure what's going on."

"Rhyn, about Andre …"

His friend's frown deepened.

"He was badly wounded and isn't among the survivors we've found. We'll keep looking."

Rhyn muttered a string of curses, pensive and agitated. "Let me know what you find," he said finally. "I gotta go."

Gabriel watched his friend storm off through a portal, worried yet certain if anyone could handle it, Rhyn could.

"Karma's missing, too," past-Death said. "I'm not surprised. She's got a lot of unfinished business. I just wish I knew why I had her and Peace in my dungeon."

Gabriel scowled. He sought his bond to the underworld and silently asked about the two deities.

The response: the only god or goddess in his underworld was him.

"You know what? I'm fed up with deities today. As long as they're out of my fucking domain, I don't care what they're doing," he said. "If any of them come back, we'll know. I'll unfreeze the world when the dealers are taken care of."

"Smart, as usual."

"Wanna take a walk to the Lake and make sure it's okay?"

Past-Death nodded.

Taking her hand, they started across the roof. Gabriel's focus went from the to-do list he was mentally generating about how to fix his realm to the woman beside him, and he began to believe every-thing was going to work out the way it should for the first time since he took over. There were no more obstacles between him and rebuilding the parts of his life he cared for most: his mate and the souls.

I can't believe this is really happening. He had the woman he'd loved his whole life at his side, and this time, nothing would ever come between them again.

Chapter Nineteen

"**G**lad you're back," Kiki said the moment Rhyn stepped through the portal back into the Immortals' fortress in the French Alps. The modern stone castle was warmer than the underworld had been. Cheerful, bright sunshine drifted through the windows of the study where Rhyn routinely went to meet his brother.

"What's up, Kiki?"

"Do you, uh, want to change first?" Kiki asked.

"Nope." Rhyn sheathed the sword at his back and placed his hands on his hips, waiting.

Kiki, the most practical and semi-loyal of his half-brothers, carried his usual iPad and was casually dressed in jeans and a sweater. He looked over Rhyn's bloodied, torn clothing critically but said nothing else about it.

"There have been a couple of changes while you were gone," he started.

"Changes? In what? Three days?" Rhyn asked skeptically.

"It's been eight here. The first is … well, you were voted off the Council."

Rhyn stared at him.

"Second, you were also voted into exile," Kiki continued with his normal crisp, factual delivery.

"What the fuck are you talking about?" Rhyn demanded. "How can you vote the head of the Council out when he's not even there?"

"That's precisely *why* you were voted out," Kiki replied calmly. "The Council felt you were abandoning your duties to the Immortals by going to the underworld for a friend. There were convincing arguments about needing someone here who was more stable."

"Wait a minute. There were two members of the Council that stayed behind. You and that chicken shit, Tamer, who was supposed to be in the underworld with me! You both were here while Andre and I were in the underworld, which means at most, the vote was tied two-two. You can't kick me out with a tied vote."

"It was three-two," Kiki said.

"Three? Did Erik come back from the dead-dead?"

"Wynn."

Rhyn went still, senses heightening. "I knew I should've killed that fucker when he showed up here."

"That fucker is our father," Kiki reminded him. "He brought up some good points about needing to rebuild the Immortal warrior corps and reclaiming the territory we lost recently because of the demon attacks."

"Tell me you didn't turn it over to him."

"He should make a good leader." The words sounded forced, and Kiki appeared uncomfortable uttering them.

Something is really off about this. "What the fuck is going on, Kiki? Really. Exile?"

"Temporary exile, if you prefer to call it that."

Coldness slithered through Rhyn. He'd left his mate and hatchling here in the fortress, the safest place for them to be.

Unless Wynn was in charge.

"Where's Katie?" Rhyn took a step towards him.

"Upstairs. Safe." Kiki backpedaled. "Look, it's not personal, Rhyn. You aren't equipped to handle the types of things Wynn can. He's not the man he was before."

Rhyn's head felt like it was ready to explode. Not only was he hungry for his mate, but he was worried about how he'd take care of her, if Wynn decided to act on the threat he'd made about hunting Rhyn down to kill him.

They were better off as far as he could take her from here.

"Fine. I'll leave," he snapped. "But you listen to me, Kiki. That man is a lunatic waiting to fuck up your world. You all have hated the way I did business, but you're about to find out just how fucked up it can get. And if any of you ever, *ever* come after my mate and hatchling, I will slaughter every last one of you. I'll make what Darkyn's demons did up here look like a fucking picnic!"

"Rhyn-"

Ignoring him and anxious to ensure his mate was indeed safe, Rhyn stormed out of the study, nearly running into Andre, who lingered in the hallway outside.

He stopped short despite his hurry. "I thought you were dead-dead," he said. "I mean, again."

Andre smiled. He was impeccably dressed as usual in slacks and a button down shirt. Rhyn smelled no blood, and Andre appeared well rested. Rhyn's brow furrowed. The battle for the underworld hadn't been over long enough for anyone to have showered let alone healed from his wounds.

"I made it back in better shape than you," Andre said, eyebrow raised as he took in Rhyn's state.

"I don't have time for this shit."

"What's wrong, Rhyn?" Andre's voice was even more soothing than usual, his presence making the tension between Rhyn's shoulders melt.

"I'm leaving. Exiled, thanks to Wynn, the new head of the Council. You vote against me, too?" Rhyn asked with a snort.

Andre's smile faded, and something sparked deep within his turquoise eyes. He pulled his hands from his pockets. Rhyn caught the glint of a ring he didn't recognize on one finger, a brilliant blue-green gem in tarnished bronze.

"I've never voted against you," Andre said quietly.

"You never outright supported me either, except to send me to Hell."

"I'm not your enemy, Rhyn."

Rhyn drew a calming breath. "I know. But this … this is wrong. Even I know that. Not that what you all do is any of my business anymore. I'm taking Katie somewhere safe where we can raise our hatchling far away from this shit."

"Which is …"

"None of your fucking business."

"Very well."

"Glad you're not dead-dead. Have a nice life." Rhyn strode away, concern for his family making him want to leave as soon as possible.

"Rhyn, if you need anything, know that I'm here for you," Andre called after him.

Rhyn rolled his eyes. *Too late, Andre. I know better than to trust any of my brothers.*

He took the stairs three at a time to the level where he shared a room with Katie, disturbed despite his attempt to act unconcerned.

He shoved the door to his room open and relaxed. His pregnant mate was folding clothing and placing it one of two suitcases on the bed. She glanced over her shoulder at him with a quick smile, her blue eyes standing out from her dark hair and golden skin.

"Hey, Rhyn," she called cheerfully. "How's Gabe?"

Rhyn cursed. "I'm standing here covered in blood, and you want to know how Gabe is?"

"I'd know if you were hurt," she reminded him.

"He's wonderful. Fine. Happy." Grunting, he peeled off his shirt, knowing she'd never let him hug her when he was soaked with blood. Covering the distance between them with ground eating strides, he wrapped his arms around her from behind and pulled her into his body tightly.

"I missed you," he whispered, nipping her neck.

She clasped her hands over his. "I missed you, too, Rhyn. Are you okay?"

"Yeah."

"I'd hug you properly, but I'm too fat." There was a note of dismay in her voice, a sign her mood was about to change.

Rhyn rested his hand on her huge belly, where their hatchling grew. Katie was due in a few weeks, and he resisted the urge to curse and destroy the entire chamber.

His baby was coming, and they were about to be homeless.

He hugged her harder. "You're packing," he said, realizing what she was doing.

"Yep. We're exiled," she said in a hushed voice. "I told Toby and Hannah to pack," she added, referring to their adopted son, a guardian angel, and her sister.

"I guess they have to come."

"Of course they do! They're our family." She tugged free and faced him. "We'll be okay, Rhyn. You won't be stressed out anymore, and we won't have to worry about all the shit that goes on here. Demons, Wynn, whatever." She took his face in her hands.

Peering into the eyes of his mate, his anger evaporated, replaced by worry. "I'm so sorry, Katie," he whispered, resting his forehead against hers. "I'm the worst provider ever."

"You're amazing, Rhyn."

"Worst ever."

"We'll be fine. Look." Leaning away from him, she bent to heft a huge gym bag sagging beneath the weight of its contents. She placed it on the bed. "Andre said you won an award and this is your prize." Her eyes were twinkling, a sign Andre had said more than he should about the trip to the underworld.

The gym bag was stuffed full of large bills, enough cash for them to buy their own castle anywhere in the world.

"It was a game we were playing," Rhyn muttered. "This is Andre's money."

"I know. And I don't care." Katie folded her arms across her protruding belly. "We're starting over somewhere else. Okay?"

He nodded half-heartedly, unable to shake the guilt and responsibility he felt for his family being kicked out of their home. It made him hate his brothers more than ever. He wanted to refuse the mandate and destroy the fucking fortress. Teach them a lesson about what it meant to fuck with those he loved.

"Whoa, boy." Katie touched him, the way she did whenever his temper was about to blow. His emotions ceased bubbling, and his body relaxed. "No explosions. Let's just pick somewhere cool. We always said we needed more us time, right?"

"Maybe when you're not an Immortal mood beast," he said before he could stop himself.

"I'm pregnant, not a mood beast!" she snapped, eyes flashing. "You had a hand in this, too, Rhyn. Don't you forget that!"

Her good mood gone, she whirled and stormed to the wardrobe to grab more clothing.

Rhyn smiled, watching her, grateful she was safe. Maybe she was right and it wouldn't be so bad to start over somewhere quieter, away from the drama of the Immortals.

Then again, he couldn't shake the instinct that warned him something here was really wrong.

Family first, he decided. Once Katie was safe, he'd do some investigating. He wasn't perfect, but he'd always taken his duty to the brothers that hated him more seriously than any of them cared to do for him.

"You sure Hannah has to come?" he teased. "She's a mood beast and isn't even pregnant."

"Rhyn!"

He laughed. With Katie at his side, they'd be all right. Somehow.

Chapter Twenty

Hours later, Deidre's heart was hammering when she set the soul of her mate on the rug before the fireplace with its black flames. She'd showered and changed into a Hell dress, paced to determine what exactly she'd say when Darkyn was back, then gave up, knowing he'd be able to read her mind the minute he awoke. It didn't matter what she tried to say, she'd end up revealing everything with her thoughts.

Kneeling beside his soul, she rested her hands over it and closed her eyes. She envisioned him waking up from a nap and waited, her blood racing at the thought of feeling his skin beneath her again.

Something moved beneath her fingers, and she sat back, watching in a combination of horror and intrigue. Black fog rose from the floor. It took on the shape of a man. Within seconds, the fog had begun to harden, the details of the body beneath it growing firm, the color of his skin turning into a familiar golden brown.

Darkyn's frame emerged from the fog. He was naked, scars visible on his exposed skin. His eyes were closed, his dark hair ruffled. The fog began to dissipate and sank again into the floor, leaving the demon lord before the fire.

"Darkyn?" she whispered. Uncertain what to expect, she

touched him lightly. He certainly felt real, and Deidre shifted forward, pulse surging within her. She rested her palm on his warm chest, reassured he was real once more.

Another moment passed, and he began breathing. A few seconds later, his heart started beating.

She almost squealed in excitement.

Deidre darted to the bed to grab a blanket, in case he awoke cold after the bizarre experience. Wrapping it in her arms, she turned to see him standing before the fire, testing his body with small, controlled movements.

Elation mixed with some anger and apprehension, and she crossed to him. Her eyes drank him in, from the lean, shapely muscles of his thighs and arms, to the wide expanse of his chest and the fangs that were already starting to grow.

She stopped close enough to touch him.

"Are you well?" she asked.

"I am."

"Good."

Deidre slapped him. Hard.

Darkyn met her gaze, fire flaring to life in the depths of his.

"That's for not giving me an instruction manual when you gave me Hell," she said, face flushing with a combination of desire and anger.

"You figured it out."

She slapped him again. "That's because … well, because you knew what was going to happen and didn't bother telling me!"

A cunning smile spread across his face.

Should've known he'd take it as an invitation. "Before anything … starts," she began, wetting her lips. "I think we should talk."

"About what?" He snatched the blanket from her arms and tossed it.

"For one, I'm the Dark One and I raised you. Gabe says you owe me a favor without restrictions," she said, growing more confident.

Darkyn drew nearer, holding her gaze to keep her from moving.

He paused just before their bodies touched. "And?" he asked, unconcerned.

"What do you mean, *and*?" she replied. "Hel-lo. I'm the Dark One!"

He nudged her cheek aside and bit her neck hard, a reminder of how thoroughly he owned her.

Hot pain slid through her, along with desire so intense, she began to forget what it was she wanted to set straight before tumbling into bed with him. Her breath caught, and she stared at him. The enormity of what she'd been through hit her in the safety of her bedchamber, with her mate alive and well before her. Hunger roared to life within her. The scent and warmth of his skin was within reach once more, his sweet blood a mere bite away. In minutes, he'd be fucking her the way he always did: with a combination of pain, pleasure and a whole lot of blood.

"Darkyn, I need something from you."

He studied her, cold gaze traveling slowly over her features. Cupping the back of her neck in one hand, he tugged her dress loose with the other and let it drop to the floor. His palm skimmed her shoulder and down her side to settle on her hip. He drew their bodies together, pressing his arousal to her lower belly in a way that made her shudder. The heat in her body pooled in her lower belly.

His fangs were growing longer, the fire in his eyes brighter. "What, love?" he asked.

"I love you. I know you don't respect that kind of emotion, but you need to know it's true," she said, voice trembling. "Darkyn, there is no part of me that can live with having your children in Hell."

"You do not wish to have my heir?" He cocked his head to the side.

"I do, but Hell is no place for a human child."

"They'll be half-demons."

"And half-humans," she said firmly. "That's the favor I ask from you in exchange for raising you. That you let me take them to the human world and give them the chance to make their own fates rather than be roped into Hell."

"I cannot deny it," he replied.

She started to smile. "You're not upset?"

He raised an eyebrow. "As long as you know there will be many, many heirs." He bit her again. "As many as there are stars, because I plan to fuck you every time I see you."

She gasped, arching against him. His arms went around her, and he began to suck blood from her neck. "So you ... did miss me!"

He was purring low in his chest, a sign of contentedness. He withdrew from her neck. "I'm only surprised you asked for this and not for me to dismantle my Army of Souls."

"About that." She cleared her throat. "I may have made a deal to return the souls to Gabe."

"I saw in your mind." He met her gaze again. "Take them. I'll just collect more."

"That's not how –"

Darkyn kissed her, the taste of her blood incensing her. She bit his lip, sighing into his mouth when the first drop of his blood reached her tongue. She sucked his lip until it stopped then began kissing his face again.

"I missed you," she said. "I missed you. I missed you. I missed you!" The tears began then, and she choked back a sob, intoxicated by the sensations of his hot skin and the scent of blood in the air.

"Wanna try something that would kill fifteen demons and an ogre?" he taunted, biting her rapidly along her shoulder. Pain melted into intense pleasure that made her the coral tips of her breasts hard and her legs too weak to hold her.

"God, yes!" she gasped.

He lifted her into his arms and took her to their bed. "Demons do not love," he whispered against her neck. "But there is no one else in the universe I'd entrust with Hell."

"I know. You trust me now, don't you?"

"To the extent I am capable of."

More tears filled her eyes. "What if I decide not to give it back?"

"You'll be begging me to take it back by dawn, love. Of that, I can assure you." The dark, husky promise in his tone made her shiver in anticipation.

She touched the planes of his face, smiling. "Let's see what you got, demon."

He set her down. "Run."

"I love you." Deidre's heart caught in her throat.

"Run," he repeated with an evil smile.

She laughed, happier than she'd ever felt. Her instincts and emotions clamoring, Deidre turned and ran.

Chapter Twenty-One

Ahumid, warm breeze swept into the small room where Fate stood before the Oracle, who was busy scribbling new events into her book.

Fate scrolled through the latest deals the Oracle had recorded. Midday sunlight spilled through the windows, ruffling his brown hair and tickling the back of his neck. He scratched it absently, eyes on the page before him.

There was nothing interesting, at least, not since he'd seen the deal between Gabriel and Deidre. Satisfied things had gone mostly the way he planned, he leaned back. He hadn't gotten exactly what he wanted in the arena of the Dark One, but it was a start.

Gabriel had come into his power and understood his place. His relationship with his mate was getting a fresh start, and he'd be busy for a while repairing the damage to his domain and raising a new army. Past-Death stopped being a bitch, which was really all Fate ever wanted.

Oh, and for her to admit I was right, Fate thought with a smile.

As for Deidre ... the woman realized she wasn't a victim, that she could hold her own in the Immortal society. Her role in Fate's game was not yet played out, and he was happy to know he had an ally of sorts.

Because when a certain, inevitable chain of events emerged, he'd need all the help he could get.

"A thousand years in Death's dungeon teach you anything, little sister?" he asked, aware of the woman peering over his shoulder. A deity with no need to see the Past, Present or Future, Karma was clearly unhappy about the book appearing blank for her.

"Yes. Don't fuck with deities," she muttered.

"The dungeon is better than what most of them would've done to you. Keep that in mind," he warned her firmly. "You're young. Don't make the mistakes I and others did when we started out."

"She knows." Her tone softened.

"Stop that shit. I know you're doing it on purpose."

"I know." Karma sighed. "It's hard to control the urge to tackle people and balance them. So much imbalance …"

"Start in the human world," he suggested, facing her. "As long as you kill no one, you'll learn. Humans are delicate. They get second chances, remember?"

She nodded. Her hair was in tight red ringlets, her features glowing and eyes pale green. One of the youngest goddesses, she was learning her responsibilities and domain gradually. With the predatory nature of a souleater and the soft heart of one capable of great compassion and kindness, it was going to take her some time to find her own internal balance.

"It's time for my vacation," he said. "I'm happy to say, things are going well."

She gazed at him skeptically. "What if I get in trouble again?"

"Don't," he advised. "I'm not rescuing you, if you fuck with the wrong god or get caught killing humans. Got it?"

She nodded. "Can I ask you something, brother?"

"Ask. I reserve the right to answer."

"You gave Deidre something. A soul."

"I did."

"Why?"

He considered his answer for a moment. "Because there's no safer place in the universe for it."

Karma rolled her eyes.

He flashed her a smile and walked out of the room where the sacred Oracle lived. As he climbed to the top of the walls overlooking the teal waters of the Caribbean, he debated dropping in on Deidre one more time, perhaps with a reminder to protect the soul he'd given her before her kidnapping. He'd offered no real explanation, partially because there was little time to, and partially because he wasn't ready to admit what was coming.

On second thought, it might raise suspicions, he realized. No, it was better to leave the emerald with someone he knew he could trust. Someone who didn't need to know the inevitable outcome of a chain of events that had not yet begun.

"Some things are better left unknown as long as possible," he murmured, watching the tide ebb and flow on the white sands of the island's beaches. "Another win for Mr. Checkmate."

With a smile, he turned away and summoned a portal, ready at last for his vacation.

About the Author

I breathe stories. I dream them. If it were possible, I'd eat them, too. (I'm pretty sure they'd taste like cotton candy.) I can't escape them - they're everywhere! Which is why I write! I was born to bring the crazy worlds and people in my mind to life, and I love sharing them with as many people as I can.

I'm also the bestselling, award winning, internationally acclaimed author of over sixty titles and counting. I write speculative fiction in multiple subgenres of romance and fantasy, contemporary fiction, books for both teens and adults, and just about anything else I feel like writing. If I can imagine it, I can write it!

I live in the desert of southern Arizona with a pack of spoiled dogs and Tubbs, the Godfather cat who rules them all.

Connect with Lizzy

Website: LizzyFord.com
Facebook: www.Facebook.com/LizzyFordBooks
Twitter @LizzyFord2010
Instagram: @LizzyFordAuthor

Also By Lizzy Ford

Young Adult Fiction

Non-Series Title

The Door (teen sci-fi)

Between (paranormal) (2019)

Esme (teen paranormal)

Halloween

Thanksgiving

Christmas

Lost Vegas Series – young adult post-apocalyptic

Aveline

Tiana

Arthur

Black Wolf

Lost Vegas Series Omnibus

Spell Realm Series – young adult romantic fantasy

Water Spell

Dragon Spell (2019)

Moon Spell (2019)

Sword Spell (2020)

Omega Series – teen dystopia with Greek Gods

Omega

Theta

Alpha (2019)

Omega Beginnings Miniseries – individual episodes

Alessandra

Mismatch

Phoibe

Lantos

Theodosia

Niko

Cleon

Herakles

Omega Beginnings Miniseries Omnibus

Theta Beginnings Miniseries

Silent Queen

Mercenary

Shadow Titan

People's Champion

Theta Beginnings Miniseries Omnibus

Anshan Saga – new adult science fiction romance

Kiera's Moon

Kiera's Sun

Witchlings – young adult paranormal

Dark Summer

Autumn Storm

Winter Fire

Spring Rain

Broken Beauty Novellas – new adult dramatic fiction

Broken Beauty

Broken World

Broken Chains

Foretold Trilogy – young adult fantasy

Elle's Journey

Shadow Rising (2019)

Journey West (2019)

Voodoo Nights - young adult paranormal

Cursed

———

Erotic Romance

Non-Series Titles

Star Kissed (erotic sci-fi)

A Night Worth Dying For (short story, contemporary erotic thriller)

Trial Series – erotic paranormal romance

Trial by Moon

Trial by Thrall

Trial by Blood

Trial by Heart

Trial Series Omnibus

Heart of Fire – sexy dragon shifter

Charred Heart

Charred Tears

Charred Hope

Incubatti Duet – Buffy meets 50 Shades

Zoey Rogue

Zoey Avenger

Writing as SE Reign, erotica writer

101 Nights Box Set (featuring all seven serials)

———

Adult Sweet Romance

(no graphic sex scenes)

Non-Series Titles – 2014 - 2018

White Tree Sound

Black Moon Draw (fantasy romance)

Highlander Enchanted (historical romance)

Last Resort (2019)

History Interrupted – Time Travel Romantic Adventures

West

East

North

South (2019)

Super Villainess Chronicles – twisted superhero romance

It's Not Easy Being Evil

It's Not Easy Being Good

Starwalkers Serials (with Julia Crane) – new adult science fiction serial

Severed

Trapped

Exiled

Revealed

Escaped

Ascended

Starwalkers – Omnibus

Sons of War – contemporary military romance

Semper Mine

Soldier Mine

SEAL Mine

Rhyn Trilogy – new adult paranormal with demons

Katie's Hellion

Katie's Hope

Rhyn's Redemption

Rhyn Eternal – Death finds love

Gabriel's Hope

Deidre's Death

Darkyn's Mate

The Underworld

Twisted Fate

Twisted Karma

Sammy's Demon

Untitled (2019)

War of Gods – paranormal with gods, guardians and exceptional humans

Damian's Oracle

Damian's Assassin

Damian's Immortal

The Grey God

Damian Eternal

Xander's Chance

The Black God

Hidden Evil – paranormal with angels and four horsemen

Hear No

See No

Speak No

Unnamed Series

Unnatural (TBD)

Short Stories

Santa's Ninja Elves: Natasha

Santa's Ninja Elves: Hunter

Snow Whisperers (retired)

Non-Series Titles – 2011 - 2013

A Demon's Desire (paranormal romance)

The Warlord's Secret (fantasy romance)

Maddy's Oasis (contemporary romance)

Rebel Heart (sci-fi romance)